Blood of Requiem

Blood of Requiem

SONG OF DRAGONS, BOOK ONE

Daniel Arenson

This novel is a work of fiction. Names, characters, places and incidents are either the product of the author's imagination, or, if real, used fictitiously.

ISBN: 978-0-9866028-7-0

PROLOGUE

War.

War rolled over the world with fire and wings.

The Vir Requis marched. Men. Women. Children. Their clothes were tattered, their faces ashy, their bellies tight. As their cities burned behind them, they marched with cold eyes. All had come to fight this day: the young and the old, the strong and the wounded, the brave and the frightened. They were five thousand. They had no more places to hide.

The dying sun blazed red against them. The wind keened. Five thousand. The last of their race.

We will stand, we will fly, we will perish with fire and tooth, Benedictus thought, jaw clenched. *Men will say: Requiem did not fade with a whimper, but fell with a thunder that shook the mountains.*

And so he marched, and behind him his people followed, banners red and gold, thudding in the wind. *Last stand of Requiem.*

It was strange, he thought, that five thousand should move together so silently. Benedictus heard only thumping boots. No whispers. No sobs. No whimpers even from the children who marched, their eyes too large in their gaunt faces. The Vir Requis were silent today, silent for the million of their kin already dead, for this day when their race would perish, enter the realm of memory, then legend, then myth. Nothing but thudding boots, a keening wind, and a grumbling sky. Silence before the roar of fire.

Then Benedictus saw the enemy ahead.

The scourge of Requiem. Their end.

Benedictus let out his breath slowly. Here was his death. The death of these hunted, haunted remains of his kind, the Vir Requis who had once covered the world and now stood, still and silent, behind him.

A tear streamed down Benedictus's cheek. He tasted it on his lips--salty, ashy.

His brother's host dwarfed his own. Fifty thousand men stood ahead: swordsmen, horsemen, archers, all bedecked in the white and gold that Dies Irae had taken for his colors. They carried torches, thousands of fires that raised smoky pillars. Countless griffins flew over these soldiers, shrieking, their wings churning the clouds. The army shimmered like a foul tapestry woven with images of the Abyss.

Benedictus smiled grimly. *They burned our forests. They toppled our cities. They chased us to every corner of the earth. If they force us to fight here, then we will die fighting well.*

He clenched his fists.

War.

War crashed with blood and screams and smoke.

Benedictus, King of Requiem, drew his magic with a howl. Black wings sprouted from his back, unfurling and creaking. Black scales rippled across him, glinting red in the firelight. Fangs sprang from his mouth, dripping drool, and talons grew from his fingers. Soon he was fifty feet long, a black dragon breathing fire. Requiem's magic filled him, the magic of wings and scales and flame, the magic that Dies Irae lacked and loathed. Benedictus took flight, claws tearing the earth. His roar shook the battlefield.

Let them see me. Let them see Benedictus the Black, for one final time under the sky, spreading wings and roaring flame.

Behind him, the Vir Requis he led changed form too. The solemn men, women, and children drew the ancient magic of their race, grew wings, scales, and claws. They too became dragons, as cruel and beautiful as the true dragons of old. Some became elder beasts missing scales, their fangs long fallen. Others were young, supple, their scales still soft, barely old enough to fly. A few were green, others blue, and some blazed red. A handful, like Benedictus, bore the rare black scales of old noble blood. Once the different colors, the different families and noble lines, would fight one another, would mistrust and kill and hate. Today they banded here, joined to fight Dies Irae--the young, the old, the noble and the common.

This night they fought with one roar.

The last Vir Requis, Benedictus thought. *Not humans. Not dragons. Weredragons, the humans call us. Shunned. Today is our last flight.*

War. With steel and flame.

Arrows pelted Benedictus, jabs of agony. Most shattered against his scales, but some sank into his flesh. Their tips were serrated, coated with poison that burned through his veins. He roared and blew fire at the men below, the soldiers his brother had tricked or forced into battle today. They screamed, cursed him, feared him; the Vir Requis were monsters to them. Benedictus swooped, lifted several soldiers in his claws, and tossed them onto their comrades. Spears flew. Flaming arrows whistled. Everywhere was blood, fire, and screaming.

War. With poison and pain.

Around him, the Vir Requis flew as dragons, the forms they always took in battle. They breathed fire and roared. Spears and arrows plucked the young from the skies. Their scales were too soft, their wings too small. They hit the ground, screaming, soon overcome with swordsmen who hacked them. Blood splashed. In death they resumed human forms; battered, bloodied, butchered children.

They take our youth first, Benedictus thought. He slammed into soldiers below, biting, clawing, lashing his tail, ignoring the pain of swordbites. *They let us, the old, see the death of our future before they fell us too from the skies.*

These older Vir Requis--the warriors--fought with fire, claw, and fang. These ones had seen much war, had killed too many, bore too many scars. Soon mounds of bodies covered the battlefield. The Vir Requis howled as they killed and died.

Our race will fall here today, Benedictus thought as spears flew and shattered against his scales. *But we will make a last stand for poets to sing of.*

And then shrieks tore the air, and the griffins were upon him.

They were cruel beasts, as large as dragons, their bodies like great lions, their heads the heads of eagles, their beaks and talons sharp. In the books of men they were noble, warriors of light and righteousness, sent by the Sun God to fight the curse of Requiem, the wickedness of scales and leathery wings. To Requiem they were monsters.

Today Benedictus saw thousands of them, swooping beasts of feathers and talons. Two crashed into him, scratching and biting. One talon slashed his front leg, and Benedictus roared. He swung his tail, hit one's head, and cracked its skull. It tumbled. Benedictus blew fire onto the second. Its fur and feathers burst into flame. Its shrieks nearly deafened him, and it too fell, blazing, to crash into men below.

Panting and grunting with pain, sluggish with poison, Benedictus glanced around. The griffins were swarming; they outnumbered the Vir Requis five to one. Most Vir Requis lay dead upon the bloody field, pierced with arrows and spears and talons. And then more griffins were upon Benedictus, and he could see only their shrieking beaks, their flashing talons. Flaming arrows filled the air.

Has it truly been only five years? Benedictus thought as talons tore into him, shedding blood. Haze covered his thoughts, and the battle almost seemed silent around him. *Five years since my father banished my brother, since a million of us filled the sky? Yes, only five years. Look at us now.* Dragons fell around him like rain, maws open, tears in their eyes.

"No!" Benedictus howled, voice thundering. He blew fire, forcing the haze of death off him. He was not dead yet. He still had some killing in him, some blood to shed, some fire to breathe. *Not until I've killed more. Not until I find the man who destroyed us. Dies Irae. My brother.*

He clawed, bit, and burned as his comrades fell around him, as the tears and blood of Requiem filled the air and earth.

He fought all night, a night of fire, and all next day, fought until the sun again began to set. Its dying rays painted the world red.

Pierced by a hundred arrows, weary and bloody, Benedictus looked around and knew: The others were gone.

He, Benedictus, was the last.

He flew between griffins and spears and arrows. His brethren lay slain all around. In death, they lay as humans. Men. Women. Children. All those he had led to battle; all lay cut and broken, mouths open, limbs strewn, eyes haunted and still.

Benedictus raised his eyes. He stared at the army ahead, the army he now faced alone. Thousands of soldiers and griffins faced him under the roiling clouds. The army of Dies Irae.

He saw his brother there, not a mile away, clad in white and gold. Victorious.

Bleeding, tears in his eyes, Benedictus flew toward him.

Spears clanged against Benedictus. Arrows pierced him. Griffins clawed him. Still he swooped toward Dies Irae. Fire and screams flowed around him, and Benedictus shot like an arrow, roaring, wreathed in flame.

Dies Irae rose from the battlefield upon a griffin, bearing a lance of silver and steel. Gold glistened upon his armor and samite robes. He appeared to Benedictus like a seraph, a figure of light, ablaze like a sun.

Benedictus, of black scales and blood and fire, and Dies Irae, of gold and white upon his griffin. They flew toward each other over the mounds of dead.

Benedictus was hurt and weary. The world blurred. He could barely fly. He was too hurt, too torn, too haunted. Dies Irae crashed into him, a blaze like a comet, so white and righteous and golden. Benedictus howled, hoarse. He felt Dies Irae's silver spear pierce his wing. He heard that wing tearing, a sound like ripping leather. It was the most terrifying sound Benedictus had ever heard, and the pain seemed unreal, too great to truly fill him. He crashed into the griffin that bore his brother. Screaming, mouth bloody, he bit down. His jaws severed Dies Irae's arm. He felt the arm in his mouth, clad in armor, and he spat it out, saw it tumble to the ground.

Dies Irae screamed, cried, and clutched the stump of his arm. Blood covered him. His griffin clawed Benedictus's side, pain blazed, and Benedictus kicked. He hit the griffin's head, crushing it. The griffin fell. Dies Irae fell. His brother hit the ground, screaming. His griffin lay dead beside him.

Benedictus landed on the ground above his brother.

The battle froze.

The soldiers, knights, and griffins all stood still and stared, as if in shock. Benedictus stood panting, blood in his mouth, blood on his scales, and gazed down at his brother. Dies Irae looked so pale. Blood covered his golden armor and samite robe.

"My daughter," Benedictus said, voice low. "Where is Gloriae?"

"Please," Dies Irae whispered, lips pale, face sweaty. "Please, Benedictus. My brother. Please."

Benedictus growled. He spoke through the blood in his maw, voice hoarse and torn. "You destroyed us. You butchered a million souls. How dare you ask for mercy now? Return me my daughter."

Dies Irae trembled. Suddenly he looked so much as he did years ago, a timid and angry child, a scorned brother cast away from his father's court. "Please," he whispered, clutching his stump. "Please."

Benedictus raised a clawed foot, prepared to strike down, to kill the man who had hunted his race to near extinction. Dies Irae shut his eyes and whimpered. His lips prayed silently and his blood flowed.

Benedictus paused.

He looked around him. No more Vir Requis flew. Their war had ended. The time of Requiem had ended.

It is over, Benedictus knew. *No. I will not end it this way, not with killing my brother. It is over already.*

With a grunt, Benedictus kicked off the ground, flapped his wings, and rose into the air.

Men and griffins screamed around him.

"Kill him!" Dies Irae shouted below. "Don't let him flee! I want him dead!"

Benedictus would not look back. He could see only the thousands of bodies below. *I will find you, Gloriae. I won't forget you.*

His wings roiled ash and smoke. Arrows whistled around him, and he rose into the clouds. He flew in darkness. Soon the screams of men and griffins faded into the distance.

Benedictus the Black, King of Requiem, disappeared into the night.

MIRUM

The Lady Mirum was riding her mare by the sea when she saw the griffins. She shivered and cursed.

The morning had begun like any other. She woke in Fort Sanctus to a windy dawn, waves crashing outside, the air scented of sea and moss. Julian packed her a breakfast of bread and kippers wrapped in leather, and she took the meal on her morning ride along the gray, foaming sea. No omens had heralded danger; no thunderstorms, no comets cutting the clouds, no strange pattern to the leaves of her tea the night before. Just another morning of galloping, of the smells of seaweed and salt and horse, of the sounds of gulls and sea and hoofs in sand.

Yet here they flew, maybe a league away, their shrieks clear even over the roar of hoofs and waves. Mirum saw three of them--great beasts, half lions and half eagles, fifty feet long. In the distance, they looked like seraphs, golden and alight.

Griffins. And they were heading to Fort Sanctus. Her home.

Mirum's mare bucked and whinnied.

"Easy, Sol," she said and patted the horse's neck, though she herself trembled. She had not seen griffins in ten years, not since Dies Irae had killed her father, not since she had sworn allegiance to the man at age sixteen, kissed his hand so he'd let her live, let her keep the smallest of her father's forts.

Sol nickered and bucked again. The griffins were flying closer, shrieking their eagle shrieks. Though still a league away, Mirum could see glints of armor, and the stream of golden banners. *Riders.* She felt the blood leave her face.

Dies Irae's men.

Maybe, Mirum thought with a chill, Dies Irae himself rode there.

The wind gusted, howled, and blew Mirum's cloak back to reveal her sword. She placed her palm upon the old pommel, seeking strength in the cold steel. It had been her father's sword, the sword he'd worn the day Dies Irae murdered him. *Please, Father, give me strength today.*

"Come, Sol," she said and dug her heels into the mare. "They're heading to Sanctus. Let's meet them."

Sol was a good horse, well trained, from her father's stables. Most of those stables had burned in the war, their horses slaughtered or stolen, but Sol had remained. She now galloped, kicking up sand and seaweed, the waves showering foam at her side. The morning was cold, too cold for spring. Clouds hid the sun, and the sea was the color of iron. The wind shrieked and cut into Mirum. As she rode, she tightened her woolen cloak, but that could not ease her tremble. Fort Sanctus still lay half a league away, a jutting tower of mossy stone and rusty iron. It rose from an outcrop of rock over the sea like a lighthouse. There was no doubt now; the griffins were flying toward it, and would be there soon. If they found what Mirum hid there....

Even in the biting wind, sweat drenched Mirum. She cursed and kneed Sol. "Hurry, girl," she said. "Hurry."

A wave crashed against a boulder, and water hit Mirum, soaking her hair and riding dress. The gray wool clung to her, salty and cold, and Mirum tasted salt on her lips. In a flash, the memory pounded through her. She remembered herself ten years ago, only sixteen, a youth caught in the war. She remembered Dies Irae murdering her father before her eyes, how the blood had splashed her face.

"He stood against me," Dies Irae had said to her then, bloody sword in hand. "He stood with the weredragons." He spat that last word, the word he'd invented to belittle his foes, as though it tasted foul. He held out a hand heavy with rings. "But you need not suffer the same fate. Kiss this hand, Lady Mirum, and join my ranks. Join me against Requiem, and I will let you keep what remains of your father's lands."

She had been a child. Scared. Innocent and shocked. The blood of her father had still covered her, his body at her feet. She wanted to spit at Dies Irae, to die at his sword, to die at her father's side. But she was too frightened, too young. She kissed his ruby ring, swore allegiance to him, swore to join his quest to destroy the Vir Requis.

"Good, my child," he said and kissed her bloody forehead. He knew her that night, raped her again and again, then left her at dawn in Fort Sanctus, alone and bloody, corpses surrounding her.

She had not seen him since that winter.

Fort Sanctus was close now, casting its shadow over Mirum and her horse. It was but a single tower, mossy and old, topped with iron crenellations brown with rust. Once it had been a proud fort, but its soldiers and servants had perished in the war. Only old Julian remained, loyal steward of her father, and several fishermen in the village that sprawled behind the tower. Mirum had done what she could to maintain the place--cleaning the fireplaces, sweeping the floors, and helping to mend the fishermen's nets. She had no money to hire help, and Julian was getting on in years. And so Sanctus had fallen into disrepair, a sore thumb here on the beach, a crumbling tower of moss, rust, gull droppings, and haunting memories.

The waves now pummeled it, raising fountains of foam. Gulls flew around the fort, cawing. Their cries seemed to warn Mirum. "Go! Go!" they seemed to cry. *Flee!*

Loud as they were, their cries drowned under the shrieks of griffins. The beasts swooped down just as Mirum reined in her horse by the fort.

The griffins were beautiful. Even as horror pounded through her, Mirum recognized this beauty. The fur of their lion bodies shone golden, and the feathers of their eagle heads glowed white as fresh snow. Gilded helmets topped those eagle heads, in the manner of horse armor, glistening with rubies. Their wings, a hundred feet in span, churned the air so powerfully that the sea rippled. When the griffins landed on the outcrop of stone where Fort Sanctus stood, their talons cut grooves into the rock.

Bane of Benedictus, Mirum remembered. *That is what they would call them.*

She sat before them on her horse, sword at her side, the wind streaming her cloak and hair. She placed her right fist on her heart, Dies Irae's salute of loyalty.

Riders sat upon the three griffins, staring down at her. Each wore steel armor filigreed in gold, a sword in a jeweled sheath, and a snowy cape. The man who rode the largest, foremost griffin was especially resplendent. He looked like a god of wealth. Sapphires, rubies, and emeralds encrusted his helmet. Garnets and amber formed a griffin upon his breastplate, and golden weave ran through his samite cloak. His gilded helmet hid his face, the visor shaped as a griffin's beak, but Mirum saw his arm, and she knew him at once.

Mirum had been there that day, the day Dies Irae lost his left arm. She had been sixteen when the battle of Lanburg Fields raged. Her father had been dead for only a moon, and already she, Lady Mirum, rode to war under Dies Irae's banner. He insisted she ride at his side, reveled in the thought of her fighting for him, he who'd murdered her father and raped her. She watched, weeping, as Dies Irae killed the last Vir Requis, the remains of that ancient race. She watched, shivering, as the legendary Benedictus--King of Requiem and brother to Dies Irae--bit off her tormentor's arm. *You wept like a babe at my feet,* Mirum remembered, but she had felt no pity for him. She had not seen

Dies Irae since that night... not until this gray morning, until he arrived at her doorstep, arrived with his griffins and soldiers and old, pulsing pain.

Like a body tossed into the sea, you return to my shore, rotten and smelling of old blood. Sol nickered beneath her and cantered sideways as if feeling her pain.

"Go! Go!" the gulls cawed. *Flee!*

But Mirum did not flee. Could not. She would not abandon what she hid here.

"Hail Irae!" she called, as she knew she must.

Upon his griffin, Dies Irae nodded to her, a golden god. He said nothing.

He wore a new arm now, she saw. It was an arm made of steel, encrusted with garnets like beads of blood. Instead of a fist, the arm ended with a mace head, spiked and cruel. It glistened even under the overcast sky.

Mirum dismounted her horse and curtsied before him.

Please, Earth God, she prayed, staring at the stone ground. *Please don't let him find what I hide here.*

She heard the three riders dismount their griffins, heard boots walk toward her. Soon she could see those boots as she curtsied, spurred leather boots tipped with steel. Then the spiked mace--the iron fist of Dies Irae's new arm--thrust itself before her face.

"You may kiss my hand, child," came a voice, the chilly voice Mirum remembered from a decade ago, the voice that had murmured in her ear as he raped her by her father's body.

Though disgust filled her, Mirum kissed the mace head, a hurried peck of her lips. It tasted like coppery blood.

Please, Earth God, please. Don't let Irae find him....

"Your Grace," Mirum said, head still lowered, fingers trembling.

"Rise, child," he said, and she straightened to face him. She could not see his face, only that jeweled visor shaped like an eagle's head, and she shivered. Dies Irae's lieutenants noticed and laughed--cold, cruel laughter like the sound of waves against stone. One was a tall, gaunt man covered in steel, his visor barred like a prisoner's mask. The other was a woman in white leggings, her breastplate molded to fit the curve of her breast, a gilded visor hiding her face. Both bore swords with grips shaped as talons.

Dies Irae turned to face them, those riders bedecked in gold and steel, and clucked his tongue. "Now now, it is impolite to laugh." He turned back to Mirum, standing too close, mere inches away. "You must forgive my riders. They do not often find themselves in the presence of a lady, and they are weary from a long flight. If you do not mind, we would much like to break our fast here, and to drink wine from your cellar. Would you be so kind as to host us at your home, if only for an hour?"

Mirum bowed her head. It was not a request, she knew, but a command. Her stomach roiled. The memories and fear pounded through her. "It would be an honor, my lord."

She led them down the outcrop of stone, her boots confident upon the moss. Waves crashed at their sides. Behind her, she heard the griffin riders struggling and muttering curses. She could walk this damp, mossy stone as though walking across a grassy meadow, but most struggled for balance upon it, and the spraying waves did little to help. Still, Mirum would not turn to offer aid, nor would she slow her pace. *Let them slip upon the moss. Let them fall against the boulders, and drown in the sea at the foot of my tower.*

Her prayers went unanswered. Soon she reached the doors of Fort Sanctus, towering doors of chipped oak, the wood dark with mold, the knobs brown with rust. The griffin riders, still cursing under their breath, came to stand beside her.

Ignoring them, Mirum placed her hands on the doors, leaned against them, and they creaked open on rusty hinges.

"By the Sun God, the place still stinks," Dies Irae muttered, though still Mirum would not turn to face him. Her hall might be dusty, its walls mossy, its tapestries tattered... but it did not stink. It smelled like salt, like seaweed, like sand and like horse. This was no stench, but a smell Mirum loved. It had stunk once, that night ten years ago when Dies Irae had slain her soldiers, her servants, and her father.

Mirum dared glance at Dies Irae's neck. She saw a golden chain there, its links thick. Those links disappeared under Dies Irae's breastplate. *Does he wear the amulet, the Griffin Heart?* she wondered, fingers trembling. She imagined leaping forward, tugging the chain, stealing his amulet, stealing his griffins. But of course, armies of Vir Requis had fought to reclaim the Griffin Heart, to reclaim the power to tame and control griffinflesh. Those armies had failed. What chance would she have?

Dies Irae jerked his head to one of his lieutenants, the gaunt man with the barred visor. Hand on the pommel of his sword, the man moved to guard the doors.

God, he knows, Mirum thought. Her heart pounded. *He knows what I hide here, he knows of him, he's blocking his escape. God, why did I let the boy fly? Somebody must have seen him, and now Dies Irae has come here, come to this hall with his sword and his promise of blood.*

Mirum clutched her fingers behind her back to hide their tremble.

"Please sit at my table, my lord," she said. She stared at that chipped old table, not daring to look at Dies Irae. Her heart thrashed. "I will serve you bread and fish."

With a snort, the female griffin rider removed her helmet, and Mirum felt herself pale. She recognized this face, and it sent shivers through her. The woman was beautiful, achingly so, with icy green eyes, red lips, and cascading golden locks. She couldn't have been older than eighteen, yet none of youth's life nor folly seemed to fill her; her face was cold and cruel as a statue.

Gloriae.

Dies Irae's daughter.

As Mirum watched, Gloriae spat onto the floor. Her spit landed at Mirum's feet.

"Bah! Bread and fish," Gloriae said, those perfect red lips curling in disgust. "We've not flown for hours to this place to eat bread and fish. Have you no boar? No deer or fowl? What kind of hall do you run, you seaside waif?"

Mirum felt the blood rush back into her cheeks. She knew the stories. She knew that King Benedictus had believed this young woman to be his own daughter, not the daughter of Dies Irae's rapes. Mirum, however, saw only the cruelty of Dies Irae in this one. She remembered the stories of Gloriae killing her first Vir Requis at age six, of killing ten more when she was but eight.

Trained from childhood in malice and murder, Mirum thought, for a moment rage overpowering her fear.

Disgust filled her mouth, tasting of bile. She forced herself to curtsy before Gloriae. "Forgive me, my lady. This is a but a simple seaside fort, the home of waifs, not the abode of great, illustrious nobles such as yourself." She wondered if Gloriae would detect the sarcasm in her voice. "But if you please, I would be glad to serve fine ale with your meal."

Gloriae stared at her, eyebrows rising over those icy green eyes. Her white cheeks flushed just the slightest. She took a step forward, drew her sword with a hiss, and placed its cold tip against Mirum's neck. Mirum stiffened. The blade was white steel, beautiful and glinting, its base filigreed in gold, and Mirum could imagine Vir Requis blood flowing down its grooves.

"Ale, you say?" Gloriae said softly, regarding her, one eyebrow raised. She tilted her head, her expression almost quizzical. "No fine wine for us great, illustrious nobles? Maybe instead of red wine, I shall content myself with red blood."

Mirum stared back, not tearing her eyes away, and clenched her jaw. They might kill her now, she knew. *Kill me if you must, but don't look in my tower. Please, Earth God, don't let them see what I hide.*

Dies Irae stepped forward. He placed a hand on Gloriae's shoulder. "Now now, sweet daughter," Dies Irae said, voice echoing inside his eagle helm. "This is not the time for blades. Mirum is being the most gracious host she can, for one who lives in a seaside ruin. Let her serve us her bread, her fish and her ale. We are not above the simple pleasures of peasants, are we?"

Mirum felt the rage boil in her, and she swallowed hard. Hers was an old, noble line. Her father had ruled many forts, as had his father, and many past generations of their line. Mirum was descended of great blood, and yet Dies Irae saw her as a waif, a fisherwoman barely worthy to serve him. Still she curtsied again. "I have no fine wine, but my ale is cold, and my bread warm."

Finally Dies Irae removed his helmet, and Mirum saw his face for the first time in ten years. It froze her blood. Here he was, here was this same face, the face that had haunted her for so long. It was ironic, she thought, that he looked so much like the beasts he rode. His face was like the face of an eagle, cold, handsome, his skin a golden hue. His hair was slicked back, blond streaked with gray, and his nose was hooked like a beak. His mouth was a thin line; his lips were so thin and pursed, he seemed almost to have no lips at all. A few more creases marred that face now, and more gray filled his temples, but it was the same face from ten years ago. The cold, golden, griffin face.

He was born to Vir Requis, Mirum remembered suddenly. He had their noble face, their high forehead. But of course, Dies Irae had been born without the gift, without the ancient blessing, without the magic to become a dragon. *It must have been so hard,* she reflected, shocked to find pity fill her. *To be firstborn of Requiem's king, yet lacking the gift. To be cast aside. To grow to hate that gift, to seek to destroy it. So much pain must dwell in him.*

That thin mouth curved into a smile, a cold smile, a smile that made that face even harsher, crueler. "Do you fear me, child?" he asked. "You tremble."

She lowered her head, realizing that she had stared at him. "It's been long since the presence of greatness has entered my hall. Forgive me, my lord. I'll fetch your food and drink."

Dies Irae sat at the chipped oak table. Gloriae removed her white leather gloves, stared at a wooden chair distastefully, and too sat down. The third rider--the gaunt, silent man--stayed to guard the door. His barred helm still hid his face.

Mirum hurried out of the hall. She paced downstairs into the cellar, legs trembling, heart thrashing. The cellar was a dark, dusty place carved into the rock beneath Fort Sanctus. The roar of waves was loud here, as were the smells of moss, dried fish, sausages, bread rolls, and oak barrels of ale. She had thought to find Julian sweeping the cellar floors. When she did not see him, she remembered that he had taken his donkey to town that morning, gone to buy turnips and onions and spices. *He will probably buy me a gift, too; flowers for my room, or a simple necklace of beads. Dear old man.* She was glad that he was gone. He was safe away from this fort. If Julian had been here, Dies Irae would have killed him for sport. Mirum was sure of that.

She collected pewter mugs from a shelf, opened a keg of ale, and began filling the mugs. As she worked, her mind raced. Had the boy in her tower seen the griffins? Surely he had. Surely he knew to fear them. She had rehearsed this day with him many times--every night. She would clutch his shoulders, stare into his eyes, and force him to repeat what she had taught him.

"Stay in the tower," he would say, bored with the words he would recite every night for ten years. "Do not turn into a dragon. Do not fly. Do not try to escape. Stay hidden, stay silent, stay inside my barrel."

Please, Kyrie, Mirum thought as she placed the mugs of ale upon a tray. *Just don't panic. Just don't fly.*

She found some chipped wooden plates and began loading them with smoked fish and bread rolls. Ten years ago, she had found the boy lying in the devastation of Lanburg Fields. Dies Irae had been flown away, armless, pale, near death. Benedictus the Black, King of Requiem, had fled. The other Vir Requis all lay dead upon the field, the last of their kind. Most of Dies Irae's soldiers had left the bodies to rot, but a squad of men, their white cloaks now red, had remained to move among the bodies, to search for the wounded and spear them. When they saw Mirum moving between the bodies too, they laughed, mocked her, called dirty words her way. She was so numb, she barely heard.

When she first saw the boy, she thought him dead. He looked six or seven years old, thin, covered in blood. Many young Vir Requis had come here to fight, flushed out of hiding with their elders, but this one was the youngest she saw. He did not move at first, but when Mirum stood above him, crying over his body, he opened his eyes.

"Mama," he whispered, voice high and soft.

"I... I'm not your mama," Mirum whispered back, glancing behind her, praying the men in bloody cloaks did not hear.

The boy spoke again, tears on his ashy cheeks. "I want my mama."

She had wrapped him in her cloak that night, placed him on the saddle of her horse, her good horse Sol. He was so small, so thin, he could be mistaken for a bundle of clothes or firewood. She sat behind him in the saddle and galloped, galloped harder than she ever had, galloped over bodies and fields drenched in blood, galloped away from the mocking men and the death of an ancient race, galloped home. To Fort Sanctus. To her sanctuary by the sea, to the fresh graves of her men, of her father, of her old life.

Kyrie Eleison was his name. She kept him in her tower, this young Vir Requis, kept him hidden for ten years now. She had stood by Dies Irae that day, stood with his banners as he murdered the last survivors of Requiem. She too was stained with their blood. If she could save one, just the life of one boy, maybe... maybe she would find redemption. Maybe the blood would be washed from her hands. So she had hidden him, and raised him, and prayed every night to forget the sight of all those bodies, the bodies of her men, of her father, of Kyrie's people. She tried to toss those memories into the sea, to let the waves claim them. For ten years she had gazed upon this angry sea, praying to forget.

She stepped back into her hall, tray of ale and food in hands.

Mirum set the table silently, eyes lowered. As she worked, Dies Irae stared at her body, and his eyes told her, *I hunger for you more than for your food.* Feeling blood rise to her cheeks, Mirum was acutely aware of her riding dress, how its wool clung to her, still wet from the waves. She forced herself to suffocate the memory of that night, that endless night of rapes. She had to bite her lip, to shut her eyes, to swallow the anger and continue setting the table. Anger would kill her now. She raised her eyes and glanced at the door, but the gaunt man still guarded it, arms crossed, face hidden. Mirum wanted to flee. Every instinct in her body screamed to run, to escape, to jump out the window if she must, even if jumping meant crashing against the boulders and drowning broken in the sea. Yet she could not. She had to stay here, serve these riders, protect Kyrie. She had vowed ten years ago to protect him. She had done so since. She would do so now... whatever it took.

When she placed the last plate on the table, Dies Irae reached under her skirt to find and squeeze the soft flesh beneath. Mirum's breath froze and her heart leaped. *I still have Father's sword at my waist,* she thought and trembled. *I can still draw it, kill at least one of them, maybe two before they kill me. I'm good with the sword.* But no. She could not die now. Not as Kyrie hid in her tower; she owed him to live, to protect him, no matter what Dies Irae did to her.

"Father, must you while I'm around?" Gloriae said, staring distastefully at Dies Irae's hand up Mirum's skirt. She sipped her ale, wrinkled her nose, and spat it onto the floor. "Honestly, Father, you can be as tasteless as this ale."

Dies Irae laughed, and blessedly, his hand left Mirum's skirt. She exhaled shakily.

Dies Irae sipped his ale and his thin, curved mouth curved even further. He put the mug down, lines of disgust appearing in that golden skin of his. "I certainly would hate to appear as coarse as this drink," he said.

These ones rarely drank cheap ale, Mirum knew, but were used to sipping fine wines. Their tastes had to be as exquisite as their jeweled armor and priceless samite capes. Dies Irae pushed the mug away, his eagle face frowning, and reached out to grab Mirum's arm.

She couldn't help but yelp, which made Gloriae laugh, a cold and beautiful laugh like ice cracking. But Dies Irae did not laugh. His fingers clutched her so painfully, Mirum wanted to scream. It felt like his fingers could tear into her, pull the muscles off her bone. She had not known fingers could cause such pain.

"Mirum... sweetness," Dies Irae said, voice soft, cold, like a slow wave before a storm. His eyes pierced her, steady and dark blue. They bored into her, a stare so cold and sharp, it almost hurt her skin.

"My lord," she whispered, unable to talk any louder. She wanted to scream or faint from the pain.

He tightened his grip on her, fingernails digging, and she bit her lip hard. "Sweetness," he said, "do you know why I am here today? Do you know why I've come to this wretched, seaside ruin of a fort, this pile of moldy stones by this cesspool you call a beach?"

She wanted to hit him, to spit at him, to draw her sword with her free hand and run him through. *Kyrie,* she thought. *I must live for Kyrie. He has nobody else. And neither do I.*

"I don't know, my lord," she whispered.

He rose to his feet so suddenly, she started. He released her arm, shoved her back, and backhanded her face. Pain exploded. For an instant, Mirum saw only white light. She took a ragged breath, wobbling, spots dancing before her eyes. She could barely see, barely breathe. *Draw your sword,* a voice inside her whispered. *Draw Father's blade and finish him now, or he'll rape and kill you, or kill and then rape you. Kill him now and then fall upon your sword.*

Yet she could not... and she didn't know if it was because she was brave, or because she was a coward.

"You're lying," Dies Irae said, voice as hard as his hand.

Mirum's eyes were glazed, and she gazed past him, gazed out the window toward the sea. She could see the waves there, hear their murmur, taste their salt on her lips. So many of her tears, so many of her whispers and mumbles those waves had swallowed. So many of her fears she had spoken into their roaring depths. The promise of hidden realms and seascapes of wonder pulsed beneath them, a world unknown to her, unknown to any human. Standing in this room, blood on her lip, cruelty surrounding her, Mirum wished like never before to dive into those waves, to disappear into their kingdoms of seashells, sunken ruins, twinkling beads of light so far from pain. *From the sea we come, to the sea we return,* were the words of her forefathers, words always murmured at births and deaths. *Who will utter those words for me? Will I be buried too in the kingdom of waterdepth, or burned upon my walls?*

Dies Irae returned to his seat. He leaned back, placed his hand behind his head, and laid his boots upon the table. "There are rumors," he said, voice soft, but Mirum could hear him so loudly, she wanted to cover her ears. "There are rumors in the village. The fishermen whisper of... a shape at night, a shape in the skies. A shape that blocks the stars."

"Could it be a cloud, my lord?" Mirum dared to ask, and Dies Irae laughed mirthlessly.

"You are an endearing creature, are you not?" He placed his boots on the floor and gestured at Gloriae. "Bring her to me."

The young woman was slim, no taller than Mirum and unlikely to be stronger, but still she stepped forward, green eyes flashing with amusement. A slight, crooked smile on her lips, Gloriae shoved Mirum.

Dies Irae caught her and pulled her down, so that Mirum sat in his lap. She tried to rise, to struggle, but Dies Irae held her firmly, his iron arm across her. She turned her face away from his, disgusted, but he clutched her cheek with his good hand and turned her face toward him. Gloriae laughed icily.

"So innocent," Dies Irae whispered to Mirum. His good hand was gloved in moleskin, and he used it to wipe the blood off her lip. "You are still a child, are you not? Like the last time I saw you. A cloud, you say. It is sweet, my child, sweet like your soft cheeks, like your bloodied lips, sweet like all of you." His eyes undressed her. "But no, child. This was no cloud. This was the shape of a dragon, swooping low over the sea at nights, sometimes roaring, scaring fishermen's children, waking them, filling their nightmares. Can you imagine the atrocity, child? A dragon flying at night... here in my lands? Over the sea of Fort Sanctus, which I let you rule?"

Mirum shut her eyes. Looking at his golden, hard face was too painful. "I have seen no dragons here."

Dies Irae squeezed her thigh, and Mirum struggled, but could not free herself. "Nobody has seen dragons, not true dragons, not in a thousand years. The true dragons left these lands long ago. No, child. This was a Vir Requis."

At the sound of that ancient name, the tittering Gloriae fell silent. Mirum froze, her breath dying within her. *Vir Requis.* Nobody spoke those words anymore. They were forbidden words, taboo, words Dies Irae allowed nobody to speak.

Vir Requis. The ancient blood. The men who carried the old magic, the magic that let them take dragon form. They were not true dragons, but nor were they true men. Vir Requis. A proud, ancient race. They were remembered now as weredragons, as if they were monsters, no nobler or prouder than beasts.

"But... but I thought they're all dead," Mirum whispered and opened her eyes.

Dies Irae was looking at her, and Mirum realized that his eyes were the same color as her sea, gray blue, as cold and dangerous as those waves that crashed against her fort.

"I thought so too, child," he whispered, so softly that she read his lips more than she heard his voice. "But they say that one may have survived. One... maybe two. Maybe three. No more. No more out of a million. But a handful might remain, pretending to be decent humans. Like cowards they hide--in basements, in caves. Maybe even, child, in a ruined seaside tower."

There could be no doubt now. He knew of Kyrie. Someone had betrayed them. One of the villagers. One of her friends. Someone had seen Kyrie, had seen him turn into a dragon, and had talked.

A tear rolled down Mirum's cheek.

"Now now, dear child," Dies Irae said and lifted the tear on his finger. "Why do you cry? Is it for your shame, your shame for having betrayed me?"

Mirum tightened her lips. *No! Do not give up now. Not yet. Live a little longer, for Father, for Kyrie.* She swallowed hard, swallowed down all her terror, all her memories. "There is no weredragon here, my lord. You may search this tower if you will. You will find none."

He rose suddenly, shoving her off. She hit the table, then hit the floor, but this time Gloriae did not laugh. There would be no laughter so soon after the forbidden words had been uttered. *Who of them will rape me today?* Mirum thought. *And will Irae kill me after, or before they've had their way?*

"Show us to the tower top," Dies Irae said, all the softness gone from his voice. That voice was now cold, commanding, and sharp as Gloriae's blade. "Let us search this ruin."

Dies Irae left the hall, holding Mirum before him, and they stepped onto the staircase. His lieutenants walked behind: the cold and dainty Gloriae, all in steel and gold, and the gaunt, silent man whose face still hid behind his helm. The staircase wound up the tower, its steps chipped, centuries old. Mirum walked numbly, Irae's fingers digging into her arm. They walked round and round, up and up, and Mirum kept looking out the arrow slits, peering at the roaring sea, wishing again that she could dive under that water, swim away, drown into the world of hidden wonders.

Please, Kyrie, she thought feverishly, lips trembling. *Please hide.*

And if they found him... she still had her sword at her side. She could not hope to kill them all, probably not even kill

Dies Irae. Even if she did kill him, that meant torture for her. They would break her spine with hammers, break her limbs and string them through the spokes of a wagon wheel, and hang her outside to slowly die. They would do the same to Kyrie, not caring that he was still a boy, only sixteen. But maybe... maybe if she could draw her sword fast enough, she could still fall upon it.

They reached the tower top. A rotting wooden trapdoor lay above her, leading outside to the crenellations.

"Open it," Dies Irae said.

With numb hands, Mirum pushed open the trapdoor, then stepped outside onto the windy, crumbling crest of Fort Sanctus.

The waves roared below, spraying foam. The wind lashed her, streamed her hair, and flapped her cloak and dress. Old iron bars surrounded the tower top, the vestiges of some ancient armaments, now rusty. The stone they rose from was moldy and chipped. *This tower has been in my family for centuries. Will it fall today?*

Below the tower, Mirum could see the three griffins, those beautiful beasts. She could not see Sol. Had the griffins eaten her, or had her mare escaped? Either fate seemed kinder than what Mirum would endure if they found Kyrie here today.

Mirum could see for leagues from here. On one side, she saw the endless sea, gray water flowing into the horizon. On her other side, she saw leagues of boulders, rocky fields, and scraggly deltas. Once all these lands had belonged to her father, and to his father before him, and many forts had risen from them. Dies Irae had taken these lands, toppled these forts, killed her father and his father. All he'd left was this place, this old tower, this old village. When Mirum looked down, she could see the fishing village, this hamlet where somebody had betrayed her, where somebody had seen Kyrie and spoken.

I told you, Kyrie, she thought and tasted tears on her lips. *I told you not to fly. I told you never to use your magic, never to become a dragon.* But he would never listen. A Vir Requis was meant to fly.

If they stayed human too long, they grew thin, pale, withered. They needed to breathe fire, to flap wings and taste the firmaments between their jaws.

"There's nobody here," Gloriae said, her sword drawn. The wind streamed her golden hair and turned her cheeks pink.

Dies Irae raised his steel fist, the spiked mace head. "Wait, my daughter. We will look."

A few old chests and barrels littered the tower top. Dies Irae eyed them.

"Old fishing gear," Mirum said, and was surprised to hear no hoarseness to her voice, almost no trace of fear. Her voice sounded dead. Flat.

Dies Irae did not spare her a glance. "We shall see. Molok, the laceleaf, please."

The gaunt man stepped forward, rail-thin, tall and gangly. Finally he lifted his helmet's visor, and Mirum saw his face. The face was cadaverous. His cheekbones jutted and his dark eyes were sunken. Mirum knew this one. Lord Molok--known in whispers as the baby killer, for he had once slaughtered five Vir Requis infants in a village, and probably many more that men did not speak of. As Mirum watched, trembling, Molok opened a leather pouch. He pulled out crumpled leaves and handed them to Dies Irae.

Mirum's knees trembled. *Laceleaf.* The pale, serrated leaves leaked white latex like milk. Laceleaf was what Dies Irae would call it, of course; a mild name, the name of a herb one might find in an old woman's garden. To the Vir Requis it had other names.

"Do you know what this is?" Dies Irae asked. He held the leaves up to Mirum's nose. He crushed one between two fingers, and she smelled it, a smell like vinegar and overripe apples.

"A herb," she whispered.

Dies Irae laughed softly. "To you or me, yes. A harmless herb. My maids often cook my meals with it. But to the weredragons... do you know what they call it, sweetness?" His nostrils flared, inhaling the plant's aroma, and he let out a satisfied sigh. "They call it ilbane, or deathweed, or devil's leaves. In their ancient tongue, which the weredragons spoke in the old days, it was simply called *valber*, which is their word for poison."

"It kills weredragons," Mirum said, hating the taste of that word on her lips. *Weredragons.* A foul word. The name of monsters.

Dies Irae shook his head. "Kills them? Oh no, my dear. It takes more than a herb to kill beasts of such evil. It sickens them. Burns them. When they are in human form, it reveals the monstrosity that lies within them, their reptilian blood. But no, sweetness, it does not *kill* them." He raised his iron fist. The sun finally peeked from the clouds, and the mace head glittered. Dies Irae's thin lips smiled. "*This* kills them."

So swiftly Mirum gasped, Dies Irae swung his iron arm. The mace head hit a rotted chest, showering splinters of wood. Mirum bit her lip, instinctively reaching for her sword, but Lord Molok grabbed her arm with a gauntleted hand, and she could not draw her blade.

Mirum took a ragged breath. Nothing but some old arrowheads, flasks of oil, and rope fell from the shattered chest.

Mirum saw two more chests, both of rotting and cracked wood, and five barrels. Which one hid Kyrie? *Fly, Kyrie,* she thought feverishly, trying to transfer her thoughts to him as by magic. *The time to fly has come. Escape!*

Dies Irae smirked and approached a barrel. Now that the clouds had parted, he truly looked like a seraph, his armor so bright it hurt Mirum's eyes, the jeweled griffin on his breastplate shining like stars. The garnets on his mace appeared like drops of blood.

That iron arm swung again and slammed into a barrel.

Splinters scattered.

Turnips rolled onto the floor.

Fly, Kyrie! Mirum wanted to scream, but she could bring no breath to her lungs. She felt paralyzed, could barely breathe, and would have fallen had Molok not been holding her.

Dies Irae swung his mace into another chest.

Wood shattered.

Splinters flew.

A cry of pain sounded, and there--in the splintered wreck of the chest--huddled a boy.

Kyrie.

"Ah, here we go," Dies Irae said pleasantly, as if he had just found a missing sock.

Mirum stared, mouth open, Molok clutching her. Huddled on the floor, glaring up with burning eyes, Kyrie seemed so young to her. He was sixteen now, but suddenly to Mirum's eyes, he seemed six again, a mere child, like when she'd found him bloodied among corpses at Lanburg Fields. His hair was fair, dusty, wild. His eyes were brown, more pain and anger in them than fear. As always, his parchment map was rolled up and stuffed into his belt. Kyrie always kept the map on him; his bit of hope, bit of memory, bit of anger.

Ice filled Mirum's stomach. Kyrie did not know Dies Irae like she did. If he had seen Dies Irae slaughter her father, rape her all night by the corpse, he would have less anger in his eyes... and more terror.

Cradling his arm--Dies Irae's mace must have bashed it--Kyrie rose to his feet. He was taller than Mirum already, but when he faced Dies Irae, the golden lord towered over him.

"All right, all right, you win," Kyrie said, eyes flashing. "You found me. Now bugger off before I bash your beak nose."

As Mirum gasped, Dies Irae laughed. It was not a cruel laugh, Mirum thought, nor angry; Dies Irae seemed truly amused. "Bold words," he said, "for a worm caught cowering in a barrel like a rat."

Kyrie glared, fists clenched at his sides. "Am I a rat or a worm? You're good at bashing things, but your tongue is as blunt as that freakish iron hand of yours."

"No, Kyrie," Mirum whispered through a clenched jaw. *Fly! Turn into a dragon and fly! Why do you linger here?*

But of course, she knew. If Kyrie flew, he'd prove to Dies Irae that he was Vir Requis. The griffins would chase him, but they would not just kill him; they would torture him, then burn him alive upon the towers of Flammis, Dies Irae's marble palace. *He thinks he can withstand the ilbane*, Mirum realized, feeling faint. Her knees buckled, and she stayed standing only because Molok clutched her arms. *No, Kyrie, you cannot; no Vir Requis can, not even the great Benedictus.*

"What's your name?" Dies Irae asked the boy, still seeming more amused than slighted.

"Kyrie Eleison," he replied, chin raised, fists still clenched.

"Kyrie, I like you," Dies Irae said. "Most weredragons are terrified of me. They tremble in my presence like the sweet Lady Mirum here. But you, Kyrie... you feel no fear, only anger. That is rare for weredragons, who are known for their cowardice."

"Yes, yes," Kyrie said, and Mirum knew that he was scared now, terrified, but letting his anger drown that fear. "I have weredragon features, and Eleison is a weredragon name. I hear that all the time. Why do you think I hide here? People always mistake me for a weredragon. My father was one. But then... so was yours, wasn't he, Irae?"

Mirum gasped. Nobody mentioned Dies Irae's father to him. Nobody who wished to live. Everyone knew that this was Dies Irae's greatest shame.

Dies Irae's thin mouth curved bitterly, and lines ran down his face. His fist clenched the ilbane, and sap dripped. "Yes," he said, "my father was a weredragon. The filthiest, most cowardly among them."

"He was their *king*," Kyrie spat out, eyes aflame. "But you were a disgrace to him, weren't you? His firstborn son... but without the ancient magic, unable to become a dragon. You were a freak in his court, weren't you? So he disowned you. He had another son, Benedictus, to replace you--"

"*Enough!*" Dies Irae shouted, so loudly that Mirum, Irae's lieutenants, and even Kyrie started. Dies Irae shook with fury, fist clenched, face red. His eyes burned. "My lineage is none of your concern, weredragon. That old, royal house of Requiem is gone now. My father is dead. My brother is dead--"

"Benedictus is *not* dead," Kyrie interrupted, and Mirum wept, because she knew that their torture and deaths were now certain. "You never killed Benedictus. You stole his amulet, and you stole his griffins, but you never killed him. Your brother bit off your arm. He could have *killed* you, but he showed you mercy, and he flew away. I know! I was there. I saw it happen--"

Kyrie froze and bit his lip.

Oh, Kyrie..., Mirum thought, tears in her eyes.

Dies Irae stared silently for a moment, a moment that seemed to Mirum to last a lifetime. Finally he broke the silence. "You were... there. Certainly you were too young a decade ago to fight under my banners." Dies Irae raised his fist, bringing the ilbane near Kyrie... and then pressed the leaves to Kyrie's cheek.

Kyrie tried not to scream. His teeth gritted, and sweat washed him, and his eyes moistened. Mirum saw welts rise on his cheek, and his fist clutched his map, that parchment forever at his belt, as if it could save him, give him strength. Mirum struggled to free herself from Molok, but could not. Finally voice found her throat.

"*Fly, Kyrie!*" she shouted at the top of her lungs.

Kyrie too shouted, a cry of pain. He leaped away from Dies Irae, cheek blistering, and suddenly fangs grew from his mouth. Claws sprouted from his fingertips. Dies Irae swung his mace, but Kyrie leaped back, and the mace missed him.

Kyrie leaped off the tower.

In the chaos, Molok's grip loosened. Mirum twisted, freed herself, and drew her blade.

She thrust her sword at Dies Irae. *You killed my father!* she wanted to scream. *You raped me! You murdered millions!* But everything happened so fast, she had time for only a wordless cry of all her rage and tears. Her blade gleamed.

Dies Irae swung his mace, met her blade, and shattered it.

Mirum fell to her knees, clutching her bladeless hilt, and saw a dragon rise over the tower's crenellations, forty feet long and roaring. Blue scales covered Kyrie. Flames rose from his nostrils, and his wings churned the air, blowing the hair back from Mirum's face. Mirum heard the thud of griffin wings, their eagle shrieks.

"Fly, Kyrie!" Mirum shouted. He was reaching toward her. "Leave me! Follow your map, Kyrie, and fly!"

Kyrie's claws almost caught her, but Dies Irae's mace slammed into them, knocking them away. Kyrie howled and blew fire into the sky. One griffin rose behind him, clung to his back, and bit his shoulder.

"*Fly, Kyrie!*"

The last thing Mirum saw was Dies Irae's mace. It swung toward her head.

She felt only an instant of pain.

White light flooded her.

Floating.

Her spirit... flying, gazing down upon her body, her blood upon the mossy old stones of Fort Sanctus, her home, the home of her forefathers.

And then... nothing but light.

Father....

Child....

She could now see nothing, nothing but white, but she could imagine the rolling lands of her realm, their proud towers standing again, the sea that called her home.

I'm going to that world, the kingdom of waterdepths, the land of seaweed and seashells, of beads of light and endless sleep, endless wonder.

It was like falling asleep...

...and she was gone.

KYRIE ELEISON

"Mirum!" Kyrie howled.

The griffin on his back shrieked and dug its talons into him. Kyrie struggled, lashing his tail, and freed himself. Two more griffins flew at him, one from each side.

Mirum....

Tears in his eyes, Kyrie pulled his wings close. He swooped from the tower top to the boulders below, the rocky beach, and the crashing waves. Water sprayed him. He twisted, skimmed across the water, and shot up. The griffins followed, reaching out their talons.

"No... Mirum...," Kyrie wept. He could barely see the waves, the clouds, the fort, the griffins that followed. All he could see was the image of Dies Irae clubbing Lady Mirum, the image of her falling, head cracked. Dead. She could not have survived that blow; Kyrie knew it. And yet... he had to go back. He had to get her body, to bury her at sea.

Fly, Kyrie! Her voice still echoed in his mind. *Leave me!*

A griffin slammed into Kyrie, and its talons ripped off scales. Kyrie screamed, pain blazing. He blew flames, roaring red flames of all his fury, setting the griffin alight. It shrieked so loudly, it hurt Kyrie's ears. It swooped into the sea, then emerged smoking and screaming.

Fly!

"I'll come back for you," Kyrie swore... and he flew.

He flew low and skimmed the water, the wind lashing him. He was soon a league from Fort Sanctus. When he looked back, he saw the griffins following. Dies Irae, Gloriae, and Molok rode them. *Damn.* Dragon eyes were sharp--sharper than his eyes in human form--and Kyrie could see that Dies Irae glared, his thin mouth curving. His mace was raised.

Let's see how fast you bastards can fly, Kyrie thought and narrowed his eyes. He pumped his wings. At night, streaming over fields and seas, he could travel hundreds of leagues in a flight. Now he flew faster than ever. There was no way those griffins could fly half that fast, Kyrie told himself. Not while bearing armored riders.

He rose above the water, moving higher and higher. He crashed through the clouds and emerged into startling blue sky, the sun a blazing disk above, blinding him. Kyrie found an air current and shot forward, body straight as a javelin. He gritted his teeth and flapped his wings madly, pushing himself forward with all his strength. He was moving so fast now, the clouds below him blurred. The sun hit his back, and the icy air bit him. He had never flown faster.

Beat that, Irae, he thought and grinned bitterly.

Then he heard it.

A griffin shriek.

He turned his head and cursed. *Impossible!* The griffins were pursuing, bodies like arrows. How could they fly so fast?

Kyrie grunted. He flapped his wings with all his might. His body ached. The air stung him, icicles covered him, and he could hardly breathe. It was cold up here, freezing, the air so thin his head spun. He would not survive much longer at this altitude. Kyrie lowered himself just a few hundred yards, dipping into the clouds. Moisture clung to him and filled his maw, eyes, and nostrils. When he turned his head again, he could see nothing but cloud, but he heard them. They were moving closer. Gritting his teeth, Kyrie kept flying, aching, moving faster than an arrow. He must have traveled thirty leagues, maybe more, but could not lose them. He pulled his wings close, dived, and emerged from under the clouds.

He saw a land of rock and water. He still flew over the sea, but great stone teeth now rose from the water, some hundreds of feet tall. The jutting rock formed towers, snaking walls, canyons of foaming sea. Rising from crashing waves, the rocks looked like forts, with pillars and bridges and tunnels, battlements of some forgotten water gods. The sea roared between the pillars, through the stone tunnels, moving in and out of crevices like the watery breath of sea monsters. Kyrie had never seen this place, this realm of rock and foam and salt, and he gasped at its beauty and danger.

Shrieks sounded above him. Kyrie raised his head and saw the griffins swooping from the clouds, talons outstretched, beaks open.

Damn it.

Kyrie veered aside, but a griffin clawed his leg, drawing blood. Cursing, Kyrie shot into the clouds again. The griffins followed. He dived to the sea, but another almost clawed him. A third flew from below, and Kyrie swiveled, dodging it, then spun again, just missing another griffin. They surrounded him.

Damn the stars!

Kyrie blew fire. The griffin ahead swerved, dodging the flames. Kyrie swooped, zoomed by it, almost hit the water, then straightened himself to skim over the waves. The boulders rose around him, black and jagged, and one almost hit his shoulder. Waves and foam brushed his belly.

You're fast bastards, he thought, *but let's see you maneuver.*

Stone walls rose ahead, a canyon between them, barely wider than his body. Kyrie flew into the canyon, the walls rushing by his sides. The sea roared below, spraying him with foam, and he could barely see the sky. Screeches came behind him, and when Kyrie glanced over his shoulder, he saw the griffins follow him into the canyon.

Rocks jutted out from the cliff sides, and Kyrie flew up and down, dodging them. He snaked around boulders like liquid silver streaming through a labyrinth. Fire pumped through him, and despite the danger and anguish, Kyrie grinned over gritted teeth. This was what he'd been born for. This was *flying*. In some places, the canyon walls met above him, forming tunnels. One tunnel was so low, Kyrie's belly grazed the sea as he flew. A thud came behind him, followed by a shriek of pain.

"Having fun, girls?" Kyrie shouted over his shoulder, and saw that one griffin was hurt, its shoulder bleeding. Kyrie grinned and kept flapping his wings, which was hard to do in a tunnel this narrow. His heart raced. *I was made for this.*

Suddenly the canyon curved, and Kyrie made a sharp turn. His shoulder grazed the stone wall, and he grunted, but he made the turn with nothing but a scratch. Behind him came a thud, a shriek, and a rider's cry; one griffin at least had not made the turn. Kyrie kept flying. When he glanced over his shoulder, he saw that the wounded griffin was gone. So was its rider, the gaunt Lord Molok. Kyrie hoped he was dead.

The canyon ended, the walls giving way to a network of jagged pillars. Some met above him, crisscrossing, molded together. Kyrie flew up and down, left and right, moving between the pillars at top speed. Around one column, a boulder rose from the waves, and Kyrie shot straight up, under an overhanging stone, left around another column, and quickly down into a tunnel.

Damn, he thought, then heard a crash behind him. A second griffin was gone. Its rider, the beautiful and icy Gloriae, crashed into the water.

One griffin remained now, and one rider.

Dies Irae.

The man who'd killed Mirum.

Kyrie grunted. *Now we're even.*

Flying between the stone boulders, he spun to face Dies Irae on his griffin. He howled and blew fire.

The flames roared, and the griffin rose, dodging the fire, but hit an overhanging arch of stone. The beast screeched, and Kyrie shot forward, claws slashing.

Dies Irae pulled the reins, and his griffin bucked, raising its talons. Kyrie's claws hit the griffin's leg, drawing blood. The griffin reached out to bite, but Kyrie was too fast. He dodged the beast, then lashed his spiked tail.

He hit Dies Irae, cracking his armor. Blood seeped from the steel. More blood flowed down the griffin's flanks. Kyrie growled.

"You're dead now, Irae," he said. Smoke rose from his nostrils. "You killed Mirum. You killed my family. And now I'm going to kill you."

He sucked in air, prepared to blow flames and roast the glittering, one-armed lord.

Dies Irae raised a crossbow.

So fast Kyrie barely saw it, a quarrel flew. It slammed into Kyrie's chest.

Kyrie howled. Pain bloomed, twisting and sizzling. He knew that pain. *Ilbane.* The quarrel was coated with the poison.

Kyrie gritted his teeth. *No! No. This does not end here.* He blew fire.

The flames roared, hit the griffin, and its fur kindled. It screeched, and Kyrie tried to fly toward it, to claw it apart, to crush Dies Irae, but his wings felt stiff. He could barely fly. He dipped several yards.

A second quarrel flew.

Wings aching, pain blazing, Kyrie managed to flap aside. The quarrel scratched his shoulder, tearing off a scale, burning.

Kyrie roared. He felt ready to pass out, but he mustered every last bit of rage, horror, and hatred in him, and he shot forward.

For Mirum. For my father, mother, brothers, and sisters. For ten years of hiding in stinking barrels. He opened his maw, howling, prepared to bite off Dies Irae's head.

For an instant, his eyes locked with Dies Irae's stare. The man's eyes blazed. He seemed full of so much hate, so much pain, that Kyrie nearly faltered. What was it? What caused the man to hate Vir Requis so much?

It happened so fast, Kyrie barely registered it. Dies Irae tugged the reins, and the griffin shot up.

No! Kyrie tried to follow. He flapped his wings, but felt so heavy. The griffin was shooting into the skies. It was getting away.

"Come back here, coward!" Kyrie howled. He blew fire, but his flames felt weak. They could not reach the griffin, who was only a distant spot now.

A third quarrel came zooming down. Kyrie spun aside, and the bolt missed him. He flew higher and higher, and his head exploded with pain.

"Irae, come back here and finish what you started!" he cried, then shut his eyes with pain. He dipped a hundred yards, another hundred. Another quarrel flew. It sank into his shoulder, and he screamed. He fell. He crashed into the sea. His wings would no longer move, and his muscles ached. Waves roared around him, icy cold, and water filled his mouth. He swam toward a boulder that rose from the waves, clutched it, and climbed onto it.

He became human again.

He clung to the rock, shivering. His shoulder and chest bled, and the ilbane coursed through him. It wouldn't kill him, he knew. He remembered what Dies Irae had said; the stuff was not lethal, but it burned. Worse than the pain was his grief.

Dies Irae had gotten away--gone to fetch more griffins, no doubt. The man was a coward. And....

Kyrie lowered his head. He tasted salt on his lips, and didn't know if it was from the sea, or his tears. *Mirum.* His best friend, the light of his life. Mirum was dead.

A wave washed over him, and Kyrie barely held onto the boulder. His clothes, which had shifted with him, now clung to him, cold and wet. His veins felt full of lava, and his head felt ready to crack. The waves kept pounding him. He looked around, but saw only furious water, jagged rocks, and pillars of stone. He was a hundred leagues away from shelter, from civilization, from life. He was stuck here on this jagged rock, shivering, bleeding, maybe dying. More griffins would arrive any moment. The waves roared so loudly, his ears ached.

Kyrie lowered his head against the stone. He closed his eyes. *It cannot end here. I cannot die here like this. Not now.*

He took a deep breath, lungs aching. With trembling fingers, he felt for the parchment map. It was still there, hanging from his belt. It was soaked, but it was still there.

There was only one thing to do now, Kyrie knew. It was a crazy quest, a fool's quest. The chase of a myth. But Kyrie knew it was the only path he could now follow.

He must find him.

He must still live... somewhere.

Kyrie nodded. He would seek Benedictus.

DIES IRAE

Dies Irae could barely hold the reins. His shoulder ached. The armor was dented, and blood seeped through its joints. His griffin, Volucris, was also wounded; his fur smoked and stank, and blood poured down his sides. Dies Irae clenched his jaw and clung to Volucris as he flew. Smoke filled his nostrils, and he grunted and coughed.

It seemed an eternity before he saw land ahead. A beach of black rocks stretched for a hundred yards, giving way to a forest of elms and birches. Gritting his teeth, Dies Irae directed Volucris to the shore. His ears ached as he descended. He landed upon the rocky beach.

Grimacing, Dies Irae alighted from Volucris, then stood before the foaming sea. He removed his pauldron. Beneath the gilded steel, his shoulder was a mess. A bruise was already spreading, and the skin was cracked and bleeding.

Disgusting reptile, Dies Irae thought. Lady Mirum had been hiding him all this time. Dies Irae wished he could club her again, hear the crack of her skull. He should fly back to her body and let Volucris eat it.

He clenched his good fist. Kyrie Eleison. A living weredragon.

Dies Irae spat. How could one of the monsters have escaped him for so long? Dies Irae decided not to kill the boy. No. Once he mustered reinforcement, he would capture the monstrosity, chain him, and display him as a freak for Osanna to jeer at. The last member of a wretched race, Kyrie would become a side show, a curiosity for a menagerie.

Dies Irae sat down with a grunt. *Where is Gloriae?* he wondered. Last he'd seen, she was swimming toward a boulder, bruised and battered. Had she flown back to land, or still remained at sea? Either way, she would live. He'd seek her soon.

Fingers stiff, Dies Irae caressed the amulet that hung around his neck, the amulet that contained the blood of the griffin king. As always, touching the amulet calmed him. The Griffin Heart. For centuries, it had hung around the necks of his ancestors, a jewel of Requiem's courts.

When Volucris saw the amulet, he bucked and clawed the air.

"Yes, Volucris," Dies Irae whispered. "Yes, it hurts to see, does it not? It burns your eyes."

The griffin growled, and Dies Irae patted him. Volucris mewled and clawed the beach. Dies Irae remembered that day long ago, the day he took the Griffin Heart, took the amulet that should have always been his.

"For one hundred generations, the Griffin Heart went to the firstborn," he had said that day, a younger man, not yet forty and still full of youth's rage and strength. "Father! How dare you deny me this?" Tears had stung his eyes, and his voice had quavered.

His father sat upon Requiem's throne of twisting oak roots, the throne now chopped up and burned. The king looked down upon Dies Irae, his firstborn, the giftless son. His shame. The shame of the court.

"My son," the king said, "I have told you. This court is forbidden to you. How dare you enter it? How dare you demand a gift from me?"

Around the court of Requiem, the lords stared silently, grim, hands on their sword hilts. They wore green and silver, dragons embroidered onto their tunics. Beyond the columns,

Dies Irae could see Requiem Forest, the hoary birches that spread for leagues. Birds chirruped and griffins flew above.

Standing below the throne, Dies Irae glared at his father. "I will not hide in my chambers any longer. I will not sit with the women of your court, learning to scribe, learning to count, learning to become some servant to you. I am your firstborn. I demand the--"

"You are a disgrace!" Father shouted, rising to his feet. Dies Irae froze and stared. So did the lords of the court. Even the birds fell silent. The King of Requiem stood, white hair wild, liver-spotted fists clenched.

"Father," Dies Irae whispered, lips trembling.

The king took a step toward him, jaw clenched. "How dare you demand anything from me? I do not know whose son you are, boy. You cannot turn into a dragon. What kind of Vir Requis are you? You think you can lead this people, sit upon this throne, use the Griffin Heart to tame them? You are no son of mine. I do not know what human my wife bedded, or how you were begotten, but--"

Dies Irae shouted, tears falling. "I am no bastard son! I am *your* son. The son of the king. No, I cannot turn into a dragon. I lack the gift. Others do too. Dozens of us were born this way, but you banish us. You make us your servants, but we're not weak. I will take the Griffin Heart. I will wear the amulet. I might not have dragon wings, but I will have griffin ones. And when I control the griffins, you will pay, Father, you will--"

"Brother!" came a voice from behind, and Dies Irae's voice died. Shaking with fury, he spun around to see Benedictus.

His younger brother was entering the hall. He wore green and gray, forest garb. He must have been out hunting, as was his wont. His black curls clung to his brow with sweat.

"Benedictus!" Dies Irae called across the hall. "*Prince* Benedictus, I should say. Heir to our throne. Baby brother." The words tasted vile.

Benedictus. Born to replace him, Dies Irae, the elder son. Benedictus, the second born. The great Vir Requis prince, able to become the great black dragon. Future king. *You too will kneel before me,* Dies Irae swore. *You too will beg for mercy when the Griffin Heart hangs around my neck.*

"Brother," Benedictus said and reached out callused hands. "Father. Please. Do not yell. Perhaps we can give the Griffin Heart to Dies Irae, Father. If I was born to sit upon the throne, he can sit beside me, rule the griffins for me."

Dies Irae spat. "I'll do nothing for you," he said. His hand strayed toward his sword. "I am first born, and I'll not see you sit upon any throne. If I cannot have this throne for myself, and myself only, I will destroy it. I will rule this kingdom, or I will burn it."

With a hiss, he drew his blade.

Bloodlust filled him, painting the world red.

Eyes narrowed, Dies Irae thrust his sword into Father's chest.

"Father!" Benedictus shouted and ran forward, but the hall was long. Long enough for Dies Irae to grab the Griffin Heart, which hung around Father's neck. Father gasped, his blood gushing, and his fingers clawed the air.

"I can't grow fangs," Dies Irae said and snapped the amulet off its chain. "But swords can bite just as deep."

A roar sounded behind. Dies Irae spun to see Benedictus shift into a dragon and leap at him.

Dies Irae snarled and raised the amulet.

With shrieks and thudding wings, a dozen griffins swooped into the hall and crashed into Benedictus. As his brother's blood spilled, Dies Irae smiled.

The griffins were his.

Requiem's greatest servants became her greatest enemies that day. They flew for him. They toppled the columns of this court. They tore down the birches. They burned all the shame and weakness from his heart; he was their master, and the world was his.

The Requiem War began.

Standing on the beach, Dies Irae clutched the Griffin Heart. The amulet bit into his palm. He forced himself to take a deep breath, to release the memories. That had been many years ago. The Vir Requis were nearly extinct now. His father was dead, the Oak Throne destroyed, Requiem in ruin. Benedictus was gone; nobody had seen him in a decade.

He released the amulet and took another deep breath. If he let the pain claim him now, let the memories fill him, he could lose track of time, drown in his rage, spend days in it. He gritted his teeth.

"There's no more time for memories," he whispered to Volucris, the greatest of the griffins, a prince among them. He mounted the beast. "Our war is not over yet. There is a weredragon to find."

As he took flight, Dies Irae imagined crushing Kyrie's bones, like he had crushed Mirum... and he smiled.

KYRIE ELEISON

As Kyrie traveled the land by foot, he learned something new about himself.

He hated walking.

Loathed it.

A blister grew on his right heel, two on his left. He didn't even know which foot to limp on. He had stubbed two toes against a root a league back, and the nails were turning black. *Disgusting*, he thought. His legs ached, and his wounded chest burned. His back also screamed.

He spoke between gritted teeth to the surrounding trees. "I. Hate. Walking."

He wanted to *fly*--to turn into a dragon, flap his wings, feel the rush of air, the power. *That* was the way to travel. But not today. Nor for the past month he'd spent walking in human form.

Flying, he knew, was just too dangerous.

Dies Irae was after him. Kyrie had seen parchments posted upon roadside taverns, crossroad signs, even the occasional oak. "Weredragon at large! Kyrie Eleison, escaped monster, transforms into a blue reptile. Bring dead or alive to the nearest Sun God temple for reward."

Kyrie snorted whenever he saw the posters. The crude drawing of a dragon was laughable; it showed him clutching a maiden in each hand, toppling a house with his tail, and chomping a baby. *Ridiculous.* If anyone ate babies, it was the beautiful and icy Gloriae; the young woman seemed just vicious enough.

Laughable as the poster was, Kyrie still dared not fly. Not with griffins patrolling the skies. An hour did not pass without Kyrie hearing a distant griffin cry. Several times a day, he saw them too, like eagles high above. And he knew they were looking for him.

Indeed, as Kyrie now limped on his blisters, more shrieks sounded above. Griffins. Three or four, by the sound of it. With a grunt, Kyrie dived into a leafy bush. He saw the griffins between the branches, talons like swords. Did Dies Irae ride one? The griffins shrieked again, then were gone, flying into the distance.

Kyrie sighed and climbed out from the leaves. He sat down on a fallen log and gazed around him. The forest was thick, and Kyrie couldn't see more than a few yards in each direction. Oak, birch, and ash trees grew here, and most seemed centuries old, thick and knotty. Their leaves rustled, scattering motes of light. Fallen logs crisscrossed around him, covered with moss and mushrooms.

"What am I even doing here?" he asked aloud.

Nobody answered but chirping birds, pattering squirrels, and rustling leaves. There was nobody here. Nobody in the entire forest.

Benedictus is dead, he told himself. *I'll never find him here. I'm the last Vir Requis. And once those griffins catch me, I too will die.*

Kyrie suddenly felt hot, his blood boiling. He wanted to scream, but dared not. Instead he gritted his teeth and punched a tree trunk. It hurt. *Good.* Physical pain could drown anguish. Pain was easier than anguish.

"That bloody, stupid, cursed map," Kyrie said and spat.

Breathing hard, he pulled the rolled up map from his belt. The parchment was old, cracked, and burned in one corner. The sea had soaked it, leaving it wrinkled. For five years, he'd carried it on his belt, refusing to shelf or box it. For five years, it had been his hope.

But the map couldn't be real. It too was just a child's dream. Wasn't it?

Kyrie unrolled the parchment. The ink was faded and smudged, but Kyrie had examined this map so many times, he could read it with eyes shut. He had found the parchment when he was eleven. An old peddler had ridden his donkey to Fort Sanctus, his cart overflowing with trinkets. Mirum bought a pan, tea leaves, and a necklace of agate stones. Kyrie wanted to buy a knife with a horn handle, but then saw a pile of scrolls. Fort Sanctus had a few scrolls in the basement; some contained prayers to the old Earth God, others epic poems of legends. Kyrie loved reading them, especially the poems. Most of the peddler's scrolls contained prayers to the new, cruel Sun God, but a few featured maps. And one map--the smallest, most tattered one--made Kyrie's heart skip.

The map showed a mountain, a river, and forest. It marked several villages and a cave. A road led between a castle and a port, and several roads led to towns. It was a map for peddlers, but Kyrie didn't care for its trade routes. What caught his eye was the map's corner, where Hostias Forest lay. Above that forest, smaller than his fingertip, appeared a picture of a black dragon. "Beware," was written over the drawing, "the black fangs."

A black dragon. Fangs.

Benedictus.

Kyrie had bought the map, the knife with the horn grip forgotten. Gasping, he'd shown it to Mirum, talked about it all day, told her that this map showed the location of Benedictus, the legend, the king in exile.

"Kyrie," Mirum would say, "it might be only a decoration, a scribble. It might mean nothing. And the map might be old, drawn when many dragons filled the land."

Kyrie would shake his head. "No. It's Benedictus. I know it."

Mirum would sigh, say nothing more, and ignore the parchment that forever hung at Kyrie's side. She let him believe, Kyrie knew, because she wanted him to have hope, to have a dream, to feel he wasn't the only one. For years, Kyrie clung to that dream, knew that Benedictus still lived, that somewhere there were others like him. Others who could turn into dragons. Others who were hunted, who hid, who remembered Requiem. Others who could some day come together, raise their race from hiding, and once more find the skies.

But standing here in the forest, wounded, hungry, hunted... it was hard to believe. Things were so different now. He had followed the map here, to this forest, to this corner where black fangs should bite. And what did he find? Birds. Squirrels. Shattered dreams.

"Damn it!" Kyrie suddenly shouted, not caring if griffins heard. He no longer cared about anything, and he pounded the tree again. Fingers shaking, he tore the map to shreds. "Damn Dies Irae, and damn Benedictus."

He stood panting, leaning against the tree, eyes shut... when a voice spoke.

"And damn loud, bratty kids scaring away deer."

Kyrie froze, then spun around, eyes opening.

A man stood before him.

Kyrie breathed in hard, fighting the urge to become a dragon, to attack or flee. This man was trouble; Kyrie could smell the stink of danger on him.

"What do you want?" Kyrie demanded, eyes narrow.

The man spat and growled. "For you to shut up. I was just about to shoot a stag, and you scared him off. How about you keep your trap shut, or go whine in somebody else's forest?"

The man wore ragged furs and carried a bow. A quiver hung over his back, full of stone-tipped arrows. He looked familiar, though Kyrie couldn't remember where he'd seen him. He seemed to be in his fifties, his face weathered like old leather. His hair was black and shaggy, strewn with gray, and his eyebrows were thick. His eyes were dark and piercing, two burning coals.

"It's not your forest," Kyrie said, anger bubbling in him. "You look like a common woodsman--or outlaw, more likely. You don't own this place, so bugger off."

Kyrie instantly regretted those words. The man took a step forward, and Kyrie suddenly realized how tall and powerful he was. He was perhaps forty years older than Kyrie, but all muscle and grit. A scar ran along his cheek, and another scar peeked from under his collar. In some ways, this ragged man, with his furs and arrows, seemed even more dangerous than Dies Irae with all his armor and griffins.

"If you don't shut your mouth," the man growled, "I'll punch the teeth out of it."

Then Kyrie realized why the man looked familiar. He looked liked Dies Irae, cold and hard and dangerous. *Only Irae is blond and golden like the sun,* Kyrie thought, *and this man is dark as midnight.* They had the same brow. The same strong, straight nose. The same... aura, an aura of pride and power.

Kyrie's heart leaped.

"Benedictus," he whispered. "It's you." His fingers trembled, and he took fast breaths. "You're Dies Irae's brother. Benedictus the Black." His head spun, and words spilled from his mouth. "You can help me! You can fly with me against Dies Irae, steal his Griffin Heart, and defeat him."

The man stared at Kyrie as one would stare at the village idiot. He spat again. "What's wrong with you, kid? I don't know no Irae. Don't know no Benedictus. My name's Rex Tremendae. Now get out of my forest, or I'll stick one of these arrows in your throat."

GLORIAE

Gloriae cut the sky.

She lashed her riding crop, and her griffin shrieked, flapped her wings, and drove forward. The wind howled, biting Gloriae's face and streaming her samite cape.

"Fly, Aquila," Gloriae called to her griffin over the wind's roar. Her riding crop flew too. "Fly hard."

As Aquila flew, Gloriae narrowed her eyes and scanned the lands below. Hills, copses of trees, and farmlands stretched into the horizons. Hearth smoke plumed from a distant village, and a fortress rose upon a mountain.

"Where are you, Kyrie?" Gloriae whispered, willing her eyes to see through every tree, into every barn, down every road. He was down there somewhere. He would travel north, travel to Hostias Forest where they whispered that Benedictus still roared. He would stay off the roads, sneak into barns for food, and sooner or later she would find him.

"You cannot hide for long," she spoke into the wind, and her lips pulled back from her teeth. Men often called her smile a wolf's grin, and Gloriae felt like a wolf, a huntress, a creature that lunges and kills and digs its fangs into flesh. "I will find you, Kyrie Eleison, and I will not take you alive. No, Kyrie. My father wants to capture you, to parade you as a freak, but not I." She caressed the hilt of Per Ignem, her sword of northern steel, which hung at her side. "I will make you taste my steel."

When Gloriae remembered the last time she saw Kyrie, she snarled. She had nearly drowned that day, but she had pulled herself from the roaring water, had survived, and now she hunted again.

Soon she flew over the village. *If you could call it that,* Gloriae thought. It was merely a scattering of cottages around a square. It was a wretched place, the houses built of mud and cow dung, the roofs mere thatch that no doubt crawled with bugs. Gloriae wrinkled her nose; she imagined that she could smell the place's stench even in the sky.

She turned her head to see the three griffins she led. Lord Molok flew alongside two riders of lower rank, men whose names Gloriae hadn't bothered to learn.

"The village below," she called to them and pointed. "We seek the weredragon there."

They nodded. Gloriae tugged the reins, and her griffin began to descend. The cold air lashed her, and Gloriae pulled down the visor of her helm. Peasants scurried below, fleeing into homes and closing the doors. Gloriae smiled her wolf's grin. Did they think their huts of mud and dung could stop her, Gloriae the Gilded, a maiden of the blade?

She landed her griffin in the village square, sending pigs and chickens fleeing. Gloriae snorted. Pigs and chickens? Truly this was a backwater; just the sort of place a weredragon would hide, cowering in the filth of beasts and the hovels of commoners. Gloriae drew Per Ignem, and its blade caught the light. She craved to dig this blade into Kyrie, to let weredragon blood wash it.

"You reptiles killed my mother," she whispered inside her visor, her jaw tight. "I was only three, but I know the story. You killed her. You *ate* her. You burned our towns, and poisoned our wells, and drank the blood of our children. Now I will wet my steel with your blood, weredragon. I am Gloriae the Gilded. You cannot hide from me."

Her men landed behind her and dismounted. Lord Molok gazed upon the village silently, face hidden behind that black, barred visor. His lieutenants drew blades and awaited orders.

"Into the inn," Gloriae said, gesturing with her chin toward the building, a scraggly place of wattle and daub. "We will ask there."

She walked ahead, leading them, and kicked open the inn's door. Her boots were leather tipped with steel, and the door swung open easily, revealing a dusty, shadowy room where commoners cowered. The air stank of ale, sweat, and grease. If she hadn't been wearing a visor, Gloriae would have covered her nose.

"Who runs this sty?" she demanded.

A wiry man hobbled forward, bowing his head. He wore an apron and held a mug and rag. "Welcome to our town, fine lady! May I offer you some bread and butter, mayhap some ale or--"

"Still your tongue before I cut it from your mouth," Gloriae said, glaring at him. "Do you think I've come for the dung you try to pass off as food, or the piss you serve as ale? I come seeking somebody. A boy."

Three men sat in the back of the tavern. Two were thin peasants, but the third was taller and broader than a peasant, his clothes finer, and he bore a sword. He'd been a knight once, perhaps; maybe a follower of Osanna's old, corrupt kings. This one was trouble, Gloriae knew. She would keep on eye on that shadowy corner.

The barkeep bobbed his head and whined, drawing Gloriae's attention away from the burly man. "Yes, my lady," he said. "I understand. But there is no boy here, as you can see." He tittered. "We are but simple folk, and--"

Gloriae stepped toward him, reached out a gloved hand, and clutched his throat. "You talk too much," she hissed. She raised her sword above him. "A boy with blond hair. A weredragon child. If I find that you've seen him, barkeep, and fed him your gruel, I will have you beg for death."

A chair scraped behind, and Gloriae turned her head to see the burly man rise to his feet. He had not drawn his sword, but his fingers lingered near the hilt

"Sit down, drunkard!" Gloriae told him, her voice filling the hovel.

The man gave her a long, hard look. He did not bow his head nor lower his eyes. "There was no boy," he said, voice low. "And you may refer to me as Taras, not drunkard."

Gloriae shoved the barkeep away, and he fell to the floor, gasping and clutching his neck. Gloriae stepped toward that burly man, that Taras, her sword drawn. Her fellow griffin riders stepped behind her.

Facing Taras, Gloriae pulled off her helmet. She tucked it under her arm and shook her hair so that it cascaded down her back. The barflies gasped, and even Taras narrowed his eyes. Gloriae smiled thinly. Men often gasped when they first gazed upon her green eyes, her golden locks, her legendary beauty.

"Whoever you are," Gloriae said softly, a crooked smile finding her lips, "you will obey me. Sit down."

Taras gave her a long, hard stare... then sat back in his chair.

"Good," she said to him, voice sweet. "Now, you say there was no boy, yet you bear a sword. Why do you need weapons here, if no weredragons terrorize your village?"

Taras still stared into her eyes, something few men dared. He had brown eyes, eyes that were tired but still strong. "I followed Osanna's old kings, and I worshiped her old Earth God. Your griffins killed our king and our monks, stripped our temples bare and crowned them with Sun Disks. Why do I bear a sword, my lady? It is not Vir Requis that I fear, but--"

Gloriae backhanded him, putting all her strength into the blow, and his blood stained her white leather glove. "You will not speak that name here," she hissed, voice trembling with rage. "You will not speak the name they gave themselves. They are weredragons; that is what you will call them. They are murderers. Do you work for them, worm? Did you hide the boy?"

She tried to backhand Taras again. He reached out and caught her wrist.

"I hide nothing," he said, glaring, and rose to his feet. He towered over her. "I know who you are. You are Gloriae. You are the daughter of the usurper, and you are no rightful ruler of Osanna. The old dynasty and monks will return, Gloriae the Gilded, and--"

Gloriae pulled back from him and swung her sword.

He was fast. He had expected this. Eyes still cold, he leaped back, drew his blade, and parried.

Gloriae kicked the chair at him. It hit his chest, tangled against his sword, and Gloriae swung her blade. The steel cut Taras's shoulder. He grunted, fell back, and Gloriae lunged with a snarl. Before he could recover, she shoved her blade into his chest, driving it through him and into the wall behind.

She stepped back, watched him die, then pulled Per Ignem free. Taras slumped to the floor, and Gloriae placed her helmet back on.

"Would anyone else like to cause trouble?" she asked, aware that she was smiling wildly, that her chest rose and fell, that her blood roared. When nobody spoke, she nodded. "I didn't think so." She looked at her men. "Torch the place; it stinks of old piss."

She walked out of the inn, snarling, as her men tossed logs from the hearth onto the floor. When she smelled smoke, she laughed and mounted her griffin.

"Kyrie Eleison was never here," she called to her men; they too were mounting their griffins. "And if he ever does come this way, well... there will be no place left to hide."

She dug her spurs into her griffin, and once more she flew, the wind in her eyes and the sky in her lungs.

KYRIE ELEISON

When the gruff woodsman walked off, Kyrie waited several moments, then followed.

What kind of name is Rex Tremendae? he wondered as he sneaked from tree to tree. *That's a fake name if I've ever heard one. This is him. Benedictus. It must be.* Kyrie's heart thrashed and his fingers trembled.

The man was easy to follow. He tramped through the forest with steps as gruff, hard, and angry as his face. His heavy boots snapped fallen branches, kicked acorns and stones, and raised dirt. *Aren't hunters meant to be stealthy?* Kyrie thought as he followed, branches snagging him and sap smearing him. This man moved as if he owned the forest, as if nothing could harm him.

After a while, when Kyrie was out of breath and dizzy, Rex's voice came from the forest ahead.

"I know you're following me, kid. Go home."

Kyrie could not see the man--the forest was too thick--but his voice sounded about a hundred yards ahead.

"I'm not leaving," he called back. This time he did not speak High Speech, the language of Osanna, but spoke in the older Dragontongue, the language of Requiem. Dragontongue felt odd in his mouth--he hadn't spoken it since childhood--but he knew this man would understand. "I'm sticking with you, so you better get used to the idea. You and I will fly against Dies Irae, reclaim the Griffin Heart, tame the griffins, and rebuild Requiem."

Rex kept walking, and it sounded like he was moving faster, his stomping boots angrier. Kyrie could barely keep up.

After weeks of journeying with little food, he was weak. But he bit his lip and kept following. This Rex couldn't just be a simple hunter. The scars. The scowl. The black hair and eyes. It had to be Benedictus.

"Because if it isn't," Kyrie muttered, pushing his way between branches and bushes, "the world is crueler than I can believe."

Kyrie walked for hours, covering at least two leagues. His feet ached. Just when he thought he could walk no further, he spotted a hut between two oaks. Rex's boots left prints in the soft earth, leading to the hut. The door was closed; Rex had to be inside.

The shack was built of crooked, mossy wood bristly with splinters and bent nails. Vines crawled its walls like green snakes. Turnips, peppers, and peas grew nearby in a weedy garden. A smokehouse stood beside the embers of a cooking fire. Kyrie frowned. *The place is a junkyard.* Was this truly the home of Benedictus, the great king? Doubt punched Kyrie's belly, as cold as Gloriae's eyes. Maybe Rex *was* but a woodsman. Maybe Benedictus the Black, the Vir Requis king who'd bitten off Dies Irae's arm, truly was dead.

No. No! He's alive. He is here.

Kyrie pounded on the hut's door.

"Go away, kid," came a growl from inside.

Kyrie pounded the door again. "I want a job."

"What language you speaking, kid? Talk to me in High Speech. I don't understand your gibberish."

Kyrie snorted, but decided to humor Rex. He switched back to the language of Osanna. "I said I want a job."

"Got no money to pay you," replied Rex's voice from inside the hut.

"I don't need money. I'll work for food. I'm a good worker. I can hunt, repair things, cook...."

For a moment there was silence. The moment lasted so long, Kyrie raised his fist to pound again, and then the door swung open. Rex stood there, black hair dusty, eyes dark. He shoved a loaf of bread, a flask, and a shank of meat into Kyrie's hands, then slammed the door shut.

"Eat that," came Rex's voice from inside the hut. "Then go away."

Kyrie considered pounding on the door again, but the food smelled too good. He sat by the fire pit and ate. The bread was homemade, not a day old, grainy but soft. The meat was slow cooked--deer, Kyrie thought--and melted in his mouth. The flask contained good, strong beer. It was the best meal Kyrie could remember eating; definitely the best he'd eaten since fleeing Fort Sanctus. He polished off every crumb and drop, then leaned back on his elbows, sighing. *I needed that. Badly.*

Maybe Rex was just in a bad mood today, but would feel better tomorrow, Kyrie thought. It was getting dark, the sun dipping between the trees, casting long shadows. Kyrie yawned. He curled up outside the hut, hoping no bears or wolves frequented this part of the forest. He closed his eyes and instantly slept.

He did not dream.

He woke at dawn to the sound of the hut door slamming open. Before Kyrie could even open his eyes, he felt a boot prod his side. He heard Rex's gravelly voice.

"I thought I told you to get lost, kid."

Kyrie blinked, rubbed his eyes, and rose to his feet. Rex stood by him, a knife in his belt, a bow in his hands. The scar peeking from his shirt looked red in the dawn.

"I wanted to thank you for the food last night," Kyrie said. "Let me work for breakfast. I can weed your garden, or skin your catch, or--"

"Or get lost," Rex said. "How about you do that for me?"

The hunter walked away, disappearing into the trees.

Kyrie hurried to follow. "You won't get rid of me that easily," he called after Rex, trudging over fallen logs and boulders. "I know who you are."

Rex spoke without turning to look back at Kyrie. "Told you, kid. You've got the wrong guy. Ain't ever heard of no Benedictus or weredragons. You're wasting your time. Go home."

Kyrie struggled to keep up. The forest was thick. Every step he took, branches, thorns, rocks, or vines nearly tripped him. Rex's large boots trod here with ease, but it was all Kyrie could do to keep up.

"I don't have a home," he said. "Not anymore. Nor do you. That hut you've got? You should be living in a palace! Dies Irae destroyed our home. Your brother. He didn't have Vir Requis magic, so your dad hated him. He stole the amulet, he controlled the griffins, he destroyed Requiem--"

Rex spun around. His face was so livid, Kyrie took two steps back. Teeth bared, eyes flashing, Rex's weathered face resembled a dragon's face. "Stories," Rex grumbled. He spat. "Fairytales. I don't know who you think I am, kid. I'm just a hunter. No weredragons. No palaces. Just a hunter, nothing more. Okay?"

Without waiting for a reply, Rex stormed off.

That night Kyrie pounded on the hut's door again. Again Rex shoved food into his hands, then slammed the door in his face, grumbling at Kyrie to go away. Again the next day, Kyrie followed Rex through the trees. Again Rex would answer him only with growls and grunts.

For a week Kyrie spent his nights outside the hut, and spent his days demanding a job. For a week he heard nothing but grumbles, saw nothing but frowns.

On the seventh night, a sound woke Kyrie in the darkness.

He opened his eyes and saw the stars above between the trees. He heard the sound again--the hut's door clanking. Kyrie closed his eyes and pretended to sleep. He heard Rex's boots walking beside him. Normally Rex thumped through the forest, but now he paced softly, as if trying not to wake Kyrie.

What's going on? Kyrie waited until the footsteps moved farther away, then opened his eyes and rose to his feet. He followed in the darkness.

Kyrie walked in his socks, but still had to tiptoe to avoid making noise. Luckily the wind moaned this night, a loud and mournful sound, masking his footfalls. Rex carried a lamp, and Kyrie followed its light, his breath quick. Owls hooted, frogs trilled, and crickets chirped. Soon it began to rain, and still Rex walked through the darkness, Kyrie slinking behind.

Finally the forest gave way to a clearing.

It was a small clearing, circular, sunken in. Kyrie had read that wroth angels sometimes tossed boulders from the sky, and where their heavenly rocks hit, no trees could grow. This looked like such a place. Pines and oaks fringed it, tall and dark, and the clearing's floor danced with pattering raindrops.

As Kyrie watched from the trees, Rex entered the clearing and stood at its center. Kyrie held his breath.

Rex looked to the sky, tossed his head back, and outstretched his arms. Wings sprouted from his back, leathery and black. His arms and legs grew longer, and claws grew from his hands and feet. Scales flowed over him, and fangs grew from his mouth. Before Kyrie's eyes, the rough woodsman became a black dragon with a scar along his chest and a torn wing.

Hiding among the pines, Kyrie tasted tears on his lips.

Benedictus the Black, King of Requiem, stood before him in the night.

LACRIMOSA

The mountain winds howled around Lacrimosa, threatening to topple her. They billowed her cloak, flapped her hair, and stung her eyes with snow. With shivering fingers, she tightened her cloak around her, but its white wool did little to warm her, and her fingers looked pale and thin to her. *My bloodline was never meant for snow and mountains, but for glens and glittering lakes,* she thought. Her family had always had pale skin, pale eyes, silvery hair; they were the color of snow, and brittle like it, but with a constitution for sun and meadows.

"Agnus Dei," she whispered, lips shivering. "Please."

She stared at the cave, but could not see inside. She saw only darkness that fluttered with snow, deep like the chasm that had opened in their family, their home, their people.

"Agnus Dei," she whispered again, voice so soft, she herself could not hear it. "Please."

The mountains rose above the cave, disappearing into cloud--cruel, black mountains covered with ice and snow, bristly with boulders like dragon teeth. The snowy winds danced around their peaks like white demons, and even when Lacrimosa turned to gaze below, she could not see the green of the world she had fled.

She dared take a step toward the cave, but it was a trembling step. She was afraid. Yes, afraid of her daughter, afraid of what Agnus Dei had become. The girl was eighteen now, no longer a child, and she had become like a stranger to Lacrimosa, as wrathful as her father.

Lacrimosa smiled sadly. Yes. Agnus Dei was like her father, was she not? So strong. Proud. Angry. Tough enough to live in forests and snowy peaks, while she, Lacrimosa, withered in these places and missed the warmth of their toppled halls and the song of their shattered harps.

Does Agnus Dei remember those halls, where marble columns stood, where fallen autumn leaves fluttered across tiled floors? Does she remember the song of harps, the poems of minstrels, the chants of our priests? Does she remember that she is Vir Requis, or is she full dragon now, truly no more than a beast of fire and fang?

"Agnus Dei," Lacrimosa tried again. "Let us talk."

From inside the cave came a growl, a puff of smoke, a glint of fire. Yes, she was still in dragon form. Why did she never appear as human anymore? She was such a beautiful child; not pale and fragile like Lacrimosa, but dark and strong like her father. Lacrimosa still remembered the girl's mane of dark hair, her flashing brown eyes, her skin always tanned, her knees and elbows always scraped. A wild one, even in childhood. She had been seven when her uncle destroyed their world, when Dies Irae shattered their halls, and the harps were silenced.

Seven is too young, too young to understand, Lacrimosa thought. *She was too young.*

She felt a tear on her cheek. *And I was too young when I married Benedictus, too young when I had my children, the loves of my life, my Agnus Dei and my Gloriae.* She had been only fifteen when she married Benedictus, twenty years her senior, to become a princess of Requiem. She had been only sixteen when she gave birth to the twins. *We were all too young.*

She sighed. But that had been so long ago. Now this was all that remained. This mountain of boulders and snow, and this cave of darkness, and this husband who hid in exile. One daughter kidnapped. The other lost in darkness and rage.

"Agnus Dei," she said and took another few steps toward the cave. She could see inside now, see the fire that glowed in Agnus Dei's dragon mouth, see the glint of it against red scales. Red--a rare color in their family. Lacrimosa became a silvery dragon, as had her father and forefathers, while Benedictus and his line had forever become black dragons. Yet Agnus Dei's scales glinted red, a special color, the color of fire.

"It means she is blessed," a monk said when Agnus Dei first became a dragon at age two, drawing gasps and whispers at her color. "It means she will forever be as wildfire."

Lacrimosa wanted to believe. She prayed to believe. When she looked at Agnus Dei's dark hair and flashing eyes, she told herself that she saw Benedictus there. Again and again, on darkest nights, she would pray to the Draco constellation. "Let Agnus Dei and Gloriae be the daughters of my husband, the daughters of Benedictus."

Yet in the deepest halls of her soul, Lacrimosa's fears whispered. She would remember the day Dies Irae found her, grabbed her, forced himself upon her. The day she swore to never reveal, to die with her secret. Had this been the day her daughters quickened within her?

Lacrimosa shook her head, banishing those memories, that old pain. *Agnus Dei and Gloriae are the daughters of Benedictus. They are good at heart like him, angry and fiery like him. They are his, and let those whispers of my heart never cast their doubts again.* She tightened her lips, the snow stinging them, and clutched the bluebell pendant she wore around her neck, the pendant Benedictus had given her.

She took another step, so that she stood at the cave's mouth. She felt the warmth of her daughter's flames, and though she feared the wrath and wild ways of Agnus Dei, she could not help but be grateful for the heat. A wry smile tickled her lips. *We silver Vir Requis of the warm glens; we'd welcome the fury of our offspring to escape the snow and winds of banishment.*

"Hello, daughter," she said softly.

Agnus Dei crouched in the cave, smoke rising from her nostrils, flames fluttering around her fangs. Her tail flicked, and her claws glinted. A growl sent ripples across those red scales. The girl spoke in a low, dangerous voice. "I am staying a dragon."

Lacrimosa sighed. She stepped toward her daughter and touched her shoulder, feeling the hot red scales. Agnus Dei growled and pulled away, flames leaving her nostrils. Lacrimosa caught her reflection in her daughter's brown, burning eyes. A slender woman, of long fair hair, of delicate features. Eyes that were haunted, too large, too sad. She was the opposite of Agnus Dei; soft while Agnus Dei was strong, sad while Agnus Dei was dark, reflective while Agnus Dei was angry. But then, she had not seen Agnus Dei for a year now, not in human form at least.

"You'll have to become a girl again sooner or later," Lacrimosa said. Her eyes moistened. "You can't stay like this forever."

Agnus Dei growled. "And why not? The true dragons of Salvandos have no human forms. They live upon great mountains of gold, and they fear no one." She growled and blew flames from her mouth. Lacrimosa stepped aside, heart fluttering, and watched the flames exit the cave to disappear into the snowy winds.

Lacrimosa shook her head, hair swaying. "The true dragons live thousands of leagues from here, and some say they are but a myth. Agnus Dei. Daughter. Beloved. You cannot stay in this cave forever, hidden in darkness, rolled up into this ball of flames and scales. You--"

Agnus Dei roared, a sound so loud, Lacrimosa covered her ears. "If I were pale like you, I could fly outside, is that right, mother? But I am red. Red like fire. And I would burn like fire upon the mountainside, a beacon for our enemies to see, a call for them to hunt us. I say let them come! I fear no man. If Dies Irae arrives, I will burn him." She bared her fangs, and her eyes blazed.

Lacrimosa again placed her hand against Agnus Dei's scales. "You could not fight Irae, my child. With a hundred thousand Vir Requis we fought him, and we died at the talons of his griffins, at the sting of his swords."

Agnus Dei smiled bitterly. "Oh, but we did not die, did we, Mother? No. Not I, the daughter of Benedictus the Black. Not you, his young wife, the girl who married the legend. No. We were the family of royalty. We were kept in safety." Her voice rose to a yell, and her fire filled the cave. "As the multitudes died, as they fought and perished, we remained hidden. As King Benedictus called the hosts to his service, led countless to die under his banners, he hid us. So we lived, Mother. Yes, we lived. We should have died, but we were blessed, were we not? Blessed with royal blood, blessed to be the family of our king, and look at our blessed life now." She gestured at the cave walls. "To live in a hall of royalty."

Lacrimosa had heard this before, had heard her daughter's rage a hundred times in this cave. "Agnus Dei, please--"

The dragon shook off Lacrimosa's hand, rising as tall as she could in the cave, this cave too small for a dragon's body. Tears filled her eyes. "I should have fought with them! I should have died with them, now drink and dine with them in the halls of afterlife."

"You were a child--"

"I am eighteen now, and I am old enough. I will fight Irae now." She growled again, flames shooting, and Lacrimosa had to step back. "I am a dragon. I fear no one."

"You are a Vir Requis--"

"I am a dragon! A true dragon. I have no more human form. I have not taken my human shape in a year, and I never more will. Vir Requis are weak. Vir Requis are gone. Let me be a true dragon--like those of the west--and I will never more hide in caves."

Sometimes Lacrimosa thought that Agnus Dei did not know who she raged against. Was it the Vir Requis? Was it her mother, her father? The color of her scales? Her life while so many others lay dead? Maybe it was all these things, and maybe Agnus Dei was simply like wildfire, and needed kindling to burn, any kindling she could find. And so in this cave she flared.

"The new moon approaches," Lacrimosa tried again, as she did every month. "Let us travel to Hostias Forest. Let us see Father, like we used to. We'll become dragons together for one night. We'll be a family again."

But like every month for years now, Agnus Dei shook her head and roared. "I don't want to see him. He could live with us here if he pleases."

"You know Benedictus cannot live with us," Lacrimosa said. "It's too dangerous. He would place us in danger."

Agnus Dei stretched her wings so that they hit the walls of the cave. She seemed like a caged beast, barely able to move. "I would welcome danger. I would welcome a fight. I would welcome death, even."

Lacrimosa cried. She had lost her parents, her siblings, and her home in the war. She had lost her husband, could see him only one night every new moon. She had lost her daughter Gloriae; Dies Irae had kidnapped her, raised her as his own, raised her to hunt Vir Requis. How had she lost Agnus Dei too? Only a few years ago, Agnus Dei loved her mother, would play with her, listen raptly to her stories, travel with her in human form to visit Benedictus. She had always been a wild child, bruised and dark and angry, but cheerful too, loving and beautiful. How had this happened? How had Agnus Dei become this enraged beast?

Lacrimosa closed her eyes. She took a deep breath, trembling, tears still on her cheeks. Her voice was but a whisper. "As the leaves fall upon our marble tiles, as the breeze rustles the birches beyond our columns, as the sun gilds the mountains above our halls--know, young child of the woods, you are home, you are home."

She hugged herself, trembling. The song of her childhood, of her people, of those marble halls now shattered, covered in earth and burned trees. The whispers of their fallen race. Her voice shook. "Requiem. May our wings forever find your sky."

When she opened her eyes, Lacrimosa saw her daughter regarding her, silent, staring. Finally Agnus Dei spoke.

"There are no more marble tiles; they are shattered and buried, Mother. There is no more breeze to rustle the birches; it stinks now with smoke and death. The halls are gone, and the golden mountains are but a memory. I remember them, Mother. But I wish I did not. I wish I forgot that I am Vir Requis. It is a dead race. You can look to the past. I will not. I will be as a true dragon--wild. Goodbye, Mother." A tear streamed down Agnus Dei's cheek. "I love you."

And then, so fast Lacrimosa could not stop it, could barely react, Agnus Dei leaped out of the cave. She shot into the howling winds, roaring, breathing fire.

"Agnus Dei!" Lacrimosa cried. She raced outside the cave and saw Agnus Dei already aflight, already distant, a comet shooting through snow and wind. Sobs shook Lacrimosa's body. She had already lost one daughter; how could she lose Agnus Dei too?

"Agnus Dei! I love you, daughter. Goodbye! I love you."

She did not know if Agnus Dei could hear. The red dragon flew, churning the clouds, roaring and breathing fire. And then she was gone... gone like the halls of Lacrimosa's youth, gone into memory.

Lacrimosa fell to her knees and wept.

KYRIE ELEISON

Kyrie was collecting firewood when he heard the griffins.

Five days had passed since he saw Benedictus shift, since he saw Black Fang--Benedictus in his dragon form, the beast that had led the Vir Requis to war, to their final stand at Lanburg Fields. Five days had passed in silence. Five days of collecting firewood, of sleeping on the ground, of trying to speak to the gruff man and hearing only silence.

Today shrieks broke this silence--the eagle shrieks that still haunted Kyrie's nightmares, the shrieks he'd heard the day Lady Mirum died.

He squinted, dropped the firewood, and saw them above.

They were close.

He had seen many griffins since his chase above the sea, but they had been distant. These ones flew just over the forest canopy. Kyrie could see their talons glint, their beaks snap, their armored riders scan the forest. They swooped, flew into the sky, looped, swooped again. They moved fast, blurred into streaks, wings churning the air. Their cries hurt Kyrie's ears.

"Damn it," he muttered and began to run back toward the hut, boots kicking up moss and dirt. He had to find Benedictus.

He stumbled over a tree root, almost fell, and managed to steady himself. He kept running, branches slapping his face. The griffins swooped. One's talons hit a treetop, and branches crashed behind Kyrie.

What if... I led them here?

A griffin swooped so close, Kyrie dropped down. The beast tore the canopy with its talons. Kyrie leaped up and ran from tree to tree, hiding under the foliage.

Ice filled his stomach. *They could have seen me... last night.*

Tears stung Kyrie's eyes. He couldn't have helped it. He'd had to turn into a dragon. Had to. It had been a month already. A Vir Requis needed to fly once a week; going longer could drive him mad, fill his blood with fire, make his fingers shake, his head ache. So he had shifted. He had flown. He had soared over the trees at night, streamed through the clouds, and let the cold air fill his maw. *Did they see me then?*

Talons tore down the tree before him. Kyrie found himself staring into a griffin's eyes.

He recognized its rider. She was a young woman, her gilded armor molded to the curve of her body. She wore white leggings, white gloves, and leather boots with steel tips. A helmet hid her face, but Kyrie could imagine those icy green eyes.

"Gloriae," he whispered.

For an instant the world froze.

Then Kyrie shouted, leaped up, and shifted.

A tail sprung from his back, wings unfurled, and blue scales flowed across him. His maw opened, full of sharp teeth, shooting flame at Gloriae.

Dragon and griffin soared into the sky, wreathed in fire.

Griffin talons shot out. Kyrie blocked them with his claws. He leaned in to bite, and his teeth closed around the griffin's neck. Gloriae screamed. Her lance stabbed Kyrie's shoulder, and he howled and blew flames.

Talons clutched his back. A second griffin landed on him, biting and clawing. Kyrie felt his blood flow, and he shouted and spewed fire, spinning above the trees, lashing his tail.

He beat off the second griffin, but he was hurt, maybe badly. He blew flames again; they roared around Gloriae's shield, staving her off. A quarrel zoomed. Gloriae was firing a crossbow, and the quarrel scratched Kyrie's belly. It was only a nick, but Kyrie felt the sting of ilbane, and he howled. The sun blinded him.

Talons scratched. Kyrie kicked, lashed his tail, and blew flames in all directions. Through the blinding light, light that shone against Gloriae's armor, Kyrie saw three more griffins swoop toward him.

For a second, Kyrie froze with horror. He saw his life like pictures in a book. His parents. His siblings. His old dog running through autumn leaves. And then his family dead, his house burned, Requiem Forest torched, columns shattered upon the ground. Lanburg Fields, and dead all around, and Lady Mirum lifting him. Fort Sanctus by the sea. Waves, salt, flights under stars over water.

And death.

Lady Mirum broken.

Griffins upon him, and claws, beaks, pain.

He tried to fight them off, but they were too many, and one griffin clutched his neck. Kyrie closed his eyes, prepared to die.

A roar shook the forest.

It was a thundering roar, impossibly deep, a roar like the darkest caves, the deepest tunnels. Kyrie opened his eyes and saw the great dragon, the Black Fang, the beast with the torn wing.

Benedictus crashed into the griffins, biting and clawing, knocking them off Kyrie. The black dragon's eyes blazed red, and fire burned from his maw.

Though bleeding, muzzy, and trembling, Kyrie cried in joy. "Benedictus flies!"

The sight of this legendary creature, its wings spread again, sent lightning through Kyrie. He soared with more passion and strength than he'd felt since Mirum died. He roared, shooting fire at the griffins who flew toward him. "And I fight alongside him!"

They fought. Two dragons. Five griffins and five more joining them from the eastern sky. Among swirling clouds and blazes of fire, the roars and shrieks rippling the air, they fought.

Four griffins latched onto Benedictus, clawing and scratching, their riders lashing spears. He was a large dragon--larger than Kyrie--burly and jagged, a few of his scales missing, a scar rending his breast. He was like Fort Sanctus, Kyrie thought--tough and proud, but old and rundown, years past his glory days. *But he is still great; our greatest warrior, our greatest legend.*

As this gnarled black beast roared and lashed his tail, Kyrie shot up. He crashed between three griffins, knocking them aside, and somersaulted.

"Benedictus, I'm here!" he cried, flew to the sun, then pulled his wings close. He swooped, whooping, and somersaulted again. He crashed into a griffin that clutched Benedictus's neck, knocking it off.

"Get out of here, kid," Benedictus growled, eyes blazing. His wing knocked a rider off a griffin. Blood coated his claws. "I'll take care of them. You go!"

Kyrie grunted and nodded. "I'll take a few off your back."

He swooped and flew over the canopy, letting the leaves skim his belly. When he turned his head, he glimpsed five griffins following him. Their riders shot quarrels, but Kyrie flew up and down, left and right, zipping around like a lightning bolt, and they could not hit him. When he saw an opening in the forest canopy, he dived and flew among the trees.

The griffins followed, through the canopy toward the forest floor. One slammed into an oak's trunk, and Kyrie whooped. He flew just over the ground, shooting between the tree trunks, spinning around boulders. Another griffin hit a tree. Another's talons hit a boulder, sending the griffin tumbling, tossing off its rider. Kyrie laughed and kept flying, and soon found himself over a forest pool. Two griffins still flew behind him, and he heard Benedictus roaring somewhere far behind, still fighting.

Grinning, Kyrie flew along the pool, and found himself before a cliff and waterfall. He turned his head, blew fire at the pursuing griffins, then flapped his wings hard. With a thundering cry, Kyrie shot toward the waterfall, then flew up the cascading water like a salmon. He emerged wet above the cliff, flew toward the sun, then swooped down upon the blinded, soggy griffins.

"Nobody," he roared, biting and clawing, "messes with Benedictus and Kyrie."

One griffin crashed dead into the water.

Only one griffin remained. The griffin bearing Gloriae.

Fury filled Kyrie, burning and red. He remembered how Gloriae had stood upon Fort Sanctus, a small smile on her lips, watching her father murder the Lady Mirum. He remembered the stories villagers would tell of her: How she had murdered a Vir Requis at age six, three more when she was eight. *She's a demon bred for cruelty.*

"I kill you now, Gloriae," he hissed.

Gloriae tilted her head. She pulled back her griffin, flew over the water, and landed on the forest floor.

"You kill me?" she cried. "You kill me, weredragon? Then face me as a human, not as the blue monstrosity you become." She dismounted her griffin, drew her sword, and stood golden in her armor.

The sounds of Benedictus's roars were far; he fought griffins half a league away. Kyrie was alone here, alone with Gloriae. He flew toward the ground where she stood. He shifted into human form while still flying, then landed on his feet before Gloriae, snarling.

"You want to duel?" he said, eyes narrowed, hair wet. "You got it." He drew his knife from his belt.

Gloriae laughed. He could not see her face--her visor hid it--but he could see her green eyes mocking him.

"Stupid boy," she said. "I will teach you some sense." She thrust her sword.

Kyrie realized that he *was* stupid. Gloriae wore armor and bore a sword. While Kyrie's clothes and knife could magically shift with him, that magic could not turn them into his own armor and sword. Stupid, yes; but the rage and horror made it impossible to think. Kyrie leaped sideways, dodging the sword, and thrust his knife. The knife hit Gloriae's breastplate, sending pain up Kyrie's arm, doing the girl no harm.

Gloriae laughed again, an icy trill. "Having fun, boy?" She swung her sword lazily, forcing Kyrie to duck. *She's toying with me,* Kyrie thought. *She's having fun before she kills me.*

"I'm having a blast," Kyrie said, eyes narrowed. He grabbed a rock and tossed it, but it only bounced off Gloriae's armor, not leaving a dent.

Gloriae took a step toward Kyrie, swiping her sword. The blade scratched Kyrie's arm, drawing blood, and Kyrie grunted. Pain burned.

"What was the girl's name?" Gloriae asked. She took another step toward Kyrie, swinging her sword, making Kyrie leap from side to side. "Lady... Mara? Mira? She was a sweet thing, was she not? Did you ever bed her, boy?" Her sword bit Kyrie's shoulder, a nick to fuel her amusement. "We did, as she lay with a bashed head, still twitching; she died there beneath us. Such a sweet thing, boy. I hope you tasted her. If not, you don't know what you missed."

She's trying to get me mad, Kyrie knew. *She's lying. She's trying to enrage me.* And it worked. Kyrie screamed and leaped forward. "You monster."

He swung his knife. Gloriae laughed and stepped aside, grabbed Kyrie, and shoved him. Kyrie stumbled and hit the ground, and Gloriae kicked his side. She kicked again. Kyrie grunted, pain filling him. Gloriae's sword flew down, and Kyrie rolled, barely dodging the blade.

"You are the monster," Gloriae said, eyes cold. She placed her boot upon Kyrie's neck, her sword on his chest. "Did you think you could beat me like this? As a human? You weredragons--your pride and honor were your undoing. It is so today too." With her free hand, Gloriae removed her helmet and shook her head, letting her hair fall loose. The golden locks shone, and Kyrie saw that angry pink patches spread across her pale cheeks. She gazed down upon him, eyes frozen. "Goodbye, Kyrie Eleison."

Gloriae raised her sword.

Kyrie shifted.

He ballooned in size, shooting up, his head growing scales and horns. Gloriae's sword bit, chipping his scales, scratching his flesh, and Kyrie's head slammed into her. The horn on his head slashed her thigh, and blood covered Kyrie's eyes. He roared and flew into the air. Gloriae's griffin shrieked, but Kyrie blew fire at it. It caught flame and writhed on the ground.

Kyrie plucked Gloriae off his horn and stared at her, disgusted. She was still alive, blood flowing down her leg. Her fists clenched and she grimaced.

"Honor?" Kyrie whispered, flapping his wings. The trees bent and rustled below him. "Pride? What would you know of such things? You'd be nothing but a spoiled girl were your father not Dies Irae. What do you know of the honor and pride of an ancient race, a magic that has flown over the world for millennia? Honor and pride could never undo us, Gloriae. Benedictus is back. We fly again."

He held her in his claws. Though her limbs shook and sweat beaded on her brow, Gloriae fixed him with a stare. Pain filled her eyes, but ice and determination too.

"Kill me then," she said. "Spare me your speeches and kill me. I am a mistress of steel. I am ready for death. I've lived my life to die in battle. Kill me, weredragon; I welcome it."

Suddenly Kyrie realized how young Gloriae was. Only a youth; not much older than him. What lies had Dies Irae told her? What cruelty had he inflicted upon her, to turn her into this heartless killer, this creature of hatred? *She's only a girl,* he thought, shaking his head. *What kind of girl yearns to die in battle?*

Kyrie felt his anger melting, replaced with pity. He had suffered in his childhood, Dies Irae hunting him. What would it be like to have Dies Irae as your father, to grow up in his hall? It sounded to Kyrie like a childhood infinitely worse than his own.

In his moment of hesitation, he barely saw her draw the vial.

She smashed it against his claws.

The glass shards stung him. More painful was the ilbane sap the vial had contained.

Kyrie roared, his claws burned, and he dropped Gloriae. She fell into the water below. Despite her wound, she began swimming away.

Kyrie wanted to follow, but the ilbane was like chains around him. He crashed into the pool, swallowed water, and floundered. His head spun and he could barely swim. Finally he crawled onto the bank, coughing, and looked around.

Gloriae was gone.

Kyrie howled. He tried to take flight, but his wings barely flapped. He spat and cursed. It was long moments before the pain of ilbane faded. When it did, Kyrie crashed through the treetops into the sky.

Where was Gloriae? Kyrie wanted to seek her, but griffins still filled the air. Three were attacking Benedictus in the distance. Three more flew toward Kyrie.

Forget Gloriae for now, he told himself. *Benedictus needs me.* Kyrie shot between clouds, tumbling and somersaulting. He flew with eyes narrowed, flew like never before, dazzling the griffins, spinning so fast, they barely knew where to follow. As he flew, he roared in pain and pride, for his king had returned.

Benedictus joined him. Together they fought. Blue dragon and black. Kyrie and Benedictus. Together they flew. One dragon slim, fast, dizzying; the other large, slow, his wing torn. Together they killed. Soon three griffins remained, then two, then one.

They killed the last griffin with fang and fire, then landed on the forest floor, wounded, panting, and victorious.

Kyrie shook with excitement. He turned back into human form. His knees wobbled, and the hatred for Gloriae, the thrill of the battle, and the pain of his wounds all throbbed in his head.

He faced Benedictus, who shifted back into human form too. The gruff man spat, breath heavy. Sweat drenched his graying curls, and his eyes seemed darker than ever.

"You were amazing," Kyrie said. "I've seen you fly before, at Lanburg Fields, but that was from a distance. To fight beside you... it was an honor." Before he realized what he was doing, Kyrie knelt; it felt right. "My king. You have returned, and you fly again."

Benedictus grunted. He grabbed Kyrie's shoulder and pulled him to his feet. "Get up," he said in disgust. For the first time, Kyrie heard him speaking Dragontongue. "I'm no king. That was a long time ago. Honor? Honor is dead, kid. I was amazing? I was slow. I was clumsy. I could barely fly with my torn wing. I probably would have died were you not here."

Kyrie felt himself glow. Pride welled up in him, like a torrent of water rising throughout his body. "Thank you." He wanted to say more, but found no words. His throat was tight.

Benedictus turned and walked toward a fallen log, rubbing his shoulder blade, the shoulder blade where his torn wing grew in dragon form. He sat down with a grunt. For the first time, Kyrie realized that Benedictus was aging. He was still closer to fifty than sixty perhaps, but not by much. Lines covered his brow, gray hairs filled his stubble, and his joints creaked. It had been ten years since Lanburg Fields, and those years had not been kind to Benedictus. The great King of Requiem moved slowly, grunted when he sat down on the log, and still panted and wiped sweat from his brow. *He's four decades older than me,* Kyrie realized, *and he thinks his time is over. But it's not over yet. He still has some fight in him.*

Kyrie sat down beside him, and for long moments, the two said nothing. Finally, when his breath had slowed and his sweat dried, Benedictus spoke in his low, gruff voice.

"I knew your parents, kid."

Kyrie spun his head toward him so fast, his neck hurt. "My parents?"

Benedictus nodded. "Aye. Your father was a bellator in my court. Do you know what that means? In our forests of Requiem, the bellators were our warriors of noble blood, commanders of our wings; like knights in the armies of Osanna. Your father was among the best I knew. I knew your mother too. I courted her once, but she chose your father instead." He chuckled--a deep, sad sound, lost in memories. He gazed into the trees, as if again seeing those marble tiles and columns that grew between the birches in Requiem's old courts.

"I... I didn't know. They died when I was six. I remember little. I never met another Vir Requis until I met you, not since Lanburg."

Benedictus rubbed his shoulder again and grimaced. His scar, peeking from under his shirt, seemed livid. "He was a proud warrior, your father. I fought with him. When Dies Irae killed your parents, I... that's when I gathered the last of us, that's when I marched to Lanburg Fields, to our final stand."

Kyrie felt his fingers tremble. He buried them in his pockets. "I thought my parents died at Lanburg Fields. I was there, but I don't remember much."

"They died a month before. Dies Irae murdered them. He torched their house and shot them when they fled. I'm sorry, kid. They were friends of mine. You survived. You were but a little one. We took you with us to Lanburg. We took all the orphans. There was nowhere to hide you, nowhere safe left in the burning world. You flew as warriors. I thought all the children had died." Benedictus's eyes were suddenly moist. "But you lived."

Kyrie bit his lip. His eyes were moist too, and he took short breaths, struggling to curb his tears. He could not cry before Benedictus, before his king. For the first time, Benedictus was talking about the past, speaking to him as an equal, and Kyrie's head spun.

Through clenched teeth, Kyrie said, "I will kill Dies Irae some day." He clutched Benedictus's shoulder and stared at him. "Fight with me, Benedictus. Fly with me again. Let us seek more Vir Requis. There are more. There must be more. Let us raise our banners, fly one more time, fight Dies Irae again. If we can grab the Griffin Heart, the griffins will fly with us. We can rebuild Requiem. We will speak the old words. I remember them." His voice shook, his body trembled, and tears flowed down his cheeks. "Requiem! May our wings forever find your sky."

The softness in Benedictus's eyes, that sadness of memory, died. At once his eyes were cold again, his face hard. He rose to his feet, shoving off Kyrie's arm. Once more he was

Rex Tremendae, the hunter, the gruff man who knew nothing of "weredragons".

"Go home, Kyrie," he said and started walking away.

Kyrie leaped to his feet and began to follow. Griffin blood and feathers covered the forest floor. "I have no home."

Benedictus did not turn to look at him as he walked, boots crunching leaves. "So just go away."

Kyrie shook his head, eyes stinging, heart thrashing. "How can you still say this? After what just happened? I want to fight!"

Finally Benedictus looked at him, eyes blazing, deep and dangerous like demon caves. "You need to know how to fly, kid, if you want to fight Dies Irae."

Kyrie bristled. "I'm a great flier. Did you not just see that? Did you not see me shake off three griffins between the trees, shoot among them in the skies, blind them with sunlight, claw them as they wobbled around me?"

Benedictus spat again. His boots kept thumping, and he seemed not to notice the branches snagging him as he walked. "I saw a stunt show. You're a great showman, you are. Doing loops. Flying up and down like a bird. Are you a dragon, or are you a sparrow? You want to fight Irae, you better straighten out, lose your hotshot attitude, and learn to fly straight."

Kyrie felt mad enough to catch flame. He forced himself to take a deep breath, to calm his anger. "Will you teach me?" he said.

Benedictus grunted. "You will learn nothing. I've known young Vir Requis like you. Showoffs. Hotshots. We had a lot like you in the war. They fall from the sky faster than raindrops."

Kyrie struggled to keep up with Benedictus's long strides. Branches slapped him, smearing him with sap. "I won't fall so easily. Fly again, Benedictus. Fly against Dies Irae like in the old days."

Benedictus stopped walking and spun toward Kyrie, glaring. "The old days are gone," he growled, voice so loud that birds fled. "My wing is torn. I can barely fly straight these days. I could barely beat those griffins. I'm old and wounded, and I'm tired. It's over, kid."

Kyrie shook his head in disbelief. How could Benedictus say this? How could their great king, the Vir Requis who had killed so many griffins, speak this way?

"But don't you hate Irae?"

In a flash, so fast Kyrie could not react, Benedictus grabbed Kyrie's throat and slammed him against a tree. Kyrie could not breathe, could not struggle, could not move, could only stare at Benedictus's burning eyes. Stars floated around him, and he thought he would die.

"Dies Irae kidnapped my daughter," Benedictus said, voice cold, his fingers tight around Kyrie's throat. "I hate him more than you can imagine. You cannot know how I feel."

Kyrie could not breathe. He could barely speak. Sure he would pass out any second, he managed to whisper hoarsely. "He murdered my family. I know exactly how you feel."

Benedictus let go. Kyrie fell to the ground, clutching his throat, taking ragged breaths. Stars still floated before his eyes.

"I want you gone by tomorrow," Benedictus said, walking away into the trees, leaving Kyrie gasping and coughing on the ground. "I told you. The war is over."

DIES IRAE

When his hall's doors slammed open, and Gloriae limped in bloody and bruised, Dies Irae did not need to be told.

He knew at once.

Benedictus still lived.

"Daughter," he said, rising from his throne.

Dirt and blood covered Gloriae's breastplate. She dragged her left leg, which was a bloody mess. She carried her helmet under her arm, and her face was ashy, her hair tangled. As she limped across the marble tiles, her blood trickled. The lords and ladies of the court gasped and stared.

"Father," she said, limping toward his throne. "I would not rest. I come bearing news. Benedictus-- he-- he's--"

"He's alive," Dies Irae said, voice icy.

Gloriae nodded, panting. "He slew us all. My men. Our griffins. The boy Kyrie Eleison flies with him. Let us go. Now! On the hunt." She drew her sword, then wobbled. Dies Irae dashed forward and grabbed her, holding her up.

"Daughter," he said and caressed her cheek. She looked up at him, green eyes so large and beautiful. Dies Irae kissed her bloody forehead. "You are hurt. Come sit by my throne."

She nodded, and they walked across the hall. The nobles of the court stared silently, the light from the stained-glass windows glinting in their jewels.

Light filled his court this day, glistening upon these jewels, upon golden statues of his likeness, upon filigreed columns and chandeliers. This court was a place of beauty, of light and truth, of righteousness and splendor... but today it seemed dark to Dies

Irae. All the gold and jewels in Osanna, his empire, could not light his eyes today.

He sat Gloriae on the stairs by Osanna's Ivory Throne. Servants rushed forward to bandage her leg, to pour wine into her mouth, to remove her bloodied armor. Dies Irae watched them work, then turned his gaze to his left arm, the deformity Benedictus had given him. And now... now Benedictus was back.

With sudden rage, Dies Irae grabbed his crystal goblet and tossed it with a howl.

The lord and ladies of his court, a hundred jeweled nobles, started and stared at their feet. Only Gloriae, the servants bandaging her leg, did not flinch. Blood speckled the marble stairs beneath her, and her eyes burned.

"You failed me," Dies Irae said to her. "You failed to kill him."

Her cheeks flushed, and for a moment Gloriae looked ready to scream. Then she lowered her eyes. "Forgive me, Father. I have failed you once, but I will not fail again. Let us fly on the hunt. I know where he is. We will find him. We will kill him. I will kill Kyrie Eleison, and you will kill Benedictus." She drew her sword with a hiss.

Dies Irae began to pace the hall. Around him the nobles spoke in hushed tones, daring not meet his eyes; a wrong glance now could kill them, they knew. Gloriae shoved away the servants tending to her, rose to her feet, and limped beside him. Pink splotches spread across her cheeks, and fire blazed in her eyes. Her hand trembled around the hilt of her sword.

"Is he plotting a return?" Dies Irae wondered aloud.

Gloriae spat onto the marble tiles. "He flies with the boy. The weredragons plan an attack against us, Father. They will gather more. They will fly upon this city."

Dies Irae nodded, the conviction growing in him, festering like a wound. "Yes, he will return now. If he found the boy, that will embolden him. Two weredragons? He will think it an army." He stared at his daughter. "Can you find the way back, Gloriae? We will kill him."

Gloriae snarled and placed her helmet on her head. "Yes, Father. Let us fly together. The boy gave me this wound. He is mine. You will kill the Black Fang."

Dies Irae nodded, fire growing in his belly. He clenched his good fist. *Yes, I will find you, brother, and I will kill you. You have hidden from me for ten years. But you cannot hide any longer.*

"There are more," Dies Irae said. "More weredragons. There have been sightings of a red one--a young dragon, female they think, slim and the color of blood. Villagers spotted her flying over the Fidelium mountains. And in the north, they speak of a silvery dragon, female too. Females can breed, Gloriae. They can fill Osanna with their spawn. I will not have my empire infested with new broods of these creatures."

Gloriae snarled and swung her sword. "I have killed their spawn before. If they breed, I will do so again."

Suddenly a lord burst forward, abandoning a group of ladies he had been courting. Dies Irae could not remember his name, but he was a pudgy man, balding, bluff and drunk. He wore a billowy fur coat and tunic to cover his girth, and wore a ruby ring on each finger.

"Bah, they cannot hurt you!" the lord blustered, cheeks red with wine. Sweat glistened on his brow. "My lord Dies Irae! You are powerful beyond measure. How can a handful of Vir Requis harm you?"

Gloriae gasped.

Silence filled the hall.

Dies Irae's jaw twitched.

For a long moment nobody spoke, and the lord stood teetering, nearly falling over drunk.

Finally Dies Irae broke the silence. He stared at this corpulent lord, fist clenched. "What did you call them?"

"Vir Requis, Vir Requis! Weredragons, whatever. Who cares? Call them what you like. They cannot harm us! Osanna is bold and strong." He drew his sword, swiped it so wide that Dies Irae had to leap back, and began singing a drunken war song.

When a guard stepped forward to grab him, the lord stumbled back, sputtering. "Unhand me, man!" he cried, grabbed a bottle of wine from a table, and drank deeply. "I am no woman for you to fondle. Let go!"

The guard shoved the man down, more guards stepped forward, and soon the large lord stood chained to a column. The other lords and ladies looked aside, too fearful to speak, to even look upon Dies Irae. They had seen too many chained to this column stained with old blood.

"Sun God," Gloriae said, blanching. She returned to the marble stairs leading to Dies Irae's throne, faced that throne, and clenched her fists.

A smile spreading across his lips, Dies Irae sat back on his throne. He watched as handlers brought in the griffin cubs. The young beasts--each the size of a horse--whimpered and screeched, claws clanking against the floor, beaks open in hunger. Their handlers kept them always famished, caged, dreaming of tearing their beaks into flesh.

"Watch, Gloriae," Dies Irae said softly. "I want you to see this."

Gloriae still faced the other way. "I do not wish to look upon this."

Dies Irae glared at her. "I command it. Watch, daughter. Watch every bite."

Gloriae turned, and when she saw the snapping griffin cubs, she shuddered. The chained drunkard was thrashing and screaming. His screams of terror soon turned to screams of pain.

The lords and ladies watched, silent, as the griffin cubs feasted, as new blood stained the column.

"Sun God," Gloriae whispered again, staring with narrowed eyes. Her skin was ghostly white.

When the griffin cubs had finished their meal, gulping down the last bites, their handlers led them away. The drunk lord was now nothing but bones, skin, and blood against the column.

"These cubs will grow," Dies Irae said softly to Gloriae. His daughter looked ready to throw up. "In a few years, they will be fifty feet long, and fine fliers. And they will fly in a world without weredragons."

Gloriae nodded but said nothing. She was a fierce warrior, Dies Irae thought; he had raised her for fierceness, for cruelty. But he had not finished the job. He had not finished molding her. Some of life's harshness still frightened Gloriae, harshness like the justice he dealt in his court. But she would learn. He was a good teacher, and he would teach her, would kill all softness and mercy within her.

He rose from his throne, caressed Gloriae's hair, and kissed her head.

"Come, Gloriae," he said and began to walk across the hall, heading toward its doors. "My brother awaits. We head to the griffin stables. We fly."

KYRIE ELEISON

"Benedictus," Kyrie said, "you can't go back to your hut."

Benedictus stopped walking.

Slow as sunset, he turned to face Kyrie. His face seemed harder than a mountainside, and his eyes burned. Words left his mouth slowly.

"Why not?"

Kyrie took a deep breath. His fingers tingled. He knew he had to tell Benedictus the truth, but he was afraid. What would Benedictus do to him? Would he beat him? Kill him, even? He took another deep breath, then spoke with a wince.

"I let one get away, Benedictus. I'm sorry. Dies Irae will know we're here. He might be on his way already."

Kyrie had expected Benedictus to be angry. The fury that suffused the man's face, however, still managed to surprise him. Benedictus's lips peeled back from his teeth. It was a wolf's snarl. He stomped toward Kyrie, eyes blazing. Kyrie tried to flee, but Benedictus caught his shoulders and shook him.

"You... did... what?" Benedictus demanded.

Kyrie lowered his eyes. "I'm sorry, Benedictus. I know I should have killed her. I wanted to. But... she's only a girl. I hesitated, and she escaped me. I was stupid. I realize now that she probably flew for reinforcements. I should have killed her right away, but I couldn't, Benedictus. I couldn't."

Benedictus seemed ready to howl and beat him, but then his eyes narrowed. He sucked in his breath. "Who, Kyrie? Who couldn't you kill?"

At the memory of those green eyes and golden locks, Kyrie shuddered. "Gloriae. Dies Irae's daughter."

Benedictus's fingers dug into Kyrie's shoulders. "Gloriae? You saw her? She lives? Did you wound her?"

What was going on? Kyrie felt dizzy. Benedictus seemed almost concerned about Gloriae, but that was impossible. "Yes, I saw her. I wounded her, but she's alive. I... what's wrong, Benedictus?"

The man was suddenly pale. He released Kyrie and turned aside. For a long moment, Benedictus stared away from Kyrie, silent. Finally he spoke again. "Don't worry about it, kid. You did fine. But she'll be back here before long, and Dies Irae will fly with her. We pack our things. We go."

Kyrie rubbed his shoulders where Benedictus had grabbed him. "Go where?"

Benedictus lowered his head. "I don't know. But we can't stay here. This forest is no longer safe. We leave tonight."

"Tonight?" Kyrie remembered Gloriae's boot on his neck, choking him, and the bite of her sword. He shook his head. "Gloriae might be back by then. Let's leave now! We can... we can go to Gilnor's swamps in the south and hide there. Or we can travel to Salvandos in the west; few griffins venture that far. Wherever we go, we have to leave now."

Benedictus said nothing for a long moment. Finally he sighed and said, "I have nothing of value in my hut. A hammer and axe. A few bowstrings and arrows. Nothing more. But there is a treasure I must save from this forest. I go there tonight. We leave at midnight." He lifted a fallen branch and tossed it at Kyrie, who caught it. "Start building a fire. We'll hide half a league from it. If griffins arrive, they'll head to the smoke, and we'll see them."

As Kyrie built the fire, he tried to ask Benedictus more questions. A treasure? Something to save tonight? What was the man talking about? And why, for stars' sake, did he seem so concerned about Gloriae's well being? But Benedictus only stood silently, staring into the forest, until the fire burned. They left the flames between stones, and walked north through the forest. Sunset began to toss shadows.

"Where are we going?" Kyrie said.

Benedictus grumbled. "You talk too much, kid."

They walked for a long time through the darkness. It began to rain, and soon Kyrie was soaked and shivering. It was a cold night, starless, and Kyrie imagined that he could hear griffins in every gust of wind. How Benedictus could navigate in this darkness, Kyrie didn't know. He tried to ask more questions, but heard only growls in reply.

Finally Benedictus stopped by an oak tree. He said to Kyrie, "Wait here."

"Wait for what?" Kyrie said. His teeth chattered, and raindrops dripped down his nose.

But Benedictus did not answer. He walked past the oak, disappearing into darkness. Just then the clouds parted, the rain stopped, and the stars shone. Kyrie saw that they had reached the crater. He remembered. This was where he'd first seen Benedictus shift. Starlight fell upon the clearing. It seemed to Kyrie like a holy place, almost like the old courts of Requiem. The crickets fell silent and the wind died.

Kyrie stared, silent, and saw Benedictus walk to the center of the crater. The moonlight limned his form. As Kyrie watched, a woman stepped into the crater and stood before Benedictus.

Kyrie froze.

A woman?

Silent, hidden between the oak leaves, Kyrie stared. His breath caught. The woman was beautiful, the most enchanting creature he'd ever seen. His body tingled to view her. Mirum had been beautiful too, but in an earthy way, a beauty of sand and salt.

This woman's beauty was ethereal, a beauty of starlight and magic. Her hair was long and fine, a blond so pale it was almost silvery. Her skin was milky, and she was tall and slender, clad in white silk. Kyrie gaped.

"Lacrimosa," Benedictus said to her. His voice was softer than Kyrie had ever heard it. "You shouldn't have come."

Lacrimosa smiled sadly. "You say that every new moon, yet every new moon I'm here." Her voice was soft and high. *If moonlight could speak,* Kyrie thought, *it would sound like her.*

"It's dangerous," Benedictus said and held her hands.

Lacrimosa nodded. "You say this every new moon too, yet I still live."

She took a step back, releasing Benedictus's hands, and shifted.

Kyrie gasped. She was Vir Requis! Like a butterfly emerging from the cocoon, she grew white wings, silvery scales, and a slender tail. Soon she stood as a dragon, tall and lithe, glistening in the stars.

A third living Vir Requis! Kyrie watched, eyes moist, as Benedictus too turned into a dragon, the great black dragon, chest scarred. The two dragons, the black and the silver, flew through the night as in a dance. They coiled under the stars, whispering to each other, a dance of sad beauty. Kyrie could no longer hear their words, but their dance spoke of old love and lost dreams.

Finally the dragons landed, one woven of darkness, the other of starlight. In the crater under the stars, they shifted back into human form: one man gruff and dark, one woman pale and glowing. They began walking toward the trees, toward Kyrie. He could only gape, awed.

"Close your mouth, kid," Benedictus said when he reached Kyrie. "A griffin might fly into it." He turned to the woman. "Lacrimosa, meet the kid I told you about."

Not sure how to react, Kyrie knelt before Lacrimosa. He tried to kiss her hand, but stumbled in the mud and fell. He pushed himself to his feet, stammering apologies, and tried to introduce himself.

"My lady! I'm Kyrie Eleison. It's good to meet you, my lady. How are you? I mean... I hope you are well. Are you?"

He realized how he sounded, winced, and cursed himself silently. But Lacrimosa seemed not to mind. She smiled, her teeth white, a smile that filled Kyrie with peace and angelic warmth.

"Hello, Kyrie," she said. "I'm Lacrimosa. I'm so happy to meet you."

Her eyes were large and lavender, and Kyrie was surprised to see tears fill them.

The three Vir Requis walked together, silent in the darkness. Kyrie had so many questions. He felt as if ants raced inside him. Who was Lacrimosa? Where had she been hiding? Were there even more Vir Requis survivors? Kyrie ached to ask, but something about the night's silence seemed holy. He dared not break it. Fireflies emerged to dance lazily like tiny dragons, as if they came to witness a sacred night, a night that would forever change Kyrie's life and his people's fate.

Kyrie noticed that more light glowed. Not the starlight, nor the light of fireflies, but a red, flickering light. He stopped in his tracks, and his nostrils flared.

"Smoke," he said.

Lacrimosa's eyes widened. "Fire," she whispered.

Kyrie stiffened. Yes, fire; he could smell it. Suddenly a crackle rose, and the trees ahead burst into flame. Sparks flew like the fireflies. Memories flooded Kyrie. He could almost see them in the darkness: the burning of Requiem, and the flames of war upon Lanburg Fields.

"Run!" Kyrie said. He turned and began fleeing the fire. Benedictus and Lacrimosa ran beside him. The flames roared behind, and smoke filled Kyrie's mouth. The heat burned his back.

"I should have killed Gloriae," he said as he ran, eyes stinging. "I should never have let her flee. It's my fault." Tears filled his eyes.

He saw the griffins before he heard them. He looked up and they filled the sky. There were hundreds.

Kyrie jumped and shifted. "Fly!" he shouted as he grew a tail and scales, as his wings sprouted and flapped. He crashed through the canopy, branches snapping against his scales. "Benedictus, Lacrimosa, fly!"

With light and fury, they flew.

They flew as griffins followed. They flew as arrows fired through the night, aflame, whistling comets in the darkness. They flew as the trees burned, as flames howled, as smoke blinded them. Into the darkness they fled, crying in the night. Below them the forests burned, and all around them griffins filled the skies.

"Benedictus!" Kyrie cried. Three griffins fell upon Black Fang, and Kyrie shot forward, screaming, and knocked them off. He turned to fight them, to claw and bite and burn, but Benedictus growled at him.

"We do not fight tonight. Fly!"

The three Vir Requis kept flying. Kyrie could barely see, and the night swirled around him, smoke and flame stinging his eyes. Stars spun and flaming arrows whistled. One clanked against his scales. A griffin talon hit him, tossing him into a spin, and he howled, lashed his tail, and hit something. He flapped his wings. He kept fleeing. Where were Benedictus and Lacrimosa? He couldn't see them.

"Fly east!" he shouted. "Fly to the sea!"

Had they heard him? Did they still live? Kyrie could barely see for the smoke and fire, and ten griffins flew toward him. Kyrie flew, spun, swooped to the treetops, shot up again. A griffin slashed Kyrie's leg, and a flaming arrow slammed against his scales. He grunted.

A cry rose over the thud of wings and roaring flames, a cry of pain and terror. *Lacrimosa!* Kyrie flew toward the sound, eyes narrowed in the smoke, knocking griffins aside. He saw Gloriae upon her griffin, clad in her gilded armor, driving a lance toward Lacrimosa. The lance glinted red in the firelight and hit Lacrimosa's shoulder, drawing blood.

"No!" Kyrie cried.

"Gloriae!" Lacrimosa called out, eyes narrowed, voice nearly lost beneath the roar of griffins and fire. "I--" Griffins shrieked and fires blazed, drowning her words. "--your mother!"

Gloriae seemed ready to attack again. She drew back her lance, but hesitated. Before she could recover, Kyrie flew toward her, clawed her griffin, and it pulled back howling. More griffins flew toward them, and Benedictus too joined the fray, biting and clawing. Kyrie looked around wildly, searching for Gloriae, but the girl was gone.

"Lacrimosa!" Benedictus said, eyes burning, smoke rising from his nostrils. She leaned against him, bloody, barely able to fly.

"Fly, get out of here!" Kyrie shouted, spreading his wings wide. A hundred more griffins came shooting toward them, their riders firing arrows. "I'll hold them off. Benedictus, get her to safety."

Benedictus paused. "Ky--"

"GO!" Kyrie shouted and blew flames at a hundred storming griffins. Behind him he heard dragon wings thud. Benedictus flew off, holding Lacrimosa.

Kyrie hovered in midair, eyes narrowed, wings churning the smoke. The hundred griffins would be upon him in seconds. Kyrie snarled.

"Come on, you bastards," he hissed. "Let's see what you've got."

He knew he would die. He was ready. He would hold them back. He would let Benedictus and Lacrimosa flee. She could be the last female of their race, the last hope of Requiem. He would not let her die.

"*Come on!*" he shouted to the griffins, hoarse, and rose higher into the air, shooting flames.

And they were upon him.

Kyrie fought like he had never fought, and he flew like had never flown. Like a comet he shot through the sky, spinning, falling, shooting up, rising from flame. He shot fire and the griffins burned. He bit, clawed, fled and charged. Talons lashed at him, beaks bit, and Kyrie roared with fury even as his blood fell.

"You will not reach them," he cried. "You will not touch them."

There were a hundred, and more were joining them. How long did he hold them off? Was it only a minute? Was it an hour? Kyrie did not know. It was a timeless eternity. But he held them off. He let Lacrimosa flee. With fang and claw and fire, he held them.

And then, with a roar that rocked the night, with a blast of flame that blinded Kyrie, the Black Fang charged into the ranks of griffins, scattering them.

"Get out of here, kid," Benedictus growled, glaring at Kyrie.

"Not without you!" Kyrie slashed at three griffins and knocked a fourth back with his tail.

"I'm right behind you, kid. Now fly!"

They turned to flee, the griffins screeching behind. Benedictus was wounded, Kyrie saw. Blood covered his left leg, and three arrows stuck out from his back. He wobbled as he flew with his torn wing.

"Where's Lacrimosa?" Kyrie shouted as they flew, the burning arrows zooming around them.

"She's safe." An arrow glanced off Benedictus's scales. He grunted. "Follow me."

They turned east. The sea spread out beyond the forest, a sheet of black in the night. Benedictus flew toward it, wobbly, and Kyrie followed. The griffins shrieked behind. The trees burned below.

When the sea was beneath them, Benedictus swooped and crashed into the water, disappearing into the depths. Kyrie took a deep breath and followed. The water so cold, he grunted. The salt stung his wounds. He forced his eyes open, though they stung too, and saw Benedictus swimming in the darkness. Kyrie could barely make out the great dragon; he only glimpsed glints on black scales. He heard several griffins dive into the water, and Kyrie swam as fast as he could. In the darkness, he felt fish and seaweed slap him.

Where was Benedictus? Kyrie could barely see. The world was but murky ink. *Wait. There!* Kyrie saw a tail. Benedictus seemed to swim into an underwater cave, and Kyrie followed.

Worry gnawed him. As a dragon, he had large lungs, but he'd been swimming for a while now. He couldn't hold his breath much longer. He swam through an underwater tunnel, seeing nothing but darkness. He felt stone walls against his sides, smooth, brushing against him. Where was Benedictus going? How had he found this underwater place?

A shriek shook the water behind him. A griffin. Kyrie slapped his tail, and it hit a griffin's head. He slapped his tail again, knocking it against the wall. It seemed to fall; he no longer heard it, and when he glanced over his shoulder, he saw only black.

Kyrie's lungs screamed. If he didn't breathe soon, this mad flight would have been for nothing; he'd die here underwater. *Damn,* Kyrie thought. Benedictus had led them to a watery death. Stars floated before Kyrie's eyes, and his limbs ached. His head spun.

The tunnel opened up, and Kyrie found himself in open water again. Not looking for Benedictus, not caring if griffins still followed, Kyrie shot straight up. He thought he saw starlight above, but it could have just been the stars in his eyes. How deep was he? He kicked and flapped his tail, shooting up as fast as he could. Was this sea endless?

And then--*thank the stars!*--he burst onto the surface. Kyrie took a huge breath, a breath that could suck in the world. He savored it. Air had never tasted sweeter. He coughed, breathed ragged breaths, and laughed.

"Benedictus," he called when he could speak again.

The black dragon was coughing beside him, head sticking out of the water. His breath wheezed. "Quiet, kid," he managed. "We might not be out of the woods yet."

"Oh, we're out of the woods all right," Kyrie said. He looked toward the forested shore; it lay half a league away, rising in flame. It was hard to believe they had swum so far. Griffins still fluttered over the trees. More griffins were diving into the waters by the shore, seeking them.

"Let's go," Benedictus said. "Best we swim underwater."

"Where's Lacrimosa?" Kyrie asked.

Benedictus grunted. "I'll take you to her. Follow me."

They dived underwater again and swam, close to the surface, and soon reached an islet. It was only several yards wide, not large enough for dragons. They shifted into human forms and climbed onto the rocky shore.

"Lacrimosa!" Kyrie cried. He saw her there. She lay between the rocks, cradling a bloodied arm. Moonlight glinted on her wet hair, and her eyes were huge and haunted.

"Keep down," Benedictus said. "Keep behind the boulders. And keep your voices low. Griffins have sharp ears. We're not safe yet."

Benedictus tore a strip from his tunic and bound Lacrimosa's wound. He touched her hair, kissed her cheek, and whispered in her ear. She embraced him. He held her, and she laid her head on his shoulder. Kyrie watched them silently.

"We have to go," Kyrie finally said, glancing nervously back at the griffins. "They'll scan these waters. They'll find us."

Benedictus glared at him. "When Lacrimosa is ready."

Lacrimosa touched Benedictus's shoulder, her eyes soft. "I can swim. Let's go."

They swam in the darkness, remaining in their human forms. They were slower that way, but smaller and harder for griffins to see. When they were far enough, they shifted into dragons again and swam faster, swam all night, until at dawn they climbed onto a distant shore.

They collapsed onto the sand as the sun rose around them. Kyrie had never felt so tired. Everything hurt. Bruises and cuts covered him, his muscles screamed, his lungs burned, and his head pounded. Blood beaded on wounds on his shoulders and left leg. On the sandy beach, he took ragged breaths and fell onto his back, shifting into human form. Dawn rose before him.

Benedictus and Lacrimosa collapsed beside him, also becoming humans. If Kyrie felt so exhausted, he could only imagine how tired Lacrimosa was, being so dainty, or Benedictus with his old wounds. For a long time, they only lay on the shore, watching the dawn. They had not heard griffins in hours, and could see none in the new light. Only gulls fluttered across the skies. No more fire, no more griffins, no more armored riders with flaming arrows.

For a long time, they just lay.

When Kyrie could move again, he sat up and finally saw Lacrimosa in daylight. She looked more beautiful than ever. Her hair was like gossamer, her skin fair, her lips full and her eyes large. Her body was slender and long. Kyrie could not guess her age. She was not young; not young like him, at least. Her eyes were too wise for youth. Neither was she old. No wrinkles marred her face, and her skin looked soft and pure. She seemed ageless. She wore a silver pendant shaped as a bluebell; it glowed purple in the dawn.

A third Vir Requis. A woman. Kyrie had never known, had never dreamed of another....

He turned to look at Benedictus. The gruff man stared back, face inscrutable, eyes dark. Sand filled his rough curls and stubble covered his face, salt and pepper.

Kyrie spoke to him. "Dies Irae will return. He will never stop hunting us."

Benedictus stared back, eyes boring into him. "I know."

Kyrie stood up and stepped toward him. "Fight with me, Benedictus. Help me reclaim the Griffin Heart. Rebuild Requiem with me."

Grunting, Benedictus struggled to his feet. He stood before Kyrie in the sand, glaring. His eyes were so dark, coal black. If Lacrimosa's face was pale silk, Benedictus had a face like beaten leather. For a long time, the man just stared silently.

Finally he spat into the sand, then stared at Kyrie. "Will you fly silently? No whooping or shouting?"

Kyrie nodded.

Benedictus gritted his teeth. "And will you fly straight? No loops? No somersaults? No showing off?"

Kyrie nodded again.

Benedictus took a step toward him, so that he stood so close, he could have reached out and throttled Kyrie. "And will you do exactly as I tell you?"

Kyrie nodded a third time.

Benedictus growled. "Look, kid. I don't like this. I don't like you. But I'm old, and my wing is torn, and I can't fight alone. You learn how to fly fast, you learn how to fly deadly, and you can fly with me. But you obey my orders. No questions, no talking back, no attitude. You show me lip, I'll bash your mouth in. Deal?"

Kyrie reached out his hand. "You got a deal, old man."

Benedictus glared for a moment, as if staring at a rotted carcass on a roadside. Then, with a grunt, he grabbed Kyrie's hand and shook it.

GLORIAE

They were gone.

Once more they had escaped her. Once more she had failed.

Gloriae stood over the smoldering hut, staring at its embers, and her eyes burned. Whether they burned from smoke or tears, she did not know.

She kicked the embers with her boot, searching for something, some clue, some answer... to what? Gloriae didn't know. There was a riddle here, a secret, but she knew neither the answer nor question.

A wind blew, streaming her hair, a hot wind smelling of smoke and blood. She stood alone; she had sent her griffins to scour the beaches, islands, and forests, to burn and destroy whatever they could not search. Her father had joined them, trembling with rage.

"What did she say, Aquila?" Gloriae asked her griffin. The beast stood beside her, lion body singed, feathered breast cut with Kyrie's claws. Aquila cawed and scratched the burned earth.

"The silver one, the female," Gloriae said. "She spoke words."

Suddenly Gloriae was trembling, and she clutched her lance and gazed at its bloodied tip. She had wounded that silvery beast, driven her lance into its flesh, and it had opened its evil maw and spoken in a voice too soft, too delicate, too... *familiar*. Those words still echoed in Gloriae's mind.

"Gloriae, I--" it had called, and here griffin shrieks and fire had drowned its words. "--your mother!"

Gloriae closed her eyes, the wind stinging her face, the smoke stinging her nostrils. A tremble took her, and she had to lean against Aquila. A dream came unbidden to her mind, but not a dream as those which invaded her sleep; it filled her like a spell. She was a child. She walked between pillars in a birch forest, and the leaves were golden like her hair, gliding around her, scuttling against marble tiles. She held her mother's hand and wore no armor, only silk.

"Mother!" she spoke in her dream, and she saw her mother's eyes gaze down upon her, lavender eyes, loving, and Gloriae played with her mother's hair and laughed.

Gloriae opened her eyes and stared back at the burned forest. She trembled and clutched Per Ignem's hilt.

"A memory," she mumbled. "A memory, no more."

She knew not its place, nor its time. Her mother had died when Gloriae was only three. Gloriae had thought that no memories of the woman remained, but here this vision had come to her, and Gloriae knew it to be from those first three, joyous years of her life.

She looked at her bloodied lance and tossed it down in disgust.

"Gloriae!" the weredragon had spoken. How dared it speak her name? What kind of devil spoke with such a soft, beautiful voice? Only the greatest evil would mask its true nature with such a voice, Gloriae knew. And what did it mean?

"I--" Shrieks and fire. "--your mother!"

"The weredragons killed my mother," Gloriae whispered, jaw clenched, staring at the hut's embers. "I know the story. My father told me. They kidnapped her, tortured her, and ate her." She screamed, drew Per Ignem, and stabbed the ashes. "How dared one speak of my mother?"

Then Gloriae knew. With trembling fury, fury more white and burning than the embers, she knew the answer. That silvery dragon, that *Lacrimosa* as the others called it, had been the one. It had killed Gloriae's mother. It had taunted her mother with that soft voice, had ripped into her with claws.

"'I *killed* your mother,' it tried to say." Gloriae spoke in icy hatred, and Aquila cawed and retreated several steps, wincing as if expecting a blow. "Come, Aquila. We fly."

Aquila was wounded, but Gloriae drove her hard that day. If the griffin whimpered or slowed, Gloriae whipped her with her riding crop, and dug her spurs into her sides, and drove her onward. Today was important. Today she would fly faster than ever. They flew over the burning forest, and over lakes, and over more trees and farmlands. They flew until night, and slept in a field, and flew again with dawn.

For three days Gloriae flew upon her griffin, eyes narrowed, clutching her lance, the wind streaming her hair.

On the fourth morning, Gloriae saw the place she had sought. It lay ahead in the distance, a great stretch of ash and rubble, a patch of death upon the land. Once this land had been called Requiem, she knew--the evil land of the Vir Requis. Today it was a mere stain upon her beautiful empire of Osanna.

Lashing her crop, Gloriae directed her griffin to fly over the desolation. Aquila whimpered, but Gloriae drove her on with crop and spur. This was a strange land, a silent land. No birds chirped here, nor did any leaf sprout. Ash, rubble, smashed columns, and skeletons littered the ground.

"We will build a palace here, a great temple to your glory, and to the glory of the Sun God," the gaunt Lord Molok had once told Dies Irae.

But Gloriae's father had only shaken his head. "No. Forever shall the lands of the weredragons lay barren and ugly; that will be their legacy."

That legacy now stretched below Gloriae, and she imagined that she could still smell the blood and fire from

Requiem's destruction ten years ago. A force seemed to guide her, like those whispers of her dream. She had never been to these lands, but somehow she knew what she sought. Somehow she knew where to fly. Gloriae flew north over the burned lands, scanning the ruins below, until she found the place she knew would be there.

She landed by toppled, shattered columns.

They were carved of marble, and must have risen a hundred feet tall in the days when Requiem still stood. The columns lay smashed now, each segment no longer than several feet. Their capitals had once been shaped as dragons; hammers, maces, and time had taken to them, beaten them down into shapes Gloriae could barely recognize. But Gloriae knew these columns; she could still see them standing among the birches.

"How... how could this be?" she whispered, clutching her sword. Cold wind blew, invading her armor, and she shivered. Bones, cloven shields, and shattered blades littered the ground. A mosaic lay cracked at Gloriae's feet, half buried in mud. The place was a ruin, but... she had been here before, seen this hall when it had still stood. She had walked here with her mother, had--

"You should not have come here," spoke a voice behind.

Gloriae spun, drew Per Ignem with a hiss, and snarled. Her heart burst into a gallop, and she tightened her lips.

Upon toppled bricks, stood a red dragon.

Sucking in her breath, Gloriae pointed her sword to the beast. Aquila stood cawing at Gloriae's side, and Gloriae mounted the griffin, never removing her eyes from the dragon's.

"These are the lands of my father's empire," she spoke, eyes narrowed, and placed her helmet on her head. She sheathed her sword and grabbed her lance. "It is you who should not have come. The weredragons' age has passed. You will join their bones here upon their toppled columns."

The red dragon sneered, smoke rising between her teeth. It was female, Gloriae knew; the dragon was too slim to be male, too graceful. Her scales were red like the fire leaving her nostrils. She looked young, only a youth.

"The only fresh bones here will be yours, Gloriae the Gilded," the dragon said. Her voice was that of a young woman. "Yes, Gloriae, slayer of Vir Requis children, I know your name. I am Agnus Dei, daughter of King Benedictus, heir to Requiem. I am the one who will kill you today."

The dragon leaped toward her.

Gloriae drove her griffin forward, steadying her lance.

Agnus Dei growled and blew fire, and Gloriae raised her shield. The flames burned around her, lapping at Gloriae's breastplate and helmet. Her lance scratched Agnus Dei's side, and the dragon grunted. Gloriae tugged the reins, spun around, and saw Agnus Dei leaping toward her again.

Narrowing her eyes, Gloriae pointed her lance. She gritted her teeth, and Agnus Dei blew fire again. The fire enveloped her shield, and Gloriae cried in pain; a tongue of flame found its way around her shield to burn her gloved hand. The leather protected her skin, but turned hot enough to blaze with pain.

"You will die, lizard!" she screamed and drove Aquila forward. The two had risen and now flew high over the ruins. Aquila too wore gilded armor. The fire had not kindled her fur or feathers, but that steel now burned hot, and the griffin screeched.

Agnus Dei was laughing. Blood seeped down her side, but still she laughed, smoke pluming from her maw. She charged, swooped, and before Gloriae could right her spear's thrust, Agnus Dei bit Aquila's leg.

The griffin shrieked and tried to bite, but Agnus Dei pulled back. Gloriae wished she could reach for her crossbow--its quarrels were coated with ilbane--but dared not drop her lance.

She could not lose a second. As her griffin cried, Gloriae dug her spurs deep.

"Fly, Aquila! Fly at her."

Agnus Dei flew toward the sun, then dived down, the sunrays blinding Gloriae. Cursing, Gloriae raised her lance and shield, and felt a great weight land upon her. She saw nothing but scales, fire, and light. Her lance clanged. Agnus Dei was clawing, pushing her down. A claw scratched Gloriae's breastplate. She dropped her lance, drew her sword, and swung it. The steel cut scaled flesh, and Agnus Dei howled.

"Weredragon!" Gloriae cried. "I spit on your forefathers' graves. I will kill you upon their bones."

Agnus Dei drove her down, pushing Gloriae onto the ground. The claws lashed again, and Gloriae leaped off her saddle and rolled across the earth. Agnus Dei's claws slammed down, missing Gloriae by an inch, and she lashed her sword. The steel hit Agnus Dei's leg, spouting fresh blood. The red dragon roared.

"I will kill you even without my griffin," Gloriae said and snarled. She charged at the dragon, screaming, sword raised.

Agnus Dei flew up, and Gloriae screamed. "Coward! Come back here, girl, and face your death."

Gloriae ran toward the fallen griffin, not caring if Aquila lived or died; she cared only for the crossbow on the saddle. She grabbed it, aimed, and fired.

She caught Agnus Dei as the dragon swooped. The bolt hit the dragon's neck, and the scream of pain thudded against Gloriae, knocking her down. Agnus Dei kicked, and her leg hit Gloriae's breastplate. Gloriae saw nothing but white light. She flew, breath knocked out of her, and crashed against a smashed column. Armor covered her, but this blow still ached. For a moment, Gloriae could not breathe, and tears streamed down her cheeks as she struggled to her feet. Shakily, she raised her crossbow.

Agnus Dei was lumbering toward her, snarling, limping, unable to fly. She blew fire.

Gloriae ducked, rolled, and raised her shield. The flames burned around her shield, and Gloriae squinted. When the fire died, she aimed her crossbow and fired again.

The bolt hit Agnus Dei's shoulder, and the dragon screamed. She fell upon the ruins, cracking a fallen statue of an old king.

"Yes," Gloriae said, smiling through her snarl. "The ilbane on my quarrels is strong and thick. It burns, doesn't it? I finish you now." She stepped toward the dragon, the wind blasting her, Per Ignem raised.

Agnus Dei struggled to rise, but could not. She glared at Gloriae, and her eyes seemed so human--brown, pained eyes--that Gloriae faltered.

"Gloriae...," Agnus Dei spoke, blood seeping down her sides, squinting in pain. There was something about that voice, those eyes.... Gloriae shook her head. *Finish her!* cried a voice inside her. *Bring down your sword, chop off her head, kill the beast!*

"Requiem," Agnus Dei whispered at Gloriae's feet. "May our wings forever find your sky."

Those words! Gloriae knew them! But how could she? Tears filled her eyes, and her arm trembled. Her sword wavered. Gloriae could not breathe. Standing over the wounded Agnus Dei, she tore off her helmet, shook her hair loose, and took deep, desperate breaths.

Agnus Dei, staring up from the ground, gasped. Those eyes--those brown, almost human eyes--widened. "I... I know you, Gloriae. I've seen you before, I...."

Gloriae trembled. She walked between columns, the birches rustling, holding her mother's hand. She heard old songs on harps, and played with a girl her age, a girl with brown eyes, and--

"No!" Gloriae screamed, a scream so loud, that Agnus Dei started. "I do not know you, lizard! I-- I know only your evil. You cast spells upon me. You cast evil magic. I will not let you invade my mind. I will not!" Her eyes swam with tears.

She could no longer bear to look into those brown eyes. She saw lies and dreams within them, trees that still rustled, and songs that still played, and smiles from... what? A different life? A different world?

No! Spells. Lies! Black magic of beasts.

Gloriae fled, boots kicking up ash, leaving the creature there. The weredragons were more dangerous and evil than she had imagined.

"Aquila!" she cried. The griffin still lived, through she was wounded, maybe badly. Gloriae climbed onto the saddle and urged the beast up. "Fly, Aquila. Fly far from here. This land is cursed."

The wind streamed her hair, stung her eyes, and blew the tears off her cheeks. Clutching her wounds, Gloriae flew, trembling, vowing to never more return to the ruins of Requiem.

LACRIMOSA

Lacrimosa walked along the beach, her shoulder bandaged, tears on her cheeks.

She walked alone. She needed to be alone. She needed to think, to breathe, to shed her tears in silence and solitude. She had left her husband behind with the boy; the two tended to a campfire she could just see in the distance, its smoke unfurling. It was dangerous to light a fire, to cast smoke into the sky like a dragon's tail, but Lacrimosa had lived her life in danger. She had been running for ten years, hiding in forests, in snowy mountaintops, in caves and along beaches of ruins such as this one.

Old bricks lay in the sand around her feet, and Lacrimosa saw the ruins of a fort toppled across a hill ahead. Its scattered bricks and broken walls had settled years ago, and the water had smoothed them, and covered them with moss. Gulls picked between the stones, and crabs scuttled along toppled battlements. What fort was this? Lacrimosa did not know. She had once known the names of many forts, but in the past ten years, memories of the old world had fled her. She could no longer remember Osanna's castles, those castles the Vir Requis had once fought and died against. She could no longer remember a time when the men of Osanna lived alongside her race, would visit their courts, would treat with them. Sometimes Lacrimosa could barely remember Requiem, the autumn leaves that scuttled along mosaic floors, the columns that rose in the forest like so many birch boles, Requiem's elders walking in green velvet embroidered in gold. Those memories were fleeting too. They emerged now only in dreams or in the moments of her greatest loneliness and fear.

Lacrimosa stepped among the ruins of the fort. Water pooled between the stones, and the waves whispered, entering and leaving the homes these stones formed for fish and crabs. Salt and seashells glistened in the sand. Lacrimosa knelt to lift a conch, pink and large as her fist, and beneath it she saw a bone emerging from the sand. A human bone.

She dropped the shell and walked on, a tear on her cheek. Thus it was these days, she thought. Whatever beauty she found hid darkness.

"Like my daughters?" she whispered.

No. She hated those whispers. Hated the doubts. Agnus Dei was beautiful, forever good and right, a future for their race, a hope. She could not conceal darkness. She could not have quickened that day, that day that hid beneath her memories of beauty. And yet the memories flooded her.

Lacrimosa had been fifteen, a wispy youth of marble skin, of hair that Benedictus said was woven of moonlight. Her father was a great lord, and her coming of age was a grand party, among the grandest Vir Requis girls had known, for she was among their fairest. She glistened in white silk inlaid with diamonds, and apple blossoms lay strewn through her hair. She had felt shy, but beautiful too, fearful yet joyous in the beauty of Requiem. She walked among lords and ladies in jewels.

Among the lords stood Prince Benedictus, the younger of the princes. He wore green velvet embroidered with gold, a sword upon his hip, and a crown atop his black curls. Lacrimosa thought him handsome, but she feared him. He was twenty years her senior, from a different world, destined to someday be her king.

Her lord father presented Lacrimosa to Benedictus that day, and they danced to the song of flutes, and drank wine.

Benedictus was a clumsy dancer, and he did not speak much, but he was courteous and sober, holding her hand gently, praising her gown and beauty. She knew she would marry him; they all knew. Perhaps they had known for years, these noble families of their courts.

That evening she walked alone, leaving the palace for some solitude, some reflection in the woods. She often walked here alone among the birches, to speak with the birds and deer, to pray, to escape the lords and ladies and servants that forever fussed around her. She would find treasures here most days: acorns, or pretty stones, and once a golden coin lost two hundred years before. But this day, the day of her fifteenth birthday, her coming of age, she found something else in the forest. She found pain, and darkness, and a secret that would forever haunt her.

Dies Irae stood leaning against a birch, dressed in white. He looked much like Benedictus--the straight nose, strong jaw, tall brow. Yet his hair was golden, not black, and his eyes were not solemn but cruel, calculating.

"Hello, my lord," she said to him and curtsied, and he only stared with those cruel eyes, blue and hungry.

He spent many days in these woods, she knew, for his father scorned him. Dies Irae had been born without the magic. He could not shift, could not become a dragon. All her life, Lacrimosa had pitied him. How horrible it must be, to be forever in human form! How painful to be the elder brother, yet not heir to the throne--an outcast, a sad child.

"Let us return to the court," she said and smiled, hoping to soothe his pain. "There are honey cakes and wine."

But he wanted more than honey cakes and wine. He wanted the Griffin Heart, revenge against his family, revenge against the race that had outcast him. And he wanted her.

He took all those things.

Between the birches, he stuffed ilbane into her mouth, and muffled her screams with his palm. The pain stunned her, dazed her so she couldn't shift. He knew her there, pinning her down. With a clenched jaw, he made her swear to secrecy, to swear by their stars, on the honor of her forefathers. And she swore, vowed to never speak of how he'd hurt her, planted his seed inside her. When she cried that night, back in her home, all assumed that she was overcome by her party, by meeting Benedictus whom she would wed. She never spoke of what happened in that forest, not even a week later when she married her lord Benedictus, not even nine moons later when she gave birth to her daughters.

They were twins, one dark, the other fair.

"Agnus Dei, I name you," she whispered to the babe with dark curls. Lamb of God, the name meant, for the child's hair was soft and curly as lamb's fleece, and she was holy.

"And I name you Gloriae," she whispered to the fair child, for this babe seemed a being of light, angelic and pure, a golden child.

One dark babe, one fair. One child of fire, the other of gold. One child Lacrimosa kept; the other Dies Irae stole from her. Agnus Dei and Gloriae; the chambers of her heart.

They are Benedictus's daughters, Lacrimosa told herself when they were born, and she told this to herself today too, walking among the ruins of this seaside fort. *They are like him. They are his. They could never be the children of Dies Irae; they are too noble, too good at heart, even Gloriae whom Dies Irae has raised. They are ours.*

Tears were salty on her lips like the waves that whispered. Lacrimosa turned and walked back to their camp, to the fire Benedictus and Kyrie were tending. She approached her husband, a trembling smile found her lips, and she kissed him. He held her by the fire and water. She laid her head against his shoulder, shut her eyes, and felt safe in his arms.

That was when she heard the whistles.

Lacrimosa opened her eyes, and she saw thousands of slivers in the sky, shadowing the world.

"Arrows!" Kyrie shouted. "Fly!"

Lacrimosa ran and shifted. Arrows peppered the beach around her. Two hit her back, but snapped against her scales. Ilbane sizzled over her, and she yelped.

"Fly over the water!" she cried and flapped her wings. She saw Benedictus and Kyrie flying beside her; they too had shifted. She heard more whistles. When she peeked over her shoulder, she saw a thousand archers in the trees above the beach. Their arrows flew, and more clanked against the fleeing Vir Requis. This time, an arrow broke Lacrimosa's scales and pierced her. She cried in pain; ilbane coated the arrowhead, sending fire through her.

"Fly faster!" she cried. They were far from the shore now, and when more arrows flew, they fell into the water. Lacrimosa exhaled in relief. *We made it.*

That was when she heard the griffins.

When Lacrimosa looked over her shoulder, she saw them there: Three griffins, their armor gilded and their wings wide. She recognized the leader. A woman sat atop that griffin, aiming a lance, her armor golden.

Gloriae. My daughter.

The sight of Gloriae sent more pain through Lacrimosa than the arrows. She wanted to fly toward her, to embrace her, to tell her who she was, to save her from Dies Irae. But how could she? How could she reveal this shattering truth to Gloriae? How would this girl raised to loath, hunt, and kill Vir Requis ever believe it?

You are Vir Requis too, Gloriae! she wanted to cry out. *You have our magic within you. You can shift, become a dragon. I know it. You are not Dies Irae's. You cannot be his. You are the daughter of Benedictus.*

All these things Lacrimosa ached to cry out, and tears filled her eyes, but she could bring no words to her lips. Gloriae and the riders she led were firing crossbows. The bolts whizzed by Lacrimosa, and one hit Kyrie's tail. The boy yelped, dipped several feet, but kept flying.

"That's it!" Kyrie said. He snarled, and suddenly he spun around to face the griffins. Lacrimosa's heart froze, and she cried out. Eyes narrowed and grin tight, Kyrie began flying toward Gloriae.

"Kyrie!" Lacrimosa cried.

Quarrels flew across the young Vir Requis. One hit his shoulder, and he grunted, but kept flying.

"Hello again, sweetheart," Kyrie said and drove his head into Gloriae's griffin.

Gloriae screamed and lashed her lance, but her griffin was bucking, and she could not aim. Kyrie clawed the beast, bit its shoulder, and shoved it. The two other griffins were clawing, but Kyrie's lashing tail kept them at bay.

Gloriae and her griffin fell and crashed into the sea. Kyrie blew fire at the other two griffins, holding them back.

"You die now, blondie," Kyrie said, growled, and swooped at Gloriae with open claws.

"No!" Lacrimosa cried and flew. Ice seemed to encase her. She was about to watch Kyrie kill her daughter. "Kyrie, no, she's my--"

The words froze on her lips. She could not reveal the secret, not like this, not here. Instead, she grabbed Kyrie and pulled him back. He struggled, and then Benedictus was flying there too, pulling the boy away.

A griffin flew at Lacrimosa. She blew fire, and it caught flame. Screeching, it dived into the water. The third griffin attacked Benedictus, and he swatted away with his tail, cutting its side.

"Fly!" Lacrimosa said, still struggling to pull Kyrie back. Gloriae was swimming away, tossing off her armor. Kyrie was trying to reach her, to claw her, but Lacrimosa would not let him.

"I'll explain later, just fly now, fly away, there are more griffins coming."

She could see them on the horizon. A hundred more flew their way, maybe two hundred. They would be on them within seconds.

Kyrie saw them too. He grunted and began to fly away. The three dragons were soon flying into the clouds, fleeing as fast as they could.

"Swim back to shore, Gloriae," Lacrimosa whispered as she flew, breath aching in her lungs. "Leave this place, and travel far, and forget about us. I love you, my lost daughter. I love you."

KYRIE ELEISON

They flew all day and into night, until they lost the griffins over a forest of oaks and pines.

Under rainclouds and trees, they ran in human form, small and cloaked in darkness. They ran for a league, maybe two, ran until Kyrie's side ached and his lungs felt ready to burst. They ran until they heard no more griffins, and then ran some more.

Lost, wounded, and exhausted, they finally collapsed in the forest.

Kyrie sat on the wet ground, leaned against an oak, and shut his eyes. Everything hurt. Lacrimosa and Benedictus collapsed beside him. Benedictus breathed ragged, creaky breaths like a saw. Lacrimosa's chest rose and fell, and she seemed paler than ever.

It was long moments before Kyrie could speak again. Finally he turned to Lacrimosa and said, "Why? Why wouldn't you let me kill her?"

She looked at him, pain in her eyes. "She is a sad child."

Kyrie shook his head in disbelief. Gloriae? Sad? He snorted. He saw rage in Gloriae. He saw cruelty. He saw a killer. There was no sadness in those icy eyes, in those cruel lips.

Lacrimosa began crying. Kyrie felt guilt like a rock in his belly.

"Lacrimosa, I--" He couldn't understand. It seemed almost like Lacrimosa loved Gloriae, loved this killer, the daughter of Dies Irae. But how could that be? "I'm sorry, I don't understand."

"Drop it, kid," Benedictus said, still wheezing. "Gloriae's tale is a sad one. Dies Irae kidnapped her when she was three, raised her to hate Vir Requis, raised her to kill. The girl is not evil at heart; she's simply ignorant."

Kyrie doubted that. He had looked into Gloriae's eyes. He had seen something cold, cruel, and calculating there. If that wasn't evil, he didn't know what was. Lacrimosa, however, was still crying, and Benedictus's eyes were shooting daggers. Kyrie decided to drop the subject.

He rubbed his aching shoulder. "All right," he said. "I'll drop it. But I'm not done asking questions. I have many. And I want answers to some at least. In the past few days, I've been shot at, clawed at, bitten, burned, and hit with about a field's worth of ilbane. My wounds ache, this rain is bloody cold, I'm famished, and I stubbed my toes about fifteen times on these roots. I think I've earned some answers." His voice was hoarse and his eyes stung. "So tell me this at least: Are there more Vir Requis? Or are we the last?"

Before anyone could answer, a griffin shrieked in the distance. Kyrie stiffened. He sat still, daring not breathe. Beside him, Benedictus and Lacrimosa also froze. An old oak rose above them, twisted and leafy. No griffins would see through its boughs, but still Kyrie's fingers trembled. He scanned the clouds for griffins. He saw a glint above--a rider carrying a torch. *Is that Dies Irae who rides there? Or Gloriae?* Then the griffin flew by, its shrieks fading into the distance.

When they could no longer hear the griffin, Benedictus turned to face him. At least, Kyrie thought he did; in the darkness, Benedictus appeared as but a shadow, burly and stiff like the oaks around them.

"There is another," spoke his gruff voice in the night.

Kyrie's heart leaped. Another! Another Vir Requis! He wanted to leap up and dance, and only the memory of the last griffin kept him still. "Who?" he breathed. "A girl Vir Requis?"

In the darkness, he heard Lacrimosa laugh softly, and Kyrie felt blood rise to his cheeks. *Nice one, Kyrie,* he scolded himself. *You sound like a lonely, love-starved boy.*

But maybe it wasn't so foolish a question, he decided. A female Vir Requis meant hope. A female could bear children. And if Kyrie himself was the father.... He felt even more blood rush to his cheeks, and he was grateful for the darkness that hid his fluster. Suddenly he was no longer cold.

"I know what you're thinking," Benedictus said. "And you can forget it right now. Yes, she's a girl. But she's not for you."

Why is he so angry? Kyrie wondered. Had he somehow offended the old warrior? It was hard to know; Benedictus was angry more often than not.

"Who is she?" Kyrie said. His fingers tingled. All his life, he'd been sure no other Vir Requis lived, except perhaps for the legendary Benedictus. And now, within a moon's cycle, he had met not just Benedictus, but Lacrimosa too. And there was a fourth! A second female! For ten years since Lanburg Fields, the world had seemed so grim, a world of hiding in Fort Sanctus, a world of pain and loneliness. Now things were different. To be sure, he still lived in hiding, and danger and loneliness were still his companions, but promise filled this night, and hope, and wonders. These were new feelings to Kyrie, and they made him feel drunk. He wanted to become a dragon and fly to find this new Vir Requis right away. Had she too been hiding all this time, alone in some fort? Had she too been dreaming of finding others, of finding Benedictus? Why wouldn't the old king speak? The burly shadow merely stood silently. It boiled Kyrie's blood.

"Well, why don't you speak?" he demanded, then bit his tongue. "I'm sorry, but-- can't you tell me?"

Benedictus only growled again, a sound like a bear in its den. "I told you, kid, forget about her."

A griffin shriek sounded, but it was a league away. Kyrie ignored it. He stood up, boots crunching the leaves that carpeted the forest floor. Rising so quickly made his wounds hurt, but he ignored the pain. "How can I forget her?" he said. He knew his voice was too loud, but couldn't help it. His fists clenched. "I've spent ten years thinking I'm alone, thinking all the others died. Now I learn there's another--a girl!--and you tell me to forget her? Why, Benedictus?"

The shadow also stood up. Kyrie was tall, but Benedictus towered over him. That growl sounded again, louder this time. "Watch your mouth, kid, unless you want it bashed in."

Now it was Lacrimosa's turn to rise. A slender shadow in the darkness, she leaped forward. If Benedictus was gnarled, tough, and wide as an oak, Lacrimosa was like a sapling. She came between them and placed one hand on Kyrie's chest, the other on Benedictus's chest. Kyrie marveled at how small and soft her hand felt, and how her hair, only inches from his face, smelled like jasmine.

"Please don't fight," she said. Though the night was starless, and they had no fire or lamp, Kyrie could see her hair glitter like moonlight. "Ben, we must tell him."

Benedictus regarded her for a moment, then turned away. He faced the oak and stood silent for a long time, fists at his sides. Finally his voice came in the darkness, low, almost sad, a voice drenched in memory and regret.

"Her name is Agnus Dei," said Benedictus. "And she will not join us. She will not fly with us."

"Why not?" Kyrie said, stepping forward, heart leaping. Fire blazed through him.

Benedictus still did not face him. "Agnus Dei is a wild one. She spends all her time in dragon form. Forgets she's a Vir

Requis. Thinks she's a true dragon, forgets her human side, forgets her humanity. More dragon than woman, that one is. I don't think she's been in her human form in a year."

Kyrie shook his head. "How is that possible? How has she survived? How do you know her? Where is she?" He had so many questions, he could have asked a hundred more, but Benedictus turned to face him. Kyrie could see but two blazing eyes in the shadowy form, and something in those eyes silenced him.

"She's my daughter," Benedictus said.

Kyrie took a step back. "Your... daughter?"

He did not know how to feel. Elated? Heart-warmed? But more than any other emotion, Kyrie felt sudden rage. His daughter! Kyrie clenched his fists. He had seen Requiem burn, had seen her courts topple. He had been to Lanburg Fields where the last of their kind perished, even the children. Yet Benedictus's family had been safe! His wife, Lacrimosa. His daughter, Agnus Dei. Where had he kept them? Had he hidden them underground while leading the others to die? Kyrie felt as if dragonfire consumed him. He wanted to pummel the old man. He wanted to shout, to accuse Benedictus of cowardice, but could bring none of it to his lips. So many emotions swirled through him, spinning his head, that he could barely speak. He could only manage two more words: "Your daughter."

Benedictus stared at him. "Yes, kid. I have a daughter. And I know what you're thinking. Yes, I kept her safe. Yes, I kept my child and wife away from Lanburg Fields." He took a step toward Kyrie; they stood only a foot apart. "Yes, I lead the rest of you to die. I lead thousands to die, but I kept my family safe. Even in the darkness, I can see that you hate me. And you're right to hate me. I've spent ten years hating myself, so a little more hate ain't gonna make a difference."

Silence filled the night. Not even crickets chirped. Lacrimosa stood by them, staring, and Kyrie did not know what to say. Finally he just turned around, walked toward the oak tree, and placed a hand against the trunk. Leaning against the tree, he lowered his head. His eyes stung.

"Kyrie," came Lacrimosa's voice behind him, soft and entreating. He felt her hand, so small and light, on his shoulder.

He turned around. He stared at Lacrimosa and Benedictus. "I want to find her."

"Forget her," said Benedictus.

"No!" Kyrie yelled, and Benedictus growled. Yelling could alert the griffins, but Kyrie didn't care. He preferred a fight to hiding. "No," he repeated. "She's your daughter, Benedictus. And she might be the only other Vir Requis who lives. The time for hiding has ended. Let's find her. We can't live scattered like this, in caves, in towers, in forests." Kyrie gritted his teeth. "We fly again, Benedictus. We fly like in the old days. And we fly with Agnus Dei."

Benedictus glowered. "She will not fly with us."

"I will get her to fly." He smiled mirthlessly. "We both saw our childhoods cut short. We will understand each other. Benedictus. Lacrimosa. Please. Let me speak with your daughter. Will you take me to her?"

He noticed suddenly, with a wrench of his heart, that Lacrimosa was weeping. Her tears glistened in the night, and her body shook. Such guilt filled Kyrie, that he felt like somebody had punched his stomach.

"Lacrimosa," he said, voice soft. "I'm sorry. I didn't mean to hurt you, I...."

She shook his head. "No, you don't hurt me. You're right, Kyrie. We'll seek her. I want her to meet you." Her voice shook and her tears fell. "I've wanted her to meet other Vir Requis for so long, others her age, of her kind. Maybe you can help her. Maybe you can help heal the pain within her." She smiled a trembling smile. "You're right. We're all in this together. Benedictus is no forest hunter. Agnus Dei is no wild dragon. We are Vir Requis. Tomorrow morning, I'll take you to her."

Kyrie was about to speak when shouts filled the forest. He heard creaking armor, swords being drawn, and thumping boots. Dogs barked.

"Actually, I think we better go now," Kyrie said and started running. "Tomorrow morning? Too late."

Benedictus and Lacrimosa ran beside him. They fled through the forest, panting, aching. *We're going to need to find more than one Vir Requis,* Kyrie thought as branches slapped him and the rain pelted him. *We're going to need to find a hidden army.* He suddenly missed Fort Sanctus; even hiding in that dank fort seemed heavenly compared to this, to running scared through the rain and darkness. Soon griffins flew above.

"They haven't seen us yet," Benedictus whispered as they ran. "Do not shift! Keep running, and keep quiet, and keep hidden. It's the dogs I'm worried about."

"Me too," Lacrimosa said, "I--"

She fell, twisted her ankle, and bit down on a yelp. His heart racing, Kyrie helped her up, glancing behind him. He could see steel blades and torchlight. Benedictus lifted Lacrimosa over his shoulder, and they kept running. Thunder rolled and the rain hammered them.

Kyrie clenched his fists. He had never harmed Dies Irae or Gloriae. Why were they so desperate to murder him? He wanted to shift, to roar, to fight them, but he just kept running. Lightning flashed, the dogs howled, and suddenly Kyrie doubted that he'd ever see Agnus Dei. He doubted that he'd live through the night.

Through rain and darkness, the Vir Requis ran.

DIES IRAE

Dies Irae slapped the girl's face, not hard enough to cut her, but hard enough to knock her to the floor. "You looked into my eyes," he said, voice icy. "Never look into my eyes."

She lay at his feet, trembling, hair covering her face. When he'd seen her that afternoon in the village, a peasant girl hawking eggs, he knew he must have her. A girl not yet twenty, slender, her hair fair and soft... she looked so much like Lacrimosa, that Dies Irae knew he would take her. Hurt her. Punish her for what Lacrimosa had done to him all those years ago.

"Please, my lord," the girl whispered, voice shaking. "My husband. Is he--"

"Be silent," Dies Irae said, staring down upon her. "Do not speak unless you are spoken to."

Her husband! Dies Irae barked a laugh. He had dealt with the farmer. The man had put up a fight, trying to protect his wife; he had even dared punch Lord Molok. Dies Irae smiled when he remembered how Molok had grabbed the man, then dragged him away screaming. If griffins had not eaten the peasant yet, it was only because Molok was still torturing him.

Dies Irae sighed. These backwater villages taxed him, with their crude peasants, impudent girls, and cold stone forts. He hated Benedictus for drawing him away from Confutatis, his Marble City of splendor and comfort. He hated Benedictus for eluding him this long, for leading him on a chase that seemed to never end. Dies Irae stared out the window of the fortress, gazing over the filthy village below, the field and forest, and the distant mountains.

"My lord, please, I beg you--" the peasant girl began, rising to her feet. Dies Irae hit her again, a punch that knocked her to the ground. Blood gushed from her lips.

"Silence," he said. These peasants lived so far from Confutatis, from his glory and statues and palaces. They forgot his power, his holiness. He would beat respect into them.

The girl was weeping at his feet. With his iron fist, the mace he now wore for an arm, Dies Irae caressed her hair. She shivered at his boots. *So young, soft, pale. So much like Lacrimosa.*

Dies Irae smiled when he remembered that day, eighteen years ago, when he'd found Lacrimosa in the forest. She had been only fifteen, fresh like an autumn fruit, and he had enjoyed hurting her, hurting his brother's prize. Yes, Benedictus had inherited the Oak Throne, Benedictus had gotten Lacrimosa to be his bride. But Dies Irae was the elder brother; if he could not inherit his birthright, he could destroy it.

"So I burned your throne, brother," he said softly. "And I broke your wife."

The girl at his feet looked up, then quickly looked away. Blood covered her mouth. The sight of her blood stirred Dies Irae's own blood.

"I will hurt you now, girl," he said, grabbed the girl's hair, and pulled her up. "And I will hurt Lacrimosa still. And I will hurt Benedictus, and that boy who flies with them. You all tried to cast me aside, to exile me, to hurt me. Look at you now."

The girl screamed, and he covered her mouth with his good hand. From outside his window, from the village stables, came more screams--the sounds of her husband, and the shrieks of feasting griffins. As the screams rose across the village, and across his empire of Osanna, Dies Irae smiled.

Soon, Benedictus, he thought as he shoved the girl down and tore off her dress. *Soon, Lacrimosa. Soon you will scream too.*

When he was done with the girl, he pulled her to the window, shoved her outside, and watched her crash to the cobblestones below. She convulsed, kicked, and lay still. Blood spread below her.

She was too skinny, Dies Irae thought.

He turned away from the window and stared into the mirror. He was old, he saw. Lines ran down the sides of his mouth, and gray streaked his golden hair. Wrinkles surrounded his eyes. But he still stood straight and strong, and he could still defeat men half his age in combat. *I still have my strength, and my rage, and the light of the Sun God.*

He left the room, stepped downstairs, and exited the fort. He walked across the courtyard, where his men were dragging the dead girl away. A cold wind blew, ruffling his robe, and Dies Irae looked up to see crows gliding under gray clouds. *Winter is coming,* he thought. *The weredragons will freeze in the snow and winds, but I will burn with the Sun God's flame.*

He walked down the hill, hand on the hilt of his sword. The stones were rough beneath his feet, and the grass and trees moved in the whistling winds. Below in the village, he saw his soldiers move from house to house, plundering food and grabbing peasant girls. When Dies Irae reached the stables, he stepped inside to find ten griffins. Gloriae stood there too, tending to her mount.

"She's hurt... badly," Gloriae said, not turning to look at him. A tin lamp hung over her, its light warm against her golden hair, her soft cheek, and her white tunic. Her griffin lay on her side, bandages covering her leg, side, and neck. She mewled.

"Kill the beast," Dies Irae said, not bothering to hide the irritation in his voice. "She's useless now."

Gloriae spun toward him, eyes flashing. Golden flecks danced in those green eyes, as ever when fury filled her. "How dare you say this? I've had Aquila since I was a child." She patted the griffin's head. "Hush, princess of the sky. You are strong. You will heal."

Dies Irae looked down at his daughter and her griffin, and couldn't decide what emotion he felt more strongly: disgust at her weakness, or admiration for her passion. The latter won, and Dies Irae sighed.

"Gloriae, I have spoiled you. I should have been harder on you, taught you to see griffins as tools, no more; not living creatures to love. But how could I? I admit it; I too have fond feelings for my griffin Volucris, and would rage should a weredragon wound him." He took her hands in his. "We will heal dear Aquila, and we will kill the weredragons who hurt her."

Gloriae looked at the griffin, chewed her lip, and said, "The blue weredragon hurt her. He'd have killed her and me, but... the silver dragon stopped him. I can't understand it. Kyrie Eleison had me; I was his to kill. The one they call Lacrimosa pulled him back." She shook her head as if to clear it. Her locks of golden hair swayed. "I don't understand, Father. I'm confused. Lacrimosa said something to me in the forest. Something about my mother." She looked back at her griffin, worry clouding her eyes.

Dies Irae winced inwardly. Of course Lacrimosa still recognized Gloriae. Of course she would stop Kyrie from killing her daughter. *Gloriae must never know,* he told himself, as he'd been telling himself for fifteen years, since that day he took one sister for his own, and left the other for the weredragons.

"Daughter," he said, "have I told you about your mother?"

"Of course. You told me that the weredragons killed her."

He nodded. "When you were three years old. Of course Lacrimosa wanted to pull Kyrie back. She wanted to kill you herself. Lacrimosa, you see, is the weredragon who murdered your mother."

Gloriae's face changed. All worry and doubt left her, and hatred suffused her expression. She whispered through a tight jaw. "I knew it."

Dies Irae stepped toward his griffin, the great Volucris, who stood at the back of the stable. He mounted the beast. "Come, Gloriae. Sit before me on the saddle. We go hunting weredragons."

Within minutes, they were flying over the countryside, a hundred griffins behind them. As the wind streamed through his hair, Dies Irae allowed himself a small, tight smile.

KYRIE ELEISON

They flew through the night. In the darkness they streamed forward, three Vir Requis--one young and blue, fire in his nostrils; one black and burly, scarred and limp; one slender and silvery, her eyes like stars. Cloaked in night and clouds, they flew like the great herds of old.

It feels good to fly, Kyrie thought. They had run for leagues on human feet, until finally shaking off the pursuit in hills of thick pines. The griffins could still return, he knew, and he kept both eyes wide open--but for a moment, he allowed himself to breathe easy.

"Are you sure she'll be there?" Benedictus called over the roaring winds. They flew hidden in cloud. Their scales glistened in the firelight from their mouths and nostrils.

Lacrimosa nodded. "She loved that cave as a child, that summer we hid there. In the snowy Fidelium, she always spoke of returning someday. She'll be there."

Kyrie watched the two Vir Requis fly side by side. He could not help but envy them. They shared a past and memories. They had a family. Kyrie had nobody to reminisce with. His family had perished. His home lay in ruins. Dies Irae had killed Lady Mirum. Kyrie had nobody who also remembered his childhood, remembered his home among the trees, and then his home in Fort Sanctus. He would never have what those two had, and it filled him with both fire and ice.

Dawn was rising, he saw. He could see Benedictus and Lacrimosa more clearly now. He could not yet see the sun, but its pink tendrils touched the clouds where they flew, kindling them. Soon the clouds blazed like dragonfire.

They had flown for hundreds of leagues. They were far now from the Marble City of Confutatis, from Dies Irae's center of power, from his armies and griffin stables... but not beyond the length of his arm. *His griffins fly far,* Kyrie knew. *They fly across this land too, and the distant lands beyond it. Maybe they fly until the end of the world.*

"We're close now," Lacrimosa said, the dawn glittering on her scales like sunlight on morning sea. The three dragons pulled their wings closer and descended, tails snaking behind them, until the clouds parted and they saw green land. Grassy hills rolled for leagues, cradling valleys of bindweed and goldenrod, leading to chalk mountains under yellow sunrise. Kyrie scanned the land, but saw only wild sheep, starlings and robins, and a fox running across a hill to disappear into a burrow. No griffins. No Dies Irae or Gloriae. No people at all.

"What is this place?" Kyrie asked.

"It's called Sequestra," Lacrimosa said. "Our kind used to herd here before--"

A roar pierced the land, cutting her off. Lacrimosa narrowed her eyes, Benedictus grunted, and Kyrie stared to the mountains. The roar had come from there. That was no griffin shriek. That was the sound of a dragon. *An angry dragon,* Kyrie thought.

The three Vir Requis kept flying, gliding lower, until they were near the mountains. Pines grew across the mountainsides, clinging with gangly roots and looking as if a sparrow could topple them. The smell of pines, chalk, and grass filled Kyrie's nostrils, and he savored it. He'd spent a decade by the sea, smelling the salt and waves and fish. He loved the seaside smells, but this place had a new scent, invigorating, healthy, and he imagined the ages long ago when herds of Vir Requis--thousands of them--filled the skies over Sequestra.

Lacrimosa was leading them toward a cave upon the mountain. Ash covered the mountainside here, the pines were burned, and great claw marks dug into the chalk and earth. A roar sounded again, coming from the cave. It echoed across the mountains and valleys, so loud that birds fled. Smoke and flames flew from the cave, and Kyrie tensed. Would a dragon attack a dragon? Kyrie knew that in the old days, Vir Requis houses would sometimes battle one another, but would Vir Requis fight even now, near extinction? He growled, gearing for a fight should it come.

Kyrie soon reached the cave and flapped his wings, hovering before it. Lacrimosa and Benedictus hovered beside him.

Lacrimosa called out, voice loud and clear across the mountainside. "Agnus Dei! Come and see us."

More fire emerged from the cave, and that roar sounded again, so loud that stones rolled down the mountainside. Then, with a puff of smoke, a red dragon burst out from the cave.

Kyrie couldn't help but retreat a dozen feet. He had never seen a dragon look so fierce, so wild. Agnus Dei looked like a creature woven of flame, her scales burning red. Her fangs and claws glinted, white and sharp. She was a long dragon, lithe but strong, her wings wide and blood red. She howled to the skies and blew more flames.

No wonder the humans think us monsters, Kyrie thought. *They must have seen Agnus Dei.*

"Hello, my daughter," Lacrimosa said. Her eyes were stern, but compassion and love filled them too. "Your leg. You're hurt."

Kyrie noticed that a long cut, as from a sword, ran along Agnus Dei's leg. The red dragon seemed not to mind. She snorted. "It's nothing, Mother. When will you stop worrying?"

"When you stop getting into fights!" Lacrimosa said.

Agnus Dei rolled her eyes, and smoke rose from her nostrils. She groaned, then seemed to notice Kyrie for the first time. The annoyance left her eyes, and amusement filled them instead. She raised an eyebrow and smirked. She looked like a girl who, in the midst of a heated argument, saw a silly dog and couldn't help but laugh. She studied Kyrie for a moment, then turned to Benedictus.

"Who's the pup?" she asked her father.

Kyrie bristled, and Benedictus snickered.

"The pup's with me," Benedictus said. "Thinks he's a hot shot."

Agnus Dei looked at Kyrie again, the sunlight glinting on her red scales. "Cute pup," she said to Benedictus. "Can he fly?"

Benedictus snorted. "Barely."

Kyrie had heard enough. He felt like roaring and blowing flames. "I can fly better than you any day," he said to Agnus Dei, baring his fangs. He spread his wings wide, trying to appear as large, wild, and intimidating as possible.

Agnus Dei laughed. She gestured with her head to a valley below the mountain. "Race you. First one to grab a deer wins."

"You're o--" Kyrie began when Agnus Dei took off, blazing over his head toward the valley.

Cursing, Kyrie spun around and shot after her. He saw her flying ahead, already distant, her tail swishing. Kyrie narrowed his eyes and flew like an arrow, diving toward the valley, wind whistling around him. His eyes scanned the grass and trees for deer. Agnus Dei was flying five hundred yards ahead, heading to a copse of trees, and Kyrie followed. Deer had to gather there. If he could just--

There! He saw one. A doe was racing across the grass, and Kyrie grinned and dived, snarling. The doe raced, fleeing to the trees. Kyrie swooped. He reached out his claws, and--

With a flash of red, Agnus Dei came swooping. She slammed into him, shoving him aside, and Kyrie howled. She drove him into a hill, and they slid across it, tearing up dirt and grass.

"Let go!" Kyrie cried, struggling to throw her off, but she clung to him, pinning him down.

"That deer was mine," Agnus Dei growled, her maw inches from his face. Her fangs glistened.

Kyrie struggled, freed a leg, and tried to push her off. She wriggled, clutching him with her legs and tail, refusing to release him. They wrestled in the grass, and Kyrie growled. He could not free himself; not without tearing into her flesh with claws and teeth, which he was not prepared to do. Not yet, at least.

"Get off," he grunted. Grass and dirt covered him.

Pinning him down, her knee in his side, she laughed and twisted his front leg. "Pup," she said.

Kyrie growled, smoke rising from his nostrils. "Benedictus warned me about you. He said you're more dragon than woman. He said you forgot what your human form is like. You must be a hideous freak, if you just stay in dragon form."

Agnus Dei laughed again, leaped off him, and shifted. Her wings pulled into her back, her scales vanished, and her claws and fangs retracted. She stood before him in human form.

Kyrie stared. Her hair was curly and black, her eyes brown and mocking, her skin tanned. She was tall and lithe, clad in tattered black leggings and a brown bodice. When he'd met Lacrimosa, Kyrie had thought her the most beautiful woman he'd seen, and he still thought so, but *this* woman.... If Lacrimosa was beautiful as moonlight, Agnus Dei had a beauty of fire, and that fire boiled Kyrie's blood.

"Stick your tongue back in," Agnus Dei said, her smile just as mocking as her eyes. "You might trip on it."

Kyrie frowned and shifted into human form too. He stood before her, covered in grass and dirt.

"I do not forget," Agnus Dei said. She drew a dagger from her belt and pointed it at him. "I merely do not fear. Others fear their dragon forms. They spend all their time as humans. I have no fear." She growled. "You are a pup." Then she shifted back into a dragon and leaped into the air, kicking up grass. She flew, heading back to the mountainside.

Kyrie too shifted back to dragon. He leaped and flew as fast as he could. He wanted to beat Agnus Dei back to her cave, to show her his speed, but he reached the cave just behind her. She looked at him with those mocking eyes and barked a laugh, and Kyrie felt his cheeks grow hot, and smoke rose from his nostrils.

Agnus Dei, he knew, would be a lot of trouble.

AGNUS DEI

Agnus Dei sat on her haunches, the cave dark around her, and growled at her parents. Smoke rose from her nostrils to sting her eyes.

"Agnus Dei, please," Mother said, soft silver in the darkness. "We've talked about the growling."

Agnus Dei shot flames from her nostrils. The fire glinted on Mother's silver scales, Father's black scales, and the pup's blue ones.

"Agnus Dei!" Mother said, rising to her feet, though the cave was too low for her to stretch to full height. "Will you *please* stop that?"

Agnus Dei turned to Father. The black dragon sat beside her, watching her with dark eyes.

"Do you see what I've had to put up with?" Agnus Dei asked him. "Do you see, Father?" She mimicked her mother. "Do not growl, do not blow fire, do not act like a dragon. Be a lady, Agnus Dei. Be like me, the noble and beautiful Lacrimosa."

"I never told you to be a lady," Mother interjected, eyes flashing.

"But you want it, don't you?" Agnus Dei said and growled, just to annoy Mother. "You want me to be like you. Delicate and fair, walking around in human form, all pretty." Agnus Dei thrust out her chest and let fire glow in her mouth. "But I'm like Father. I'm like the Great Benedictus, a wild thing."

Still Father said nothing, and that pup Kyrie also only watched from the shadows, eyes burning. *He doesn't care for me much, that pup,* Agnus Dei thought. *Or maybe he cares for me too much, and can't stand it.* She gave him a crooked smile, but he only bared his fangs at her.

"Pup," she said to him, and he growled.

"Now don't you start growling too, Kyrie," Lacrimosa said to him. "Don't let my daughter spoil you. I knew your parents, Kyrie Eleison; you are a child of nobility. Noble children do not growl."

Grinning now, Agnus Dei gave the loudest, longest growl of her life, a growl that shook the cave. Kyrie couldn't help but smile, the menace leaving his eyes, and he joined her, growling so that his whole body shook and his scales clanked. Even Father, always so stern and angry, began to growl deeply, eyes glinting with mischief. Birds fled outside, and Mother covered her ears.

"All right, all right!" Mother said. "I get the point. Benedictus, really. I expect this behavior from the young ones, but not from you. So stop it."

For the first time in her life, Agnus Dei saw her father look sheepish. He let his growl die, and Agnus Dei laughed. Father, cowed into silence! Her laughter seized her and she rolled around on the cave floor, tail lashing in all directions, slamming into the walls and several times into the pup.

"Cut it out," Kyrie said, rubbing his side where her tail had struck. "The spikes on your tail are huge. Stars. Your parents warned me about you."

"Did they, pup?" she asked.

"Stop calling me that!" he demanded, smoke rising from his nostrils.

Agnus Dei laughed at the sight of him bristling; he reminded her of a baby porcupine. "Okay, pup. Pup pup puppy pup."

He objected some more, as did Mother, but Agnus Dei could not hear. She was laughing too hard. It felt good to laugh. For so long, she had hidden alone in this cave. She had not spoken to anyone in days. After a year upon the snowy mountains, she had fled to this place, this green land on the far side of the world, this land where few men and griffins ventured. This land near the fabled kingdom of the salvanae, the true dragons.

I fled here to escape Mother, but... I missed her, Agnus Dei thought. She hated to admit it, even to herself, and would never tell Mother. But Agnus Dei knew it was true. Though she clashed horns with Mother whenever they spoke, figuratively and sometimes literally, she did love her. She had missed her. She had missed Father. Her laughter died, and she regarded her parents in silence for a moment.

"You two always said it was dangerous being together," Agnus Dei finally said. "You said we must live separately; Father in the forest, Mother and I in the snowy mountains, that we could not risk the griffins killing us all together. So why are you here? Why are we together? Why did you bring the pup?"

"I'm not a--" Kyrie began, flames leaving his nostrils, but Mother touched his shoulder, hushing him.

"I'll tell you," Mother said. "It begins with Kyrie on a seaside fort...."

For a long time, Mother spoke and Agnus Dei listened. She lowered her head as Mother told of Dies Irae arriving at Fort Sanctus and killing the Lady Mirum. She gasped when Mother spoke of Kyrie and Benedictus fighting off griffins in Hostias Forest. She shook her head in wonder as Mother talked of their flight from the woods, their plunge underwater, their journey here to Sequestra Mountains. When Mother finally fell silent, Agnus Dei rose to her feet, head brushing the cave's ceiling, and nodded.

"Well," she said, "there's only one thing to do now."

They all looked at her: Father with his dark eyes; Mother, her eyes sad; Kyrie, eyes gleaming and curious and fiery. Agnus Dei looked back at each one, took a deep breath, and struggled for the courage to speak what she thought. *Yes,* she told herself. It was the only way. The only hope they had, if they were to fight back, if they were to fly again. She was surprised to find tears in her eyes. *I will not hide again, I will not spend my life in caves. We are Vir Requis. Once more, our wings will find the sky.*

She spread out her wings and snarled. "We will find the true dragons. We will have them join us."

Agnus Dei watched their reactions. Benedictus lowered his head and let out a long, tired breath. Mother sighed and shook her head softly. Kyrie, however, widened his eyes and nodded, teeth bared. "Yes," he whispered, voice eager like fire seeking kindling.

"No." Father spoke for the first time, voice deep and gruff. "And that's that."

Agnus Dei spun toward him, glaring. "Why not?" she demanded, flames tickling her teeth.

"Because I said so," Father said, baring his fangs, fangs twice the size of Agnus Dei's. "We will not seek any of these salvanae, these 'true dragons'. As far as anyone knows, no such creatures even exist."

Agnus Dei could not believe it. The fire burned inside her belly, and she blew it at the ceiling, lighting the cave in red and yellow. Her roar echoed. "How can you say that?" she demanded. "Father! They are real. I know it."

Agnus Dei expected Mother to rage, but the silvery dragon only looked at her with sad eyes and touched her shoulder. "My daughter. Sweetheart. Those are only stories. Stories I told you when you were a child. There are no salvanae in real life. They are only legends humans told, mistaking us Vir Requis for creatures with no human form."

Agnus Dei did not know if to feel more foolish or more angry. She glared, fangs bared, all eyes on her. Could Mother be right? Had she simply believed fairytales from her childhood?

No, impossible! Salvanae did exist, flying serpents with no human forms, creatures who could join them, fly with them, breathe fire across the skies. The legends were true. The salvanae simply lived far away, far over mountains and lakes and forests, hiding in the fabled land of Salvandos, a land where no griffin dared fly.

Agnus Dei turned to Kyrie. She grabbed his shoulders. "You believe, don't you?" she said. "I can see you do! Don't deny it. You too know the stories are real. Imagine, pup!" She shook him. "Imagine... a mountain covered with dragons, *real* dragons, not Vir Requis. Wild, untamed beasts who have no human forms, who live for fire and wings and battle." Agnus Dei growled. "We can find them. You and I. We can have them join us, fight with us against Dies Irae."

Kyrie's eyes shone. He believed her; Agnus Dei could see it. He turned toward Benedictus, as if seeking permission from the old king. Agnus Dei grabbed Kyrie's face and pulled it back toward her.

"Don't look at him!" she said. "He is old and tired. He does not believe. Look at me. I'm young and hungry like you, and I want to fight. I want to fly. I want to fly with the true dragons like in the legends. Come with me to find them, pup. Kyrie, I mean. Come with me. I remember the stories of Salvandos, of this distant land of golden trees and misty mountains. A land so far, not even griffins fly there. But I can fly there."

Father stepped toward Agnus Dei, kneeling under the cave ceiling. He glared at her, and she stared back, refusing to look away though his gaze burned.

"Daughter, if you remember the stories, you will remember this too," Father said, voice grave, that cold voice of the Black Fang, King of Requiem. "You will remember that the salvanae were treacherous, untameable. Beastly. In the stories, they hate Vir Requis. They see us as demonic shape shifters, as profane, an insult to their kind. If humans hate us for having dragon forms, the salvanae hate us for having human forms."

Agnus Dei growled. "I am like a true dragon. I do not have to take human form again. They hate Vir Requis? I will remain a dragon. I will tell them I am a dragon true, that I need their aid." She grabbed Kyrie. "Kyrie and I are going. What else could we do? Stay in this cave until Irae finds us? I want to fight. Fly with me to the west, Father, Mother."

Not waiting for a response, not caring if she was reckless, not caring that griffins might be flocking outside, Agnus Dei ran to the cave opening. She burst outside into the wilderness and sunlight, spread her wings, shot up toward the sky, and roared. Her fire flew, raining sparks.

She heard a roar behind her and saw Kyrie flying toward her, also breathing fire. His blue scales shimmered, blinding her. "I'm with you," he said. "Kitten."

She lashed her tail at him, but he ducked, narrowly escaping it.

"Who are you calling kitten?" she demanded and blew fire at him.

He swerved, dodging the flames, and grinned at her. Mother and Father were flying toward them too, and Agnus Dei looked at them, and saw in their eyes that they would join her, would fly west with her, fly to seek that land of legend. Land of the salvanae. The true dragons.

As Agnus Dei roared and flapped her wings, she was surprised to feel icy fear trickle down her spine.

The war, she knew, would flare again.

DIES IRAE

Dies Irae stood in the courtyard of another fort on another cold, dreary hill, and gazed down upon the lashed body of a shepherd.

He admired the bruises and welts covering the man and smiled.

"Gloriae, your work is beautiful," he said.

His daughter stood by him. The wind streamed her hair and rustled the weeds between the cobblestones. Ice filled her eyes. She stared at the moaning peasant and spoke, her face blank. "He was hiding information about the weredragons. He got what he deserved. There is no beauty to this, Father. I took my information with my lash and my boots. There is beauty to the white towers of Confutatis, and to her banners that fly golden. This?" She nodded her head at the tortured man. "This is no art; it is justice, harsh and unforgiving."

The shepherd groaned at her feet, blood trickling across the cobblestones. Dies Irae caressed his daughter's cheek, so soft and cold. "I've taught you well, Gloriae."

He nodded at his guards, and they dragged the man away, leaving a trail of blood. Dies Irae caressed his mace, this new left arm. Benedictus had eluded him for too long, but he could not hide forever. When shepherds saw the monstrous shapes against the stars, they would speak, or they would die.

"They fly to Sequestra Mountains in the west, and they're hurt," Gloriae said, staring at those stains of blood. Her face was blank. "Soon we'll be upon them.

Dies Irae nodded. "Benedictus, Kyrie Eleison... and Lacrimosa."

Lacrimosa. Dies Irae loathed displays of emotion, but now he twisted his lips into a small, thin smile. Lacrimosa--of pale skin, lavender eyes, and moonlit hair. He remembered how he'd bruised that skin, filled those eyes with tears, pulled that hair. His blood boiled at the memory. He wanted to hurt her again, to tear her clothes, grab her breasts, hear her scream.

Gloriae looked to the west, over the crumbling fort to the distant mountains and forests. Dark clouds covered the sky, elk herded in the distance, and the grassy plains undulated in the wind. "There are those three... and there is a fourth," she said. "A red one. A female."

Dies Irae stared at his daughter and frowned. A red dragon. A female. Could it be? Dies Irae clenched his jaw. There was only one such living weredragon.

"The shepherd spoke of her?" Dies Irae asked, struggling to keep the rage from his voice.

Gloriae nodded. "He did, and I saw her myself. Her name is Agnus Dei."

Dies Irae turned from his daughter and stared into the distance. Vultures were circling under the clouds. A cold wind chilled him. *Yes, Agnus Dei.*

Two girls, one dark and wild, one fair and cold. One could shift, become a red monster. The other had no curse; she would remain forever beautiful and pure. Agnus Dei and Gloriae. Daughters of Lacrimosa. Benedictus believed they were his own; Dies Irae knew better.

Does Gloriae know? Dies Irae thought in sudden fear. *Does she know the truth, know that Agnus Dei is her sister, that Lacrimosa is her mother?* He stared at his daughter, seeking the answer in her eyes, and saw only steel. No, Gloriae did not know. That was good. Dies Irae loved her more than anything; he would shield this horrible truth from her. If she knew, it would crush her.

Agnus Dei, he thought, staring at his iron fist. *The cursed, monstrous twin. You I will not kill, no. You will serve as my mount, daughter. You are fairer even than Volucris, the king of griffins. I will ride the last living weredragon, conqueror of the race.*

Dies Irae turned and walked away. He carefully avoided the blood on the cobblestones; his boots were priceless, those boots made from the golden scales of a Vir Requis child. Two of his men stepped forward, eyes lowered, and placed his samite robe around his shoulders.

"Come, Gloriae," Dies Irae said. He walked down a crumbling staircase, past saluting soldiers, weedy walls, and tethered griffins. "We have lingered in this fort long enough. We resume the hunt."

He was surprised to find a smile still on his lips, twitching, and his gut felt like ants raced through it. Dies Irae prided himself on controlling his emotions, but this chase thrilled him.

I destroyed the weredragons who shunned me. I killed the father who disowned me. But you, Benedictus... you are the one who stole my throne, who took my arm, who turned Father against me. Now, finally, I will hurt you like you hurt me. Now I will punish you for what you did.

Dies Irae clenched his good fist. Fury flooded him, turning the world red, and he licked his lips. When the fire burned inside him, that was when he felt alive. This was what he lived for.

Because fire and anger, whispered a voice inside him, *are better than pain.* Hatred was better than fear. Dies Irae hated the pain that surfaced at nights, hated the nightmares that haunted him. All the statues, all the women, all the gold in the world could not drive that pain away, the shunned child inside him. But anger could. Hatred could.

I am no longer a frightened, lonely boy, an outcast, a freak. You are the freak now, Benedictus. You are the outcast, and you now cower. You fear like I have feared. I am a terror and light to the world. You will see this, Benedictus.

The passion blinded him. Dies Irae barely noticed time pass. He found himself on his griffin, taking flight from the stables, soaring into the sky. Gloriae flew behind him, and behind her flew a hundred more armored riders upon a hundred griffins. The fort disappeared in the distance, and cold wind slapped Dies Irae's face. He lowered the visor of his helmet, the visor shaped as a beak, and reached around his neck to clutch the golden amulet. When he remembered how he'd taken the Griffin Heart, Dies Irae felt a heady mix of fear, joy, and power. He snarled.

They flew for a long time.

They flew over forests of oaks and mist, and over fields of wheat and barley, and over lakes. They flew over farms where peasants labored and fields where shepherds roamed. *A beautiful land,* Dies Irae thought. *My land.* They flew over cities of stone towers, statues, murals, and Sun God temples. They flew over toppled cities too, now only ruins covered with moss and ash, piles of shattered columns and burned trees. Dies Irae smiled when he saw them; they were the most beautiful sight in this land. Here were the ruins of weredragon cities, great cemeteries to his enemy. He would let them lie forever ruined, a reminder of the weredragons' evil and his conquest of it.

"The weredragons will be lost to memory," Lord Molok had said to him once, on a day they burned a weredragon town and cleansed it of the beasts. The man's black eyes had burned.

Dies Irae had shaken his head and stared at the thousands of weredragon bodies littering the ruins. "No. I want all to remember the weredragons. History must remember their evil, and remember it was we, men of light, who defeated them."

That had been years ago, and still those ruins remained. Still weredragon bones lay among them.

"Look what you did, Benedictus," Dies Irae whispered as they flew over the ruins of Requiem. His griffin heard him and looked back, but Dies Irae barely noticed the beast. He was seeing his brother in his mind. "See what you did when you stole my birthright, took Requiem's throne, took the woman who should have been mine."

The griffins were soon tired, eyes rolling, fur matted with sweat, but Dies Irae refused them rest. How could they rest when they were so close, maybe moments away from killing Benedictus? Night was falling when they finally saw Sequestra Mountains ahead, deep purple veiled in shadows.

Dies Irae snarled a grin. He scanned the darkness. This was the place the shepherds had spoken of. Where were the weredragons? *Where are you, brother?*

"Fan out!" Dies Irae barked and gave a few signals with his good arm. The griffins split into five squads, twenty griffins in each. They began scanning the mountain and valley. Dies Irae led his squad to a piney mountainside. He narrowed his eyes, searching for caves. Weredragons liked cowering in caves, hiding their shame in the darkness.

They searched the mountains for a long time. The sun set, and the moon shone. *Where are you, Lacrimosa?*

"Father!" came Gloriae's voice beside him. She flew toward him, moonlight on her armor. Her griffin panted, eyes rolling back. "Father, the griffins must rest. They are weary enough to fall."

Dies Irae shook his head. "No, daughter. We must find the weredragons." His own griffin panted, but Dies Irae knew he could push the beast a while longer.

To his right, one griffin faltered and crashed to the ground. Dies Irae snorted; that one was a weakling. If any griffin could not survive this flight, they did not deserve to fly in his herd.

"Father, I--" Gloriae began again, but Dies Irae interrupted her.

"Look, Gloriae. There."

A cave yawned open in the mountainside ahead. Dies Irae led his griffin toward it. His heart raced and his fingers tingled. He imagined that he could feel his missing hand tingle too, as if fingers still moved there instead of an iron mace. He landed his griffin outside the cave and dismounted.

"Men, join me," he called and waved to the others. Soon twenty griffins covered the mountainside, panting, collapsing. The riders dismounted and joined Dies Irae outside the cave.

Dies Irae grabbed a torch from his griffin's saddle and lit it. His men too lit torches, drew swords, and Dies Irae led them into the cave. He gritted his teeth and raised his iron arm, prepared for a fight.

Inside the cave, he slowly exhaled. The place was empty, and Dies Irae lowered his mace, pulled up his visor, and spat. So the cowards had fled him. They had camped here. Ash covered the walls and ceiling, speaking of recent dragonfire. Claw marks covered the floor, and the place stank of them. Dies Irae could recognize that stench anywhere, a smell like smoke and oil.

Where are you, sweet Agnus Dei, sweet daughter? Dies Irae narrowed his eyes. He spun around, shoved his way past his men, and stepped outside into the night. He gazed up at the sky, sniffing the air. *Where did you fly to, weredragons?*

Dies Irae shut his eyes. He could imagine that he smelled their trail through the sky. They would not fly east, no. They would not fly north into the cold, nor south into the deserts. They could flee west, hoping to fly beyond his arm, but Dies Irae's arm was long enough to hunt weredragons anywhere.

Dies Irae opened his eyes and turned to his men. They stood behind him, torches and swords still raised. "Feed and water your griffins. You have ten minutes. Then we fly west... and hunt weredragons."

LACRIMOSA

As the four dragons streamed between the clouds, Lacrimosa shook her head. *We're on a fool's quest,* she thought. *Chasing a legend, a dream.*

The clouds filled her nostrils, tickled her cheeks, and stung her eyes. She could see Agnus Dei's red tail ahead, lashing from side to side. Benedictus and Kyrie flew by her, but the clouds hid them; she glimpsed only flashes of sunlight on their scales.

We're safe here, she thought. No griffins would see them in these clouds. Still Lacrimosa shivered as she flew. She wished she were in human form, walking upon the land; it was safer that way. Griffins could fly far, and Dies Irae would never stop hunting her, Lacrimosa knew.

We're risking our lives. And why? For a bedtime story I'd tell Agnus Dei years ago. A story, that's all. And for hope.

Lacrimosa sighed. The clouds darkened and moisture covered her. *Maybe that is enough. Maybe Agnus Dei needs some hope, a journey, a future to cling to. There might be no true dragons, but if I can give Agnus Dei hope, even fools' hope, maybe that will help her. Maybe that will soothe the pain inside her.*

As if to answer her thoughts, Agnus Dei turned her head. The clouds veiled her, but Lacrimosa could see her daughter's blazing eyes and the fire in her mouth. "Come on, catch up!" she said. Excitement, even joy, filled her voice. It had been years since Lacrimosa had seen her daughter happy, and she felt droplets on her cheeks, and knew it was not the clouds, but her tears.

"We're flying as fast as we can," Lacrimosa called back, and couldn't help but laugh and cry. "I'm old and slow, Agnus Dei."

That was a lie, of course; Lacrimosa was neither old nor slow. But Benedictus was, and his wing was torn, and he was too proud to admit weakness. Lacrimosa looked at her husband and smiled. He looked at her with one eye and grunted. The clouds flowed around him.

Kyrie, a stream of blue scales through the clouds, gazed anxiously at Agnus Dei. His claws flexed, and Lacrimosa knew he was aching to fly ahead by Agnus Dei, to spend time alone with her among the clouds. But the young Vir Requis looked at Benedictus, tightened his lips, and kept flying by the black dragon.

As much as my daughter's charmed him, he worships my husband more, Lacrimosa thought with a sad smile. He was like so many young Vir Requis in the war, so many who had fought for Benedictus. *I myself once worshiped him thus; he was a being of legend to me. Maybe he still is.*

Lacrimosa sighed and turned her gaze to her husband. He flew solemnly, staring ahead, his torn wing wobbly. *The wing Dies Irae tore with his spear.* Lacrimosa closed her eyes as she remembered that day so long ago, that day more terrible than any other. Benedictus had returned from Lanburg Fields, bleeding. He was half dead, and he only said to her, "It is over." Then he collapsed and slept for days, and Lacrimosa thought he would die, and she wept so many tears. Their race had died then, its last remnants fallen upon the fields, the elderly and the children. Only her family had remained: her husband, her daughters, and herself.

But no, Lacrimosa thought as she flew through these clouds. Kyrie Eleison survived. *Our leader, Benedictus the Black, still flies. We still fly by him. And one day Gloriae will return to us, and fly with us too.*

Lacrimosa tightened her lips and blinked tears out of her eyes. Sometimes she felt like a youth again, a youth in love with her prince.

"I still fly with you, my lord, my love," she whispered.

When night fell, the Vir Requis flew down under the clouds, cloaked in darkness. Agnus Dei's nostrils glowed with fire, and Lacrimosa nudged her until the girl sniffed back the flames.

"Do not blow fire, do not growl, fly like a shadow," Lacrimosa whispered, and Agnus Dei nodded.

Lacrimosa scanned the darkness. In the distance she saw the lights of human fires; it looked like a town, but it still lay leagues away. Below them Lacrimosa saw no lights, no sign of life. She glided down, silent, and landed in a field of wheat. The others landed by her. The youths landed silently and gracefully, but Benedictus hit the ground with a thud and muffled grunt.

Lacrimosa glanced around, hoping nobody heard. In dragon form, her eyes were sharp, but she could see nothing but wheat and a farmhouse half a league away.

"Mmm, a barn!" Agnus Dei whispered, drooling. "I'm going to get us some sheep."

"Go in your human form," Lacrimosa whispered. "All of you--shift now. It's safer."

Lacrimosa let her magic fill her, tickling all over, and shifted. Her scales vanished, her claws and fangs retracted, and soon she stood on human feet. It was suddenly cold, and she shivered in her thin, white dress and hugged herself. Around her, the others too shifted, even--with a grumble--Agnus Dei.

Lacrimosa walked toward her daughter and embraced her. Agnus Dei grunted and tried to shove her off, but finally capitulated and just sighed. Lacrimosa didn't care. It felt so good to see her daughter in human form again, taming her wild side. It had been so long.

"You flew well today," Lacrimosa whispered into her daughter's mop of curls. "I'm proud of you. I love you."

Agnus Dei wriggled out of the embrace. "Mother, really. I'm not a child."

She was right, Lacrimosa knew. Agnus Dei was no longer a child. The girl was eighteen now, and as tall as Lacrimosa. *When I was eighteen, I was already married and had two daughters. Agnus Dei, I'm so sorry I raised you in this world, that you grew up in caves and tunnels. I'm so sorry we couldn't give you a better world.*

"Mother, will you stop looking at me like that?" Agnus Dei demanded, eyes fiery. "Wipe your tears away. Stars above, I'm fine, okay? You're always worrying. Even when you say nothing, your eyes are nagging me."

Lacrimosa laughed. "Okay, Agnus Dei, okay. Go grab us some chickens or sheep. And here, take this." She pulled a silver coin from her pocket. "Don't let the farmers see you, but leave this in place of the animals you take."

Agnus Dei's eyes flashed, and she seemed ready to complain, but Lacrimosa glowered at her so severely, that her daughter only sighed, snatched the coin, and stormed off.

"I'll go with you," Kyrie offered and followed her. "You'll need help carrying back the grub."

When the young ones vanished into the shadows, Benedictus and Lacrimosa sat down. She leaned her head against his shoulder, and he placed an arm around her, kissed her hair, and sighed. For a long time they sat together, staring into the night. The clouds thickened and a drizzle fell, so light it barely wet them, but cold enough that Lacrimosa trembled. Stalks of wheat rustled around them, and Lacrimosa wrapped her arms around Benedictus, seeking warmth from his body. He was all muscle, bones, and scars, but there was warmth and softness to him too.

"How are you, Ben?" she finally asked.

He stared ahead into the night and said nothing. Lacrimosa waited. She knew that he needed time to gather his thoughts, to form his words. Benedictus rarely spoke freely. When he spoke, it was because he had considered every word and meant it. After a long moment, he spoke into the darkness.

"I'm scared," he said.

Lacrimosa looked at him and bit her lip. Benedictus the Great, the Black Fang, the King of Requiem--scared? Lacrimosa touched his dark curls lined with gray, and her hand seemed so small and soft against his gruff, tousled head.

"I'm scared too," she whispered.

Benedictus ran his hand against her thigh, a rough hand, the hand of a hunter and fighter, calloused. "The kid, he... he believes in me, Lacrimosa. He looks up to me; worships me, even. I used to demand that from young Vir Requis. I used to expect it. They died under my command, Lacrimosa. Thousands of kids like Kyrie died under my banners. If anything should happen to Kyrie, or to our daughters...."

Our daughters. Lacrimosa closed her eyes, the secret of her shame burning within her. *Yes, Agnus Dei and Gloriae are ours, mine and Ben's, and not grown from Dies Irae's seed.*

Sometimes Lacrimosa ached to tell him, could almost speak her secret. Tonight she wanted to whisper to her husband, to hold him, touch his hair, speak of that night long ago. Tell him what Dies Irae had done. But she could not. Not yet. The pain still burned too strongly, even after all these years.

She kissed his stubbly cheek. "They may die," she whispered. "I know that. And I want to protect them. But how much longer can we hide, Ben? We've hidden for years, but they keep hunting us, sending us fleeing. You know how Agnus Dei was. Half mad with cabin fever and pain. I watched her and I wept and feared. I thought she would become wild, untameable, that she would become fully mad with rage. I thought that she would fly with fire and let the griffins find her. You sent men to die, Ben, yes. And you sent women to die, and children, and I know, my lord, I know how much blood covers your hands, and how it haunts you. But you are a hero to Kyrie. And you are a hero to Agnus Dei; she will not admit it, but I know it's true." Tears filled her eyes, and Lacrimosa smiled. "She always tells me: I am not fair and graceful like you, Mother, I am strong and proud like Father. That is how she loves you. You are brave, and noble, and you are doing right. If you were not scared, you would be heartless. Your fear speaks of your goodness."

He smiled in the dark, one of those rare, soft smiles of his. "You were always better at words, my love," he said, and she leaned her head back against his shoulder.

The sounds of stomping feet and crackling wheat filled the darkness, and Lacrimosa stiffened, suddenly sure that Dies Irae had found them... but it was only Kyrie and Agnus Dei walking back toward them.

"Pup, you are wrong as always," Agnus Dei's voice carried through the night. "The word for sheep meat is mutton; lamb is what you call a baby sheep."

Kyrie grunted. "So why do you call them lamb chops, not mutton chops? Lamb is the meat; the child sheep is called a kid."

"You're thinking of goats, pup," she said.

"Stop calling me that!"

Lacrimosa rose to her feet and shushed them. They were a dozen feet away, and when they saw her, they closed their mouths and approached silently. They carried lambs under their arms. Lacrimosa found herself again smiling with teary eyes. *Are you going soft, Lacrimosa?* she asked herself, but she couldn't help it. For the first time in years, she saw two Vir Requis, a boy and girl, walking together through a field, talking, happy. Memories of the old days, of her own youth among her kind, flooded her so that she could barely breathe.

They dared not make a fire, so after scanning the field again for unfriendly eyes, they shifted into dragons and ate the meat raw. They then lay on their backs, digesting, letting the drizzle fall upon their bellies. Lacrimosa nestled against Benedictus, while the young ones whispered to each other. Lacrimosa could not hear them, but she smiled because she knew that, for the first time in years, Agnus Dei had a friend.

"I'll guard first," Lacrimosa said. "Best we sleep as dragons tonight, at least until we digest those lambs. But stay low, and try to look like haystacks."

"I'll guard second," Agnus Dei said, licking her lips. "If any griffins show up, I'll pound them!" She clawed the air and snarled.

Kyrie agreed to guard third, and Benedictus last. When they all slept, Lacrimosa watched them, smiling softly. The drizzle fell upon them, and their scales glinted wet, but they seemed not to notice. All three slept soundly, and Lacrimosa felt warm even on this cold, wet night. *We are family,* she thought, *and we are together again. Kyrie too is part of our family now.*

The Eleisons had been a proud line, and close to her own blood, Lacrimosa remembered. Kyrie's parents had been blue too, fiery like their son. *They are gone now, gone like so many others, bones and ash in our burned forests. But we will look after you, Kyrie. We will protect you like a son.*

She thought, too, of her lost daughter, of Gloriae. The fair twin. The babe who rarely cried, who stared, who seemed lost in thought even in her cradle. *I will find you, Gloriae. I will bring you back to our family.*

Weariness tugged Lacrimosa. She wanted to stand up and walk to keep awake, but dared not. She would not walk in dragon form, not so close to a human farm, not even on a starless night. Nor did she dare turn human again, not until she digested the meat in her belly. So Lacrimosa bit her tongue, twisted her tail, and tried to recite old poems to ward off sleep.

Then she saw something that made the poems die on her lips.

Lacrimosa stiffened, frowned, and stared.

A shadow in the sky. No, only her imagination. Or maybe.... Lacrimosa raised her head and her claws. There! She saw it again. A snarl came to Lacrimosa's lips, and she wanted to wake up Benedictus. She nudged him.

"Ben," she whispered.

He moaned but did not wake. Lacrimosa stared into the sky, seeking that shadow, that black patch against the clouds. She saw nothing. It was gone.

It was just a shadow in my mind, a fear in the night. She kept watching the sky for a moment longer, then blew out her breath.

Nothing.

Then--

Griffin wings spread open above. A bolt of metal shot down, and pain stung Lacrimosa's neck. She opened her mouth to scream, but could not utter a sound. Ilbane flowed through her, and her eyes rolled back.

"Ben!" she tried to call, but no voice found her lips. She fell back, trembling, and griffin talons clutched her.

DIES IRAE

Dies Irae flew, the wind biting his cheeks, his griffin clutching Lacrimosa.

"Fly, damn you," he hissed. "Faster, Volucris!"

Volucris was large and heavy, twice Lacrimosa's size, but the chase had wearied him, and he flew slowly. Dies Irae dug his spurs into his flanks.

"Fly!"

Already the sounds of the other Vir Requis, roused from sleep, sounded behind him. "Lacrimosa!" one howled, and soon the others joined the howling. "What happened? Lacrimosa!" and "Mother! Mother, where are you?"

Dies Irae cursed under his breath. This night was not going as planned. He had hoped to catch the Vir Requis with a hundred griffins at his back. After finding the cave deserted, he had broken up his herd, then sent individual griffins to scan the fields and forests. Now he flew alone.

"Lacrimosa!" came a deep cry in the distance. It had to be Benedictus.

I should have killed him in his sleep, Dies Irae thought. *I should have killed them all as they slept.* But of course, that had been impossible. He'd arrived alone, and in the second he had before Lacrimosa could raise the alarm, he'd done what he must.

She squirmed in Volucris's talons, voice weak. "Ben... Benedi..." Her voice faded and she fell limp.

"Lacrimosa!" came the howls behind, and Dies Irae heard flapping dragon wings. "Lacrimosa, where are you?"

Dies Irae laughed. He turned in his saddle and gazed into the darkness. He could see nothing under the dark, raining clouds, but he could hear them, smell them.

"Do you want her back, Benedictus?" he shouted. "Do you want your Lacrimosa? I have her, Benedictus! I have the creature. If you want her, you'll follow."

Howls of pain and rage filled the night, widening Dies Irae's grin. So he was alone. So he could not kill them all. So Benedictus still lived. But this night was still proving useful. They would follow, Dies Irae knew; their pathetic weredragon "code of honor" demanded it. They would follow Lacrimosa, try to rescue her, and fly into his camp.

"Where are you, Benedictus?" he cried over his shoulder, the wind whipping him. They were blowing fire behind him, still distant, trying to see him. "Is that the fastest you can fly?"

He turned back forward and spurred his griffin. "Fly, Volucris. Faster."

The griffin grunted. His talons tightened around Lacrimosa's slender body. She was still mumbling, but Dies Irae could not make out the words. He had coated his quarrels with potent ilbane; the stuff would keep her dazed for hours. Despite the howling behind him, the thud of wings, and the roaring flames, Dies Irae felt his blood boil at the thought of Lacrimosa. True, she was in dragon form now, a hideous beast of scales, but he would force her to take human form later. He had ways to force her. In the night, the memories resurfaced, the sweet memories of that night in the woods, the night he caught her alone, the night he pulled off her dress and--

"I see him!" came a cry behind. It was the young blue weredragon from Fort Sanctus, Dies Irae realized; the Eleison kid. "I see him--there, follow me!"

Dies Irae turned in his saddle, aimed his crossbow, and fired at Kyrie. The weredragon was easy to spot; he was blowing fire and burning in the darkness. The crossbow shot true, and Kyrie cried and fell back. Dies Irae loaded another quarrel and shot again. Again he hit Kyrie, and again the weredragon yelped. He tumbled from the sky.

Dies Irae smirked. *One gone, two to go.* Benedictus and Agnus Dei still followed him, blowing flames. *Pathetic,* he thought. *They reveal themselves with fire, while I fly hidden in darkness.* He was tempted to turn and charge them head on, but dared not with his griffin's talons clutching Lacrimosa, unavailable for battle. He kept flying.

"Faster, Volucris, faster."

Benedictus was falling behind. When Dies Irae glanced over his shoulder, he could not see the great black beast. But Agnus Dei still flew there, moving closer and closer, gaining on him. Her red scales glinted in her firelight.

"Hello, my daughter," Dies Irae whispered and shot his crossbow.

Agnus Dei cried. The quarrel hit her neck, coated in ilbane. Her wings wobbled and she fell, crashing from the sky like a comet, flaming and howling.

"Join me in Confutatis, Benedictus!" Dies Irae shouted back into the night. "Join me in my palace, if you wish to see Lacrimosa again. You know where I live." His voice was hoarse, and he laughed. "I will see you there, weredragon, or I will torture this silver beast until she breaks. Goodbye for now, Benedictus! I will see you soon."

They howled in the distance, and Dies Irae spurred his griffin onward. They shot through the night, the howls of the weredragons fading behind.

BENEDICTUS

Benedictus flew as fast as he could, cursing, fear an iceberg in his gut.

"Lacrimosa!" he howled, voice hoarse. "Lacrimosa!"

He could see nothing but blackness, and the rain and wind whipped him. He blew fire, but could not see Dies Irae ahead. Benedictus cursed his brother, and cursed himself for sparing Dies Irae that day, for biting off an arm but not finishing the job. *I spared your life, brother. I let you live then. I will not let you live today.*

"Lacrimosa!"

He heard Volucris's shriek ahead, and Benedictus narrowed his eyes and flew in that direction. *Damn this torn wing.* In the old days, he could fly faster than any griffin, but now he lagged behind. Where was Kyrie? Had he survived? Where was Agnus Dei?

Benedictus blew fire again, and it glinted against red scales half a league ahead. Agnus Dei! Benedictus flew toward her, his wings churning the clouds. Darkness cloaked her, and he blew fire again, saw the red glint again.

"Agnus Dei!"

Soon she was only feet away, and Benedictus felt his heart tighten. She was hurt. Her wings flapped weakly, and her head lolled. She barely stayed in the sky. Blood trickled down her neck.

His fire died in his mouth, and Benedictus could see nothing again. He grabbed Agnus Dei in the darkness.

"Get out of here," he said. "You're hurt. Fly back. Find Kyrie. He was hit."

She shook her head, struggling to free herself from his grasp. "Mother!" she whispered, tears in her eyes. Her voice was hoarse, heavy, thick with the pain of ilbane. When lightning flashed, Benedictus saw that her eyes were glazed. "Mother is ahead, I have to save her, I have to...." Her voice died, drowning in pain.

"I'll save Mother," Benedictus said, pulling Agnus Dei to the ground. She was too weak to resist, and Benedictus knew he must hurry. Every second he lingered here, Dies Irae was flying farther away. He reached the ground and laid Agnus Dei on the grass. He blew fire, lighting the world, and examined her wound. It was not lethal, but the ilbane would hurt for hours. With a quick tug, he removed the quarrel that had pierced her. Her blood dripped.

"Find the salvanae," he said to her. "Fly west and find them with Kyrie. I'll go after Mother."

Her eyes stared at him, pleading. "I want to go with you. Let's hunt Dies Irae together, we'll save Mother--"

"No!" Benedictus rose to fly again. "Find the salvanae; that's what I need you to do. Fly west. With Kyrie. Fly as far as you can--to the end of the world. That is your mission now."

With that Benedictus took off, leaving her below, heading into the eastern sky. Clouds and rain and wind lashed him. There were no salvanae, of course. Dragons with no human form? That was a myth. A bedtime story. But it was a myth that would send Agnus Dei and Kyrie flying west, far from Dies Irae, far from all this war and blood. If there was safety for them, it lay in the distant lands where perhaps Dies Irae's arm could not reach.

I might never see them again, Benedictus thought as he flew. *But maybe that's safest for them. I put my daughter in danger. I put Kyrie in danger. May they fly far, and fly well, and may they find safety on their quest.*

Where was Dies Irae? Benedictus could not see the man nor his griffin, could no longer hear griffin shrieks. But he knew where Dies Irae headed. He was taking Lacrimosa to Confutatis, to chain her, to torture her, to lure him--Benedictus--into danger. *It's me you want, Dies Irae. It's me you'll get. We'll face each other again in battle, and this time, one of us will die.*

As Benedictus flew, piercing the night, a chill ran through him. He knew that he most likely flew toward his death.

Fly west, Agnus Dei. Fly west with Kyrie. You two are the last hope for our race.

Benedictus howled in the night.

KYRIE ELEISON

Kyrie struggled to rise from the ground. Everything ached, and lava seemed to flow through his veins. He strained his muscles, but the pain flared, and he collapsed. Mud and moss squelched around him.

"Lacri... Lacrimosa--" he managed, gasping for breath. The pain was worst on his chest, where the quarrel had struck. The bolt burned, and blood seeped around it. The ilbane sent sluggish ache through Kyrie from horns to tail.

"Agnus Dei--" he said, struggling to utter each word through clenched teeth. He wanted to shout, but his voice was so hoarse and soft. "Benedictus--"

He coughed and struggled to breathe. With blazing agony, he raised his head and stared into the sky, but saw only blackness. Rain pattered against him. Kyrie heard nothing but wind, thunder, and creaking trees.

I have to save them. I have to fly. Gritting his teeth, he managed to push up one shoulder, then the other. With a grunt, he pushed himself to his feet, though the ilbane felt like shackles tugging him to the ground.

Lightning flashed, and Kyrie saw a dozen eyes blazing, staring at him from shaggy black forms. *Wolves.*

"Stay back!" he warned, but his voice was weak. He tried to breathe fire, but only a small puff of flame left his mouth. Lightning flashed again, growls rose, and the wolves were upon him.

Kyrie cried in pain. The wolves covered him, biting and clawing. Though ilbane burned, Kyrie rolled around, struggling to shake them off, but they moved like devils. The wolves on his back could not break his scales, but no scales covered his belly, and one wolf bit him there.

The new pain made Kyrie buck, and in his rage, he blew fire at the wolf. The beast caught flame and fell off his belly, howling. Kyrie swiped his claws at the blazing wolf, tossing it into the grass. Soon the grass too caught fire and burned around Kyrie. The other wolves howled and fled.

The pain and fear were enough to let Kyrie limp forward, flap his wings, and fly a hundred feet. He landed, aching, wings stiff, and kept limping.

"Agnus Dei!" he cried hoarsely. "Benedictus!"

Where were they? Were they dead? Had more griffins arrived? Kyrie cursed himself; he had fallen first, had flown clumsily, had let Dies Irae shoot him down. He clenched his jaw, wanting nothing more than to find Dies Irae and kill him. *If I catch him, I'm going to rip off his other arm, then beat him to death with it.*

"Agnus Dei!" he called out in the night. Wolf howls answered him. Thunder boomed and the rain grew even stronger, pattering against him. Hail rattled against his scales. He wanted to blow fire, a beacon for the others, but could bring none to his breath. When lightning flashed, he saw only clouds. No dragons, no griffins.

"Agnus Dei!" His voice was only a hoarse call; he doubted it carried a hundred yards.

The wind slammed against him, carrying a whimper.

Kyrie stiffened and gazed into the darkness.

The whimper sounded again. He thought he heard a voice calling, distant and weak.

"Who's there?" Kyrie cried, but his voice was only a whisper. He began to trudge forward, slipped into the mud, shoved himself up, and kept limping. His wings hung uselessly at his sides. "Benedictus? Agnus Dei?"

"Pup!" came a cry from ahead.

Kyrie felt his eyes moisten. He laughed, as horrible as everything was. "Agnus Dei!"

He tried to run toward her voice, fell, and groaned in pain. He struggled to rise, fell again, and reached out into the darkness.

Dragon claws reached out and clutched him.

"Agnus Dei!"

"Pup!"

And then she was upon him, embracing him, weeping. She was hurt, and Kyrie felt his anger bubble. Fire burned in her nostrils, and in its light, he saw blood trickle down her neck.

"Where's Benedictus?" Kyrie asked, hoarse.

Agnus Dei trembled. "He went after Mother. We have to find the salvanae, Kyrie! We have to. Only they can help us now. Only they can help us save Mother and Father. We must find them. We must!"

She struggled to her feet and kicked off the ground. Her wings flapped, she flew a few yards, then crashed to the ground. She raised her head weakly, looked at him with pained eyes, and whispered, "We have to."

Her eyes rolled back, and she collapsed.

Kyrie crawled toward her and embraced her. She still lived; he could feel her chest rise and fall. The rain fell upon them. Kyrie managed to pull himself above her, shielding her from the rain. In a few hours, he knew, the ilbane's pain would die, and they would fly again.

It would be a long, cold night.

AGNUS DEI

Strange dreams filled Agnus Dei's sleep.

She walked on human legs, but had a dragon's head. The heavy, scaly head wobbled on her human body, the thin body of a child, a child lost in a burning forest. Ash flew around her like the ghosts of butterflies, and shattered columns littered the forest floor. Though the trees were burned, dry leaves fell from them, gold and orange and rufous, gliding to fizzle into steam upon hitting the ground.

"Mother!" Agnus Dei cried, but her voice was hoarse, beastly, the shriek of a dragon. She clutched her scaly head with soft hands, tears in her eyes. "Mother!"

Ahead she saw a ruined palace--the palace of Father, the Vir Requis King. Its columns and walls had fallen, and scattered fires burned where statues had stood. Skeletons littered the ruins, all with human bodies and dragon heads, the skulls glaring at her, turning to follow as she walked.

"Mother!" she cried again, a twisted shriek. *I am a creature, a freak, a thing not human nor dragon.* She tried to turn all dragon, or all human, but could not.

"Look at the monster!" came voices from ahead, and Agnus Dei started. A group of Osanna's soldiers stood ahead atop a fallen column, clad in steel, their capes billowing though there was no breeze. Above in the skies, countless griffins streamed, row by row of them, silent, flying without flapping their wings.

"I'm not a monster!" she replied, but her words came out a horrible shriek, a sound like a dying hawk. As the soldiers laughed, a scream came from the sky, and Agnus Dei looked up to see a griffin clutching her mother. The griffin was the size of the whole sky, casting a shadow across the ruins. Mother seemed so small in its talons, like a house lizard in the clutches of an owl.

"Mother!" Agnus Dei tried to cry, but again only a screech left her mouth. The griffin holding Mother turned and flew away, vanishing into the distance. Agnus Dei tried to follow, but the soldiers shot flaming arrows at her, and she caught fire.

"Mother!" she cried, burning, and fell into wet grass.

"Agnus Dei," spoke a voice in her ear, and she felt a hand on her head.

She rolled around, trying to extinguish the flames. Wet grass squelched beneath her. "No, no. Please no! Leave me alone, I'm burning." Tears flowed down her cheeks, and she wondered if they could put out the flames.

"Agnus Dei, wake up. You're having a nightmare."

She opened her eyes, panting, and saw Kyrie above her. He had taken human form, and looked like a drowned cat, muddy and bloody and wet. The sun was rising, casting pink and red light across a soggy field.

Agnus Dei leaped to her feet. She realized that she had taken human form in her sleep, possibly when trying to shift in her nightmare. She looked to the sky, seeking Mother or Father, seeking griffins. Nothing but clouds and sunbeams filled the sky. She spun to face Kyrie.

"What happened?" She heard anger in her voice, and she narrowed her eyes. She pushed muddy hair back from her face. Her clothes too were caked with mud, grass, and blood.

Kyrie stared to the east, eyes dark. "Dies Irae flew east, taking Lacrimosa. Benedictus followed." He tightened his fists. "I tried to follow too, but... the ilbane. It was too much. I... I passed out. You did too." He trembled and his face was red.

Agnus Dei jumped into the air, shifted into a dragon so quickly that her head spun, and flapped her wings. Hovering, she turned to look at Kyrie. "Come! We fly."

Kyrie hesitated, standing below in human form.

"Come on!" She growled. "What are you waiting for?"

"I...." He frowned. "Agnus Dei, are you sure we can catch Dies Irae? Free Lacrimosa? He has armies, Agnus Dei. Armies. Tens of thousands of griffins. I want to rescue Lacrimosa." His eyes were suddenly moist. "More than anything. But how could we? If we fly east, aren't we flying to death?"

Agnus Dei growled and blew flames toward the clouds. "You pup. We're not flying east. I know I can't save Mother by dying. We're flying *west*, pup. We're flying to get the salvanae. And then we too will have armies." She snarled. "We fly."

She flapped her wings, shooting into the west. She heard a roar behind her, a dragon's roar, and soon Kyrie flew beside her, a great beast of blue scales. They left the ground far below and flew hidden between the clouds. The clouds were sparse this morning, dispersing after the stormy night, and Agnus Dei found herself flying in and out of blue skies. Anyone could see them here, she knew, but she narrowed her eyes and kept flying. She dared not walk in human form, not as Mother and Father were in danger. Walking was slow; as a dragon, she could fly hundreds of leagues a day.

She looked at Kyrie. He seemed to be thinking the same thing. Whenever they emerged from cloud cover, he narrowed his eyes, tightened his jaw, scanned the ground and sky, but kept flying.

I'm glad you're here with me, Kyrie, she thought. The thought surprised her. She was a loner. She needed nobody else. For years, she had prided herself on fierceness, strength, independence. *Are you growing soft?* she asked herself, but when she looked at Kyrie again, she understood. *Kyrie is like me; young, fiery, the last youth of an endangered species.*

Kyrie noticed she was staring and met her gaze. Concern filled his eyes. "Do you think there really are salvanae?" he said, the wind whipping his words. "That it's not just a legend?"

She bared her fangs. "Of course there are salvanae." She growled, blew fire, and clawed the sky, because inside her dread swirled. Ice filled her belly, and a shiver ran along her spine. If there were no salvanae, there was no hope. She would never save her parents. She would never defeat Dies Irae.

At the thought of Mother in prison, Agnus Dei felt a lump in her throat. She could imagine griffin talons scratching Mother, spears piercing her, ilbane burning her. Would Dies Irae kill her? Torture her? Agnus Dei couldn't help it--tears fled her eyes and flew back across her cheeks.

"Agnus Dei," Kyrie said, voice almost drowned under the wind. "Agnus Dei, I... I'm sorry about what happened. But Benedictus... I've seen him fight, Agnus Dei. He is amazing. I've never seen such a warrior. And he's after Dies Irae. He's flying to save Lacrimosa. If anyone in the world can do it, it's your old man."

She looked at him, tears still in her eyes. Clouds and sunbeams streamed between them. "If he's still alive."

"He is," Kyrie said, but uncertainty filled his voice.

The final clouds vanished, and they flew in clear skies. The land was wild below, covered with brambles and twisted oaks. Boulders jutted like teeth from tall grass. Rivulets glistened, and Agnus Dei saw a herd of deer raise their heads from the water, look up at them, and begin to flee. Agnus Dei was hungry, and her stomach growled, but she dared not swoop to hunt. Eating would delay her, and Agnus Dei wanted to fly, to cross thousands of leagues far into the misty realms of the west, lands beyond the maps of men and Vir Requis.

"Let's fly higher," Kyrie said. "We're too easy to spot here. If we fly high enough, we might appear as great birds."

She snorted. "You maybe, pup. I would never pass for a bird."

Still she flew upward. Kyrie flew by her, eyes narrowed, jaw clenched. They shot up in a straight line so fast, her stomach churned, her head ached, and spots danced before her eyes. But she kept flying. Soon they were so far up, she could barely breathe, and the thin air chilled her. When she looked down, the land was so distant, she could make out no trees or boulders or bushes, only patches of green and brown in all shades: bright green like fresh leaves, and deep gray-green like old forests, and brown like the barks of oaks, and pale green like the leaves of birches back in Requiem. The streams and rivers were but strands of silver, glinting. She had never flown so high.

Kyrie slapped her with his tail. "Fly straight," he called over the roaring wind, "and breathe well. If your head spins, or your eyes go dark, we'll go lower."

She growled at him. "I don't need flying lessons from a pup. Come on. See if you can catch up."

Agnus Dei flew as fast as she could, like she would as a girl when fleeing her scolding parents. As a child, none could keep up with her, not even the bigger kids, but Kyrie flew beside her the whole time. She tried to fly faster, to beat him, but could not. *Hot shot,* she thought with a snort. *Hot pup.*

Osanna moved beneath them, endless lands of wilderness, an empire stretching across the known world. *But there is a land beyond Osanna,* Agnus Dei thought. There had to be more lands. Had to! The world could not be just Osanna, just the realms of Dies Irae and his griffins. Once there had been other lands--Gilnor in the south, snowy Fidelium the north, and Leonis across the sea. Once there had been a land called Requiem, too, a land of marble columns among birch trees, a land where dragons flew.

Requiem lay in ruins now, forgotten, her glow drowned under Osanna's fire. But she had once stood; Agnus Dei remembered. She would never forget the courts of Requiem.

Like there was a Requiem, there is a Salvandos too, a land far in the western mists of legend. Agnus Dei nodded as she flew. Salvandos was real. She knew it with every heartbeat, every breath. This land would not have fallen under Osanna's rule.

They flew for hundreds of leagues before Agnus Dei's head began to spin, and they had to dive down. She saw no towns, only a forest and grasslands where deer grazed. She and Kyrie landed in the grass, caught a deer, and ate silently. They drank from a stream. Agnus Dei's wings, lungs, and heart ached, but she dared not rest for more than a few moments. Then she was flying again, Kyrie at her side.

"You look tired, pup," she said to him.

He grunted, flapping stiff wings beside her. "I can keep up with you." He snorted fire at her. "Kitten."

"We'll see, little puppy."

They flew until nightfall, the most Agnus Dei had ever flown in one day. They must have crossed a thousand leagues, moving so far from Sequestra Mountains, so far from the marble city of Confutatis where Dies Irae lived. In the darkness, they found a forest and shifted into human form.

"It's best we sleep as humans," Agnus Dei said. "Just in case Dies Irae has dragon hunters roaming the woods."

Oaks, elms, and birches rustled around them like ghosts in the night. The air smelled like mold and earth, cold in her lungs. They had no blankets, so they curled up on the ground, holding each other for warmth. Kyrie smelled like grass and wind and clouds, and she clung to him in the darkness, her face against his chest. He began to stroke her hair, but then his hand stilled, and he snored softly.

I miss you, Mother, Agnus Dei thought and tears fled her eyes. *I miss you, Father.* She shivered against Kyrie, more lost and lonely than she'd ever felt. Flying all day had left her stiff, sore, and exhausted, but she couldn't sleep. In the darkness, she kept seeing Dies Irae chaining, stabbing, and torturing her mother.

"I'll save you, Mother," she whispered. "I'll find the salvanae, you'll see."

The trees rustled and wind moaned. An owl hooted. Agnus Dei wondered if wolves or bears filled these woods, or worse--men. She shivered and wept for a long time, grateful that Kyrie slept and couldn't see her weakness. When he peeked at her, then closed his eyes again, she realized that he feigned sleep to spare her embarrassment, and that soothed her. Finally, nestled against him, she fell into slumber.

LACRIMOSA

Lacrimosa did not remember losing consciousness. She did not remember the sun rising. She did not remember landing in this rocky field. Last thing she remembered was a starless night, her husband and daughter beside her, then--she grimaced to recall it--searing pain and griffin talons.

Where am I?

She gazed around, eyes blurry. She was still in dragon form, and everything hurt. Boots stomped around her head, spurred leather boots with steel tips. Lacrimosa tried to raise her head from the ground, but could not. A chain bound her neck down, she realized, and more chains bound her body. The boots stirred up dust, and she coughed and blinked.

"The creature!" called a voice, the voice of a young man, a soldier. "The creature is waking up."

She could see only his boots; their steel tips had skulls engraved upon them. He sounded like a youth, and Lacrimosa felt a deep sadness that Dies Irae should infect youth with his hatred. More boots raced toward her, and Lacrimosa cried out. Several pointy objects, spears or sticks, jabbed her sides, her back, her tail. She roared and tried to raise her head, but could not, and her roar was muffled. She tried to blow fire, but an iron muzzle held her mouth closed.

"The creature is struggling, yeah?" said one soldier and laughed, and more laughter sounded. Boots kicked Lacrimosa, their steel jabbing, and tears filled her eyes.

"Please," she tried to whisper, but could not speak through the muzzle. The soldiers laughed and kept kicking and jabbing her.

She wanted to shift, to take human form, to try and escape her chains, but dared not. As a dragon, her scales offered some protection. If she became human, the boots and spears could kill her. She remained chained, beaten, spat on. The torture seemed to last forever, an eternity of pain, leaving her squirming and unable to beg for mercy. Finally--it must have been ages before it happened--a voice spoke over the soldiers' laughter.

"Enough."

It was only a cold word, spoken softly, but at once the boots and spears ceased their torture. The boots backed off, slammed together in attention, and one soldier cried out, "The Commander, his lordship Dies Irae, Light of Osanna!"

As the dust settled, Lacrimosa moaned and blinked feebly. She could still not raise her head, and saw only the men's boots and dust, and droplets of her blood upon the ground. A new pair of boots strode between the soldiers, but these boots were not leather. They were made of golden Vir Requis scales--the rarest color--and steel claws grew from their tips, like the claws of a dragon. *Dies Irae's boots,* Lacrimosa knew.

For a long time, Dies Irae merely stood above her, and though she could not see his face, she felt his eyes boring into her. Then he turned to face his men. "All right, men, you've had your fun. This beast must reach Confutatis alive. If we reach my city, and the weredragon is dead, it will be your hides. Understood?"

"Yes, Commander!" a dozen voices shouted together.

"Leave us," Dies Irae said, and the boots marched away.

For a long time, Lacrimosa lay on the ground, struggling not to whimper. His boots faced away from her, as if he still watched his men depart, or maybe gazed upon his camp in reflection. Finally he turned back toward her, placed his boot under her chin, and forced her head back painfully. Lacrimosa grimaced, the muscles in her neck creaking, and found herself staring up at Dies Irae.

He looked down upon her, cloaked in samite, his armor bearing the jeweled likeness of a griffin. His visor was raised, and Lacrimosa could see his face--a hard face, golden and cruel, so much like the face of Benedictus, but colder. His eyes stared at her, ice blue, and she shivered under his gaze.

"Hello, Lacrimosa," he said. "Hello, sister-in-law."

She could not speak for the muzzle around her mouth, nor had she any words to say to him.

"How is Agnus Dei?" he asked, his boot still under her chin, its steel claws painfully close to piercing her. "How is my daughter?"

Lacrimosa growled, and smoke rose from her nostrils. How dared he? Fury and pain bloomed inside her, a hundred times more powerful than when the men tortured her. She struggled against her chains, but could not free herself, and only froze when she felt the claws of his boots press closer against her. She froze but fumed, a growl in her throat. *Agnus Dei is not your daughter, snake,* she thought. *She is everything like Benedictus and nothing like you. There is nothing pathetic, base, and cruel to her, and you are all pathetic cruelty. I will kill you, Dies Irae, or my husband will.*

It was as if he heard her thoughts. "She is my daughter, sweetness. I remember that day in the woods. That day you surrendered to me. You want to kill me now. I see that in your eyes. You may think, even, that you *can* kill me, or that your husband can. Yes, I imagine that he will emerge from hiding now, that he will fly to Confutatis on some bold rescue mission. I am sure he is flying now in pursuit. I will kill him, Lacrimosa. I will kill him, but I will not kill you, and I will not kill our daughter. No. You two will live."

The way he said it, Lacrimosa knew: Benedictus was getting the sweeter deal.

She growled again, and blew flames from her nostrils, but Dies Irae only laughed. He pulled back his boot, letting her head hit the ground with a thud. He marched away. Soon Lacrimosa heard the cries of griffins, the thud of their wings and the scratching of their talons, and the scurrying of soldiers as they gathered their camp.

Griffin wings fluttered above, a shadow covered her, and talons grabbed her. Dies Irae cried "Fly!" above her, and the griffin lifted her. The ground grew far below her, and a hundred griffins flapped wings.

They flew over fields and forests, and over marble cities where statues of Dies Irae glittered. They flew over mountains and lakes. They flew over Requiem Forest, where the ruins of the Vir Requis courts lay burned and toppled, and when Lacrimosa saw her homeland below, she shed tears.

They flew, a hundred griffins, a bound Vir Requis, crossing hundreds of leagues, heading to the Marble City, to Confutatis, to Dies Irae's home.

Fly west, Agnus Dei, Lacrimosa thought, willing the words into her daughter's mind. *Fly away from here, fly to find your true dragons, fly with Kyrie into distant lands. And my sweet husband, I pray that you too flee, that you too fly west, though I know you're coming here, that you're following.*

That last thought made fear wash over her, colder and crueler than any fear she'd ever known. As the talons clutched her, and Dies Irae barked commands above, Lacrimosa shut her eyes and trembled.

BENEDICTUS

Benedictus cursed as he flew.

He cursed such foul words, he thought birds might fall dead from the sky, and the clouds themselves wilt. He cursed his old bones, and the wound on his chest that ached in this high, cold air above the clouds. He cursed himself for sleeping while Dies Irae had kidnapped Lacrimosa. Most of all, he cursed his torn wing; it meant he flew so much slower than griffins, flew so slowly as Dies Irae bore Lacrimosa to imprisonment and torture.

"You got what you wanted, brother," he said as he flapped that wobbly, torn wing. The clouds streamed around him. "You got me out of hiding. I'm flying to meet you again."

He knew what he must do. He knew what he should have done years ago. He would meet Dies Irae, kill the man, and steal back the Griffin Heart. With the amulet, he could reclaim the griffins. With the amulet, he could topple Confutatis, that city of marble and gold and malice. With the amulet, he could save Lacrimosa, save his children, create a world safe for Vir Requis.

"I will face you again, brother, and kill you. I spared you last time. No more."

Benedictus sighed, a deep sigh that felt close to a sob. Were these but fantasies? In his mind, he saw himself biting his brother, spilling his blood, killing him for all the evil he'd done. He saw himself with the Griffin Heart, the old hero, King Benedictus risen to reclaim his glory.

He sighed again. *Fantasies.* Deep inside his old heart, he knew that he flew to his death, a death at Lacrimosa's side. *I will die with you in the Marble City, Lacrimosa, but in our hearts, we will be in Requiem.*

He thought of his daughters--of Agnus Dei, who grew hunted, and of Gloriae, who grew molded into evil--and a tear fled Benedictus's eye. It had been so long since he'd cried, and when he looked down to see where his tear fell, he saw the ruins of Requiem. Once those forests had rustled with countless birch trees, and Vir Requis children raced between statues, and wise elders walked in robes upon cobblestones. Now the birches were burned, still blackened, and ivy grew over smashed columns. So many lay dead there--a million skeletons burned and broken. His parents, his wise old uncles, his fussy aunts, the cousins he would wrestle and hunt with, his friends... all dead now, all bones and ash.

Benedictus forced his gaze away. He narrowed his eyes and stared east. Confutatis lay beyond that horizon.

Dawn was rising, the sky was clear, and this was griffin country. *It's too dangerous to fly in the open,* Benedictus thought.

As if to answer his thought, shrieks sounded below. Benedictus stared down to see three griffins upon a fortress.

Benedictus cursed. He tried to fly faster, but could not. As he watched, riders leaped onto the griffins, and they flew toward him.

Benedictus flapped his wings as powerfully as he could, but his left wing blazed with pain, and he grunted. "So much for out-flying them," he muttered.

He roared, reached out his claws, and then the griffins were upon him.

He took out the first one with a blaze of flame. As it fell burning, the other two griffins attacked, one at each side. Benedictus slammed his tail into the right griffin. He hit its rider, sending the man tumbling to the ground. The left griffin bit Benedictus's shoulder, and he roared.

He clawed the griffin, etching red lines down its flank. The right griffin was riderless, but still attacked, and Benedictus howled as its talons scratched him. He lashed his tail, bit, and clawed. He hit one griffin, and it tumbled. The second bit again, and Benedictus roared and blew fire. It caught flame, and Benedictus bit into its roasting flesh, spat out a chunk, and kicked.

The griffin's rider thrust his lance. It dug into Benedictus's shoulder, and he growled, clawed, and snapped the man's head. The body slumped in the saddle. Benedictus clawed again, and the griffin fell dead from the sky.

Benedictus looked around. Were the griffins all dead?

No. The first griffin he'd burned was still alive, fur and feathers blazing. It shot toward him, screeching, its rider also burning and screaming. The man had removed his armor, and his skin peeled and blazed. His eyes had melted, but his mouth was still open and screaming. Still the griffin flew at Benedictus, talons outstretched.

Benedictus blew more fire. The blaze hit the griffin, pushing it back. It tumbled a few feet, then again flew at Benedictus. It looked like some roasted animal now, smoking and furless, its skin red and black and blistering. The beak was open and screeching, the rider writhing and screaming, a ball of fire and blood.

Benedictus howled and lashed his tail, driving its spikes into the griffin, and finally it tumbled toward the ground. It fell like a comet, still screeching, until it hit the ground and was silent.

Benedictus turned and kept flying after Lacrimosa.

"Damn the fire, and damn the blood," he said, jaw tight. He had seen so many burned this way, so many dying in agony. What was one more to the weight already on his soul? His wounds ached, blood dripped down his shoulder, but Benedictus ignored the pain. What were more scars to those he already bore, and what was more pain to the weight of his memories?

He gritted his teeth and flew.

Distant figures flew a league ahead, mere specks. Benedictus narrowed his eyes. More griffins, he knew. He didn't have to get any closer to know these were no birds, but riders Dies Irae had sent after him. Benedictus cursed under his breath and turned south. Storm clouds gathered there, maybe two leagues away. They would serve as cover. It was out of his way, but clear skies swarmed with griffins. If Benedictus wanted to reach Confutatis alive, he'd have to take the long route.

"I'm sorry, Lacrimosa," he whispered. He flew south toward those storm clouds, glancing east toward the griffins until he no longer saw them. "I'm sorry, love of my life. You'll have to hold on a little longer, but I'm coming for you. I'll be there soon."

His wing ached more than ever, a searing pain that drove down his entire left side. Soon Benedictus flew through rain and thunder. He told himself that the drops on his cheeks were only rain, not tears. Again, as with his hope of defeating Dies Irae and saving his family, he knew that he was lying to himself.

DIES IRAE

As they flew, Dies Irae couldn't help it. He kept looking over his shoulder, scanning the distance for Benedictus. At times he thought he saw the beast, but it was only a distant vulture, or another griffin on patrol, and once--Dies Irae shook his head to remember it--even a crow had made him squint and stare and hope.

Soon twilight fell, and Benedictus had not caught up. *Of course not,* Dies Irae told himself with a grunt. His brother still had a torn wing; he could not fly as fast as these griffins. It was pathetic. Benedictus, great King of Requiem, was but a slow, lumbering beast.

Should I send griffins after him, hunt him down? No. He will come to me. He will follow.

The setting sun gilded the mountains below. Their western slopes, snowy and undulating, glimmered like beaten gold. Their eastern slopes melted into mist, deep blue and purple strewn with black lines where rocks broke the snow. Yellow and orange wisps ran across the sky, and the clouds burned. *The glory of Osanna,* Dies Irae thought, admiring the masterpiece that was his empire. *My land, beautiful, no longer tainted by the scaled beasts that once covered its skies.*

But of course, some weredragons remained. A moan sounded below, and Dies Irae looked down. Volucris still clutched Lacrimosa in his talons. Her scales were dented, and blood seeped from nicks and scratches that covered her. *Why does she not take human form?* Dies Irae wondered. *Why does she remain this beastly lizard?* Dies Irae wanted to see her human shape again--

ached for it. He remembered that night in Requiem Forest, how he'd pressed his body against hers, grabbed it, squeezed it. His blood boiled at the thought. He wanted that human body again, to clutch it, crush it, hurt it. He'd wanted this for years.

"Down, Volucris," Dies Irae said and tugged the reins. The sun dipped behind a western peak, and though Dies Irae was tempted to fly through the night, he would not. His griffins needed rest. So did his men. And Dies Irae wanted something this night, wanted it now. He looked back down at Lacrimosa, imagined her human form, and licked his lips.

He found a snowy valley and began to descend. His men followed, leading their griffins down in spirals, until talons kicked snow and men dismounted with creaking armor. Volucris tossed Lacrimosa down, and she rolled in the snow, hit a boulder, and moaned. Chains still bound her limbs and wings, and a muzzle clutched her mouth.

"Set camp," Dies Irae told his men. "We spend the night."

His men scurried to raise tents, tether and feed griffins, kindle campfires, and distribute rations. As they bustled across the valley, and griffins gulped chunks of raw cattle, Dies Irae walked toward Lacrimosa. His boots crunched the snow, their golden scales glinting. A cold wind blew, rattling the tents and rustling Dies Irae's cape. He smiled thinly when Lacrimosa saw him approach and whimpered. Snow whitened her chains, and droplets of blood speckled the snow around her. Dies Irae saw the lines of Volucris's claws across her flanks, and his smile widened.

"Hello, Lacrimosa," he said when he reached her.

She stared up and said nothing. A tear streamed down her cheek.

"Darling," Dies Irae said. He placed his good hand upon her head. Her scales were cold, surprisingly smooth, shimmering like mother-of-pearl. "Will you not take human form? I've waited long years to see you again."

She stared up at him. Still she said nothing.

Dies Irae pursed his lips, looked aside, then with a sudden movement, he kicked Lacrimosa's head. She cried out and fresh tears sprung into her eyes. Blood dripped between the iron bars of her muzzle.

"Turn into a human," he said.

She snarled, smoke leaving her muzzle. Finally she spoke, voice muffled behind the iron. "I know what you'll do if you see my human form. I will not allow it. I will not let you rape--"

"I will not rape you," Dies Irae interrupted her. He snorted. "Look at you. Bloody. Covered in ash, snow, and mud. What kind of unclean creature do you think I am? I have my standards, Lacrimosa. Once you were fair; a princess in silk and jewels, young and beautiful, and yes, I took you then. Look at you now. Old. Filthy. What man would touch you?"

She stared at him, eyes blazing, and fire glowed inside her muzzle. Her tears dried, and her stare blazed with such hatred, that Dies Irae snickered. He raised his foot to kick her again.

Lacrimosa flinched, looked away, and shifted.

Her wings pulled into her back, her scales vanished, and she shrunk in size. Her chains and muzzle, shaped to fit a dragon, fell into the snow. She lay before him, bloody and wet, her silvery dress tattered. Her hair like moonlight covered her face.

Dies Irae was surprised by the force of his memories. They hit him so hard, he took a step back. Requiem rushed back into him, not Requiem today of ruins and ash, but the Requiem where he'd lusted for Lacrimosa, a land of passion and anger.

"Stand up," he said softly.

Lacrimosa raised her head to look at him, and Dies Irae saw that she was still beautiful. He hadn't seen her in... what was it? Fifteen years? And yet her beauty had only grown, even as blood and dirt caked her, even as her hair was tangled and her dress torn. He stared at the tatters of that dress, and at the flesh he could see through it. Her left thigh was bare, and he could see the tops of her breasts, pale and small. Yes, she was filthy, bloody, deplorable, but he wanted to renege on his promise, to grab her, hurt her, take her right there.

"You promised," she whispered to him.

He spat. "Stand up."

Legs trembling, she struggled to rise, and finally stood in the snow. She glared at him, chin raised, snowflakes in her hair. Her body shook; from fear or cold, Dies Irae did not know.

"You promised," she whispered again.

He grabbed her arm, digging his fingers into her white skin. "I lied," he said.

She glared and bared her teeth, as if she were still a dragon with fangs to flaunt. "If you touch me," she said, voice strained, "I will turn into a dragon. I will become one as you're in your passion, as you're inside me, and I will kill you."

Dies Irae hesitated. He hadn't considered that. It was possible, he conceded; she had nothing to lose. If he dragged her into his tent, and took her there, he'd be vulnerable. If she became a beast, her claws and fangs could tear him apart.

"Not if I drug you with ilbane," he said. "I'll fill your mouth with it, like I did that day."

She barked a laugh. "Try it then. I'm no longer fifteen, Irae. I've suffered enough ilbane to shift though its pain. You've given me this strength."

Damn it. Anger flared in Dies Irae, and he shouted and slapped her, knocking her down. Fresh blood speckled the snow. He stormed off, leaving her there, bloody.

"Chain her," he ordered his men. "And keep guard, three griffins around her at every moment. If she escapes, I kill every one of you."

Men and griffins rushed toward Lacrimosa, and Dies Irae entered the tent his men had raised for him. Inside the embroidered walls, he fumed and paced.

"You made a mistake, Lacrimosa," he said, though none were there to hear. "You will pay for it. You will suffer. Once we reach Confutatis, you will suffer more than any weredragon ever has."

Outside he heard her cry in pain, and he smiled, a mirthless smile.

The tent flaps flew open, and Gloriae stormed inside. She carried her helmet under her arm, and her cheeks were flushed--from anger or cold, Dies Irae did not know. *Probably both,* he thought.

"Let me kill her," Gloriae demanded, eyes flashing. "Let me kill the weredragon." Her chest rose and fell, and her hand trembled around the hilt of her drawn sword.

"In time," Dies Irae said.

"Now. She killed Mother. I will avenge her." Tears filled Gloriae's eyes. "Please, Father. I will kill her like you've taught me to kill."

She must never know, Dies Irae told himself. *She must never know that Lacrimosa did not kill her mother... but* is *her mother.* The truth would crush her, Dies Irae knew. If Gloriae learned she was descended from monsters, it would be a pain too great to bear. He would spare her this. He would keep Lacrimosa gagged, he decided, to stop her from speaking the truth.

He gestured at an upholstered chair in the corner. "Gloriae, sit down."

She shook her head wildly. "I will not. Father, I--"

"Sit down, Gloriae," he said again, a little more firmly.

She held her breath, bit her lip, seemed about to scream, then finally stormed to the chair and sat down. She still held her sword raised.

Dies Irae sat beside her in a second chair. "Daughter, you know that I love you."

"And I love you, Father." Her voice was ice over fire.

"If you love me, you'll stay away from Lacrimosa. You will not kill her. You will not remove her muzzle to speak with her. You will not even approach her."

Gloriae rose so quickly, she knocked back her chair. It hit the tent wall, and a flurry of snow blew in. "I refuse."

"Gloriae. Sit down." This time his voice was cold, and he raised his mace. When she was a child, he would never beat her. Instead, he would whip her handmaiden, bloodying the girl as Gloriae watched and bit her lip, stifling tears. The handmaiden's back still bore scars, and Gloriae still harbored a fear of him. Face pale as the snow, Gloriae righted her chair and sat again.

Dies Irae touched a strand of her hair. So golden, so beautiful. It was like his own hair. Inwardly, Dies Irae snorted. And Benedictus thought he was her father? That a beast like him could beget a child as fair as Gloriae? Benedictus could keep Agnus Dei, that beastly child of scales and flame. Gloriae was pure.

"You are beautiful, my child, and your spirit is still soft."

Gloriae glared. "My spirit is cold and strong as my blade."

"It is still soft. The weredragon would ensorcell you. She might even inflict her disease upon you, so that you too grow scales, wings, and turn into a lizard."

Gloriae narrowed her eyes and gasped. "They can spread their curse?"

Dies Irae nodded, forcing a sad expression to his face. "Most cannot, but Lacrimosa is fouler than her kin. She killed your mother, and so your soul is vulnerable to her black magic. I fear for you, daughter."

Gloriae snarled. "I don't fear her." She raised her blade. "She will fear my sword."

"Do it for my own fear, then," Dies Irae said. "I confess that I'm afraid. Please, Daughter. I grow old. In only several winters, I will be sixty, did you know? An old man. You are the light of my life, Gloriae. All that I do, all the wars I fight, all the cities I build... it is for you. I try to clean this world, to turn it into a empire of light and goodness, so that when I die--"

"Father!"

"Hear me out, Gloriae. I will die someday, maybe in a year, maybe in twenty years, but I will die. And then you will sit upon the Ivory Throne. I want to leave this a good world for you to rule. If you should fall to Lacrimosa's magic, I... I could not bear it."

"I will not fall to her curse."

Dies Irae caressed her hair with his mace. "You are brave, Gloriae, but I am not. Not when it comes to your safety. So do an old man a favor. Don't kill Lacrimosa; not until she lures Benedictus to us. Don't speak to her. Leave my men to hurt her."

"But *I* want to hurt her."

"If you do, you will hurt me. Do you want to hurt me, daughter?"

Gloriae stared at him, green eyes icy, face expressionless, and Dies Irae saw the answer in her eyes. *Yes. She does.*

"I will not kill her yet," Gloriae finally said, staring into his eyes, not blinking. "I will let her live until Benedictus flies to rescue her, until we catch and kill him, and Kyrie Eleison, and Agnus Dei. I will keep our bait alive. But once we kill the others, then, Father... then I will hurt her like she hurt me. Then I will kill her like she killed Mother."

Not waiting for him to reply, Gloriae rose to her feet and stormed out of the tent. Snow flurried in, and Dies Irae stared at the embroidered cloth walls for a long time. Finally he spoke, as if she were still there to hear.

"Very well, Gloriae." He sighed, remembering that day in the forest, Lacrimosa's soft skin, her screams, her hair in his hands. "Very well. Then you may kill her."

KYRIE ELEISON

Kyrie had never felt more pain.

He and Agnus Dei had not touched ground in a day and night. Through darkness and hail, and sunlight over burning cloudscapes, they flew faster than wind, higher than mountains. Again the sun was setting, blazing orange and red over a sea of clouds, casting rays between the Vir Requis. How far had they flown since that night Lacrimosa fell captive? It must be close to three thousand leagues, Kyrie thought. Maybe more. He had never flown so fast, so far.

His wings ached. His lungs burned. His joints felt like rusty metal hinges. He looked at Agnus Dei. She flew beside him, her scales blazing red in the sunset. Her eyes stared forward, narrowed and fiery. Her fangs were bared. Yet Agnus Dei too needed rest, Kyrie knew. Pain lived on her face alongside her anger, and her wings looked stiff and aching.

"Let's rest!" he called to her over the wind.

She glowered. "Not until we find the salvanae."

"Maybe they're below the clouds," Kyrie said. "Let's land and look for them on the ground."

She gave him a look that said, *Nice try, pup, but no cookie.*

Kyrie attempted to think of another argument, found none, and resigned himself to grabbing Agnus Dei and pulling her down.

"Let go!" she cried as they tumbled through the clouds.

But Kyrie would not let go. He wrapped himself around her and swooped through the clouds, into clear sky, and toward the earth. She wriggled in his grasp, and he tightened his grip, eyes narrowed and teeth clenched. Luckily she was too weary to break free.

No trees covered the land, and the grass was thin and yellow. Hills rose from the earth, round like upside down bowls on a tabletop. A stream ran between them, gray under the clouds, and deer drank from it. Still pulling Agnus Dei, Kyrie landed by the water. The deer snorted and fled, hoofs kicking up dirt and grass.

"Let go, pup," Agnus Dei said, panting. She finally shook herself free from Kyrie. She looked to the sky, as if considering to take flight again, then shook her head and approached the stream. She drank deeply.

Kyrie joined her. He dipped his head underwater and drank. The water was icy, and it filled him with such goodness that he sighed. He drank until his belly bulged, then raised his dripping head from the water.

"I needed that," he said.

Agnus Dei gestured toward the next hill, which lay nearby. More deer stood there in the dusk, promising a meal. "I'm hungry," Agnus Dei said. "Feel like mutton?"

"Their meat is called venison," Kyrie said.

Agnus Dei rolled her eyes. "Now don't start that again."

They flew toward the hill where the deer grazed, and caught one before the others escaped. It was mostly skin and bones, and its meat was tough. After a day of no food, however, Kyrie wasn't complaining.

Agnus Dei swallowed her last bite and licked her lips. "Let's fly. Ready, pup?"

Lying on the ground, Kyrie turned his head toward her. He wanted to be ready. He wanted to fly, to find help, to find the salvanae. In his dreams, he saw himself leading an army of dragons to Confutatis, saving Lacrimosa, and avenging all those whom Dies Irae had killed. But were those only dreams? Kyrie sighed.

"What if there are no salvanae?" he whispered. "What if we're only chasing a myth?"

Agnus Dei's nostrils flared. Her eyes blazed, and flames escaped her lips. "Kyrie, you know how I feel. You know I believe."

Kyrie nodded. He wanted to believe too. After flying all of last night, however, he also ached for sleep. The thought of flying another night and day made his head, body, and soul hurt. Of course, that pain was nothing compared to what Lacrimosa must be enduring. Dies Irae would torture her; Kyrie knew that. He had to do something, anything, even if it was just chasing a dream.

"All right," he said. "Let's fly."

He struggled to his feet and stretched, his joints and wings aching. He looked at the setting sun; it would soon disappear behind the horizon. Kyrie sighed. It would be a long night.

Before he could take flight, however, a herd of deer upon a distant hill bugled. They began to run together, wailing. They fled toward Kyrie and Agnus Dei, as if mere dragons--hungry dragons who had just eaten one of them--were gentle compared to what chased them.

"What the--" Agnus Dei began, then her voice died and she stared.

Kyrie stared too. Four creatures emerged from behind a hill, dragon-sized and covered in bloodred fur. Bat wings grew from their backs, and their claws tore grass and earth. The beasts stared at Kyrie and Agnus Dei. Flames crackled in their eyes, and their fangs oozed drool. Their stench carried upon the wind, a stench like corpses. Lanburg Fields had smelled the same.

Kyrie growled and bared his fangs. Agnus Dei snorted a blast of fire. They stood side by side, silent and watching.

"Ugly buggers," Agnus Dei muttered to Kyrie.

"And smelly ones," Kyrie muttered back.

One of the four red beasts was larger than the others. A crest of black hair ran along its head and back, and three serrated horns grew from its brow. It took three steps forward, smoke rising from its nostrils. Saliva dripped from its maw.

"Are you griffins?" it asked, voice low, a growl like broken rocks.

"Not too bright, are they?" Agnus Dei whispered to Kyrie from the corner of her mouth. She then stared at the creature and raised her voice. "Griffins? Do we look like griffins? We hate those things. What are you?"

The creatures ignored her. The beast with the black crest, apparently their leader, snorted smoke. It licked its lips with two slobbery tongues.

"Are you dragons?" it asked with that low, crackling growl. The other three beasts growled too and scratched the ground, their claws red in the sunset.

"Dragons?" Kyrie said, narrowing his eyes. "We're Vir Requis. We seek the salvanae. Do you know where we can find them?"

The black-crested beast snarled and snapped its teeth. "You are Osanna stock. You may not pass the Divide. You may not enter Salvandos. We are dividers. We guard the Divide; it is holy. You have touched the Divide. Flee now, or you will die."

Kyrie took a step closer to the creature, this *divider*. Its stench was so powerful, he nearly gagged, but Kyrie forced himself to stare into its eyes.

"We must pass the Divide," he said. "We must enter Salvandos."

The dividers howled, a sound that shook the hills. Lightning slashed the sky, and dark clouds gathered. The chief divider snarled, eyes blazing, and took another step toward Kyrie. It now stood so close, it could claw Kyrie.

"No griffins may pass the Divide."

Kyrie gulped. The divider was sixty feet long; a good twenty feet longer than Kyrie. Muscles moved beneath its fur, and its claws glistened when lightning struck. Its tongues licked its chops again, dripping drool that burned the grass and sizzled, eating holes into the earth.

"I told you ugly buggers!" Agnus Dei said and stepped up beside Kyrie, flames leaving her nostrils. Her eyes blazed nearly as angrily as the divider's. "We're not griffins."

The dividers considered her. Their chief said, "You are dragons. No dragons or griffins may pass the Divide. We are dividers. The Divide is holy. Leave now, or we will feast upon you."

All four dividers licked their chops.

Agnus Dei rolled her eyes. She flapped her wings and said, "Oh, give me a break."

Then she took off and began to fly over the dividers' heads.

"Agnus Dei, no!" Kyrie shouted, ice flowing through him.

The dividers howled and leaped toward Agnus Dei, bat wings flapping.

Agnus Dei blew fire at them.

Kyrie cursed, kicked off the ground, and flew toward her.

The fire roared. It flowed over the dividers above, and then covered Kyrie. He shut his eyes, grunted, and veered left and out of the flames. The fire blackened the scales across his right side.

The dividers were blazing. If Kyrie's scales protected him from fire, the dividers' fur now crackled and burned. Kyrie expected them to die, or at least flee, but the fire seemed only to enrage them. They screamed, horrible sounds like slaughtered animals, and flew toward Agnus Dei. Their claws scratched and their teeth snapped.

"Hey!" Kyrie called. "Leave her! Take me on."

He swiped his tail at one blazing divider. He knocked it aside. The others were clawing at Agnus Dei, who was lashing her tail and snapping her teeth.

"Oh sure, save the damsel in distress, my hero pup," Agnus Dei called to him over the shrieking dividers. She lashed her tail and hit one divider, knocking it into a spin.

Two dividers turned toward Kyrie, maws open. Fire raced across them, raising sparks, but seemed not to slow them. They flew toward Kyrie. Kyrie lashed his tail and hit one, driving his tail's spikes deep into its side. The other bit Kyrie's shoulder. He howled. The divider's fangs pushed through his scales and into his flesh, and its fire blazed against Kyrie.

"Get off!" Kyrie grunted and shook, but the divider kept its fangs in his shoulder, shaking its head like a dog biting a bird. Kyrie shoved his claws into its side, grunting as its flaming fur burned him, and kept clawing until its innards spilled. Even in death, it kept its jaw locked on his shoulder. Kyrie could barely keep above the ground. The dead divider weighed more than him. Its entrails dangled.

"Agnus Dei!" he called. She was fighting above him. Scratches covered her, and five dividers surrounded her. *Five dividers?* Kyrie grunted. Where had more come from? Then he noticed that a dozen dividers now surrounded him.

"Damn it," Kyrie muttered. One flew toward him. Kyrie lashed his tail at it. The dead divider clung to his shoulder, jaw locked in its death bite, tugging him closer and closer to the ground. Kyrie growled, pulled its jaw open with all his might, and sent the body crashing down. Fresh blood spurted from his shoulder.

Kyrie was close to the ground now. Agnus Dei fought a good thousand feet above. Kyrie flapped his wings, shooting straight up, knocking through a crowd of dividers. They clawed and bit, and Kyrie clawed and bit back, shoving his way through them. Twenty flew around him. In the distance, he saw a hundred more flying toward the fray.

"Agnus Dei!" he shouted. "Let's get out of here!"

She was fighting above, scratching and biting and blowing fire. Her eyes blazed. Scratches covered her, and several of her scales were missing. A gash ran along her tail.

"Agnus Dei!" Kyrie cried. He blew fire at one divider, clawed another's face, and flew beside her. A hundred dividers surrounded them, a sea of red fur, fangs, and fire. Thunder boomed and lightning rent the sky.

"Hello, pup," Agnus Dei said as she fought. Blood trickled from her mouth. "What were you doing down there--taking a nap?"

Kyrie blocked a swipe of claws from a divider, clawed back, and grabbed Agnus Dei's shoulder. "Agnus Dei, this is no time for jokes. Come with me."

The dividers screamed around them, lashing their tails, and Kyrie grunted when one hit him. He wanted to blow fire, a Vir Requis's best weapon, but flames only enraged the dividers.

Agnus Dei shook him off. "We must enter Salvandos! I won't back down." She slashed at a divider, sending it crashing down, but one scratched her back. Her blood poured, and she cried in pain.

"Agnus Dei, come on!" Kyrie shouted, grabbed her again, and pulled her back. Maybe the pain of her wound changed her mind. She flew with him. They crashed through a dozen dividers, heading back toward Osanna.

The dividers followed, howling, bat wings flapping.

"We're back in Osanna!" Kyrie cried over his shoulder. "Leave us."

The black-crested divider leered. Its fur had burned off, revealing scraggly, blackened flesh covered with scratches and blood. Blood filled its mouth, and smoke rose from it. "You have touched the Divide," it said. "You will die."

The hundred dividers, eyes like raging stars, stormed forward.

Kyrie cursed under his breath, grabbed Agnus Dei, and pulled her with him. They flew east and down, moving close to the grass.

"Let go!" Agnus Dei demanded, squirming as she flew, trying to release his grasp. "I flee from no fight."

"I have an idea," Kyrie said. "Just do what I do."

Lightning crashed, and the clouds roiled. The dividers screamed, their bat wings churning the air. Kyrie flew behind a hill crowned with boulders. For a moment, he couldn't see the dividers behind him. The boulders shielded him and Agnus Dei from view.

Kyrie landed by a stream and turned human. His wounds ached even worse this way, and the deer meat grumbled in his belly.

Agnus Dei glared at him, still in dragon form. "What are you doing? They'll eat you."

"Agnus Dei, shift now!" he shouted.

She grunted, blew flames to the sky, and shifted into human form. She stood by him, her clothes tattered, her black hair a knotty mess.

A hundred dividers came roaring over the hill, flying east. They glanced down at the humans, barely registered them, and looked around in puzzlement.

"They went that way!" Kyrie shouted, pointing east.

The dividers howled. "Who are you?" their chief asked, its last patches of fur still burning.

"We're neither dragons nor griffins," Kyrie cried up to them. "We're only two-legged travelers. The dragons you seek fled east. You can still catch them. Fly, fly after them!"

The dividers hovered above them for a moment. It seemed like an eternity to Kyrie. Then they howled and flew east, a few still flaming.

Kyrie and Agnus Dei stood panting, watching them disappear into the distance.

"They're mean bastards, but they're dumb as dung beetles," she said. She sat down hard and took deep breaths. Blood dripped down her shoulder.

Kyrie collapsed onto the ground. His head spun, and his wounds ached.

Agnus Dei tore strips off her shirt, including both sleeves, and bound their wounds. Though Kyrie ached, and felt more weary than ever before, he couldn't help but notice Agnus Dei's exposed flesh. With her shirt mostly torn off, and her leggings tattered, only thin strips of cloth covered her. Her body was bloodied, bruised, and cut... but also tanned, lithe, and intoxicating. As Agnus Dei leaned over him, bandaging his shoulder, Kyrie's blood boiled. He gulped and looked away quickly.

"Cool it, pup," Agnus Dei said wryly. She tightened the cloth around his wound painfully enough that he winced. "Put your tongue back in your mouth before it hits the dirt."

Kyrie shut his mouth and muttered under his breath, face hot. He forced himself to stare at the ground rather than at Agnus Dei, but could still sense the mocking smile on her lips and in her eyes. Strangely, that look of hers, and that crooked smile, only boiled his blood hotter.

What was it about Agnus Dei? Kyrie had seen beautiful women before. Lacrimosa was beautiful, her beauty like starlight. Lady Mirum had been beautiful, a beauty like the sea. Gloriae was beautiful, a beauty of ice and snow. Yet Agnus Dei... she stirred something new inside Kyrie. She was no starlight nor sea nor snow; she was *fire*. And Kyrie liked fire.

"You're done," Agnus Dei said, bandaging his last wound. She punched his shoulder. "You okay?"

He nodded and looked back at her. "And you? You took a beating up there." Bruises and cuts covered her. The worst wound was behind her shoulder; it was a bleeding mess. "Let me help you with that."

He cleaned her wound with water from the stream, then bound it with cloth he tore from his shirt. Sweat covered her brow, and her jaw tightened when he bound her wound, but she made not a sound. When he was done, he wiped the sweat off her brow... and found himself smoothing her tangled hair. Despite its knots, her hair was soft, damp, and--

"What," she asked him, "do you think you're doing?"

He pulled his hand away, muttering. "You have blood in your hair."

She stared at him, eyes flashing. He stared back, jaw tightened. *Why should I look away? Let her stare at me with that fiery stare; it won't cow me.* She leaned forward, still staring, and grabbed the back of his head, painfully tugging a fistful of his hair. He grunted.

"You do too," she said, pulled his head toward her, and kissed him.

Her lips were soft and full, and her hand still clutched his hair, pulling it. Kyrie closed his eyes. He kissed her, head spinning, and placed his hand on the small of her back. She pushed him to the ground, and he grunted at the pain of his wounds, and then Agnus Dei was atop him, kissing him deeply, her tongue seeking.

The sun sank behind the hills, and the distant cries of beasts still carried on the wind, but Kyrie knew nothing but Agnus Dei, and fire, and her lips and body against him. Darkness and flame covered his world.

BENEDICTUS

Benedictus trudged through the snow, his hands pale and numb, his feet icy in his boots. He pulled his cloak close around him, shook snow out of his hair, and cursed again. He'd never felt such chill, both the chill that filled his body and the ice that filled his gut.

He wished he could fly. Walking like this was so slow, and every hour he delayed was an hour Lacrimosa suffered. But he dared not fly. Not with the griffins that filled the skies, the eyes in every town that watched for him.

"Lacrimosa," he whispered, plowing through the snow, his fists trembling from anger and cold. "I'm going to find you. Just hang in there, and I'll--"

Shrieks tore through his words. Griffins. Benedictus cursed and dived down, pulled his cloak over his head, and lay still. His cloak was coarse charcoal wool, now covered in snow. Benedictus knew that lying here, he could look like just another boulder. The snow filled his mouth, stung his face, and the griffins shrieked. They flew above every hour, their riders scanning the mountains, bearing crossbows and lances. Benedictus lay still, not even daring to breathe.

The griffins' cries came closer. Benedictus cursed again. *They're going to find me this time,* he thought and clenched his jaw. How many were there? He hadn't had time to look. A dozen? Twenty? Last time they flew above, he had counted seventeen. He could not beat that many. Not these days, old and lame. Not without Kyrie and Agnus Dei at his side.

The shrieks were so close now, they loosened snow from the mountainside. Chunks of the stuff hit Benedictus's back, heavy and icy. Benedictus tightened his fists. What if the falling snow became an avalanche, burying him? Lacrimosa would remain in captivity, Dies Irae torturing her for sport--

No. Benedictus shoved the thought away. *I'm going to live. I'm going to save Lacrimosa. And I'm going to save Gloriae too. I'm finally going to bring my daughter back.*

Griffin wings thudded above. Benedictus heard talons landing, kicking up snow. It wasn't fifty yards away. More talons landed, scraping snow and rocks. There were many griffins this time; at least twenty, maybe thirty. They cawed and scratched the ground.

Get up and fight, spoke a voice inside Benedictus. *You are King of Requiem, Benedictus the Black. You do not cower. You do not hide under a cloak. Get up and kill these bastards.*

"I saw something," spoke a voice ahead--one of the riders. "A man walking through the snow."

A griffin shrieked. Leather and metal moaned and chinked--saddles and armor. Scabbards clanged against cuisses. Benedictus heard the sound of a crossbow being drawn.

"Bah!" came another voice, deeper than the first. "I see nobody here. No man can survive these mountains. You saw a goat, that's all."

Rise up and fight them, spoke the voice in Benedictus's head. *I will not be caught cowering like a dog.* He gritted his teeth. *No. Stay still. You can't save Lacrimosa if you're dead.*

A griffin walked toward him; he could hear the talons sinking into the snow and scratching the stone beneath. It took all of Benedictus's willpower to stay still. He could feel the rider's gaze upon him, and Benedictus thanked the gods that their shrieks had loosened the snow on the mountainside. That snow now buried him.

The griffin's talons hit the ground inches from him. One talon, long and sharp as a sword, pierced the snow near his eye. Old blood coated it.

"I told you," came the deep voice from farther away. "There's nobody here. Come on, we're wanted back by nightfall."

The griffin above Benedictus lingered a moment longer. Then its rider spat noisily, Benedictus heard jingling spurs, and the griffin's talon pulled out from the snow, missing Benedictus's face by a hair's length. The griffins took off, wings thudding.

Benedictus breathed a sigh of relief. He remained under the snow for several long moments, then dug himself out. He was now drenched and colder than ever. He watched the griffins disappear into the horizon.

Benedictus hugged himself, but found no warmth. He craved a fire, but dared not light one, and he doubted he'd find firewood here anyway. More than anything, he wanted to fly. In dragon form, he could be in Confutatis within a week, could storm the city and save Lacrimosa. But no. He dared fly no more; during his last flight griffins had attacked within moments. The beasts filled these skies, tens of thousands watching the world.

"Be strong, Lacrimosa," he whispered. He knew she was still alive. Dies Irae would not kill her, not when he could torture her, use her to lure Benedictus to him. *It's me he wants most.*

Benedictus kept walking, shoving aside snow with his arms. He thought of Agnus Dei and Kyrie. Where were they? Were they safe in the west? Were they flying out of Osanna, heading into the realms of myth where no griffins flew? Benedictus did not know. They could be dead.

He lowered his head, grief and fear pulsing through him. With clenched teeth, he kept moving.

LACRIMOSA

She saw Confutatis at dawn, rising from the east, shining like a rising sun.

Lacrimosa blinked feebly. She struggled to raise her head, but could not. Volucris's talons clutched her, and the winds lashed her. She was in human form today, limbs bound and mouth gagged. Her dress was tattered, her body bruised and bloody, and her hair streamed behind her like the banners Dies Irae and his men bore. The other griffins flew around her, shrieking at the sight of their home.

Gloriae too flew there, Lacrimosa saw, but her daughter never approached her. The other men mocked and beat her. Gloriae remained at a distance, and Lacrimosa thought she knew why. *Dies Irae ordered her away from me. He fears she'll learn the truth... that she's my daughter, and that I love her.*

"Ben," Lacrimosa whispered, lips cracked. Though her hand was so weak she could barely move it, she clutched the pendant that hung around her neck, a silver pendant shaped like a bluebell, their flower. "Fly away, Ben. Fly away from this place."

Confutatis glittered, growing closer, a city of white spires, marble columns, and statues of Dies Irae with his fist upon his chest. A city of a million souls, cobbled streets snaking between proud buildings and temples, a city swarming with countless griffins--griffins atop every wall and tower and fortress. The Marble City. City of the Sun. Jewel of Osanna. Confutatis had many names, but to Lacrimosa, it was one thing: a prison.

"Turn into your reptilian form," Dies Irae's voice spoke above, colder than the wind. "I will have the city see your monstrosity."

She considered disobeying him, but dared not; that would only mean more cuts from the spears, more pain, more ilbane rubbed into her wounds. She shifted into a dragon. Volucris grunted at the greater weight, tightened his talons around her, and flapped his wings harder. A tear fled Lacrimosa's eye and fell to the fields of barley and wheat below.

When they flew above the first walls, Dies Irae's men blew trumpets, and the griffins cried in triumph. *Heroes returning in glory,* Lacrimosa thought. *I am their prize.*

Confutatis rose upon hills of granite and grass. Three towering walls surrounded the city, moats between them. Guards covered the walls, armed with arrows and catapults and leashed griffins. When they saw their emperor, they slammed fists against their breastplates and called his name. Behind the walls, the city folk saw the banners of Dies Irae, and they bowed. All looked upon her, soldiers and commoners, fear and disgust in their eyes.

"Weredragon," she heard them whisper, a vile word. "Weredragon."

Once a wise king had ruled Confutatis, she remembered, a kindly old man with a long white beard. She would visit here as a child, tug that white beard, run along the cobbled streets. Once Requiem and Confutatis had shone together--proud, ancient allies. But that had been years ago, before darkness had covered Lacrimosa's world.

Clutched in Volucris's talons, she watched the city below. They flew over courtyards where soldiers drilled with swords and spears, forts where great walls rose, towers where archers stood, stables of griffins. She saw catapults and chariots, armored horses, gold and steel everywhere. Statues of Dies Irae stood at every corner, statues of him raising a sword, or swinging a mace, or riding a griffin. Banners of war fluttered from every roof, white and gold and red, swords and spears embroidered upon them.

So many soldiers, she thought. *So many things of war.* And yet the war had ended, had it not? Dies Irae had destroyed the Vir Requis, killed every one other than a handful. Why did steel and military might still fill these streets? Why did she see more swords and shields than flowers or trees? What enemy did Dies Irae fight now, and what peril could justify this city? No, not a city; Confutatis was a huge fortress now, a barracks of a million people all taught to worship their emperor and hate their enemies.

A palace rose upon the highest point of Confutatis. Golden roofs topped its white towers. A hundred marble statues stood upon its battlements.

A square stretched out before the palace, five hundred yards wide and twice as long, marble columns lining it. The palace's greatest statue stood here, a hundred feet tall and gilded--a statue of Dies Irae in armor, holding aloft a sword. The statue's cold gaze stared upon the city, proud and judging.

Dies Irae and his griffins flew over the palace towers, and Lacrimosa saw a cobbled courtyard below. The griffins descended, and Volucris tossed her down. She slammed into the cobblestones, banging her shoulder, and bit back a cry of pain. Walls surrounded her, archers and griffins atop their battlements. A statue of Dies Irae stood upon a column, glaring down at her.

"Collar her," the real Dies Irae said, dismounting his griffin. He marched across the courtyard toward a gateway. "Muzzle her and chain her to the column."

She raised her head and tried to stand up. A dozen men rushed forward, kicked her, and slammed shields against her, knocking her head to the ground. They closed an iron collar around her neck, muzzled her, and chained her to a column.

"Gloriae, help me," Lacrimosa tried to say, but could not speak with the muzzle. Her daughter stood across the courtyard, eyes cold and arms crossed, staring at her. *She hates me,* Lacrimosa knew.

Dies Irae approached Gloriae and spoke to her. The two walked through the gateway, leaving the courtyard, capes fluttering. The gates slammed shut behind them, leaving Lacrimosa at the mercy of their soldiers. Those soldiers leered, and several kicked her, spat at her, and mocked her.

Lacrimosa mewled and tried to free herself, but could not. The collar hurt her neck, and she dared not become human; those kicking boots would kill her without her scales offering their meager protection. She weakly flapped her tail at the men, but they only laughed and kicked her harder.

She lowered her head. *Fly away from here, Ben,* she thought. *I cannot bear this fate to be yours too. I cannot live if I see you too chained and beaten. Fly away, Ben, fly and be with Kyrie and Agnus Dei. Never return here.*

Finally the soldiers tired and left the courtyard. The archers above kept their arrows pointed at her, staring down with narrowed eyes.

They all think I'm a beast, a monster.

She closed her eyes and tried to remember Requiem, the golden leaves upon the birches, the marble columns, the courtyards where she would walk with Benedictus, dressed in gowns and jewels. As night fell, she let those memories fill her, and her tears fell like jewels in the starlight.

KYRIE ELEISON

"How long has it been?" Kyrie asked Agnus Dei, wings flapping. The sun rose over the horizon, a disk like a burnished, bronze shield from Lanburg Fields. Snowy mountaintops peaked from clouds below. Where the cloud cover broke, Kyrie saw piney mountainsides. Rivers roared between boulders, feeding pools of mist. He saw no game, and his belly grumbled.

"Seventh morning since the Divide," Agnus Dei said, flying beside him. She looked at him, and Kyrie thought that her eyes had lost something of their rage. A week ago, fire and pain had filled them, but now he saw weariness and fear there. Her eyes, normally brown, appeared golden in the sunrise. Dawn danced on her scales.

"Is this all Salvandos is?" he asked. "Mountains, and rivers, and lakes, and...."

His voice died off. During the past week, they'd flown over more landscapes than he'd thought the world held: hills of jasmines that rolled for a hundred leagues, lakes full of leaping trout, plains of jagged boulders like armies of rock, and many realms his weary mind could no longer recall. But no humans. No griffins. And no salvanae. Salvandos--fabled realm beyond Osanna, beyond the dividers. A realm of great beauty that, at times, brought tears to Kyrie's eyes... and, it seemed, a realm of great loneliness.

"There are salvanae here," Agnus Dei said, though her voice had lost its former conviction. She was reciting. "We'll find them soon. Maybe today."

The clouds parted below, and Kyrie eyed a stream. "Let's grab some breakfast," he said, watching the silhouettes of salmon in the water. Without waiting for an answer, he dived toward the river. Cold winds and mist hit him, and soon he reached the river and crashed into the water. He swam, then rose into flight again, three salmon in his jaws. He swallowed them, dived, and caught two more.

His hunger sated, he landed on the river bank. Agnus Dei swooped and crashed into the water too, spraying Kyrie. Soon she stood beside him, chewing a mouthful of salmon. Kyrie watched her as she ate. She was beautiful in dragon form, her scales brilliant, her eyes glittering, her fangs sharp... but Kyrie couldn't stop thinking of her human shape. He hadn't seen her human form since that day, that horrible and wonderful day on the border. He remembered her bruised, hot body pressed against him, her lips against his lips, her--

No. Kyrie pushed the thought away. She had lost blood that day, had been confused and frightened. Whenever he tried to speak of their love making, she glared at him with dragon eyes, fangs bared, and he shut his mouth. He knew that he better forget it soon, or she'd beat the memory out of his mind.

But... spirits of Requiem, how could he forget the most intoxicating and wonderful night of his life?

"I love sardines for breakfast," Agnus Dei said. She dunked her head into the river, then pulled back with spray of water, another salmon in her jaws. She gulped it, then drank from the river.

Kyrie drank too, remembering those breakfasts of porridge and bacon back at Fort Sanctus, and he thought of the Lady Mirum, his heart heavy. When he finished drinking, he licked his chops and said, "Where now, Agnus Dei? How much longer can we fly? Maybe there is no golden mountain. Maybe there are no salvanae."

He looked around at the clear waters, the mountains covered in snow and pines, the valleys of grass and boulders. He wished he could stay here forever with Agnus Dei. No griffins filled these skies. They could rebuild the Vir Requis race here--him, her, their children. This land could promise a future for the Vir Requis, and... Kyrie felt his blood boil again. It could mean many more nights with Agnus Dei.

He sighed. No. He could not just hide here, not when Lacrimosa and Benedictus needed him. He would not abandon his friends.

Agnus Dei too looked around the valleys and mountains, lost in thought. She also sighed, then said, "Maybe you're right, pup, maybe--"

A roar pierced the air, sending birds fluttering.

Kyrie and Agnus Dei stared up and froze.

Nothing.

Nothing there.

The roar had sounded above them, maybe a league away. Griffins? No, that was no birdlike shriek, it was--

Again the roar shook the world. And there--a serpentine shadow above the clouds.

Agnus Dei burst into flight. Kyrie followed, wind whipping him. They crashed through the clouds and looked around.

"Where is it?" Agnus Dei demanded, looking from side to side. Kyrie looked. He saw nothing but leagues of clouds, mountain peaks, and the sun above.

"Where did it go?" Agnus Dei roared and blew fire. "True dragons! Hear me. Answer my call."

Kyrie heard nothing but the wind and, below him, the distant calls of birds. But he had seen the silhouette of that serpentine creature, had heard that roar. That had been no griffin nor divider; it had no wings, and yet it flew, a hundred feet long and coiling.

Kyrie scanned the clouds. He saw a wisp in a field of white fluff; something had dived through those clouds.

"There!" he said and flew. He reached the place where the clouds were disturbed, pulled his wings close to his body, and dived. Agnus Dei followed. Under the clouds, the mountains and rivers spread into the horizons, and again Kyrie saw no dragon. But....

"Look!" he said. Birds were fleeing a distant mountaintop. Something had disturbed them. Kyrie flew toward that mountaintop, Agnus Dei by him. He was tired, but he had never flown faster. Could it be? Had they found the true dragons of old, the lords of Salvandos?

They flew around the mountaintop, a tower of stone and snow. *There!* He saw a green, scaly tail disappear around a cliff. He narrowed his eyes and followed, Agnus Dei at his side.

A flash of brilliant green. The dragon ahead soared into the clouds.

"Wow," Kyrie said. He could think of nothing more to say. He glimpsed the dragon for only a second, but it was beautiful, the most beautiful creature he'd ever seen. This was definitely no Vir Requis. The creature was half as slim and twice as long. It had no wings, but moved like a snake in the sky, coiling and uncoiling. Emerald scales covered its body, and its horns and claws glowed. It sported a flowing mustache and beard, snowy white and flapping in the wind.

In a flash, it was gone into the clouds, leaving a wake of glittering blue.

"Come on, Kyrie!" Agnus Dei shouted, and Kyrie realized he was hovering in place. He blinked, shook his head, and flew hard. He broke through the clouds and saw the salvana in the distance, already a league away, undulating as it flew. It dived under the clouds again, disappearing from view, like a snake diving under water.

"Come back here," Kyrie cried, but doubted the salvana could hear him. It was such a strange creature, Kyrie wondered if he'd just gone mad with weariness. Flying green serpents with golden horns and white beards? What was next, pink elephants with swan wings?

Kyrie and Agnus Dei kept racing, chasing the coiling green dragon. It was fast--faster than them, growing smaller and smaller in the distance. Kyrie knew that on a good day, well rested and well fed, he could catch up, but he was too tired now. He could barely keep his wings flapping, but he pushed himself as far as he could go.

After an hour of flight, the salvana--now just a speck on the horizon--dived under the clouds again.

Kyrie and Agnus Dei, both so weary they could barely fly, followed. They too dived under the clouds... and their breath died.

Tears filled Kyrie's eyes.

"It's real," Agnus Dei whispered, eyes moist.

A mountain of gold rose before them. Kyrie had seen gold before--Dies Irae certainly wore enough of it--but here was an entire mountain of the stuff, a league high and blinding in the sun. Rings of mist surrounded the golden mountain. Snow capped its peaks. It dwarfed the smaller, jagged mountains that surrounded it. Most beautiful of all, however, was not the gold and mist and sunbeams, but the thousands of salvanae who flew here. Some were blue and silver, others green and gold, and some were white. Their eyes were like crystal balls, large and spinning. They bugled songs like trumpets, and flowed in and out of round caves in the mountainsides.

"Har Zahav," Kyrie whispered in awe. "The Golden Mountain of Salvandos." He looked at Agnus Dei and saw that she was weeping.

Three salvanae flew toward them. Two had green scales, golden horns, and long fangs. The third was golden and seemed elderly; his beard was white and flowing, his eyes pale blue with long white lashes. He flew first, leading the others, like a stream of gold.

The salvanae flew up to hover before them. Their eyes glittered, large as watermelons. They blinked, lashes sweeping, and said nothing.

"Hello," Kyrie said, then paused and cleared his throat. What did one say when meeting legendary creatures? He doubted they would understand Osanna's High Speech, but would they speak Requiem's older Dragontongue? Kyrie decided to speak the latter. "My name is Kyrie Eleison of Requiem," he said in that ancient, rolling language. "This is my companion, Agnus Dei, daughter of Benedictus and Lacrimosa. We flee danger and suffering. We come seeking your aid."

The old dragon listened, the wind in his beard. Sparks like lightning rose between his teeth. He looked at Kyrie and Agnus Dei with crystal ball eyes. He spoke then with an old, crinkly voice, heavily accented but definitely speaking Dragontongue. "Greeting, travelers and strange things. I am Nehushtan, High Priest of Draco's stars. May they bless you. I welcome you to Har Zahav. You are fellow things of flight and fang. The light of Draco shines upon you, though it glimmers oddly. You may spend the darkness, and pray to the Draco constellation, and return to your lands when the sun wakes."

Kyrie opened his mouth, then closed it again, dumbfounded. Agnus Dei's eyes flared, and smoke rose from her nostrils.

"No!" Agnus Dei said to Nehushtan. "We do not come to rest. We need help! Our people are hunted. We're nearly extinct. The griffins have killed all but four of us. They captured my mother. Please help us." Tears filled her eyes.

The salvana guards growled. Nehushtan only nodded slowly. He blinked, his great eyelashes like fans. He puffed out several rings of smoke. Finally he spoke again, turning his eyes from Agnus Dei, to Kyrie, and back again.

"We of Har Zahav convey our grief. We weep to hear your tragedy, and we pray that the spirits of your dead find peace in the afterlife. You may stay three darknesses and recover your strength. Then you may fly to your home, and we will pray that the Draco constellation glows upon you there, and protects you in the afterlife should you perish."

Kyrie shook his head and grunted. Were these salvanae daft? He blurted out his words, anger boiling his blood. "Is that all you can offer us? Three nights' stay? Then you'll send us back to die? Won't you help us? Don't you care that griffins are slaughtering fellow dragons?"

Nehushtan puffed out more smoke, seeming lost in thought. The smoke formed tiny, dancing salvanae.

"You are not fellow dragons," he finally said, "though you speak our tongue. You are the Vir Requis, creatures of old stories in our land. Yet our light shines with you, for many years ago we were allies, and fought together against the griffins, when the griffins were still wild, and no amulet could tame them. This was many seasons ago. Today we dragons of Salvandos no longer fight the wars of Requiem. Like the snow upon the mountains, we live through sunshine and rain, and thrive both in light and shadows. Ours is a peaceful life, a life of prayer and meditation, of stargazing. We cannot fight the wars of griffins and Vir Requis. You may stay here for seven darknesses, but then you must leave, and I can offer no more."

Agnus Dei roared so loudly, the salvana soldiers growled and blew smoke, and their eyes flared. "If you don't help us, we'll die," Agnus Dei cried. "Our race will vanish."

Nehushtan blinked and nodded. He puffed more smoke, which now looked like a Vir Requis dragon, wings spread, mouth blowing fire. "As fire may rise in smoke, so may the life of a dragon rise as a spirit; it does not vanish, but joins the winds and the rain that falls. Fear not, Vir Requis, for your spirit is strong. When its time to rise comes, it will find its way to the temples of your forefathers." He turned around. "Follow me, and I will lead you to rest, food, and meditation."

Agnus Dei panted with anger, eyes flaring, flames dancing between her teeth. The salvana soldiers eyed her, fangs bared. Kyrie trembled with rage, but forced himself to take deep breaths. He wasn't ready to give up yet. So long as they remained here at Har Zahav, there was hope.

"Come, Agnus Dei," he said to her. "Let's go with them. We might convince them yet."

The salvanae began flying toward the golden mountain. Kyrie and Agnus Dei followed. Watching how the salvanae coiled through the air with no wings, Kyrie felt clumsy as he flew. He marveled at how long, thin, and glittering these air serpents were, with their glowing horns, fluttering mustaches, and eyes like orbs of colored glass.

As they flew closer to the mountain, Kyrie saw many other salvanae flying around him. They flew in every color, from the deepest black flecked in silver, to bright reds and greens. Some tossed bolts of lighting from their maws. The light blinded Kyrie.

Nehushtan led them higher, moving toward the crest of Har Zahav. Flying so high, the mountains surrounding Har Zahav seemed small as hills, their pines mere specks. When they flew above Har Zahav's crest, Kyrie gasped. The golden mountain ended not with a peak, but with a gaping hole.

"It's a volcano," he whispered.

He saw darkness and stars inside the volcano, as if gazing into night sky. The salvanae coiled down toward the volcano's mouth, straightened their bodies, and entered the hole. They disappeared into the darkness.

Kyrie and Agnus Dei hovered over the volcano's mouth. The opening was five feet wide, suited for the slim body of a salvana. How would Vir Requis--with their bulky frame and wings--enter?

Kyrie and Agnus Dei landed on the mountain beside the opening. Winds lashed them, and snow flurried around their feet. Nehushtan and his soldiers were gone, and the only other salvanae flew far below.

"Well," Kyrie said, struggling to speak as snow flew into his mouth. "I guess it's time to reveal our human forms, if we're to fit through this hole."

The two shifted into humans. Though wind lashed him and he shivered, being human again felt good. Kyrie had flown for so long, he'd missed the feeling of ground beneath human feet. In his smaller form, the mountaintop seemed even more colossal, the winds wilder, the height more dizzying. He could barely breathe the thin air.

Kyrie looked at Agnus Dei. Again he realized how much he loved her human form. As beautiful as Har Zahav was, with its golden slopes, coiling salvanae, and snowy peaks, Kyrie thought that Agnus Dei was the most beautiful thing around. She was a mess, her clothes tattered and muddy, her skin bruised and battered, her hair a great tangle of knots. But she couldn't have been more beautiful to Kyrie, not if she wore gowns and perfumes and jewels.

"Kyrie," she said, "they're... not happy."

Kyrie tore his eyes away from her. Salvanae were flying up toward them from the mountainsides. They roared and blew lightning from their maws. "Demons!" they called. "Shape shifters invade Har Zahav."

Before Kyrie and Agnus Dei could react, the High Priest Nehushtan reemerged from the volcano, body flowing out from the narrow opening. He faced the charging salvanae, blew lightning, and called out, "Starlight be upon you! They are my wards."

The charging salvanae paused, tongues lolling, sparks rising from their nostrils. Kyrie released his breath slowly, fingers trembling.

"These are Vir Requis," the priest said, "our allies of old. They are strange things, but bring no evil into Har Zahav." He turned to Kyrie and Agnus Dei. "I offer sorrow; they do not remember the ancient songs. The Inner Realm is wide and warm. You may enter in your small forms, and regain your dragon beings inside."

Nehushtan reentered the hole, once more disappeared into darkness.

Kyrie peered into the volcano. He saw only inky darkness strewn with floating orbs of light. He turned his head back to Agnus Dei.

"Should we just jump in?" he asked.

Agnus Dei rolled her eyes. "Oh, pup, don't tell me you're afraid of the dark."

Before he could respond, she shoved him into the volcano.

Kyrie bit down on a yelp. He fell through darkness, the lights streaming around him. He glimpsed countless salvanae around him. With a groan, he shifted back into dragon form, flapped his wings, and steadied himself.

"Hey pup!" Agnus Dei said. She was falling in her human form. She shifted, then hovered beside him. "That wasn't too bad, was it?"

They gazed around. Thousands of orbs floated around them, glowing white and yellow and gold. Salvanae flowed between them, moving so fast, they appeared as glimmering streaks. This Inner Realm seemed endless, a universe. Kyrie had expected to see golden walls--the inner mountainsides--but the darkness and light seemed to spread forever.

"Where is Nehushtan?" Kyrie asked. "Do you see him?"

Agnus Dei pointed. "Down there."

Kyrie looked below. The orbs clustered there, glowing more brightly, a nexus of light. The Inner Realm seemed to Kyrie like some great flower, its glowing center casting pollen into the darkness. Many salvanae coiled among the cluster of orbs below, and Kyrie glimpsed Nehushtan's tail.

He flew down, Agnus Dei beside him. Salvanae stared from all directions, eyes spinning. Soon the Vir Requis crashed through hundreds of orbs, scattering them, and emerged into a bubble of light the size of a cathedral. The orbs resettled behind them, sealing them in this glowing chamber. Hundreds of salvanae flew here. Great rings of lightning spun upon the floor like an electrical storm. Every second, another salvana dipped toward the rings of lightning and blew upon it, feeding it sparks. As they coiled, the salvanae sang wordless songs like the sound of flutes and harps.

Nehushtan saw them and flew toward them. "Here is the Light of Har Zahav, which we guard with our spirits. Here is the heart of our land. Welcome, Kyrie Eleison and Agnus Dei, to our Inner Realm. Warm yourself by the Draco Light, pray, and rest."

He gestured toward a hollowed bowl in the stone floor, like a small crater. It lay a hundred feet from the electrical rings.

A thousand other holes covered the floor, Kyrie noticed, and salvanae slept inside them.

Kyrie and Agnus Dei landed in the depression. It was a tight squeeze for their dragons forms, so they shifted into humans again, and sat side by side. The electrical rings rose to their right, warming them.

Salvanae flew down, bearing glowing bubbles, which they lay by Kyrie and Agnus Dei. Some bubbles held water, some held nuts, and others held pomegranates.

"Eat, drink, and meditate," said Nehushtan, floating above them. With a nod and blink, he turned and disappeared into the lights above.

"What a place," Kyrie said, watching the electrical rings and the coiling salvanae above. "Have you ever imagined such a thing? Agnus Dei?"

He looked at her, and saw that she wasn't listening. She was popping the bubbles and devouring the food inside. Kyrie joined her, wolfing down the nuts and fruits.

The bubbles were the size of pots, meant to feed dragons. Even in their human forms, however, Kyrie and Agnus Dei put serious dents into the meal. When they could eat no more, they lay on their backs, the hollowed stone smooth and warm. They patted their bellies and sighed. Bowl-shaped, the depression forced them to lay pressed together. Agnus Dei's body was warm against his.

"You were right, Agnus Dei," he said. "The salvanae are real. You were right all along."

But Agnus Dei was already snoring, her head against his chest, her tangle of curls tickling his face. She tossed an arm over him.

"Good night," he whispered and kissed her head. He closed his eyes, just for a moment, marveling at how her hair smelled like flowers and trees even after all the fire, pain, and blood they'd flown through. He wanted to wake her. He wanted to find Nehushtan again, to demand aid at once, to demand they flew now to save Benedictus and Lacrimosa. But sleep grabbed him too powerfully to resist. Before he knew it, he was asleep, his arms around Agnus Dei.

LACRIMOSA

Dreams whispered in the darkness.

"Lacrimosa!" her mother called, voice a whisper, a flutter. "Come hear the harpists, daughter, come hear the song."

She ran, bare feet upon fallen petals, laughter like ice drops on glass, frozen in time, frozen in memory. Her mother stood before her all in white, smiling, arms open, skin like alabaster and blond hair streaked with white, drowned in light, forever out of reach.

"Mother!" she called, but her voice floated in the air, more ice drops that hung, floated, whispered and echoed.

The harpists walked between the columns of Requiem, bleached, white robes fluttering and silent, eyes a startling blue, peering through her. The birch leaves glided among them, silver, and only their harps seemed real. She could see every leaf of gold upon them, every line and knot in the wood, and the strings cut through her vision, sharper than claw or fang. They played among the columns in their courts, but she could not hear them. Not anymore. Not here, not now.

Darkness.

Darkness and pain.

She gasped, and her fingers clawed the stone ground.

"Mother." A whisper. She tried to clutch the memory, but it fled; it was not real, nothing but a wisp. She could not enter it. She could not find it. Never again, not from this darkness, not from this silence.

"It is a world," she whispered. "We were a world entire, and we are gone. Who will remember us? Who will remember the courts of Requiem when ivy grows over our ruins, and our shattered statues turn smooth under the rain of too many springs? We will be vanished then; we will be lost. Whispers. Then silence. And darkness."

But this darkness was not silent, not hers, not anymore. A rumble sounded in the black, a distant roar of a hundred thousand voices. A crowd chanting, Lacrimosa realized. She had heard crowds in Requiem, clapping people gathered in woodland theaters to see minstrels play. This was different. This crowd roared, clamored, and called for blood. They were angry, they were thrilled, and they were hungry.

She opened her eyes, but saw only shadows. Chains bound her to the floor, and stone walls surrounded her. How long had she been in this prison cell? She had drifted in and out of sleep for days, it seemed. She was in her human form, her dress mere tatters, her head spinning and her arms weak. A bowl of water lay before her, but her arms were bound behind her. She drank like a dog. Outside the stone walls, the crowds roared and thumped feet. Trumpets blew.

A door behind her clanked, and torchlight spilled into the room, blinding her. Lacrimosa squinted and moaned.

"Come on," spoke a deep voice, a voice like death. It sounded familiar, and sent fear through her, but she could not place it. Hands grabbed her, pulled her to her feet, and dragged her to the door. Others walked around her, but she could still not see in the blinding torchlight. She thought they moved down a hall of stone, and the crowd's cheering grew. Soon they entered a towering room. The chanting roared behind bronze doors.

Hands grabbed her arms, and with a clack, somebody removed the shackles from her wrists. She gasped with pain and moved her arms, rubbing them, letting the blood flow through them.

"Turn into the beast," spoke that cold voice, a voice like cracking wood in the heart of winter. Lacrimosa blinked, her eyes adjusting to the light, and then she saw him. She knew him at once.

Molok.

Gaunt and tall, the man looked like a torture device. His armor looked like an iron maiden, spiked and black. His helmet looked like a prisoner's mask, its bars like the bars of a cell. He raised that visor now, revealing a cadaverous face and sunken eyes.

"I know you," Lacrimosa hissed. "I saw you murder five infants in Requiem. I saw you r--"

He backhanded her, knocking her down. Her cheek burned, and her knee banged against the stone floor. She gasped in pain and tears filled her eyes. She glared up at Molok between strands of her hair. He'd always been Dies Irae's foulest pet--a murderer of children, a rapist and torturer. *Someday I will kill you,* she vowed silently.

"Turn into the beast," he repeated and raised his sword. His blade was black and spiked.

"I--" she hissed, and he kicked her. His boot drove into her stomach. She gasped and new tears filled her eyes.

"Turn into the beast."

Tears on her cheeks, pain saturating her, she shifted. Scales covered her, a tail and wings grew from her, and soon she crouched in the chamber, a dragon, smoke leaving her nostrils. Molok seemed so small now, a fraction of her size, and she wanted to tear her fangs into him. But that would mean death for her. That would mean she'd never see Benedictus, Kyrie, and her daughters again.

Molok collared her, then pulled her on a chain toward the bronze doors. When the doors opened, the cheering hit Lacrimosa so heavily, her head spun. Molok dragged her into a sandy arena. Tens of thousands of people cheered around her. It was an amphitheater, Lacrimosa realized, but not like the small theaters in Requiem where her kind would gather to hear minstrels or storytellers among the trees. This was a colossus, a great ring of stone. How many of Osanna's sons and daughters howled and jeered her? There were fifty thousand at least, maybe twice as many, an army of people hating her. They pelted her with rotten vegetables and cursed her. The colors and sound swirled around her, deafening, overwhelming.

Molok attached her chain to a metal post in the center of the ring. He backed away, leaving her in the middle of the amphitheater, alone, the crowd cheering. When Lacrimosa looked up, squinting in the sunlight, she saw a gilded boxed seat high upon the stone tiers. Purple curtains draped it, and griffin statues guarded its flanks. Dies Irae sat there upon a throne of ivory and jewels, wearing samite and gemstones, a crown atop his head. He gazed down at her, face blank.

What's the point of this show? Lacrimosa wondered, glaring up at Dies Irae. *Why does he chain me here? Just so Confutatis can see me, mock me, throw their rotten vegetables at me?* She growled, smoke leaving her nostrils, incurring wild cries from the crowd. *Why does he do this?*

Dies Irae rose from his seat. He raised his arms, and the crowd fell silent. For long moments, Dies Irae passed his gaze over the crowd, as if he would stare at every man, woman, and child. The sudden silence was eerie to Lacrimosa; silence before a storm. Nobody in the crowd so much as whispered. Lacrimosa could hear distant birds chirp. Finally Dies Irae spoke.

"Behold our enemy," he called out, voice loud in the silence. "Behold the beast, the weredragon. These are the creatures that threaten your children."

The crowd hissed and glared. Dies Irae spoke louder.

"These weredragons bring evil into our city. When plagues strike, it is because the weredragons poisoned our wells. When fires burn our homes, weredragon breath kindled them."

The crowd jeered so loudly now, the amphitheater seemed to shake. Dies Irae shouted to be heard.

"When rain does not fall, and crops die, it is because weredragons moved the clouds with their wings. When earthquakes tremble, it is weredragons shaking the earth. When there is not enough bread, or fruit, or milk, it is because the weredragons stole them."

The crowed howled. Several men tried to run down the tiers, into the arena, and attack Lacrimosa. The guards held them back, but the guards' eyes too burned with hatred.

Lacrimosa understood. This city was no heaven of splendor and riches; only its palaces were, only the courts of Dies Irae. The rest of Confutatis was a hive of poverty, a simmering pool of fear and misery.

"And we're the scapegoats," Lacrimosa whispered, tears in her eyes. This was how Dies Irae raised his armies, earned their loyalty, convinced them to burn Requiem, to murder babes in the cradle.

Lacrimosa glared at Dies Irae. She called out, her voice barely heard over the crowd, but she knew Dies Irae would hear. "Is this because of your father?" she cried. "Is this because he hated you for lacking the magic of Requiem, because he chose Benedictus to be his heir? Dies Irae! You have betrayed your home, you will...."

Her voice trailed off.

Bronze doors were opening behind her, and she heard grunting.

Three beasts burst into the arena.

At first she thought they were bulls. They had shaggy bodies, bull horns, and golden rings in their noses. But these were no ordinary bulls; instead of hooves, they had clawed feet, and fangs grew from their mouths. Smoke and fire left their nostrils.

They charged toward her.

Lacrimosa's heart leaped. She tried to escape, but the chain ran from her collar to the metal post, barely fifty feet long. She blew fire toward the charging bulls, and they scattered, howling.

The crowd cheered.

One bull skirted the flames and nearly gored her. Lacrimosa lashed her tail, hit it, and knocked it ten feet back. Another bull charged toward her other side. Lacrimosa pulled back, nearly choking as the chain tugged her collar. She blew more fire, hitting the bull in the face. It howled and fell, burning.

The third bull charged. Lacrimosa moved aside as best she could, the chain restricting her movements, and the bull's horns grazed her leg. Her blood flowed.

Lacrimosa howled in pain. She kicked the bull, sending it flying. The beast crashed into two guards, knocking them down, and the crowd cheered louder than ever.

The wounded bulls struggled to their feet and surrounded her. They growled, blew smoke from their nostrils, and clawed the earth. They realized her strength now, and they began pacing around her, judging her with narrowed eyes, waiting for an opening to attack.

Lacrimosa wanted to weep. She wanted to die. She missed her husband and daughter so badly. But she could allow no despair to overcome her. She had to live for her family. She kept lashing her tail, glaring at the bulls, keeping them back. If one seemed ready to charge, she blew fire until it retreated. Still they walked in circles around her.

"I love you, Benedictus," Lacrimosa whispered when the bulls charged together. She blew fire, kicked, and screamed. Pain and flames covered her world.

GLORIAE

She walked through the dungeon, hand on Per Ignem's hilt. She wore her gilded breastplate and helmet. Her boots clanked against the stone floor, tipped with steel, and a dagger hung at her side. Gloriae wondered why she brought arms and armor here today. The beast was chained. The beast was hurt. It could not harm Gloriae, and yet she felt naked without her armor, vulnerable, only a girl, a princess with soft cheeks and golden hair.

But I am a lady of steel, she thought, gloved hand tightening around her sword's hilt. *This blade is steel, and so is my heart, and so is my resolve, and so is the punishment I deal to those who hurt me.*

Soon she reached the doorway. The guards recognized her, blanched, and slammed their fists against their hearts. Gloriae did not bother returning the salute.

"Open the door," she said. The guards glanced at one another, and Gloriae drew her sword. "Do as I say, or I'll have you flayed and hung upon the palace walls."

They obeyed. Gloriae grabbed a torch from the wall and stepped into the chamber, sword drawn. She blinked as light and shadows swirled, and then she saw the beast.

Lacrimosa lay on the floor. She was in human form today, and Gloriae's breath died. She had come here expecting a reptile, a monster. On the floor lay a beautiful woman. Lacrimosa was slender, and her hair shone like moonlight, a blond so pale it was almost white. She seemed ageless to Gloriae. Lacrimosa was not young like her; when those lavender eyes looked up, Gloriae saw the wisdom of age in them. And yet no lines marred Lacrimosa's face, and her beauty seemed eternal, the beauty of a flower coated in frost.

Gloriae took a step back, raising the torch. She wanted to hate Lacrimosa, but how could she hate a creature that took such a delicate, beautiful form? It was a spell, Gloriae told herself; an illusion to hide lurking evil.

"Hello, Gloriae," Lacrimosa said, and tears filled her eyes. She rose to her feet.

Rage flared in Gloriae, nearly blinding her. She reminded herself why she had come here. She had wanted to see the creature that had murdered her mother... and to hurt it. She walked toward Lacrimosa, sword raised, and was surprised to find tears in her own eyes. She let her anger sear them away.

"You murdered my mother," Gloriae said, voice little more than a whisper.

Lacrimosa wept. Her slender body trembled and she shook her head. "Gloriae... my beloved. Is that what they told you?" Lacrimosa reached out toward her. "Gloriae, I am your mother."

"You lie!" Gloriae screamed.

Lacrimosa shook her head, tears streaming down to wet her dress. "I gave birth to you in the courts of Requiem. You are Vir Requis, child. You're one of us. I don't know who your father is, whether he is Benedictus or Dies Irae. But I know that I gave birth to you, that I nursed you, that I raised you for three years before Dies Irae took you."

Gloriae trembled. *No... no! It can't be.* Images slammed against her. She saw herself as a toddler among marble columns, heard harps, saw light and leaves and--

"Liar!" Gloriae screamed, shaking her head so wildly, that her hair covered her eyes. She trembled. "No. No, beast. I am not one of you." She snarled. "You are cursed, you are evil and you trick and you lie and you kill. You murdered my mother.

You try to enchant me now. I see those images you place in my head. I laugh at them. You think you can fool me, lizard?" She raised her sword, laughing and crying and shouting. "You will die, Lacrimosa. You will die like the vermin that you are. My father will torture you. He will break you until you pray for death. And then, when that time comes, I will be the one who kills you, who lands this sword upon you."

Lacrimosa reached out toward her, eyes entreating. "Daughter, Gloriae--"

"Do not speak my name. All your words are spells. I killed a Vir Requis child when I was only six. I killed three more when I was eight. Do you think I don't know your kind? That I don't know your evil and your magic?"

"Listen to me, please!" Sobs racked Lacrimosa's body. "They have hurt you, lied to you, but I love you. I love you, daughter. You can shift too. You can become a dragon like us. I know it, you--"

"Silence!"

"I will not be silent. You must know the truth, Gloriae. Dies Irae never taught you your magic. He is Vir Requis too, but he was born without the gift. You have it! I know you do. It's deep within you, hidden, repressed. You are scared and ashamed of it. They taught you to hate it, to hide it. But the light of Requiem glows within you. It's buried but still lives. Try it, Gloriae! Shift here in this chamber. Look into your soul, find your dragon light, and you can--"

Gloriae shoved Lacrimosa, and she fell, weeping, finally ceasing to speak. Gloriae stared down at her. Her heart thrashed, her fingers trembled, and she longed to bring Per Ignem down upon this creature. "You will not cast your curse upon me," she said, voice cold. "You will beg me for death before I grant it."

With that, Gloriae spun and left the chamber. She slammed the door behind her.

She marched down the hallway, up onto the surface of the world, and to the stables. She mounted Aquila and flew to the Palace Flammis, this jewel of marble and gold that rose upon the highest hill in the Marble City of Confutatis. After tethering Aquila, she marched across the gardens and into the palace. She marched down hallways past lords and ladies, suits of burnished armor, and scuttling servants. The people she passed saluted her, fear in their eyes. Gloriae did not need a mirror to know that her cheeks were flushed, her eyes enraged, her lips tightened into a cruel line. She carried Per Ignem drawn, prepared to slay anyone who spoke to her. None did.

She reached her chamber, stepped in, and closed the door behind her. Finally she allowed herself to close her eyes, lean against a wall, and take a deep breath.

"My lady?" came a voice, and Gloriae opened her eyes to see May, her handmaiden. The girl was her age, and had been with her since childhood. Her hair was long and auburn, her skin pale, her brown eyes soft with worry. "My lady, are you all right?"

Gloriae sheathed her sword. "Come to me, May."

Her handmaiden stepped forward, and Gloriae embraced the girl, leaned her head against her shoulder, and closed her eyes. "When will the pain leave, May?" she whispered.

May caressed her hair, untangling a knot in its curls. "Shall I draw you a bath? Bring you wine or food, my lady?"

Gloriae shook her head, opened her eyes, and looked at May. The girl smiled at her, and that smile soothed Gloriae. There was still some loyalty in the world, some goodness. "May, you've always been my friend. You always will be. No matter what. No matter what you may ever learn about me, promise that you'll remain mine."

"Of course, my lady."

Gloriae nodded. "Leave me."

May curtsied and left the chamber, dress rustling. When she was gone, Gloriae surveyed her room. This was not the room of a princess. She had no lap dogs, no dolls, no jeweled mirrors and gowns. Swords hung over Gloriae's fireplace, and daggers and crossbows lay upon her tables. Instead of bottles of perfumes, bottles of ilbane lined her shelves. Instead of gowns, suits of armor filled her room. She had dedicated her life to this war, to hunting weredragons. That was all she knew, all she'd ever lived for.

She sat on her bed, head spinning. She thought back to Lacrimosa's words. *I love you, daughter. You can shift too. You can become a dragon like us.*

Gloriae snorted. Now that she was back home, those words seemed less frightening, and more ridiculous. Lacrimosa must have been desperate. Her lies were feeble. Turn into a dragon? Her, the greatest hunter of weredragons?

Gloriae closed her eyes. "I'll prove you wrong, beast. Want me to try it?" She snorted again. "Fine." She would prove the weredragon a liar.

With a deep breath, Gloriae tried to imagine herself as a dragon. She pictured herself with scales golden like her hair, like the golden scales of Father's boots. She imagined herself with glinting claws, fangs, leathery wings. In her mind, she flapped her wings, flying over mountains and forests, tail swishing. Wind streamed around her. Cold air filled her nostrils. She roared, and fire left her maw. She could feel it, hot and wonderful, stinging her lips. The light of the Draco constellation filled her eyes, and she could hear the harps of Requiem calling, see the glint of her towers and--

Stop.

Stop it.

Gloriae snarled and tried to open her eyes, but could not. The light tugged at her. "No!" she cried.

Clouds and winds flowed across her. She could see her mother flying ahead, silvery, glinting in the sunlight. She could see her sister, a red dragon flowing on air. She could see her father, a black dragon, and--

Gloriae was weeping now. "No, no," she pleaded. She opened her eyes... and screamed.

Scales covered her arms, small and golden. Claws were growing from her fingertips. She wanted to stop it. She wanted to resist. But she also needed this, she craved it, loved it. She wanted to fly, to roar, to breathe fire. It claimed her, better than wine, better than anything. The magic flowed through her, and she both fought and welcomed it.

With a gush, wings sprouted from her back. She felt a tail beneath her, and she was huge, no longer a slim girl, but a great creature that filled her chamber. Her tail crashed against her table, knocking over the arrows, crossbows, and daggers. Her limbs were so long now, they knocked over her wardrobe. Her head hit the ceiling, no longer the head of a girl. She could see herself in a fallen, burnished breastplate. Her head was a dragon's head, golden, its eyes green as emeralds.

Gloriae froze.

She wanted to roar. She wanted to flee. But no. She must remain silent. She must alert no one. Had anyone heard her tables falling over? Would anyone burst into this room, see her like this, see the monster she'd become?

Silence, Gloriae, she told herself. *Breathe. Think. Calm yourself. Do not panic.*

She shut her eyes, forced deep breaths, and imagined herself as a girl again. She forced the image of her human form into her mind. A girl, slender but strong, of golden locks, of green eyes, of marble skin. She took deep breaths and opened her eyes.

Once more she was a girl.

"Was it all a dream?" she whispered. No. She could see claw marks on the floor, and her room was a mess. Gloriae trembled. Cold sweat drenched her, soaking the shirt under her breastplate. She had never known such terror, not in all her battles.

A thought struck her. She tugged open a drawer and grabbed a leather pouch. Inside were crumbled ilbane leaves. Fingers shaking, Gloriae reached into the pouch and touched the leaves. She yelped, dropped the pouch, and pulled back her hand. She stared at her fingers. They were red and blazed as if she'd touched open flame.

Sun God... I'm infected.

Gloriae clutched her head. She understood what had happened. Lacrimosa had given her the disease, the curse. Gloriae now carried that evil within her.

She too had become a weredragon.

Gloriae began to weep. She curled up on her bed, hugged her knees, and sobbed. She had never cried so much in her life. She was a freak now, diseased and monstrous. How would she continue? How could she face her father again? How would she ever get married, have children, raise a family? Would her children inherit this curse? She wanted to scream, to call for help, but dared not.

A knock sounded on the door. "My lady?" came May's voice. "My lady, are you well?"

"Leave me!" Gloriae cried. She rose to her feet, frantic, hair wild. *I must hide this mess,* she thought. *Nobody must know. Nobody must ever know.*

Gloriae nodded. *Yes, yes.* She would keep it secret. She would tell nobody. How would they know? If she never shifted again, they could not. It was simple.

She allowed herself a wild, weepy smile. "I can hide this."

She placed a rug over the claw marks on the floor, righted her furniture, and arranged everything as it had been. *Perfect.* Finally she spent a few moments fixing herself. She removed her sweaty clothes and brushed her hair. She pulled on leggings, a cotton shirt, a leather belt, tall boots--her clothes of battle. She owned no gowns or dresses. She had never been much of a girl, she thought, but now she wanted to be nothing more.

"May!" she called.

Her handmaiden stepped into the chamber, and Gloriae pulled her into an embrace.

"Hold me," she whispered, trembling. "Tell me it'll be all right. Please." Tears filled her eyes.

They sat on the divan, and May held her and smoothed her hair, and Gloriae slept in her arms.

She woke up to discover that night had fallen. May slept against her, her arms around her. Gloriae gazed upon the girl, her best friend since childhood, her only friend. *I won't let you down, May,* she thought. *I won't let evil fill this world. You're my friend. You're pure and good. How can I let you live in a world so dangerous, so cruel?*

Gloriae knew what to do. She had known for years perhaps, but never dared. Tonight she would dare.

Moving slowly, she wriggled out of May's embrace and placed a blanket upon the girl. Eyes narrowed, she silently put on her armor: her breastplate of steel, molded to the curve of her body, gilded and jeweled; her helmet, its visor a golden mask of her face; her greaves and vambraces, their steel bright. Finally she donned Per Ignem, lifted her shield, strapped her crossbow to her side, and left her chamber.

She found her father in his hall. He sat upon the Ivory Throne, talking to the gaunt Lord Molok. When Gloriae entered the hall and walked across it, the two men turned to face her.

Molok wore no helmet today, and she could see his ashen face, sunken eyes, and slit of a mouth. Her father was frowning.

"Father," Gloriae said when she reached his throne. She slammed her fist against her breastplate.

He nodded. "Daughter."

"Take me to the Well of Night."

Dies Irae rose to his feet, his face reddened, and for a moment Gloriae thought that he would strike her. But he only stared at her, eyes harder than his fists. "No."

Gloriae took a step closer to him. She snarled. "I saw Lacrimosa, Father. I spoke to the beast. They are fully evil creatures, more than I knew. They die this night. No more ilbane. No more griffins. No more games. We release the nightshades. We wipe them out."

Dies Irae bared his teeth, and his eyes looked ready to gore her. He grabbed her arm, fingers digging into her flesh. He leaned forward and whispered through clenched teeth. "You disobeyed me, Gloriae. You do not know what you ask."

"I do, Father. I know very well. I know their power is greater than--"

"You have not seen the nightshades," Dies Irae said, grinding his teeth. His fingers sent such pain through Gloriae, that she wanted to cry out, but held her voice. "I will show you. You think weredragons are evil? You think they are strong? You haven't seen these creatures."

He began to drag her across the hall. She struggled to free herself from his grip, but could not. He dragged her through the doorway, down stairs, and along more halls. They walked for a long time. They moved down more stairwells, and down dark corridors, and finally into dungeons and tunnels.

"You've never seen the darkness that lies beneath this city," Dies Irae said, still clutching her arm, still dragging her. "I raised you in light and beauty, surrounded with gold and jewels and goodness. You haven't seen what lurks beneath this place, far from the light of the Sun God."

Gloriae gazed around, her father's digging fingers almost forgotten. She'd heard whispers of dungeons beneath Flammis Palace, but never seen them. The walls were roughly hewn, the floor raw stone, the ceiling dripping mold. It seemed that they traveled for leagues. The air was cold and clammy, the ground slippery. They plunged deeper and deeper underground, until Gloriae thought they would reach the end of the world.

Finally a tunnel lead into a chamber where a hundred soldiers stood. They wore plate armor and carried battle axes. They slammed fists against breastplates, saluting their lords.

"Soldiers, here underground?" Gloriae asked. "Father, wha--"

"They are guards, Gloriae," he said. "They guard the terror that dwells behind these doors." He gestured at towering doors set into the stone wall.

Gloriae looked at those doors and shivered. They were made of iron. Golden skulls were embedded into them, twice the size of men's skulls, soft light in their eye sockets. The skulls seemed to watch her, and Gloriae knew; the nightshades dwelled behind these doors.

She shivered. *Nightshades.* In her childhood, she would fear them, see them in shadows under her bed, dream nightmares of them.

"These creatures cannot be tamed like griffins," Dies Irae said. "They cannot be killed like weredragons. And you want to wake them?"

Gloriae stared at that door. She thought back to her secret, her shame. *I'm infested with the weredragon curse. I have the evil within me. I must make this land pure. For May. For all the other innocents. I cannot let anyone else catch their disease.*

"I want to see them."

Dies Irae nodded to the guards, and several grabbed chains that hung from the doors. They began to pull, and the doors creaked open, inch by inch. Lights flickered in the eye sockets of the doors' skulls.

Cold wind blew from beyond, sneaking under Gloriae's armor, and she shivered. She saw only blackness. When the doors were open, Dies Irae dragged her through the doorway, into the cold and darkness.

She found herself in a chamber lined with torches. It was a great chamber, round and large as the amphitheater where Lacrimosa fought. It looked like a cave, its walls and floor rough, its ceiling hidden in shadows. In the center, Gloriae saw the well. She had always imagined a normal well, maybe three feet wide. This well was a hundred feet wide--more a pool than a well, Gloriae thought--and not built of bricks, but carved of solid stone. Mist hovered over it.

"Step up to the well, child," Dies Irae said, finally releasing her. "Gaze into the abyss."

Suddenly Gloriae was fearful. Suddenly she wanted to flee back to her chambers, back to May. But she would not show her father any weakness. He had beaten this strength into her as a blacksmith beats strength into steel. She was a maiden of steel. She would face this. Whatever lay in the abyss, she would stare it down.

She walked forward, knelt over the well, and gazed into the darkness.

At first she saw nothing but black smoke, inky and swirling. She wanted to laugh. Had she been so frightened of nothing but this--smoke and shadows? She was about to turn away, but could not. The darkness seemed... endless, of a size unimaginable to her. Gloriae clutched the well's rim, fingers pushing against the stone. She thought that she gazed into the night sky. Was she gazing below into the earth, or above into the stars? This abyss had the same depth, endless, leading into realms unknown and light that did not shine. This was the opposite of light. Not darkness, no. Darkness was merely the lack of light. This... this was its antithesis, and it was greater, deeper, tugging at her soul.

"What evil is this?" she whispered. It seemed to pull her soul downward, out of her body, so that her consciousness ballooned and filled the well like spreading ink. All her life, she had seen the world from the confines of her skull. Such a small enclosure. Now she knew that the world was larger, infinitely so, not only of three dimensions, but of endless layers and eternal time. The enormity made her grimace, fall to her knees, and cry.

Then she saw them.

They coiled in the darkness--maybe yards away, maybe millions of leagues away. They were long, murky black, not made of solid matter, but of darkness and smoke and lightning. Their eyes shone like stars, their teeth dripped smoke, and they stared at her, and spoke to her, and filled her mind and body, and *enough, enough, please-- Please, Father, enough! I cannot bear them. I cannot stand them inside me, cannot stand the size, the darkness, the dimensions, I want to leap into the abyss, I want to become one of them, to expand and fill the universe, and... God... Sun God, please, if you have power here, save me, I—*

Hands clutched her. Someone pulled her back.

"Where... where am I?" she mumbled. She was lying on a rough stone floor. She gazed up and saw a man there, a man with a face like a griffin, his nose hooked like a beak, his skin golden, his hair slicked back. Who was he? He'd been her father once, a thousand lifetimes ago, but what did that mean?

"Do you understand, Gloriae? Do you understand why we must never release them?"

Gloriae blinked. "I... the world is so large, Father. It is larger than this place, I... we can fill it. We can see it!" Tears streamed down her cheeks. "It's horrible, please, save me, make it stop, make them stop pulling me." She curled up and wept.

Dies Irae pulled her to her feet. He slapped her face. The pain shot through her, and suddenly she felt herself... sucked up, pulled back, drawn inside her body. Her soul slammed into her skull, and she wobbled. It felt like smoke retreating back into a jar.

"I..." She blinked, looked around, and saw that they no longer stood in the chamber of the nightshades. They were back in the room with the guards. She had not even noticed herself returning to this place.

"Come, daughter, we return to the air and light and music of the world."

She followed him in a daze, climbing endless stairs, and neither spoke. It was not until she stood in the gardens of the palace, breathing the sweet night air, watching lords and ladies travel paths between cypresses, that Gloriae shook her head and blew out her breath. She had returned to herself; the nightshades were gone from her mind.

"They cannot be tamed," Dies Irae said, and Gloriae started, for she hadn't realized that he still stood by her. "And you cannot release them. Only the one who sits upon Osanna's throne can open the Well of Night, and I will not. I will not release the terror that lurks there. One day you will sit upon the Ivory Throne, daughter. You will have the power to guard or release these creatures. When that day comes, remember this night. Remember what you saw there. Remember to keep it forever sealed."

Gloriae nodded. "The abyss will remain sealed, today and always."

Dies Irae nodded. He left her there in the garden. She spent a long time walking its paths, gazing up at the stars, lost in thought.

BENEDICTUS

Benedictus trudged toward the gates of Confutatis, cloak wrapped around him, two daggers at his belt.

Other travelers covered the roads around him. Benedictus saw pilgrims in robes and sandals; Sun God priests in samite riding white horses; merchants in purple silk riding in carriages; shaggy peddlers riding mules, leading wagons of wares; thin peasants and farmers, their tunics muddy and patched; and many armored soldiers, their shields emblazoned with griffin heads.

Benedictus scowled under his hood. He remembered days years ago, before Dies Irae, when he'd visit Confutatis with his father to meet its wise king. Few soldiers had marched these roads then, and the farmers were not bedraggled, but healthy and bearing wheelbarrows of crops. Monks had worn homespun robes and worshiped the benevolent Earth God, not this vengeful Sun God who cloaked his priests in gold and jewels. Now the priests were wealthy, the soldiers many, the peasants hungry, the Vir Requis dead. *Sad days,* Benedictus thought, staring at his boots so as not to gaze upon these processions of might and vicious piety. *Cruel days.*

The sound of hooves came behind him, and Benedictus turned to see a knight on horseback leading twenty marching soldiers. The knight wore plate armor and bore a banner with a red, two-headed griffin upon a yellow field. The peasants on the road leaped into the muddy gutters and knelt. Benedictus stepped to the roadside and kept walking, refusing to cower in the mud.

"You there!" came a voice. "Peasant."

Benedictus stared from inside his hood. The knight reined his courser and stared down upon him. "Into the gutter with you," he said.

Benedictus forced his growl down. He bowed his head. "The road is wide, and you have room to pass. I don't disturb you."

The soldiers clinked in their armor, reaching for their swords. The knight raised an gauntleted fist. "I said into the gutter. I want you kneeling in the mud as I ride by."

This time Benedictus did growl. He wanted to shift. He wanted to turn into a dragon and kill these men. He recognized this knight's banner. A two-headed griffin upon a yellow field--this was the banner of House Crudelis, a banner of foul memories. Ten years ago, Benedictus had flown to aid a burning village in Requiem. When he'd arrived, all the villagers were already dead, their bodies tortured and raped. The griffins and soldiers of Osanna had come, destroyed, and left. Only the banner of Crudelis remained, flapping over a pile of dead Vir Requis children.

"Ride by, Crudelis," Benedictus said from the roadside. He reached into his cloak and grabbed a dagger's hilt. "Ride by and let me be. I don't want trouble."

The soldiers stood at attention, but sneaked glances at one another. Crudelis stared down, silent for a long moment. Then he dismounted, walked toward Benedictus, and reached for his sword.

Benedictus thrust his dagger into the knight's visor, deep into his head, spurting blood.

As the knight fell, the soldiers charged. Benedictus ran into the forest. He dared not shift. If they knew a Vir Requis was here, garrisons would storm this forest. Benedictus ran, his old wounds aching, his fists pumping. The soldiers clanked behind him in their armor.

Benedictus grunted. He might just escape them. He was thirty years older than these soldiers, but their armor slowed them. Just as he began to feel safe, something whizzed by his ear. A quarrel hit a tree ahead. More quarrels flew.

"Great," Benedictus muttered as he ran. "They have crossbows."

One quarrel scratched his shoulder, tearing his cloak and drawing blood. Two more hit a tree before him. Benedictus ran from tree to tree, cursing. He saw a declivity ahead, leaped down, and fell. He rolled over roots and rocks, hit a fallen bole at the bottom, and pushed himself up with a grunt. The soldiers stood above, firing down. One quarrel scratched Benedictus's leg. He ran behind more trees, kicking up mud.

"Damn," he muttered. He was too old for this. His lungs ached. He kept running until he reached a cliff, thirty feet tall and covered with vines.

Benedictus spun around, his back to the cliff, and faced the soldiers. Boulders and brambles rose at his sides. He was trapped.

As the soldiers approached, Benedictus raised his hands.

One of the soldiers had a red griffin inlaid into his helmet. With Crudelis dead, this one seemed to have taken command. He grinned at Benedictus, a wolf's grin.

"Are you surrendering, old man?" the soldier said with a sneer. "You do not surrender to us. We are soldiers of Dies Irae. We take no prisoners." His grin widened and he stepped toward Benedictus.

"I'll have to kill all of you," Benedictus said. "I can't let any escape to call for help. If you do this, you will all die."

The soldiers laughed. Their leader raised his sword.

Benedictus shifted.

He did as he'd promised. A few tried to flee, calling for help. Benedictus crashed through the trees toward them, claws outstretched, and tore them down. They were too far from the road; if anyone heard their cries, they wouldn't know where to look. It only took a few moments. It was like stomping on bugs.

Benedictus shifted back into his human form. The soldiers lay dead around him, armor broken, blood feeding the earth.

As he walked back through the forest, seeking the road, Benedictus lowered his head. He hated killing. What he'd just done lay sour in his belly like rotten meat. He knew these men were no innocents; their leader had murdered many Vir Requis, and even the younger soldiers, those who'd not fought in the war, had been brainwashed into malice, tools of death for Dies Irae. Still Benedictus hated the blood on his hands.

"I will never forgive you for this, brother," he whispered. "I will never forgive you for forcing me to kill, for turning me into this. You have called me a monster. You have made me one."

Soon he found the road, and he kept walking. By evening he stood before the white walls of Confutatis. Lacrimosa and Gloriae waited for him there... and Dies Irae.

AGNUS DEI

"But you must help us!" Agnus Dei demanded, eyes teary. "Please."

Her claws dug into the cave floor, a floor made of gold and diamonds. The cave walls were golden too, and gems sparkled in them, reflecting the fire in Agnus Dei's nostrils. On any other day, Agnus Dei would find this vast, glittering chamber inside Har Zahav a place of beauty and wonder. Today she cared little for beauty; she was ready to blow fire, lash her tail, and topple the golden mountain.

"Won't you help us?" she asked again, smoke leaving her nostrils.

The council of salvanae hovered before her and Kyrie, undulating. Sparks of electricity danced between their teeth. The high priest, Nehushtan, hovered at the head of the council. Six other salvanae, their mustaches long and white, hovered behind him. All their eyes--those large, round eyes like glass orbs--stared at the two Vir Requis.

"Agnus Dei," Kyrie whispered from the side of his mouth, "maybe it's a lost cause. They're peaceful creatures. I'm not sure they can help us fight." He too stood in dragon form, claws upon the golden floor.

Angus Dei looked back at Nehushtan. "Please," she said. "They'll kill my parents. They've killed so many Vir Requis already. Fly with us! Bring your warriors. Their fangs are sharp. Their lightning is hot. Fight with us. Fight Dies Irae."

Nehushtan regarded her silently for long moments. He puffed rings of smoke from his mouth, then spoke in his creaky voice. His words were slow and calm. "We of the land of Salvandos, of the holy Har Zahav mountain, do not concern ourselves with the ways of humans, or of griffinflesh. We are salvanae, the true dragons of ancient times. We concern ourselves only with dragonkind. The way of the dragon is our way, and it is a good way. A way of peace. Of meditation. Of reflection and prayer."

"But we're dragons too," Agnus Dei said, eyes stinging. She bucked and clawed the air. Her tail lashed, hit a wall, and knocked down a shower of gems. The priests winced.

"Agnus D--" Kyrie began, but she ignored him.

"Look at these wings!" Agnus Dei said. "Look at these fangs." She blew fire against the cave ceiling, blackening its gold and incurring more winces. "Look at these flames. These are dragon flames. I am a dragon maiden. And my way is the way of honor. Of helping friends. Of fighting for life and goodness." Tears rolled down her cheeks. "We are dragons too, so fly with us. Shoot your lightning with our fire."

Nehushtan raised his tufted white eyebrows. "But you have human forms. How could you be dragons? We have seen you walking upon two legs."

As Agnus Dei fumed, Kyrie touched her shoulder and answered for her. "The smoke rings you blow also change form. They sometimes looks like dragons, sometimes like men, sometimes like, well... nothing at all. But it's always the same substance. Same with us Vir Requis."

Nehushtan blinked, blew smoke rings, and watched them take the shape of coiling dragons. He thought for a long time, moving his eyes from Agnus Dei to Kyrie. The other priests did the same. Finally Nehushtan spoke again.

"You have spoken well, Kyrie Eleison of Requiem, so I will offer you this. Beyond Har Zahav, and the mists of Arafel Canyons, rise the Stone Rings. There do young dragons prove their worth. There you too must fly. If you survive the Stone Rings, you'll have proven yourselves worthy dragons, that your blood and soul shine under the Draco stars. We will then fly with you."

"And if we fail?" Agnus Dei asked.

Nehushtan blinked sadly. "If you fail... you will die."

Agnus Dei growled. "Let's go."

The salvanae took flight, bodies snaking into a tunnel. Agnus Dei followed, growling. Kyrie flew behind her. The tunnel was just wide enough for their dragon forms, and it led them past gems, subterranean waterfalls, caverns of golden stalactites and stalagmites, and finally out a cave onto the mountainside. They flew into the cold air, following the salvanae. Soon the mountain of Har Zahav was far behind, a golden triangle, and then it was only a glint in the distance. Clouds streamed around Agnus Dei, cold against her face, filling her mouth and nostrils and eyes. She blew fire and roared. Whatever these salvanae had in store, she would face it. She would overcome.

"For you, Mother," she whispered, and her eyes stung with tears. "For you, Father. I love you so much."

She sniffed, shook her head to clear her tears, and glanced at Kyrie. *I hope he didn't see me cry. He is a pup, and I am a creature of fire, and he must never see my weakness.* If he saw, however, Kyrie had the grace--and good sense--to pretend he hadn't.

"Pup," she said, "what do you reckon these salvanae have planned for us?"

Kyrie looked at her, fangs bared. He looked ready to fight an army. The salvanae flew far ahead, too far to hear.

"A test of courage," he said. "A test of strength. A rite of passage for salvana warriors. Whatever this challenge is, we're going to beat it. I'm a good flier. You're not bad, either."

She bristled and blew flames. "I can beat you at any challenge they give, pup. But this time we're not competing against each other. We're going to prove that we Vir Requis have just as much strength, speed, and spirit as they do."

She tried not to think of Mother in captivity, or of Father flying into battle. Today she would think only of proving her worth, of flying to save them.

They flew for hours, following the salvanae who snaked ahead. They flew over canyons of stone, and over forests of pines, and over grassy fields and rushing rivers. Finally they reached a land of towering stone columns, each column a league high, carved into the shape of great faces. Eyes the size of palaces glared at them, and mouths larger than cathedrals gaped in silent screams. The columns--and the faces carved into them--seemed ancient. They were smooth and mossy. It seemed that centuries of rain and wind had pummeled them into weary, grotesque figures. The salvanae flew between the columns, seeming as small as dragonflies around men.

"What is this place?" Agnus Dei asked Kyrie. "Those faces are strange."

Kyrie nodded. "Feels like they're staring at you." He flew before one face's eye. It was larger than him. They couldn't even see the ground; the columns disappeared into darkness leagues below.

The salvanae led them toward an empty space of mist and shadows. Though it had been day only minutes before, night cloaked this place. Agnus Dei saw stars above, and three purple moons. They were strange stars, and strange moons, things of a different sky, too close, too large, and Agnus Dei had to look away. She felt like that sky could swallow her.

"Look!" Kyrie said. Agnus Dei followed his stare and gasped. Ahead in darkness, distant but growing larger as they flew, hovered three stone rings. No columns held them; they floated on air. One ring was large, a dozen feet wide; the next was half the size, and the third half again. When Agnus Dei flew closer, she saw that blades filled the rings, rusty and bloodied.

"What are those?" she asked and hissed. Smoke rose between her teeth.

"I don't know," Kyrie said, "but look below them."

Agnus Dei looked and growled. Jagged rock and metal rose below the floating rings, and upon them lay the skeletons of a hundred salvanae. Some bones were ancient, bleached white like dragon teeth. Others were newer and bloodstained. Some bones looked fresh; bits of skin and scales covered them, rotting in the mist.

"What is this place?" Agnus Dei demanded of the salvanae. They hovered ahead, bodies coiling beneath them, eyes blinking at her. "Answer me! What graveyard have you brought us to?"

Nehushtan regarded her. After a long silence, he spoke. "This is our gauntlet. This is the blood of dragons. Here we prove our worth, and here you will prove you are true dragons, worthy of the name, worthy of your wings. If you are demons cloaked in dragon flesh, you will die here. If your forms are true, and if Draco starlight shines upon you, you will survive. We will fight with you then."

Agnus Dei roared and lashed her tail. "What do we do?"

Nehushtan gazed at the bloody blades that filled the stone rings. "Fly through the stone rings, from largest to smallest. The blades inside the rings are poisoned; a scrape is lethal. If you fly too clumsily, the blades will kill you. The blades will lengthen as you fly, blooming like steel flowers. If you fly slowly, they will kill you. Fly straight. Fly fast. Or you will die."

Agnus Dei and Kyrie stared at the stone rings. Those rusty, bloody blades seemed to stare back. Fly through the rings? *It's impossible*, Agnus Dei thought. *Impossible!* The first hoop was twelve feet wide. That was large enough for a slim, serpentine salvana to clear. They had no wings, no limbs, and a body lithe and long. But how would she, a Vir Requis with long wings and limbs, fly through this ring of death? And even if she cleared the first ring, the second was only six feet wide, and the third--only three.

"Impossible," Agnus Dei said. "These hoops were built to test slim salvanae, not bulky Vir Requis. Give us another test."

Nehushtan shook his head. "This is the gauntlet of the dragon. If you cannot pass this test, you are weak, or you are demons in dragon form. A soul of Draco stars, worthy of our help, will fly through the Stone Rings. Fly now! Or leave our land and return to Osanna."

Agnus Dei stared at Nehushtan, the smoke from her maw obscuring her vision. Rage flared inside her. She wanted to fly at the priest and rip him to shreds. But she needed him. She needed his warriors. Agnus Dei closed her eyes, took deep breaths, and thought about her mother.

Mother has always loved me, she thought. *Even when I yelled, or rebelled, or hated her--she loved me. She raised me, protected me, kept me alive as Dies Irae hunted us across the world.* And now Lacrimosa was captured, maybe dead, maybe tortured. Father had gone to save her, but even the great Benedictus, the Black Fang, could not fight the might of Dies Irae and his hosts. *Only I can save them,* Agnus Dei knew.

She opened her eyes. "You're on," she said to Nehushtan. She flapped her wings.

"Wait!"

Kyrie grabbed her tail, holding her back. Agnus Dei howled and snapped her teeth at him, new fire filling her. "Let go, pup."

"No!" he said, eyes pained. "Agnus Dei, you'll die. Please. This is not the way."

She shook her head wildly, struggling to free herself. "If we cannot pass this gauntlet, we'll all die. You, me, Mother, Father, the memory of Requiem, the blood of Vir Requis. This is the only way, Kyrie. I can do this." She stopped struggling, flew toward him, and nuzzled his cheek. "I can do this," she whispered into his ear. "I love you, Kyrie. Believe in me."

His grip on her tail loosened. Agnus Dei flew toward the stone rings.

BENEDICTUS

Benedictus stood outside the city gates. People crowded around him--beggars in rags, peddlers riding wagons of trinkets, peasants leading oxen laden with grains and vegetables, merchants in fur coats, and pilgrims bearing coins for Sun God temples. Guards stood at the gates, golden griffins embroidered onto their red tunics, their armor burnished and their swords at their sides. They were searching everyone for weapons, collecting the gate tolls, and letting people into Confutatis one by one.

Benedictus grumbled, bent his head, and tugged his hood lower. Few people would recognize him in his human form--most knew him only as the black dragon--but he'd take no chances. He reached into his pocket and felt his coins--enough to bribe the guards should they become suspicious. He then felt at his side, where his dagger hung. The guards would confiscate this dagger if they let him in. If they caused trouble, he might bury it in their throats. Under his cloak, his fist clutched the hilt.

The people shuffled closer to the gates. Benedictus could hear the guards now. "Right, what's that then? No staffs. Give me that, old man. Nothing that can be used as a weapon. What's this here? I'll take that knife. Hand it over. All right, that's good copper; two coins a head. In you go. You there, two coppers toll, no blades, no arrows, no sticks or stones. Two coppers, you're good."

Benedictus scowled under his hood. Once he would fly into this city bearing banners, dine with the king in palaces, hear music in gardens between statues of angels. So much had changed. This city. Himself. The world. Benedictus ached for his daughters. *My daughters will never know the world I did as a youth, a world of peace and beauty.* To his daughters, it was this: a world of violence, hatred, and fear.

He shuffled closer in the crowd, one hand clutching his coins, the other his dagger. When he was ten people away, a chill ran through him. The guards held leaves, which they pressed against the chests of all who passed.

Benedictus growled.

Ilbane.

Benedictus wanted to turn away, to push back through the crowd, to find another gate. But he dared not. Too many people had seen him. To flee after seeing the ilbane would look suspicious. A few whispers in the crowd, and the guards would chase him. No. He'd enter these gates.

Ilbane burned hotter than fire, Benedictus knew. He could still feel that fire, all these years after Lanburg Fields where ilbane-coated arrows had pierced him. If the ilbane touched him, he would sweat, grunt, even scream. No Vir Requis could withstand its torture and remain composed; not even him, the great Benedictus the Black, the King of Requiem.

"Move along, come on, maggots. Move, damn you!" Two old peasants, possibly a husband and wife, were shuffling into the city. The guards had seized their canes, and they moved on shaky legs.

The guards growled, and one shouted. "Move it, peasants. We haven't got all day." Two guards shoved the old couple. They laughed as the peasants fell onto the cobblestones.

Grunting, Benedictus shoved his way through the last people in line. He tried to go help the peasants who lay on the ground beyond the gates.

"Hold there!" shouted a guard, and rough hands grabbed Benedictus's shoulders. He turned his head, scowling, to see two guards clutching him. Their faces were unshaven and their eyes red.

"I'm going to help them," Benedictus said in a low, dangerous growl.

The guards laughed, showing rotting teeth. Their breath stank. "No you're not, worm," one said. "Toll's two coppers. Pay up and open that cloak of yours. No weapons. No sticks or stones. And no lip."

One guard held ilbane a foot away from Benedictus. Even at this distance, Benedictus felt the heat and pain of those leaves. Sweat beaded on his brow.

"All right," he said, speaking slowly and carefully. He wanted nothing more than to kill these men, but then the entire city guard would fall upon him. Then he would let down Lacrimosa. *Control your temper,* he told himself. *Be careful.*

He grabbed three silver coins from his pockets. It was more than these guards would earn in a month. His teeth clenched, Benedictus slammed the three silvers against a guard's chest. "Your birthday present is early this year," he said in a low voice. "Now let me through, no questions asked, and you'll get another gift when I leave tonight."

The guard stared at the coins, and his eyes widened. He bit one and raised an eyebrow. "Who are you, peasant?" he asked, voice low.

"A private man," Benedictus said. "Now let me through."

Without waiting for a reply, he took a step toward the gate. He took a second step. A third. He forced himself to move slowly, to breathe calmly.

A hand clutched his shoulder.

"All right, stranger, no questions," spoke the guard who'd taken the coins. "You like your privacy, and you can pay for it. But we must do one thing."

The guard shoved the ilbane against Benedictus's chest.

AGNUS DEI

Agnus Dei shot toward the first stone ring, eyes narrowed. She could still hear Nehushtan's voice echoing in her mind: *The blades will lengthen as you fly, blooming like steel flowers. If you fly slow, they will kill you. Fly straight. Fly fast. Or you will die.* Agnus Dei snarled, pulled her limbs and wings close, and became a long, thin shape.

The ring's blades creaked.

Agnus Dei shot forward.

The bloody blades began to extend.

Agnus Dei screamed, shooting into the hoop. A blade scratched one of her scales, and Agnus Dei howled, but she was safe; it had not touched her blood, had not infested her with poison.

"I made it!" she cried.

"Quick, the other ring!" Kyrie shouted.

The blades in the second, smaller ring were also extending; the opening was barely four feet wide now. Agnus Dei snarled and shot forward, knowing it was too narrow for her dragon body. The ring was close now, inches away. Agnus Dei screamed as she shifted. In midair, she became human and somersaulted through the hoop. A rusty blade sliced a strand of her hair. She was through! She shifted back into a dragon and howled.

"The third ring, hurry!" Kyrie cried, and Agnus Dei grunted and flew. *No, impossible!* The third ring was so small, three feet wide, and its blades were extending inward. There were barely two feet between the blades now.

"Hurry!"

Agnus Dei sucked in her breath, flew, and shifted again. She was human, tumbling through the air. Instead of somersaulting through this hoop, she dived. She held out her arms, and pulled her legs together, and held her breath.

She shot through the last hoop, the blades shredding her clothes.

She fell through air.

"I'm through!" she cried, falling toward the skeletons below. Before she could hit them, she shifted into a dragon again, and shot into the sky with a roar and shower of flame. "I'm through!"

The salvanae began bugling, heads tossed back. Agnus Dei panted, hovering in midair. The blades in the rings pulled back into the stone, leaving just their rusty tips. *I made it. I'm going to save you, Mother.* Tears stung her eyes.

Kyrie roared and flew toward the stone rings. He too flew through the first, wide ring in dragon form. He then shifted in midair and tumbled through the second, smaller ring in human form. He shifted into dragon shape, flapped his wings, shifted again. He dived through the last, smallest ring. The blades ripped his cloak, tore off his left boot, and sliced strands of his hair.

Once through the third ring, he became a dragon again and flew beside Agnus Dei, panting. The salvanae cried to the sky, their roars shaking the world. Three pillars cracked and tumbled into the darkness.

"We did it!" Agnus Dei roared to the salvanae. "We passed your test. We proved our dragon worth. Now fly with us. Tonight! Fly with us to war."

The salvanae blew lightning into the skies. They looked at one another, at Agnus Dei and Kyrie, at one another again. They spoke rapidly, some shouting, some whispering, some spitting lightning.

"Well?" Agnus Dei said and roared. "Stay true to your word! Fly with us. Or are you cowards and liars?"

The dragons roared, and blew more lightning, and spoke louder. Finally Nehushtan shouted above them, and the others silenced. The High Priest turned toward Agnus Dei. His eyes were narrowed, and smoke left his nostrils. He coiled through the sky, flying toward her, and stared into her eyes. Angus Dei saw lightning in those eyes.

"Tonight," he said, "the salvanae fly to war."

As the salvanae flew, and the Vir Requis followed, Agnus Dei tightened her lips and shivered. Confutatis lay many days away. She was bringing help... and she prayed that she wasn't too late.

"Hang in there, Mother," she whispered. "I'll be there soon."

BENEDICTUS

Pain like shattered glass filled him.

The guard held the ilbane against his chest, and Benedictus wanted to die. The fire spread across his ribs, into his heart, down his spine, and scorched his fingertips. He had not felt such agony since Lanburg Fields.

"How does it feel, old man?" the guard asked, eyes narrowed.

With every last drop of will, Benedictus forced himself to remain silent, to keep his face calm. He even tried to will sweat from appearing on his brow.

"Fine," he whispered. He could speak no louder. He wanted to fall to his knees. He wanted to kill the guard. He wanted anything but to remain standing, casual, the ilbane against him. *Take it off!* he wanted to scream. *I've stood my ground. Remove the leaves!*

But the guard held them against Benedictus. "Are you sure?" he asked, frowning. "You look pale. And there's sweat on your brow."

Benedictus growled, though he wanted to scream in pain. *The fire!* The fire filled him. It was too much, too much. *This must be how women feel at childbirth,* he thought, almost blind with pain. Stars and mist flooded his vision.

"It's been a long journey," he somehow managed to say, mustering all his will to stop his voice from cracking. "If I were a bloody weredragon, this stuff would kill me, not just bring sweat to my brow."

The guard's frown deepened. *Take it off, take it off!* Benedictus did not think he could last a second longer. He was just about to shift into a dragon, to kill every guard he saw, to storm the city, when....

"All right," the guard said and pulled the ilbane back. "Sorry to trouble you, and I know you pay well. In you go."

Benedictus turned around quickly, and once the guard was behind him, he grimaced. His knees trembled, but he forced himself to keep walking. Once in the city, he knelt by the fallen old man and woman, who were still struggling to rise from the cobblestones. He knelt not only to help them; he could no longer stand upright.

"Here," he said to the old peasants when he'd caught his breath, "let me help you up."

He took several more deep breaths, assisted the peasants to their feet, and walked deeper into Confutatis, leaving the gates behind.

"I'm almost there, Lacrimosa," he whispered. "Almost there to save you, my love." He clenched his fists. "And I'll find you too, Gloriae. I'll find you, daughter, and I'll free you too from Dies Irae."

He moved through the city, cloak pulled tight around him, hood low. His old wound ached with new fire, his joints burned, and his head pounded. The ilbane had taken so much of his strength. Benedictus could barely walk. If soldiers attacked him now, he would not fight well. He grunted, leaned against a wall, and clutched his chest.

Some hero, he thought as he stood, catching his breath. *Look at the great king now. Just a gruff old man sneaking through alleys, grunting in pain.*

As he took ragged breaths, Benedictus noticed people rushing down the cobbled streets. Kids were jostling one another as they ran, smashing dragon dolls with wooden swords. Adults were placing bets and talking about "the beast" fighting new creatures today, "something truly deadly; lions I hear, or elephants in armor." Most of those hurrying down the street were commoners, but Benedictus also saw two wealthy merchants in a carriage, and even a noblewoman on a palanquin.

The beast.

Benedictus steadied himself and kept walking. He stumbled down the cobbled road among the commoners, nobles, and horses. Crenellations and towers rose at his sides, laden with guards sporting the golden griffin upon their shields. Real griffins stood atop towers and walls, armored, staring down at the crowd.

At every square he passed, Benedictus saw a marble statue of Dies Irae. The statues all stared toward the heavens, one fist against the heart, the other around a sword hilt. In the statues, Dies Irae still had both his hands. But Benedictus remembered biting off the left one, spitting it out, then taking pity on his brother. *I left you alive, Irae. If I meet you again, you will find that my mercy has left me.*

Benedictus did not want to meet his brother. He wanted only to find Lacrimosa and Gloriae, to steal them back, to flee with them into the west. He'd had enough of fighting, of killing, of his monstrous brother. And yet, another part of him did want to meet Dies Irae here. Craved it. That part felt like a shark in bloodlust, wanting only to bite, to kill. Benedictus hated that part of him, and hated Dies Irae for placing it within him.

The streets of Confutatis widened as he walked, clutching his chest. The crowds thickened, some chanting "Blood for the beast!" Fortresses towered here, and griffins circled in the skies. Soldiers stood at every street corner, and monoliths of Dies Irae gazed down from hills, jeweled eyes watching the crowds. Troops patrolled between the commoners, armor chinking.

The Marble City--once a place of gardens, of peace, of poets and artists. Now a city of sword and shield, of beak and talon.

Soon he beheld the amphitheater of Confutatis, a ring of white marble. Its walls rose two hundred feet, set with alcoves that held statues. Years ago, solemn stone statues of kings had filled these alcoves; today he saw figures of Dies Irae holding the Sun Disk. A golden idol stood outside the amphitheater's gates, a hundred feet tall, hands raised. It was carved as a young Dies Irae, cherubic, a halo encircling his brow.

"The beast is hungry today, I hear," said a bearded man beside Benedictus, speaking to his friends. "Whatever Dies Irae has in store for her today, it ain't gonna be enough. I bet a bronze coin on her."

One of his friends snickered. "That beast ain't nothing but a tired old lizard. Irae's been feeding her dust, I hear, and whipping her. The creature's too thin and weak to win another fight. I'll take your bronze."

The first man laughed. "Torture makes that one hungry and mean. Who else? Bronze on the weredragon!"

Weredragon.

Inside his hood, Benedictus growled. That was a cruel word, a slur that should never be uttered, least of all by scraggly men who bet on misery and blood. He stepped toward them.

"A fool bets against a proud, dying race," he said, voice low. "And a greater fool stages fights for fools' bets."

The men laughed. "What are you, a poet or something?" the first man said, scratching his beard. Fleas filled it.

"You know me," Benedictus rasped. "You know my name. Your lord wants me forgotten, but it will not be so. You will hear our roar again."

With that he left them, stepping toward the amphitheater's gates. *Foolish thing to say,* he knew. Why did he risk his cover for these men? He forced himself to focus, to forget these cruel crowds, to remember his task. *I will save you, Lacrimosa,* he thought. *Soon you'll be flying west with me to find our children.* Kyrie too was his child now, by adoption if not by blood. All the last Vir Requis were his children, his torch to keep aflame.

And I have not forgotten you, Gloriae. In the deepest corners of his heart, Benedictus knew that Gloriae was evil now, corrupted and cruel. She might be unreachable to him, a maiden of steel in her palace, but Benedictus dared to dream, dared to pray that he could save her.

He paid to enter the amphitheater, stepped inside, and found himself dizzy. Tens of thousands of people surrounded him, cheering from a hundred tiers of marble seats. Slave girls danced in the arena, chains binding their necks, raising sand under their feet. They were nude, their bodies painted red and gold. Benedictus knew that their heavy makeup hid bruises, and one's nose was bandaged. Guards watched the dancers from the sidelines, clutching whips.

Benedictus imagined those whips cutting Lacrimosa, and he clenched his fists and ground his teeth. Below the lowest tier of seats, Benedictus saw doorways and stairwells leading underground. *Which leads to Lacrimosa?* Benedictus wanted to bash down every door, storm down every passageway, and save his wife. He forced himself to wait. There were many doorways here, and many guards, and he would not find her. If he charged brazenly, like Kyrie might, he'd only get himself killed, and probably earn torture for Lacrimosa.

"Patience," he told himself. "You're not a rash, hot-headed youth like Kyrie or Agnus Dei. You can wait. Bide your time. Learn where she is."

Nobody noticed him talking to himself. The crowds were too busy cheering, stamping their feet, and leering at the dancers. Benedictus found his seat on the thirtieth row and sat on the cold stone. A father with two children sat to his left. To his right sat two young maidens, henna on their eyelids and perfume on their fair skin. Both wore white silk that revealed more flesh than it hid.

Families with children, Benedictus thought in disgust. *Young women on a day out. The blood of Requiem is sport for them.*

The dancers finished their dance, bowed to the crowd, and disappeared into an underground passageway. Silence fell upon the crowd, and everyone leaned forward, waiting for the beast to emerge. Only Benedictus did not stare at the arena. He scanned the crowds until he found the man he sought.

Dies Irae.

His brother sat across the amphitheater, a palanquin of samite shading him. Two griffin statues guarded his sides, and a slave girl lay collared at his feet. Dies Irae wore his white, jeweled armor. Sun God warriors stood at his sides, his elite guard, their helmets shaped as sunbursts, their swords shaped as sunbeams.

"Hello, brother," Benedictus whispered. "It's been a long time."

Three hundred feet away, Dies Irae raised his eyes and stared at Benedictus.

Ice shot through Benedictus. He froze, unable to look away. How could it be? How could Dies Irae have heard him? Benedictus was about to run, but then Dies Irae looked away. Heart racing, Benedictus took a deep breath. *He couldn't have seen me. My face is hidden in my hood. It was only chance.*

His heart was still thrashing when Sun God priests stepped onto the arena, saluted Dies Irae, and began to sing a hymn. The crowd rose to their feet. Benedictus did not want to rise, but forced himself to. The priests were clad in white, and white masks hid their faces. They sang for the Sun God to bless Dies Irae, the favored child of the heavens, and to grant death to his enemies.

"Child of the heavens," Benedictus grumbled. "He's calling himself the son of gods now."

When the song ended, the priests pulled forward a child in silk, her face also masked. The priests cried for the glory of the Sun God, and before Benedictus realized what would happen, they had set the girl on fire.

"No!" Benedictus cried, jumping to his feet. Nobody heard him. The crowd was cheering for the Sun God, crying out for his glory and blessings. The girl was still alive; she thrashed and screamed, a ball of fire, before falling dead to the ground.

The priests extinguished the flames with sand, then raised the small, smoldering body over their heads. They sang, calling for the Sun God to accept this offering, to grant them triumph, and to curse the weredragons who tainted the world. The crowd cheered.

The burned girl twitched and moaned.

She's alive! Benedictus wanted to retch. The small figure, blistered and smoldering, was whimpering. The priests placed her down and stabbed her dead.

Benedictus sat down, shaken. He'd seen much cruelty during the war against Dies Irae years ago. He'd seen people burn to death. He'd seen Dies Irae murder children. But this... this was different. The war had ended. Dies Irae had won his glory, his throne. Why this killing? Why still the torture and murder of innocents? Benedictus had always known his brother was evil, but for the first time, he realized how truly insane the man was.

The entire city seemed just as insane, Benedictus thought. Dies Irae and his god had turned these people into... what? Monsters? Demons? Benedictus had no name for it. In their eyes, he was the monster. Benedictus was no scholar. He could not explain this. He only knew he had to end it.

I can't just take Lacrimosa and Gloriae and flee, he realized. *I have to stop my brother. Not only for the memory of* Requiem, *but for the fate of the world.*

Before he could wonder how, gates opened below, and guards dragged out a chained, beaten Lacrimosa.

LACRIMOSA

Lacrimosa limped when the guards pulled her chains. They had sent strange creatures to fight her yesterday--furry beasts wielding hammers--and she had killed them, but not before one hammered her leg. What would Dies Irae unleash against her today? Creatures of horn, or talons, or fangs? More slaves with swords, or bears in spiked armor? How long before one of these creatures killed her, ending her pain?

As the crowds cheered around her, and the sunlight blinded her, Lacrimosa lowered her head. Today she would not fight. Whatever beasts attacked her, she would let them. She would endure their horns, claws, or fangs, let them tear her apart and end her misery.

"I'm sorry, Ben," she whispered, tears in her eyes. "I'm sorry I wasn't strong enough, that I couldn't hold on. I love you. Find our children. Fly away from here. My time is ended, and I will soon join the spirits of Requiem, and see those halls among the birches once more." She smiled through her tears. The spirits of her forefathers awaited her, and she would drink wine in their halls.

When she'd reached the arena's center, the guards attached her leash to a post. They left her there. The crowds jeered and pelted her with rotten fruit.

A trapdoor on the floor opened. Three red tigers emerged, blew flames from their maws, and raced toward her.

Lacrimosa lowered her head. "Goodbye, Ben," she whispered, waiting for the tigers. "Goodbye."

And then she heard a voice.

"Lacrimosa."

She opened her eyes.

"My love."

The tigers reached her, and Lacrimosa lashed her tail, sending them flying. She looked around wildly. Who had spoken? She could see nobody. The voice had not come from the crowds; it seemed to have spoken within her. A tiger leaped at her. She clawed it, kicked it aside, and lashed her horns against another tiger.

"Lacrimosa, of moonlit hair and eyes of stars. Lacrimosa, daughter of Requiem. You do not die today."

Light broke through the clouds, falling upon her, and she felt Benedictus with her. She couldn't see him, but she knew he was near. She knew these were the whispers of his soul, his ancient magic, flowing through her.

The tigers leaped and bit, but they could not hurt her today. Today the light of her ancestors, and love of her king, filled her with more strength than Dies Irae could conquer. She slew these tigers of fire upon the sand, and roared to the city of Confutatis, and flapped her wings, and watched them cower.

"For Benedictus, and for Requiem," she whispered, tears on her cheeks. "Let this city see our pride one last day."

The guards dragged her back into her cell underground, and chained her to the wall, and slammed the door shut, but even in the darkness Lacrimosa could see that light, feel that warmth.

"Benedictus is here," she whispered.

BENEDICTUS

Benedictus walked through the shadows. It was a starless night, a black night of the soul, and he held his breath as he padded across the cobblestones. The amphitheater was deserted now. Only three soldiers had guarded it; he had knocked them out with barely a sound. The arena now held nothing but silence, sand, and him--King Benedictus.

Once he had led armies in war. Once he had led men, women, and children to die under his banners. Once, years ago, he'd have stormed this place with fang and fire and fury, would have brought the might of Requiem upon its walls and shattered them. Tonight he lurked, a shadow, alone in darkness and pain.

He'd seen where they kept her. He crept to that old, iron trapdoor in the arena's floor. He tugged at it. It was locked, but Benedictus had taken the keys from those guards he sent to sleep. He tried the keys now, one by one, until one fit. The lock clicked, and Benedictus opened the trapdoor.

Cold air blew from below. At first Benedictus saw only darkness, but soon he discerned soft light, like a glint from silver scales.

"Lacrimosa," he whispered.

Before he could enter the dungeon, a caw sounded behind Benedictus. He spun around, eyes narrowed. A shadow darted, then vanished. Benedictus stared, heart racing, but saw nothing. *An owl,* he decided. Nothing more. He turned back to the door.

"Lacrimosa," he whispered again.

For a moment there was only silence. Then he heard a voice from below, a voice soft and pure as moonlight. "Ben?"

Tears filled his eyes. He shivered and could barely breathe. "Hang on, my love. I'm coming down, I--"

Something creaked behind him.

Benedictus spun around, and then he saw him.

Upon the seats of the amphitheater, high above and watching him, stood Volucris, the King of Griffins. Dies Irae sat upon the beast, clad in armor.

"Hello, brother," Dies Irae called down. "Hello, Benedictus, King of Weredragons, Lord of Lizards. Welcome to my home."

With a growl, Benedictus shifted.

Volucris swooped.

A black dragon blowing fire, Benedictus leaped toward the griffin.

His joints still ached from the ilbane. His heart was still heavy. But tonight Benedictus ignored the pain. With a howl, he slammed against Volucris, crashing with a ball of fire, his roars shaking the world. Volucris shrieked, clawed, and bit. They broke apart. They leaped again.

"Tonight you're mine, brother!" Dies Irae called from atop Volucris, aiming a lance. "Did you truly think that I didn't see you earlier today?"

Benedictus roared and snapped his teeth. Volucris pulled back. Benedictus's teeth clanged against Dies Irae's shield.

"I saw you, brother," Dies Irae laughed. "I saw you today, and I have seen you for years in my mind. I saw you whenever I crushed a bug under my foot, or cut the head off a serpent that crawled through dust."

Volucris bit, Benedictus pulled back, and the beak scratched him. Benedictus howled, raised his claws, and blew fire. Volucris soared and prepared to swoop. Benedictus shot up, crashed into the griffin, and sent it tumbling.

Dies Irae spurred Volucris and flew high. Benedictus followed. The amphitheater was soon distant below, and Volucris swooped toward Benedictus. He met the griffin head on, crashing into him with biting teeth and scratching claws. Feathers and scales flew. Blood rained. They pulled apart, roared, and crashed again. Fire crackled.

"You've slowed down, brother!" Dies Irae howled, laughing, mad. Volucris burned but still fought. Dies Irae's cape caught fire, but still the madman cackled. "You have slowed, you have aged, and now I will kill you. Tonight you die."

They were high above the city now. The marble streets and forts of Confutatis seemed like toys below, small fires burning among them. Benedictus swiped his claws, but his brother was right. He was slow now. His torn wing screamed. Volucris pulled back, dodging the blow, and scratched. More scales fell, and blood seeped down Benedictus's leg.

He shouted with fire and pain. "Return the Griffin Heart, brother. Return the amulet that you stole. These beasts are not yours to tame. This throne is not yours to--"

Dies Irae pulled a crossbow from his saddle and shot. The quarrel hit Benedictus in the shoulder.

Pain flowed through him, the pain of ilbane, not old leaves like the guards had used, but the pure juice of the plant. It coated the dart, spreading fire through him. Benedictus howled. The city spun below. The statues and temples and streets all blurred. More griffins lurked there, but Benedictus could barely see them. Tears filled his eyes.

With all his will, he flapped his wings and lunged at his brother. "It ends tonight, Irae. Tonight you--"

Dies Irae fired his crossbow again. A quarrel hit Benedictus's chest. He howled, blood in his eyes, blood in his mouth.

"Oh dear, brother," Dies Irae said. He raised his visor, and through squinting eyes, Benedictus saw that he was smiling. "Oh dear indeed. All these years you've hidden, Benedictus. All these years you've dreamed of revenge. Only to fail like this... an old man, tired, Lacrimosa now my slave and--"

"You will not say her name!" Benedictus said. He did not know how he still flew. He'd never taken so much ilbane, had never felt such agony, but Lacrimosa's name on Dies Irae's tongue tore him with more anguish than the poison.

Somehow, impossibly, he flew against his brother. He bit and he clawed.

Dies Irae shot a third time.

The quarrel hit Benedictus's neck.

He tried to scream. He tried to blow fire. He tried to bite, to claw, to kill his brother. But he could not even flap his wings. He could not even breathe.

I'm sorry, Lacrimosa, he thought, tears falling, before darkness spread across his eyes. *I'm so sorry.*

Benedictus the Black, King of Requiem, closed his eyes and fell from the sky.

DIES IRAE

Dies Irae stood, arms crossed, and watched his brother wake up.

Of course, his arms were not crossed, not really. You could not cross your arms if you had only one. That groggy, bloody man below him--no, not a man, a *creature*--had bitten off his left arm. Now he had but an iron mace, a freak thing, a deformity. It was a deadly deformity, to be sure, and one that he enjoyed flaunting, intimidating with, killing with... but a deformity nonetheless.

"You crippled me, Benedictus," he said softly, so softly the sound did not carry past his griffin-head visor. "You made me what I am."

Knocked into human form, Benedictus groaned on the cobblestones. Blood covered him, and his eyes blinked feebly, struggling to stay open. Red lines stretched across his chest, lines of infection from the ilbane. Dies Irae spat at him.

"You turned me into this. Yes, Benedictus. You and our father. You drove me into shame, into pain and rage. I am a year your senior. I was to be Requiem's heir, even without the dragon curse. But you stole my place. You sweet-talked Father into casting me aside. You forced me to become this man, Benedictus. To kill Father, to raze Requiem. You have suffered for it, brother. Today I end your suffering."

Benedictus struggled to rise, but chains held him down. Dies Irae wanted to spit on him again, but his mouth had gone dry. It only curled bitterly. "Today I show you final mercy. I will not torture you, Benedictus. I have tortured you for many years, but you're still my brother. Despite all you've done, all your sins, you're still my brother. I will kill you painlessly. I give you that last gift."

Finally Benedictus managed to focus his gaze and speak. "I go to the halls of my ancestors, of the spirits of Requiem. When you die--and all men must die, Dies Irae, even those who style themselves deities--may the Sun God burn your soul in eternal fire."

Dies Irae kicked him in the stomach, and Benedictus doubled over. Dies Irae kicked him again in the back, driving his steel-tipped boot into him. "You die tonight, weredragon."

He kicked Benedictus a third time, then turned and marched across the courtyard. His boots sloshed through Benedictus's blood, which had fallen from the sky. *Fitting,* he thought. His boots were made of a weredragon child; let them now walk upon the blood of the Weredragon King.

Walls and towers rose around him, the fortifications of Confutatis. Griffins manned their battlements. Soldiers stood at attention and saluted as he walked by. Dies Irae ignored them. He walked past his hosts, past the courtyards and forts, until he reached Volucris. The griffin was feeding upon the bones of a prisoner, blood staining his beak.

"Come, Volucris", Dies Irae said. He placed a hand upon the griffin's head. Volucris cawed, and Dies Irae mounted him. His body ached from the fight--bruises were probably spreading under his armor--but he ignored the pain. "To the palace."

They flew over the forts and streets, and Dies Irae watched his palace from above. He gazed upon his statues that stood, shadows in the night, with two arms. He gazed upon his menagerie of caged tigers, elephants, and other beasts. He gazed upon his banners flapping from a dozen towers. It was a palace of splendor, of endless lavishness and power. But it wasn't enough. Nothing would be enough until he killed Benedictus, killed him a million times, profaned his memory. Fire filled Dies

Irae, for he realized that even in death, Benedictus would taunt him, realized that even the destruction of the last Vir Requis could not calm the shame, the rage.

"Damn you, brother," he whispered.

The anger pulsed through him, hot and red like blood. He clenched his fist and watched it shake. When his griffin landed, Dies Irae marched through the halls of his palace, lips tight. He passed a maid, a girl no older than his daughter, and grabbed her arm so painfully, tears filled her eyes.

"My-- my lord--" she began to mumble, and he slapped her.

"Silence."

He dragged her up one of his towers, slammed the door behind him, and shoved her prostrate onto a divan. He took her there, his palm covering her mouth to stifle her screams. When he was done, he removed his palm, and found that she no longer breathed. That only enraged him further. He tossed her body out the window.

"How?" he asked himself, staring out that window into the night sky. "How do I kill him?"

In the amphitheater? No. That was a place for games, not for this, not for such a victory. In his palace gardens? No; he'd never get the stench out. In a dark alley, in a fortress, upon the city walls? *No, no, no.* Dies Irae slammed his mace against a table, shattering it. Benedictus deserved a special place to die, a place more ghastly, more humiliating than--

Dies Irae froze.

Of course.

He burst out of the room and marched down the hallway, scowling, ignoring the terrified servants who saluted him.

"Of course," he muttered between clenched teeth.

Within an hour, Dies Irae had mustered ten thousand griffin riders. He would bring an army to see this. He flew at their lead under grumbling black clouds, his bannermen flying behind him. Volucris held Lacrimosa in his left talons, Benedictus in his right. The two were in human form, wrapped in chains that would crush them should they shift. Their mouths were gagged, their backs lashed, their spirits broken.

"Tonight, I do what I should have done years ago," Dies Irae spoke into the wind, though he knew none could hear. A smile spread across his face.

He hadn't woken Gloriae to see this; she still slept in her chambers. *Why?* Dies Irae wondered. He'd spent years raising her to hate, to hurt, to hunt weredragons. Why on this night should he leave her to her dreams? Was it because Lacrimosa was her mother, and no child should witness the death of her mother? Was it because he feared for her, even with Benedictus and Lacrimosa gagged--feared that they'd hurt her, or tell her the truth of her parentage?

No, Dies Irae decided. It was not those things. It was because of something he saw in Gloriae's eyes of late. A fear and rage that burned above... what? Compassion? No. It was more like *recognition.* It had begun when they captured Lacrimosa, that strange glow in Gloriae's eyes.

Could it be that Gloriae had the curse too? Could she also shift? She had never done so before, at least not within his sight. But the possibility had begun to gnaw on Dies Irae. So he had left her in the palace. He would keep her away from these weredragons, away from their curses and magic.

Clouds still hid the stars, grumbling. Dies Irae flew over hills and farms, leaving Confutatis behind. When he looked over his shoulder, he could see his army there, thousands of riders upon thousands of griffins, their torches blazing, their armor and swords glittering. Smoke rose from their torches, trails of black and red like rivers of blood. Dies Irae snarled a grin. He wanted to see Vir Requis blood again, smell it, taste it. He spurred

Volucris, and the griffin flew faster, and the wind whipped Dies Irae's face. His grin grew, his lips peeling back from his teeth.

It began to rain when he saw the place ahead. Darkness cloaked the land, a sea of tar, but Dies Irae knew this was the place. He could feel it, smell it on the wind.

"We're here," he said to Volucris, pulled the reins, and the griffin began to descend in circles. The ten thousand griffins behind him followed, wings thudding. Soon they were close enough to the ground that their torches lit the place, and Dies Irae snarled again and laughed. The torchlight flickered against bones, some the bones of men, others of women and children. The skeletons of five thousand weredragons littered the place, half-buried in dirt, a graveyard of victory and blood. There were no bones of dragons, of course; in death, these creatures returned to their human forms, fragile.

When they were several feet above the ground, Volucris tossed down Benedictus and Lacrimosa. They hit the earth with grunts and rolled, still chained. Volucris landed beside the skeletons of two weredragons--a mother huddling over her child. Dies Irae dismounted and inhaled deeply. It still smelled like fire, old blood, and metal.

They had reached Lanburg Fields.

Dies Irae walked toward Benedictus and Lacrimosa, this couple of "eternal love" that sickened him. His boots scattered bones. Dies Irae wondered if the bones came from the same Vir Requis child whose scales made his boots. The thought tickled him. When he reached Benedictus, he stood staring down upon him. The man was filthy. Wretched. His hair was unkempt, his face scruffy, his skin like old leather. His clothes were torn and muddy.

"Look at yourself," Dies Irae said, disgusted. His own raiment glinted, a masterpiece of white steel, gold, and jewels.

This was how a king looked, he knew; not like that maggot at his feet. "You are disgusting."

Benedictus stared up between strands of black hair streaked with gray. Hatred burned in his stare. The man said nothing.

"Good," Dies Irae said. "Hate me. I've hated you for a long time, Benedictus. When you sat by Father, and I wandered the forests in shame, I hated you. When you married Lacrimosa, and I was left alone, I hated you. I do not hate you now, brother. I pity you. But I will still kill you. I will cut off your arm, the way you cut off mine, and then I will cut off your head."

Benedictus tried to say something, but he was gagged, and his voice was but a moan. Dies Irae kicked him in the chest. Benedictus coughed and moaned, and Lacrimosa screamed behind her gag.

"What is it, Benedictus?" Dies Irae asked. He ripped off his brother's gag. "There is nothing more for you to say. Look around you, brother. Look at the bones that lie strewn like a playground for ghosts. Do you know this place, Benedictus? Do you remember all those you led to die here? Women. Children. You led them here to their deaths. You chose not to flee with them. You chose to bring them here to me, to die at my sword, and the talons of my griffins, and the heels of my boots. You kept your wife safe, Benedictus, and you kept your daughter in hiding. And you led the rest to die upon the fields. You are a coward. You are a hypocrite. You fled me that day; you yourself dared not die with the women and children you killed. Today I kill you for those sins. Today it ends, here at the place where you lost your soul to blood and cowardice."

Benedictus stared up, saying nothing. Tears streamed down his cheeks. Dies Irae spun around and cried out to his men. "Gather here! Gather to see the great Lord of Lizards die."

The griffins shrieked, and their riders gathered around. They covered the land and circled above. The Griffin Heart was hot under Dies Irae's armor, nearly burning his chest. The amulet of his father.

Dies Irae raised his mace over Benedictus's head--this arm of steel where once a true arm had lived. "You die now with the weapon you gave me."

Benedictus mouthed something, but it was impossible to hear over the roar of fire and griffins.

Dies Irae laughed. "What is that? You wish to speak last words? I cannot hear your croaks. Speak loudly. I will give you these last words, for you are my brother."

Benedictus spat and spoke again, and this time Dies Irae heard his voice, and the words made him frown.

"Fight me."

Dies Irae raised his mace higher. "Fight you? Why should I fight you, brother? Why should I not bash in your skull now and be done with?"

Benedictus's lips were dry, his face bruised, his chin bloody. "We should have fought to the death ten years ago. That's how it should have ended. Let us end this now. Fight me, great and courageous Lord of Light. To the death."

Dies Irae laughed. "As it should have been? A fight to the death? Ten years ago, Benedictus, you faced my army alone. We had slain all the women and children you brought to fight your war. You faced an army of men, and you fled."

Benedictus growled. "I showed you mercy. I left you to live. I will not repeat that mistake again."

Dies Irae shook his head and sighed. "Very well, brother. You want to turn back time, to return ten years ago? I will grant you that. You will fight to death. But you will fight not only me, brother." He swept the mace head around, displaying his army.

"You will fight all of us... like you fought ten years ago. We turn back time tonight."

BENEDICTUS

"Requiem... may our wings forever find your sky."

As Dies Irae's men unlocked his shackles, Benedictus closed his eyes and whispered the Old Words. His voice was hoarse, his throat aching, and his limbs burned as he stretched them. When they had bound him, they had beaten him, covered his body with bruises. Yet through the pain, he remembered. He could still speak those ancient words, the prayer of his people. He struggled to his feet with eyes closed, the courts of Requiem resplendent in his mind.

He heard Dies Irae laughing scornfully; as a child, no doubt Dies Irae had hated the Old Words, those words every child in Requiem must speak in mornings. Dies Irae had never had the magic, never had wings; for him Requiem's sky had been unreachable.

"Are you ready, brother? Are you ready to die here?" Dies Irae's voice was icy with hatred and fiery with rage.

Behind closed eyes, Benedictus gazed upon those courts of Requiem, the marble columns that rose from the forest floor, the birch trees that grew beyond them, the rustling leaves. He could see autumn leaves skittering across the tiles of their forest courts, could see Father's throne of twisted oak roots, could see his friends, his family, his love Lacrimosa wearing silks and jewels, could see them ruling wisely under skies of blue and gold and white. *Let me die with this memory,* he thought. *I go now to to the halls of my ancestors, to drink from their wine in our courts among the stars. I now take my greatest flight.*

He opened his eyes. Around him spread the ruin of his people, the ribs rising like the teeth of dragons, the bashed skulls like so many rocks. But bones, ash, and blood could not make him forget the beauty of those old courts.

He stared at Dies Irae. His older brother. The shadow that would lurk beyond those courts, hiding and hating in its forests, planning revenge. Dies Irae was no longer a shadow; he was now a Lord of Light, a beacon of cruelty and fire to the world. Usurper of Osanna, destroyer of Requiem. Strangely, Benedictus no longer hated his brother. Neither did he fear him. As he looked upon Dies Irae, this glittering deity of steel and gold, he felt only sadness.

"We made you into this," he said quietly. "We created you. We scorned you. We turned you into this monster."

Dies Irae mounted his griffin. "Shift, brother. Turn into the dragon. Show us who the true monster is. You will die in the lizard's form."

Benedictus looked at Lacrimosa. She lay on the ground, still chained, blood trickling down her lip. The rain soaked her hair and tattered dress, and she gazed up at him with tragic, haunted eyes.

Benedictus looked back to Dies Irae. "She fights with me."

Dies Irae barked a laugh. "Are you trying to redeem yourself on this last night? Ten years ago, you would not let her fight. You hid her then, while letting the other females of your kind perish. Very well; she too will die here at my griffin's talons. Men, free the lizard whore."

When they unchained her, Benedictus helped her to her feet, and held her, and kissed her brow, and told her of his love.

"I love you, Ben," she whispered back, eyes teary, the rain streaming through her hair, hair like molten moonlight. Her eyes were the most beautiful he'd ever seen. He kissed her lips, and remembered kissing her in Requiem so long ago.

Dies Irae scoffed from atop his griffin. "You love the whore, do you?" he said.

Benedictus turned toward him, his rage finding him. He clenched his fists. "You will not call her that."

Dies Irae laughed. "But it's true, brother. That's what she is. Do you know that I broke her in for you? Yes, Benedictus. Eighteen years ago, before she married you. I took her in the forests, I placed Agnus Dei and Gloriae within her womb, I--"

"You will speak no such lies!" Benedictus shouted. He took a step toward Dies Irae, raising his fists.

Dies Irae only laughed again. "I speak the truth, brother. I raped your wife. Though to be honest, I think the whore enjoyed it. Yes, Benedictus. Agnus Dei and Gloriae are my daughters, not yours. If you do not believe me, look in the whore's eyes, and you'll see the truth."

Benedictus's head spun. His fingers trembled and his heart thrashed. He turned to look at Lacrimosa, and saw tears in her eyes. Her body trembled.

It was true.

He wanted to howl. To kill. To destroy.

Instead, Benedictus embraced his wife.

"You should have told me," he whispered, tears filling his own eyes.

She shook her head and hugged him. "I could not."

"I love you, Lacrimosa, now and forever. We go now to our courts in the sky. We will be together there. Goodbye, daughter of Requiem."

He released her gently, then turned around, shifted into a dragon, and leaped at Dies Irae.

LACRIMOSA

Tears in her eyes, Lacrimosa shifted too. Dies Irae had beaten her, tortured her, unleashed unspeakable horrors against her. *He made me strong.*

She had learned to fight in his arena, learned to kill. Tonight, upon this field of death, under this rain of fire, she would kill again before they took her down. She saw Benedictus roaring beside her, blowing flame. He slammed into Dies Irae's griffin, and more griffins mobbed him.

Lacrimosa shouted and flew skyward.

Hundreds of griffins attacked. She lashed her tail, blew fire, snapped her teeth, and clawed them. Blows rained upon her. Talons scratched her. Beaks stabbed her.

"Requiem!" she cried, weeping, and blew fire. The griffins' fur blazed around her, lighting the night, lighting the thousands of Vir Requis skeletons.

She could no longer see Benedictus. She could no longer see the skeletons below. She saw only griffins, and light that rolled over them, drowning them, not light of fire but the good light of death, the light of her courts in the heavens. Starlight.

I am flying to them, she thought, *to the Requiem beyond the stars.* She whispered last words.

"Requiem! May our wings forever find your sky. I love you, Benedictus. I love you, Gloriae. I love you, Agnus Dei and Kyrie. Goodbye."

And from the west, they answered her voice.

"Mother!" came the voice of Agnus Dei, choked with tears. "Mother, I'm here!"

Lacrimosa smiled in the light of death, the pain that was numbing. Agnus Dei had died too; she was waiting for her in the stars.

"Lacrimosa!" cried Kyrie, and Lacrimosa wept that they had died so young.

Agnus Dei's howl filled her ears. A figure of red scales and flames shot before her, rending the mists of death, crashing into griffins. "Mother, fly!"

Lacrimosa could not believe her eyes. Agnus Dei flew before her. Not a ghostly daughter of starlight, but a living, howling dragon, blowing flame, biting and clawing. Kyrie flew there too, and all around them flew serpents of lightning.

"Agnus Dei!" Lacrimosa cried, weeping, and bit a griffin that was clawing her daughter. "Agnus Dei, you're alive!"

Agnus Dei blew fire at three griffins and lashed her tail at a fourth. "No time for teary reunions now, Mother. Fight!"

Lacrimosa fought, head spinning. She could barely believe her eyes. Thousands of wingless, limbless dragons flew around her. Salvanae! True dragons from Salvandos! Agnus Dei and Kyrie had found them. The creatures howled, swarming around the griffins, biting and setting them aflame.

A griffin flew toward Lacrimosa. She blew fire at it, then clawed its neck. Its rider tumbled to the distant ground, screaming.

"Ben!" Lacrimosa called. She saw him half a league away, battling Dies Irae in the sky, fires lighting them. The other griffins were battling the salvanae. Every second, a griffin or salvana fell dead from the sky to slam against Vir Requis skeletons.

A shriek tore the air, and a large griffin flew toward her, ablaze. Its rider burned too, but still wielded a lance, driving it toward her.

Lacrimosa recognized the man's armor at once, armor like an iron maiden, the helmet like a prisoner's mask.

Lord Molok.

Lacrimosa narrowed her eyes, snarled, and flew toward him.

She screamed, ducked, and cried as his lance scratched her shoulder. She clawed his griffin, drawing blood. They flew in opposite directions, turned, and charged again.

Lacrimosa snarled. She remembered that night ten years ago, when she had seen Molok murder a dozen Vir Requis children. She remembered him beating her in Confutatis, laughing at her pain.

"For all those you tortured, murdered, and raped, I kill you now," she said, smoke rising from her nostrils.

He drove his lance again. Lacrimosa dived low, but still his lance hit her shoulder. She cried, tumbled, and struggled to keep flapping her wings. Molok cackled above her, blazing.

He pointed his lance and swooped. Lacrimosa blew fire, but nothing could stop him. She saw death driving toward her with steel and flame.

A flash of red scales.

Agnus Dei slammed into the fireball that was Molok and his griffin. They tumbled aside, Agnus Dei screaming and clawing. Molok swung his sword and sliced Agnus Dei's leg. She cried.

Rage claimed Lacrimosa, rage as she'd never felt. *No. You will not hurt her.* She screamed hoarsely, so loud that men and griffins turned to stare. Lacrimosa flapped her wings, dazed and pained, burning with fury. She flew toward Molok and drove her claws into his griffin's belly. Guts spilled like bloody serpents.

Molok's griffin tumbled, but Lacrimosa was not done. No. She would not let the ground kill Molok; he was hers. As the griffin fell, Lacrimosa bit, tearing Molok off the saddle. He struggled in her jaws, burning, and Lacrimosa bit into his armor, bending it, pushing it into his flesh. He screamed, and she tasted his blood, and she kept grinding her teeth until he struggled no more.

She spat out his body. It tumbled to the ground and thudded against his dead griffin.

Lacrimosa stared down at Molok's corpse, eyes dry and burning.

"Nobody," she said, "hurts my daughter."

Agnus Dei flew toward her, and the two shared a quick embrace. There was no time for words, no time for tears. The battle still raged around them. The salvanae were terrible to behold. They streamed like rivers, roaring, tearing into griffins with their teeth. They shot thunderbolts from their mouths, setting griffins afire. The griffins fought with equal vigor, biting serpents in half, clawing out their innards. Half the griffins now rose in flame, but still they fought; the fire only seemed to enrage them. Everywhere she looked, Lacrimosa saw griffins, roaring serpents, blood, swords, arrows, and lances. The clouds themselves seemed alight, grumbling and raining ash. Thunder boomed and lightning rent the sky. Bodies kept falling.

"Where is Father?" Agnus Dei shouted over the din, and Lacrimosa winced. *Father.* It could mean Benedictus or Dies Irae. In either case, the answer was the same.

"There," she shouted and pointed.

They looked to the east. Over a hill, griffins and salvanae surrounding them, the brothers battled. Dies Irae fought atop Volucris, driving his lance forward. Benedictus howled, the firelight shimmering on his scales. His wings churned the smoke that rose all around.

"The Great King fights again!" Kyrie said, voice awed, flying toward them. Wounds covered him, but still his eyes flashed. A tear flowed down his cheek. "King Benedictus is sounding his roar."

Lacrimosa wanted to fly to her husband. Griffins and salvanae surrounded her, and when she tried to fly forward, beaks and talons attacked. They held her back, held her from Benedictus. As Lacrimosa fought, she watched the duel, anguish gnawing her.

BENEDICTUS

War.

War rolled over the world with fire and wings.

No Vir Requis marched today under his banners. No armies mustered to his call. They lay below him now, skeletons ten years dry, fresh blood raining upon them. As fires blazed, smoke billowed, and salvanae and griffins fought, Benedictus saw but one thing.

Dies Irae.

"You should have killed me ten years ago," Dies Irae shouted over the roar of battle. His voice was maniacal, emerging like an echo from his griffin-head helm. "Your serpents cannot save you now."

Benedictus narrowed his eyes. His torn wing ached; he could barely flap it. Wounds covered him, and ilbane stiffened his joints. He didn't care. Tonight his pain ended, with death or with vengeance. Tonight all this pain--of wounds, of genocide, of haunting memory--would burn in fire. Tonight he came full circle, defeated his demons or died trying. Tonight was a blood night.

Volucris flew toward him. Dies Irae leaned forward in the saddle, aiming his lance. Benedictus charged, blowing fire, refusing to back down. The lance drove toward him. Benedictus roared.

The lance grazed his shoulder, and he shouted. His claws swung and hit Dies Irae in the chest.

Benedictus kept shooting forward, howled, and turned to face Dies Irae again. His brother had been knocked back, but pulled himself back into the saddle. Scratches ran along his breastplate, peeling back the gold and jewels to show steel.

War.

With claws and metal.

Dies Irae charged again, lance red in the firelight. Benedictus too charged, flapping that aching, torn wing. He blew fire, and Volucris caught flame, and the lance drove forward. Pain filled Benedictus's good wing. The lance pierced it, then pulled back, widening the wound. Blood fell and Benedictus roared.

"Look at you!" Dies Irae screamed and cackled. "The great Benedictus. After all these years, to die like this!"

Volucris swooped. The lance hit Benedictus's shoulder, tossing him into a spin. He tried to flap his wings, but barely could. He couldn't right himself. Talons scratched him, and a beak bit his wounded shoulder, and the lance struck again.

Benedictus howled in rage and pain.

Then, in the darkness rolling over him, he saw the Griffin Heart.

In the battle, the amulet had emerged from Dies Irae's armor. It hung around his neck on a golden chain, glowing and humming, binding the griffins to its power.

The amulet of their father.

"You stole that from Requiem," Benedictus said, finally managing to steady his tumble. Though pain filled them, he flapped his wings, flying up toward Dies Irae. He felt weak, weaker than he'd ever been, but kept flying. "I take it back from you today."

Dies Irae swooped on his griffin, lance glinting.

Benedictus was slow and wounded, but he was fast enough. He swerved, and as Volucris flew by him, he swung his claw. He hit Volucris in the head.

The griffin screamed, bloodied, and flapped his wings madly. The wings hit Benedictus, blinding him, but he no longer needed to see. He bit and clawed, digging into griffin flesh. Volucris thrashed above him, and Benedictus clutched the griffin, refusing to release him. He bit again, tearing into Volucris's chest. Blood covered him, and he drove his head up, goring the griffin with his horns.

Dies Irae screamed.

Benedictus tossed Volucris off him. The griffin and Dies Irae tumbled to the ground.

Suddenly Benedictus could see the battle again. Thousands of griffins and salvanae howled around him, staring at him and the fallen Dies Irae. Thousands more lay dead or dying upon the ground. The skeletons of the war ten years ago were red with fresh blood and fire. Below, Dies Irae still lived. He pushed himself off Volucris.

Benedictus landed before his brother and blew fire. Dies Irae ran through the flames, swinging his mace. The mace slammed into Benedictus's leg, so hard it nearly broke his bone. Benedictus kicked his brother, knocked him down, and placed a foot upon him. Dies Irae struggled, but could not free himself.

The battle froze around them.

Everyone watched silently: salvanae, griffins, men, Vir Requis. The only sounds now were the moans of the dying, the wind and rain, and the fire.

"So we end up here," Benedictus said to his brother, "the same as we were. This is how you lay ten years ago. On your back in this field. Me with my claws against you."

Dies Irae's visor had been knocked back, revealing his face. Blood trickled from his lip, and ash covered his skin. He spat out a tooth, then laughed with blood in his mouth. "You're a coward."

Benedictus growled. "And you're a dead man."

Dies Irae shook his head. "No, Benedictus. You will not crush me to death. I know you. I unchained you; I let you fight me to the death. You want to kill me? Do it as a man, not a lizard. Shift, Benedictus. Face me as a man, or forever be known as a coward."

Growling, Benedictus kicked Dies Irae aside, then shifted into human form.

"Swords!" Dies Irae cried. Two soldiers leaped off their griffins and ran forward. They gave one sword to Dies Irae, the other to Benedictus.

Benedictus drew the blade. It was heavy, well balanced, with a grip wrapped in leather. A good sword.

Dies Irae drew his own blade and swiped it, testing it. It whistled.

"Father!" came an anguished cry above. Benedictus looked up, and his heart leaped. Agnus Dei! Agnus Dei flew there! And Kyrie flew by her.

"Agn--" he began, but then she screamed. Benedictus looked back down to see Dies Irae lunging at him.

Dies Irae's sword flew. Benedictus parried. The blades clanged and raised sparks.

The blades drew apart, clanged again. Around them the fires burned, the armies watched, the winds howled, and the rain fell. Benedictus had not dueled with blades for years, not since Requiem had fallen. His shoulders ached, his wounds burned, and he felt sluggish as he swung his blade.

Dies Irae thrust his sword, and Benedictus grunted as he parried. Dies Irae thrust again. Benedictus parried again, but barely. His boot slipped, and he fell to one knee.

The armies gasped. Agnus Dei screamed.

Dies Irae's blade came swinging down, reflecting the fires. Benedictus parried and punched, hitting Dies Irae's helmet. His knuckles ached; he might have broken them. Dies Irae fell into the mud. Benedictus leaped up and swung his sword.

His blade hit Dies Irae's helmet.

Dies Irae, grinning with blood in his mouth, pushed himself up and swung his sword.

Benedictus blocked, thrust, and hit Dies Irae's breastplate. His blow sent jewels flying, but could not break the steel. Dies Irae thrust, and his blade sliced Benedictus's arm. Blood flew, and Agnus Dei screamed again.

Benedictus howled and charged in fury, swinging his sword. Dies Irae blocked the blade with his mace, that left arm of steel.

Benedictus's blade shattered. Shards flew, leaving only a hilt and jagged steel in Benedictus's hand.

"It's over, Benedictus!" Dies Irae cackled and swung his blade. Benedictus parried with his broken sword. He managed to divert the bulk of the blow, but the sword still sliced his shoulder, and Benedictus fell to his knees.

Dies Irae swung his sword again.

Benedictus rolled aside, grabbed a shard of broken blade from the mud, and thrust it up.

The metal drove deep into Dies Irae's left eye.

Dies Irae screamed. It was a horrible scream, a shriek like a dying horse. He clawed at his face, but could not pull out the shard in his eye.

"Damn you, Benedictus!" he screamed, a high pitched sound, inhuman. Blood spurted. He fell to his knees, hand covering his wound. Suddenly he was blubbering, blood and mucus and tears flowing down him.

Benedictus rose slowly to his feet. Blood covered him, and he could barely feel his arm. He limped toward his brother. Dies Irae had dropped his sword, and Benedictus lifted it. He held the blade over his brother's head. Everyone watched around them, but dared not move or speak. The rain pattered.

"It *is* over now, brother," Benedictus said and raised the sword. Dies Irae was weeping. "Goodbye."

Dies Irae shook his head and held out his hands, one hand of flesh, the other a fist of steel. "Please, please, brother," he said. "Spare me, please. I beg you." He bowed, covering his samite and jeweled armor with mud and blood. He wept. "I beg you, Benedictus. Spare me. Show me mercy. I am your brother."

Benedictus stared down. The rain kept falling, steaming against burning bodies. Benedictus looked at those bodies, thousands of them, and around them thousands of old skeletons from the war years ago. So many had died already. So many deaths because of these struggles between him and his brother.

"What are you waiting for?" Kyrie shouted somewhere above. "Kill him!"

But Benedictus could not. He could not ten years ago, and he could not now. Not after all this blood, all this death. His brother was a monster. A murderer. A despot who had committed horrible crimes. But he was still Benedictus's blood, still a man who begged for life, a man who was surrendering to him.

Benedictus looked down at this groveling, pathetic creature. Disgust filled him.

"You will return with me to the ruins of Requiem," Benedictus said, tears choking his voice. "We will stand among the columns which you toppled, among the graves of the children you murdered, and there you will stand trial. No, I will not kill you, Dies Irae. But I will judge you. For the rest of your life, you will live imprisoned to me. You will watch as I return Osanna to its old kings. You will watch as I show the world the crimes you've committed."

Benedictus, King of Requiem, lowered his sword.

Sobbing on his knees, Dies Irae crawled toward him in the mud. "Thank you, thank you," he blubbered, blood covering him, and reached out as if to kiss Benedictus's boots.

But instead, so quickly Benedictus barely saw it, Dies Irae drew a hidden dagger.

The blade flashed.

Agnus Dei screamed.

The dagger buried itself into Benedictus's gut, and Dies Irae turned the blade, grinning a bloody, insane grin.

The birch leaves rustled around him, bright green, and dapples of light danced upon the marble tiles. The columns rose around him, white marble, and he saw Lacrimosa walking among them, clad in white silks, her hair braided. Agnus Dei ran toward him, so small, her hair a tangle of black curls, and he lifted her and laughed. Gloriae ran to him too, hair golden, laughing, and he lifted her with his other arm. It was spring in Requiem, and it was beautiful, so beautiful that he wept.

Benedictus fell to his knees. Dies Irae grinned in the mud, twisting the blade. Benedictus looked up, eyelids fluttering, and saw his family there, and he smiled. "I love you," his lips uttered silently.

"I will rape Lacrimosa again," Dies Irae whispered into Benedictus's ear, blood dripping from his lips. "A thousand more times. I want you to die knowing that."

With blurry eyes, Benedictus saw Kyrie swooping toward them. He saw Dies Irae crawl through the mud. He saw Volucris stir, still alive. Then Benedictus could see no more. He fell into the mud, and rain pattered against him. He turned his head, and he beheld a sight so beautiful, that he wept.

Before him stretched the halls of his fathers, all in silver and mist, columns rising among the stars.

KYRIE ELEISON

Kyrie saw Benedictus fall. His heart shattered. That day ten years ago returned to him, the day King Benedictus had led him to this field.

Kyrie wanted to rush to Benedictus, to his king.

Instead he flew to Dies Irae.

The destroyer of Requiem, the man who'd murdered Kyrie's family, was dragging himself through the mud toward Volucris. The griffin was cut and burned, but still alive.

He's going to get away with the amulet! Kyrie thought. He could not allow that. He leaped onto Dies Irae, who squirmed beneath him. Dies Irae's armor was slick with blood. His visor had opened, revealing a shattered face, a shard of steel deep in his eye. The man was cackling, mucus and tears and blood flowing down his face. Kyrie nearly gagged.

"You murdered my parents," Kyrie said. "You murdered Lady Mirum. Benedictus showed you mercy. I will not."

Dies Irae was struggling, but growing weaker, his face paler. He looked moments from death. Kyrie shifted into human form. He placed his boot against Dies Irae's neck, reached down, and grabbed the Griffin Heart.

"It's over, Irae," he said. He pulled the amulet back, snapping it off its chain. "I have the Griffin Heart. The griffins are mine. I want you to die knowing that. I...."

Kyrie wanted to say more, but could not. The amulet blazed in his hand, sizzling hot, cutting off his words. Kyrie cried in pain and almost dropped it.

The griffins screeched.

Dies Irae shouted.

The amulet vibrated and hummed in Kyrie's hand. The griffins went mad; they were flying to and fro, and their riders could not control them. Kyrie felt their fury. They hated him, hated the amulet; Kyrie had never known such hatred. They wanted to tear him apart. Volucris, wounded in the mud, seemed to gain new strength and took flight.

"Men!" Dies Irae cried. He began crawling away from Kyrie, and soldiers rushed to him. A few men lifted him, and others surrounded him with drawn swords.

"Irae!" Kyrie shouted. He wanted to stop him, to kill him, but could not. The amulet claimed him, spinning his head, burning his fist. He could barely stay standing.

Gritting his teeth, Kyrie held the amulet over his head. He shut his eyes, ignoring the pain in his hand. The griffins began to swoop toward him, talons outstretched, blood in their eyes.

How did the amulet work? How could he tame the griffins? He felt the magic burning down his arm, flowing up his spine...

...and then he felt a million griffins in his mind, flapping wings inside his skull.

They were his.

LACRIMOSA

"Benedictus!" Lacrimosa cried, tears blurring her vision.

The griffins were flying around her, enraged and confused. Dies Irae had vanished in the shadows and chaos. The salvanae stared with their golden orbs. Lacrimosa flew, shoved her way through them, and crashed to the ground by her husband.

"My king," she wept. She shifted into human form and grabbed him. She held Benedictus in her arms, and she saw the dagger in his belly, and a sob racked her body. "Do not die today, my love."

He blinked and soft breath left his lungs. He tried to speak, but could not. Blood soaked his shirt. His fingers moved weakly.

"I need a healer!" Lacrimosa cried.

Agnus Dei landed beside her, shifted into human form, and knelt by her father. She held him and gazed upon him with huge, haunted eyes.

Kyrie too stood by them in human form, but seemed not to see them. He held the Griffin Heart over his head. The amulet vibrated and hummed and glowed. The griffins screeched above and clawed the air. For a moment it seemed they would attack. Kyrie snarled, holding the amulet to the skies, and pointed to the south, back to Confutatis. With shrieks, the griffins flew away, their riders powerless to stop them.

"A healer, quickly!" Lacrimosa cried. Benedictus moaned in her arms, blood still flowing, eyes glazed.

A bugle sounded among the clouds, and a great salvana came coiling down, furling and unfurling like a snake in water.

His golden scales shimmered in the firelight. His eyes like crystal balls blinked, and wind whipped his white beard. He was larger than the other salvanae, and older, and Lacrimosa guessed that he was their leader.

Agnus Dei seemed to recognize him. She leaped to her feet and waved to the salvana. "Nehushtan!" she called. "Nehushtan, please help us!"

The salvana kept coiling down. The firelight glinted against him so brightly, it nearly blinded Lacrimosa. When he was near, Nehushtan hovered above them, his head lowered over Benedictus. The head seemed so large next to Benedictus's human form, all golden scales and white hair.

"Nehushtan," Agnus Dei said between sobs. She placed her hands on his head. "You are a great priest. Can you heal him? Please. He's my father."

Benedictus was barely breathing, barely moaning. Nehushtan sniffed him. As he inhaled, Lacrimosa saw golden powder and wisps of light. The priest's eyelashes, each like an ostrich feather, fanned her as he blinked. The rain streamed down his scales.

"Please, Your Highness," Lacrimosa said to him, not sure if the title was appropriate, but not caring. Her husband's blood soaked her hands. She could not live without him. Without Benedictus, life was meaningless for her. *Don't leave me now, my love. Please. Stay with me.*

Nehushtan sniffed again, inhaling wispy light that floated from Benedictus, as if he were smelling the king's soul. Finally he turned that great, golden head to Lacrimosa. He blinked again, eyelashes fanning the ash, and spoke in an old voice like flowing water.

"The Draco Stars shine bright in him." Nehushtan nodded. "I have rarely seen such bright light, such powerful dragon spirit. He is a mighty king."

"Can you save him?" Lacrimosa pleaded. She placed a bloody hand against Nehushtan's scales. They felt warm against her palm.

Nehushtan blinked again, turned his orbs to Benedictus, then back to her. "The stars of the dragon shine forever upon all who follow their light. Such light cannot be extinguished; it flows forever in our wake, from birth, to life, and to the great journey to those stars. Do not grieve for those who join the constellation, daughter of dragons, for his light will shine bright among them."

Benedictus's eyes fluttered, then closed. His breath was so shallow now, Lacrimosa was not sure that he breathed at all. Agnus Dei sobbed, and even Kyrie was crying.

Lacrimosa shook her head, her hair covering her face. Tears and raindrops streamed down her cheeks. She placed her second hand against Nehushtan's head. "Not yet. Please, Your Highness. I'm not ready to lose him."

Nehushtan lowered his head to Benedictus, blinked several times, and sniffed again. "Yes, his dragon force still pulses, and starlight flows through him. But his human body, this one that lies before me, is dying. This body I cannot heal."

Agnus Dei looked at the salvana desperately. "But can you save his dragon form? If he shifted, could you heal him?"

Nehushtan looked at her. "I do not know, daughter of dragons, but I can try. His human body is beyond my skill; its form is made of ash, and to ash it will return. I can pray for his dragon form. Whether his human body survives, I do not know."

Lacrimosa wept. To lose Benedictus's human body forever? To lose his kisses, his embraces, the stubble on his cheeks, his calloused hands, the crow feet that grew around his eyes during his rare smiles? How could she lose this, to sleep at nights without his form by her side, to walk without his hand in hers? Yet she nodded, trembling. "Please, Nehushtan. Do what you can."

For the first time, Lacrimosa noticed that all the other salvanae--thousands of them--were watching from above. Their bodies were as strands of gold, and as Lacrimosa watched them, she gasped. The salvanae flowed to form a ring in the sky, and in the center of that ring, the clouds parted and no rain fell. It was like the eye of a storm. Through her tears, Lacrimosa saw that stars shone between the salvanae. *The constellation Draco. Light of dragons.* The beams of light fell upon her and Benedictus.

Nehushtan began to sing, a song in an old language, a tune that sounded ancient beyond knowing. His voice was a deep rumble, beautiful like crystals in deep caves, and the starlight moved to the notes he sang. Lacrimosa could see chords of light flowing through the air, notes descending, spinning, and landing upon Benedictus. The music lived around her in light and ancient piety. The other salvanae began to sing too, some in bass, others in a high, angelic choir of light. Lacrimosa wept, for she had never heard anything more beautiful.

The notes of light lifted Benedictus from the mud, and cleaned the dirt and blood from him. Lacrimosa wanted to hold onto him, to clutch him in her embrace, but she had to trust the music. She released her grip, and let the dragon song lift him on its light. He hovered above her, and soon he floated high under starlight, and he was no longer a man, but a dragon, a great dragon with midnight scales, with wings that were no longer torn. Benedictus the Black, King of Requiem, opened his jaws and roared, and the roar shook the land. No fire left his mouth, but starlight that flowed, danced, and sang.

"Hear the Black Fang sound his roar," Kyrie whispered, watching with moist eyes, the amulet clutched in his fist. "Hear the song of Requiem."

Strands of starlight woven around him, Benedictus descended to the earth, and stood by Lacrimosa, healed. His wing was whole now, and his scars gone. He looked so much like the old Benedictus, the great dragon who had led them to war so many years ago. He lowered his head to Lacrimosa, who stood in the mud in human form, and she embraced him.

"Benedictus," she whispered, and she smiled a teary smile, and then she was weeping. There was so much she wanted to say to him. She wanted to speak of Dies Irae torturing her, forcing her to fight in his arena. She wanted to speak of her years in hiding, raising Agnus Dei in the snowy mountains of Fidelium. She wanted to speak of Dies Irae raping her all those years ago, how she did not know who fathered Agnus Dei and Gloriae. Lacrimosa wanted to speak of two decades of horror, of pain and of longing, but she could bring none of it to her lips. Benedictus knew. She did not need to speak, and her smile widened as she cried. She leaned her head against him, and for the first time in years Lacrimosa felt that beautiful light lay in her future, and great love and timeless music.

"Is... your human body dead?" she whispered to him, embracing his dragon head. "Can you feel it within you?"

Benedictus nodded gently. "I can feel it. It's hurt, and it's weak. It will be many days before I dare shift. But my human form lives, Lacrimosa. We can heal it."

Lacrimosa closed her eyes and wept against him.

And then Agnus Dei and Kyrie were embracing Benedictus too, and jumping onto his back, and climbing his neck, and laughing and playing as if they were still children. Benedictus too laughed, a deep rumbling dragon's laugh. *Dies Irae took their childhood,* Lacrimosa thought, looking at the young ones. *Let them be as children now.*

Nehushtan watched, and it seemed to Lacrimosa that the old priest smiled. She turned to him and bowed her head.

"Thank you."

Nehushtan too bowed his head. His body hovered several feet above the ground. "Will you return with us to Salvandos, and dwell with us in Har Zahav, the mountain of gold?" he asked. "We have learned today that Vir Requis are noble, and great followers of the Draco stars. Return with us to Har Zahav, and fly with us there in golden clouds."

Benedictus bowed to the priest. "I thank you, Lord of Salvandos. But I must decline. Our home is Requiem, and that home now lies in ruin. I am still king of that land, though it is burned to ash, and I still lead my people, though only five remain. I must stay true to my fathers, and to the courts of Requiem." His eyes glimmered in the starlight. "I do not know if I can rebuild the halls of my fathers. I do not know if our race can survive. Many dangers still await us. Dies Irae will still hunt us. The men and women who live across Osanna, and over the ruins of Requiem our motherland, still fear and hate us. Our song does not end today, great priest, nor does our quest. I remain in the east. If more Vir Requis still live in hiding, I must find them, and for the memory of my forefathers, I will rebuild our kingdom among the birches. Goodbye, dear friend. Forever will Requiem be an ally to Salvandos, and forever be in its debt." He bowed again to the High Priest, and he uttered the Old Words. "May our wings forever find your sky."

Nehushtan smiled, a deep smile that sparkled in his eyes. And then the priest was flying away, and the other salvanae were coiling behind him and bugling. Within moments they were gone into the west.

KYRIE ELEISON

Kyrie watched the salvanae leave, and he felt a sadness in him, a deep sadness that he could not explain, a sadness of beauty and music. He turned toward Agnus Dei. She stood by him in human form, her clothes tattered, blood and mud smearing her skin. Ash covered her face, and her hair was a mess of tangles. Yet still she was beautiful to Kyrie, more beautiful than the salvanae or their song.

"Will you go live in Salvandos now?" he asked her, suddenly fearful. "You've often spoken of wanting to be a true dragon, to forget your human form." Strangely Kyrie wanted to cry again, and he hated his weakness. For so many years, fire and pain had blazed within him, but this day was a day of tears.

Agnus Dei snorted so loudly, it blew back a strand of her hair. "Pup," she said, hands on her hips, "there are some things dragons can't do."

"Like what?" Kyrie asked.

She walked toward him in the mud, grasped his head with both hands, and kissed him deeply. The kiss lasted for long moments, and Kyrie shut his eyes. Her lips were soft and full, her fingers grasping in his hair. When finally she broke away, leaving him breathless, she said, "This. And I intend to do a lot of it with you."

Kyrie laughed. His placed an arm around her waist, pulled her close, and kissed her hair. "I love you, Agnus Dei," he said, and suddenly tears filled his eyes again, and he turned away lest she saw them.

She smiled and pulled his face back to hers. "Right back at you, pup."

When they looked back to Benedictus, they saw that Lacrimosa had become a silvery dragon, and stood by her husband. She was only half his size, so delicate and lithe by his bulky form, her scales like starlight.

"Do you really think we can do it?" Kyrie asked her and Benedictus. "Can we rebuild Requiem?"

Benedictus looked at the horizon, beyond which Requiem lay, then at Kyrie. "I don't know, Kyrie. But we're going to try."

Kyrie raised the amulet. It felt hot in his hand, still humming and trembling. "We have the griffins with us. I sent them to Confutatis, but I can bring them back. With their help, we can--"

"No," Benedictus said, shaking his head. "The servitude of griffins to Osanna or Requiem ends today. Hand me the amulet, Kyrie, so that I can destroy it."

Kyrie gasped. He shook his head wildly. "No! Benedictus! I mean, Your Highness. I mean... I don't know what I'm supposed to call you now, but we can't release the griffins. Dies Irae still has armies that can hunt us. You yourself said so. The people of Osanna hate us, and--" Kyrie blew out his breath, exasperated. "I can't believe this. We need the griffins." He clutched the amulet so tightly, it hurt his palm. "With their power, we can reclaim our land, and reclaim our glory."

Benedictus only gazed at him, waiting for Kyrie to end his speech. When finally Kyrie could think of nothing more to say, Benedictus spoke softly.

"We cannot rebuild our land with the slavery of others, Kyrie. We have seen where that can lead. Enslaving the griffins was the downfall of my father; once Dies Irae stole the amulet, his rule crumbled. No, Kyrie. Griffins cannot speak, but they are wise beasts. They can be as wise as men, when they are free. If we can rebuild Requiem, it will be with justice and light, not as overlords of another race."

Kyrie took deep, fiery breaths. Anger pulsed through him, tingling his fingers, but he forced himself to clench his teeth. Benedictus was right, he knew. He hated that it was so. Hated it! But he knew the king spoke truth.

Wordlessly, lips tight, he held out the amulet in his open palm.

Benedictus lifted it with his mouth, smashed it between his teeth, and spat out the pieces. Somewhere in the distance, a league away, rose the cries of ten thousand griffins.

"They're free now," Lacrimosa said quietly. "They will no longer serve us, nor will they hunt us. May they find their way back to Leonis, their fabled land across the sea, and prosper there."

Kyrie stood with arms limp, not sure how to feel. Without the griffins, the road ahead seemed impossible to travel. How could they rebuild Requiem now, just the four of them? Could they truly find more Vir Requis survivors? Did any even exist? Would Dies Irae heal and resume his hunt, or was he dead already? Kyrie did not know, and the world seemed darker and more confusing than ever.

He thought of Lady Mirum, how she'd protected him for ten years in her fort, and knew the first thing he would do now. He would find her body. He would give her a proper burial. He would rededicate the fort in her name.

"We return to Fort Sanctus," he said, and did not need to say more. The others understood and nodded. There his journey had begun; there it would end.

Agnus Dei kissed his cheek, ruffled his hair, and said, "You are a pup." Then she shifted into a red dragon, all fire and fang, and took flight.

Kyrie shifted too, and soon the four Vir Requis, perhaps the last of their kind, flew together. The clouds parted, and the dawn rose, and they flew into that good, golden light. The sunrise gilded the clouds, spreading pink and orange wisps across the land, and the stars still shone overhead.

As they flew into that sunrise, Kyrie dared to hope, to imagine. The world was still dangerous for the Vir Requis. Many still feared them. Many would still hunt them. But as he flew now, his new family at his side, he breathed the cold air and smiled. He imagined flocks of thousands of Vir Requis flying, the glory of their magic. He would help rebuild that race with Agnus Dei, whom he loved more than life, and maybe someday, years from now, many dragons would fly again.

"Requiem," he whispered into the dawn. "May our wings forever find your sky."

AGNUS DEI

As Agnus Dei flew beside her parents, a thought kept rattling in her mind. She chewed her lip, but could not rid herself of it. The wind blew around her, scented of morning and dew, and sunlight filled the sky, but Agnus Dei did not see this beauty. She thought back to the ruins of Requiem, where she had fought Gloriae the Gilded, and ice filled her belly.

Father had spoken words to Nehushtan, words that kept echoing. "I still lead my people, though only five remain."

Kyrie had not noticed, but Agnus Dei had.

Five.

Five Vir Requis.

She looked at Mother and Father, and at Kyrie, and tears filled her eyes.

"Mother," she whispered. Her whisper barely carried in the wind, but Lacrimosa still heard. She turned to face Agnus Dei, eyes soft.

"Mother," Agnus Dei said. She hated that her voice trembled, that tears filled her eyes, but could not help it. "Mother, Father said that-- He--" She trembled. "Mother, who is the fifth?"

Lacrimosa was crying too. She smiled through her tears. "Agnus Dei," she said, "you have a sister."

GLORIAE

Gloriae was pacing the throne room when Dies Irae stumbled in, a shard of sword in his eye.

Gloriae's jaw unhinged. For a moment she could do nothing but stare. Blood, mud, and ash covered her father. Fresh blood spurted from his eye and filled his mouth. He cackled as he limped into the throne room, stunned guards at his sides. Blood trailed behind him.

"Benedictus!" Dies Irae shouted, mouth full of blood, and laughed madly. "He lives. He lives! He killed me. Daughter!" He collapsed at her feet.

Blood spattered Gloriae's leggings, snapping her out of her shock. She raised her eyes to the guards. "Fetch priests!" she said. "And ready the griffins."

Dies Irae laughed at her feet. He stared up at her with one eye. The other eye too seemed to stare up, if a shard of steel could stare. "The griffins abandoned us, Gloriae. Look what they did to me. Look what the weredragons did." He was weeping now.

Priests burst into the room. Their servants carried a litter.

"Take him to the temple," Gloriae ordered them. She allowed no tremble to fill her voice, no emotion to show on her face. She ruled Osanna now; she would rule with steel. "Pray for him. Let the Sun God heal him. If he dies, so will you."

For an instant, hatred blazed across the priests' faces. Gloriae knew they were not used to hearing threats, not even from emperors. Yet they only nodded, placed the cackling Dies Irae on the litter, and carried him away.

Gloriae stared at the blood smearing the marble tiles. Splotches of it stained her clothes. Finally her head began to spin. She wanted to follow the priests, to be with her father, but her feet would not support her. The closest seat was Father's throne, and she fell into it. For the first time in her life, she sat upon the Ivory Throne of Osanna.

The lords and ladies of her hall gazed at her, shocked. Fury filled Gloriae, and she let her stare pierce them. "My father is hurt. Until he's healed, I rule in his stead. Now leave this place."

As they left the hall, Gloriae shut her eyes. Blood pounded in her head. She clutched the throne's arms, and felt its power flow through her. Osanna. A realm of endless forests, towering mountains, great armies. Hers. From here flowed her dominion over the empire.

Her eyes snapped open. She left the throne and strode across the hall. She did not walk to the temple. She would be of no use there. But there was something she could do now, something Father should have done years ago.

Gloriae left her hall, walked down stairs, marched down tunnels, climbed down and down into the belly of the world. She walked for hours perhaps, lips tightened, eyes dry. She walked until she reached the chamber with the guards, where golden skulls bedecked iron doors, gazing upon her with glowing eye sockets.

Gloriae stepped through that doorway and approached the Well of Night.

She stood over the abyss and hesitated. *The nightshades.* Gloriae could not forget the time she saw them, how they had sucked her soul into their endless cavern, turned her to smoke and darkness. Then Gloriae remembered the steel shard in Father's head, the blood on his face, and the blood on her leggings. She remembered, too, the curse she carried now, the lizard curse Lacrimosa had given her.

Gloriae took a deep breath, tightened her fists, and jumped into the well.

She floated through darkness. It was calm, soothing, an inky blackness that caressed her.

Then she screamed.

The nightshades appeared around her, creatures that were the opposite of light, creatures of smoke and fear and blackness. Their eyes shone as diamonds, and she felt them tugging her spirit, pulling it from her body, as if it were wisps of steam.

"Hear me!" Gloriae shouted. "I sit upon the Ivory Throne. I have the power to free you. I release you from this well! Emerge from the abyss and serve me."

They swirled so fast, Gloriae was tossed in all directions, spun like a top, and shot into the air. She screamed and laughed and spread out her arms.

"Fly into the world, creatures of night. I am your ruler now. I tame you now. Kill the weredragons! That is my order to you, the price I charge for your freedom. Hunt them until the last one begs for death."

The creatures swirled around her, disappearing and appearing, teeth like shards of glass, bodies like clouds, eyes crackling. They laughed, a sound of storms. Gloriae's body was like a coin rattling in a cup. They flowed out of the well, raising her upon them, and swirled through the chamber. They howled and laughed and ballooned. Gloriae floated among them, high above the well. She tilted her head back, laughing, arms spread to her sides.

I will kill them, she promised herself. *I will do what Father could not. I will rid the world of the weredragon curse.*

"I will lead you there," Gloriae said, a smile tingling the corners of her mouth. "I will lead you to Benedictus and Lacrimosa, and we will kill them."

They flowed out of the chamber, down tunnels, up stairs... and into a world of dying daylight.

The story continues in...

TEARS OF REQUIEM

Song of Dragons, Book Two

NOVELS BY DANIEL ARENSON

Standalones:

Firefly Island (2007)
The Gods of Dream (2010)
Flaming Dove (2010)
Eye of the Wizard (2011)

Song of Dragons:

Blood of Requiem (2011)
Tears of Requiem (2011)
Light of Requiem (2011)

KEEP IN TOUCH

www.DanielArenson.com
Daniel@DanielArenson.com
Facebook.com/DanielArenson
Twitter.com/DanielArenson

Acknowledgements

I'd like to thank several people for their help with *Blood of Requiem.*

Thank you, beta readers Greg Baum, Janelle DeCelis, Mary Garber, Debra Martin, and Jonathan Thompson.

Thank you Anne Victory for copyediting the manuscript.

Thank you authors Michael Crane, David Dalglish, Robert Duperre, Amanda Hocking, Jason Letts, David McAfee, and Sean Sweeney for advice and friendship.

Made in the USA
San Bernardino, CA
07 December 2013